Without Warning

A Novel

Without Warning

A Novel

Ward Tanneberg

Without Warning

Originally published in 1994 under the title *September Strike.*

Published by Kregel Publications, a division of Kregel, Inc., P.O. Box 2607, Grand Rapids, MI 49501.

This book is a work of fiction. Names, characters, places, and incidents are either the product of the author's imagination or are used fictitiously. Any resemblance to actual events or locales or persons, living or dead, is entirely coincidental.

English translation quotations from the Qur'an are from Abdullah Yusuf ʿAli, *The Meaning of the Holy Qur'an* (Brentwood, Md.: Amana, 1992).

Library of Congress Cataloging-in-Publication Data
Tanneberg, Ward M.
Without warning / by Ward Tanneberg.
p. cm.
1. Terrorism—Fiction. I. Title.
PS3570.A535W57 2003
813'.54—dc22 2003015990

ISBN 0-8254-3820-9

Printed in the United States of America

03 04 05 06 07 / 5 4 3 2 1

To all who seek a certain
Hope
in uncertain times.

Acknowledgments

There are numerous people to whom I am indebted. This work was first published in 1994 as *September Strike.* It was my first novel and tragically became all too prophetic with the events of September 11, 2001. The story has since been updated from its original setting to a post-9/11 period.

I'm grateful to Dennis Hillman and Stephen Barclift of Kregel Publications, who decided that this story should enter the reader's world once more.

David Brannon, Jim Treacy, and Joshua Schmidt offered invaluable technological and philosophical insights into the troubling world of politically and religiously based terrorism, cyber-terrorism, and counterterrorism. Several television newspeople patiently helped unravel for me the mysteries of the media process.

My thanks to Stephen Barclift, Janrye Tromp, Elizabeth Hillman, and all those at Kregel Publications who worked with and encouraged this project. Dave Lindstedt contributed significantly with his editing and consulting skills. Thanks, Steve, for bringing Dave and me together. And a special thanks to my agent, Joyce Hart, for believing in me and my work.

I can never offer enough thanks to my family, or to my best friend, encourager, and loving wife, Dixie, who good-naturedly sets an extra plate at the table for each new fictional friend or foe I bring home. She patiently puts up with the many plots and preoccupations she finds stacked in all the corners of our lives. And when it gets to be too much, she closes the door. It's one of the thousand reasons I love her.

—WT

We didn't make the alcohol, but our highways have drunk drivers. We don't sell drugs, but our neighborhoods have those who do. We didn't create international tension, but we have to fear the terrorists. We didn't train the thieves, but each of us is a potential victim of their greed. We are tiptoeing through a mine field which we didn't create.

And the Angels Were Silent
—Max Lucado

I have told you these things, so that in me you may have peace. In this world you will have trouble. But take heart! I have overcome the world.

—Jesus Christ
John 16:33

Prologue

March 18 (*Reuters*)
PEACE! ISRAEL AND PALESTINE DECLARE TRUCE

Wallach and Arafat signal a truce.

March 19 (*Jerusalem Post*)
PEACE IN THE MIDDLE EAST: CAN IT LAST?

In a move hailed by the UN Security Council as both opportune and courageous, Israel and the Palestinian National Authority have agreed to an immediate cessation of hostilities and have pledged to begin a serious negotiation of key sticking points within thirty days. While Arab children dance in Bethlehem's Manger Square and Tel Aviv's sidewalk cafés overflow with happy customers, many political observers remain skeptical of this latest turn of events in the Middle East.

March 24 (*London Daily*)
TWO WOMEN LIVE UP TO THEIR NAMES IN SECRET MEETINGS

In a surprise move, Soreka Wallach, Israel's first woman prime minister since Golda Meir, and Barika bint Abaza bin Junaibi Al-Kassem, Palestinian National Authority minister of higher education and scientific research, have brokered a peace agreement between the State of Israel and the Palestinian people, one that has remained illusive to world leaders for decades.

Details of secret meetings taking place over a three-month period are just now coming to light. PM Wallach is calling on the Knesset to begin consideration of the proposal on Wednesday.

Barika Al-Kassem has been serving the ailing Yasser Arafat and the PNA as its behind-the-scenes negotiator, drawing upon a fascinating lifelong relationship between the two women. Some believe this stunning achievement will eventually lead to Arafat naming Al-Kassem the new Palestinian Prime Minister. The revolutionary leader's health continues to deteriorate markedly. He faces growing unrest among PNA cabinet members regarding his ability to lead the people into a new era of statehood.

Wallach and Al-Kassem grew up playing together in the streets and alleyways of Old Jerusalem. As teenagers, their experiences and friendship deepened when they were chosen to visit American schools on a goodwill tour with a select group of Israeli-Palestinian youths in the *Seeds of Peace* program. After decades of a decaying and volatile relationship, both Israel and the Palestinian people now stand on the threshold of peace, largely through the leadership of a woman named Soreka, meaning "love your neighbor as yourself," and Barika, meaning "bloom, be successful." Truly, these two seem to be living up to their names.

August 27 (*New York Times*)
PERMANENT STATUS AGREEMENT BETWEEN PALESTINE AND ISRAEL SET FOR SEPTEMBER VOTE

The terms of this initiative encompass the vision of President William Sanderson as conveyed in a speech by Secretary of State Charles Freeman, and agreements first proposed in 2002 by the crown prince of Saudi Arabia. Together with UN Security Council Resolutions 242, 338, and 1397, they form the basis for a permanent status agreement between Palestine and Israel.

The initiative provides for permanent boundaries to be set at the June 4, 1967, Armistice Line, with a permanent territorial corridor established between the West Bank and Gaza Strip.

East Jerusalem will become the capital of the State of Palestine and West Jerusalem will become the capital of the State of Israel. Jerusalem, venerated by the three major monotheistic religions, will remain open to all peoples of the world. Palestine will transfer sovereignty over the Jewish Quarter and the Wailing Wall in East Jerusalem to Israel, while retaining sovereignty over the remainder of the Old City.

Palestine and Israel will provide for security cooperation arrangements that ensure the integrity and sovereignty of each state, with international forces playing a central role. Neither Palestine nor Israel will participate in military alliances against each other, or allow their territory to be used as a military base of operation against each other or against other neighbors.

Palestine and Israel's respective sovereignty and independence will be guaranteed by formal agreements with members of the international community. The issue of water will be resolved justly and equitably with international treaties and norms. Palestine and Israel will be democratic states with free-market economies.

This permanent status agreement will mark the end of conflict between Palestine and Israel and the end of claims between them. A fixed timeline will be agreed upon in order to ensure that the process does not stall.

The Israel-Palestinian Permanent Status Agreement will be voted on by members of Israel's Knesset and PNA leadership on September 24. World leaders hail the proposed arrangement as the best possible solution to the decades-old hostilities in the region. And it seems the people may be ready to embrace it as well. For six months the words and weapons of war have been silent. No suicide bombings in Israel. No tanks rolling ominously into the West Bank. What was at first thought impossible by many observers now seems within reach, a distinct possibility. May it be so; let us all pray for the peace of Jerusalem.

SUNDAY, 27 AUGUST, LOCAL TIME 2224
IN THE SOUK DISTRICT, BEIRUT, LEBANON

Hafez Tabatai leaned back in his chair and scratched his ample belly. He squinted at the other two men through smoke curling up from a homemade cigarette that dangled from his lips. The room was cold, but he was oblivious to the lack of heat and to the ashes that were about to drop onto his lap.

The three sat around a table strewn with a jumble of papers amid the remains of an earlier meal. A single bare bulb overhead cast its pallid light on the dreary scene. From the far side of the room a scrawny orange and black tabby padded its way across the stone floor. Tabatai kicked at it with his foot. The cat hissed in protest and quickly retreated to a dark corner.

For a long time, no one spoke. The only movement was the smoke swirling in the dim light.

Suddenly Tabatai leaned forward, cursed, and sent papers and dishes flying off the table with an angry sweep of his arm.

"What are you doing?" Mahmoud Assad lunged forward in an awkward attempt to catch one of the plates as it dropped to the floor and shattered.

"There is nothing here!" Tabatai emphasized his disdain by spitting through tobacco-stained teeth at the scattered papers. "These plans are good for nothing. They are the dreams of incompetent women. Blow up this building. Kidnap that person. The world has become jaded by these inept operations. For months we have done nothing. The increase in U.S. security since 9/11 has resulted in one setback after another. It is more difficult than ever for us. And now Arafat tears out the souls of our people by hiding his ineptness in the skirts of a woman who makes secret agreements with the Jews. He thinks he speaks for the Palestinians, but he does not. He betrays us. He speaks only for himself."

Tabatai shifted his bulk in the chair and leaned over the table, his finger stabbing the air, lending emphasis to his words. "The world thinks we will settle for this. We will not. But we are losing the world's attention. We must do something big—something so astonishing, so unusual, so shocking, that the media will once again fall over themselves to present our story and our demands to the world. The American infidels are the key. They must be pushed to the edge. Only they can bring the Jews into line. Until that happens we have nothing. All we have are children's games. Even our own people are caving in. There must be something we can do that will wake up the world!"

"You are right, of course," Mahmoud Assad sighed, getting up from his chair.

"What we need is an atomic bomb. Unfortunately, we are no closer to possessing one than we were ten years ago. Look, maybe we should kill Arafat. That would remind the world that we are still here."

The third man had remained silent throughout Tabatai's outburst and Assad's unlikely fantasizing, leaning back impassively in his chair, his features indistinct in the dim light of the room. Both men now looked at him expectantly. Marwan Dosha, one of the most notorious terrorist leaders in the world, leaned forward and folded his hands on the table, looking first at Assad, then at Tabatai. His piercing brown eyes commanded their attention, but Hafez couldn't keep himself from glancing at the knife scar that ran from Dosha's cheek to his ear, a reminder of a prison brawl with three cellmates nearly five years ago. They were dead. He was still in the game.

"There is a plan already in motion," Dosha said quietly. He stared into each man's eyes for a long, silent moment. "If we are successful, it will be better than placing an atom bomb under the White House. And we will not have to kill Arafat. Others will do it for us."

Hafez Tabatai and Mahmoud Assad were silent. They watched Dosha intently.

"What's going to happen?" asked Tabatai, a skeptical look on his face.

"All you need to know for now is that something *will* happen," Dosha answered, "and soon."

"You are neither Hamas nor Islamic Jihad," Assad declared. "Are you al-Qaida?"

Marwan Dosha pushed back from the table and got to his feet. "Aren't we all?"

His face cloaked in the half light, eyes burning with contempt, his voice became passionate, lighting a wild and adoring fire in the others.

"Do not worry. If we are successful, the American infidels will die by the thousands. Those who remain will be afraid to come out of their houses. At the very same time, we will cut the heart out of Israel once and for all!"

PART ONE

Our battle with the Jews is long and dangerous, requiring all dedicated efforts. It is a phase which must be followed by succeeding phases, a battalion which must be supported by battalion after battalion of the divided Arab and Islamic world until the enemy is overcome, and the victory of Allah descends.

—from Introduction to the Charter of Hamas

Nay, We hurl the Truth against falsehood, and it knocks out its brain, and behold, falsehood doth perish!

—The Qur'an
Sura 21: Anbiya':18

The angel of the LORD also said to [Hagar]:

"You are now with child
and you will have a son.
You shall name him
Ishmael,
for the LORD has heard of
your misery.
He will be a wild donkey of
a man;
his hand will be against
everyone
and everyone's hand
against him,
and he will live in hostility
toward all his brothers."

—The Holy Bible
Genesis 16:11–12

1

TUESDAY, 06 SEPTEMBER, LOCAL TIME 1847
ALBERTA, CANADA

Dusk was settling over the mountains as the blue minivan came to a stop alongside the tiny, olive-colored shelter. Park ranger George McClintock glanced up in time to see the driver's side window slide downward, revealing the dark, handsome face of the man behind the steering wheel. McClintock's memory stored the man's features in an instant, an ability developed over many years of this kind of work, and a skill of which he was quite proud. His eyes darted across the van's interior, pausing momentarily to take in the passenger, a striking woman with olive complexion and high cheekbones. Her jet black hair was pulled straight back and her eyes were hidden behind a stylish pair of sunglasses.

Early twenties, McClintock guessed, returning her smile. *A real looker, too. What a nice way to end the day.*

"Hello. Welcome to Waterton International Park. Hope you've had a pleasant day of travel."

"It's been very nice," the driver answered with a smile.

"Where are you folks from?"

"We're from Toronto, but today we've come from Lethbridge," the man replied.

"Enjoying your vacation?"

"Yes. But actually, it isn't a vacation. We're on our honeymoon. We were married two weeks ago."

"Well, wonderful. Congratulations to you both." *Wouldn't you know it. The gorgeous ones are always taken.*

"Staying long in the park?" McClintock could see camping gear packed in behind the driver.

"Three or four days," the man answered. "We want to do some rafting. Maybe a little hiking. Nothing too strenuous."

"Planning any fishing?"

"No."

McClintock smiled to himself as he gathered brochures together for these end-of-the-shift visitors to his park. Glancing up again at the attractive couple, his eyes rested for a moment on the woman. *She really is beautiful.*

"Okay, this is a map of the area," McClintock said, passing a small handful of printed matter through the shelter window. "That'll be eight dollars for your park pass. See here? Camping sites are marked with a tent symbol. Should be some available for you this time of year. Plenty of great hiking trails in every direction. Downtown Waterton is small, but you can get supplies there. Everything you need, really. Good restaurants, too. Some motels, but rooms are scarce. At this hour of the day a room may be hard to come by, unless you already have a reservation. I expect you'll see a few wild goats and deer in town, too. Leave them alone, though. Don't ruin your honeymoon by getting too friendly with the animals."

The man handed McClintock the exact amount.

As the vehicle pulled away, McClintock made a mental note of the inflated raft tied to the van rooftop and the vehicle's Ontario license plate. Actually, not much ever escaped McClintock's keen eye. He took pride in the fact that his powers of recall regularly impressed his fellow rangers.

Today, however, he had missed a few important details. He had not seen the four additional passengers who lay motionless on their backs beneath the pile of camping gear. Nor had he been able to see the four automatic weapons tucked between them.

For his sake, it was just as well. Ranger McClintock would not have lived to tell what he had seen, had he seen it.

2

The van continued up the road leading past the Prince of Wales Hotel. The venerable old inn stood on its high hill as it had for so many years, a solitary wooden monarch, reigning over the tiny village and lake below. High mountain peaks, still capped with last season's snow, embraced the lake in surrealistic beauty. Rays from the late afternoon sun ricocheted off towering slopes and burst into fiery dances of light on the hotel's immense lobby windows.

Couples strolled across the grassy knoll in front of the hotel, now and then brushing at pesky mosquitoes, the only reminder left to the senses that heaven had not yet been entered. Children waved their arms and laughed with delight as gray squirrels raced ahead of them along their well-traveled miniature highways. At the bottom of the hill, encased in this bowl of majestic mountains, Waterton Lake was turning from its afternoon emerald green to a deep, dark blue.

Akmed el Hussein drove slowly until the van reached the bottom of the hill, then turned left onto a narrow road that passed by several camping sites. He had visited the park in July, so the twists and turns of the road had a familiar quality as he steered along the lakeshore. He and the woman drove in silence for several miles, keeping an eye on the side mirrors. There did not appear to be any other vehicles on the road. During his earlier visit, Akmed had carefully researched the habits of the locals and their summer guests along this particular stretch. He'd observed that most people were back in the main camping sites by this time of day. That was perfect.

Eventually they came to a small parking area. They had seen no other cars along the way and this site was empty. It was nearly dark when they came to a stop at the water's edge.

Things are as they should be. They could not be better. Allah is with us!

The woman was the first out of the van. Quickly she opened the sliding side door.

"It's clear," she said.

The pile of camping gear began to move. First feet, then legs emerged, followed by one stiff body after another as each man made his exit from the van and stood upright, weapon in hand. They stretched tired, sore muscles, their backsides aching from lack of exercise and the merciless road-pounding absorbed while lying for so long in the same position. Still, their adrenaline was pumping as they peered into the shroud of semidarkness settling around them.

"This is the place then?" asked one of the men.

"Yes," replied Akmed. "It's the end of the road. From here we take the boat. Now hurry. We must leave immediately, before someone sees us and starts asking questions."

Swiftly, the men loosened the raft from the van's rooftop, carried it to the shore, and dropped it silently into the dark water. With well-choreographed movements and no wasted motion, each person moved quickly to complete their oft-rehearsed assignments.

Mousa Ekrori grasped the rope attached to the raft and wrapped it securely around a large rock to keep the small craft from drifting away. His younger brother, Mamdouh, put the outboard motor in place while Ihab Akazzam attached the fuel tank. Two sets of canoe paddles. Five sleeping bags. A single canvas tarp, rolled tightly. Knapsacks filled with enough food for several days' journey. Canteens. Rope. Five AK-47 automatic weapons. Ammunition. Two canvas bags filled with grenades. A first-aid kit. Small shovels. Five rain-repellent parkas. Three bags filled with plastic explosives and timing devices. Two PDAs with wireless handheld modems. A single copy of the Quran.

By the time they finished, total darkness concealed every movement. When the work was complete, one of the men, Ali Shabagh, stepped forward and embraced each of the other four men in turn, murmuring, *"Allah u Akbar."*

"Allah u Akbar, Ali Shabagh," Akmed declared solemnly. "God is greater. May he give you and us a safe journey."

Ali turned and walked slowly toward the van, gravel crunching beneath his boots. Opening the door, he pulled himself up into the driver's seat. For a brief moment the dome light illuminated his face, reminding the others of how easily he could be mistaken for Akmed el Hussein. That was, of course, the whole idea. They had thought of everything. Even the possibility that if the van and driver were observed leaving the park, no one would give it a second thought. People drove out and returned every day.

"I wish I was going with you," Ali said wistfully.

"I know," replied Akmed.

Ali started the engine. The others watched in silence as the van backed away from the water's edge and angled toward the road.

"May Allah go with you," Ali called out softly, signaling farewell to his friends with a wave of his hand. The van rolled away slowly at first, then gathered speed as it disappeared around the bend.

Quietness settled around the group that remained. The awesome quiet of the wilderness at night. At first, the only sound they heard was that of their own breathing. Standing at the water's edge, they stared into the darkness, each one coming to grips with a sudden, unexpected feeling of abandonment. For the past several hours, their close proximity in the van had provided a sense of security. Now that feeling, however false it had been, was gone altogether. They were strangers in a strange land.

Gradually, their ears tuned in to the unfamiliar music around them. Crickets playing nature's nightly symphony. Frogs croaking their throaty applause. A cool breeze rustling in the treetops and pushing wavelets gently against the shore. Mousa shuffled his feet in the gravel, breaking the short-lived reverie.

"Get in," Akmed commanded, turning his attention to their task. The three men climbed into the raft, followed by the woman. Akmed removed the rope from around the stone anchor. With one smooth motion, he pushed the raft free and jumped aboard. For a few moments they drifted, straining to hear any sounds that would denote danger. Fifty feet from shore, Mamdouh huddled over the engine, double-checking to be sure its clamps were secure. When they had drifted another fifty feet out into the open water, Akmed raised a clenched fist in a silent, forward motion. With a practiced turn, Mamdouh manipulated the starter. It sprang to life instantly, pushing the craft forward on the next leg of their journey.

As the boat moved steadily through the calm water, Akmed's gaze followed the darkened outline of the mountains surrounding the lake. He recalled the soul-subduing awe he had felt during his July scouting visit here. The regal combination of water, mountain, and sky had overwhelmed his senses. On the day he'd boarded one of the several tourist vessels that regularly traversed the lake each summer, he had been apprehensive. It had been crowded and he'd felt vulnerable standing shoulder to shoulder with all those strangers. Soon, however, he'd forgotten himself and his concerns. There was nothing like this in his homeland. Frigid, ice-blue mountain water. Tall, stately evergreens. Azure blue skies. Even Switzerland could not offer a more majestic panorama than this.

"Somewhere out there is the swath cut through the forest that I told you about," he announced to his disciples above the steady drone of the engine.

Pointing to his left, he continued, "It comes straight down that mountain to the water's edge, disappears, then rises on the opposite side of the lake, continuing to the west. If we were traveling in the daylight, we would easily see it." Tonight, however, the swath was invisible to the "honeymoon couple" and their three companions. Still, they peered into the darkness, trying to imagine this unnatural phenomenon.

The line that cut through tall forests of Douglas fir and birch was a benchmark of international accomplishment. It identified a long stretch of unguarded border between two of the world's great nations, Canada and the United States. On one side lay the province of Alberta. On the other, the state of Montana.

But for Akmed and his companions, it was an invisible landmark on the most glorious adventure they would ever know, and from which none of them would return. An adventure that would bring an unbelieving, unheeding, unholy world to its knees.

—~—

Ali Shabagh smiled to himself as he drove the blue van up the road leading past the Prince of Wales Hotel. The rustic old building was well-lighted now, its one hundred rooms filled with happy tourists.

If only they knew, they would not be so happy.

Before long he saw the outline of the ranger's shelter at the park entrance. He touched the brakes, slowing until he observed the headlights of two oncoming cars. As the cars pulled to a stop at the ranger's window, the blue van passed unheeded, heading in the opposite direction.

It wouldn't have made any difference anyway. Ranger George McClintock had been off duty for more than two hours. He was sitting by himself in a small village restaurant, eating pizza and drinking beer, thinking about the honeymoon couple that had entered the park near the end of his shift. No doubt they were settled into a nearby motel room by now.

No, probably in a tent at one of the campsites.

He took another sip of beer as the memory of the man's striking companion flashed across his mind.

He's one lucky guy.

—~—

The raft was still more than a mile from Goat's Head when Mamdouh cut the motor. A strong north wind whipped at their backs as Akmed handed a paddle to each of the men.

"It's another sign that Allah is with us," he said as the woman shifted to the front of the boat, giving the others room to work. She turned to face them as Akmed continued. "If this wind were coming from the opposite direction, we would have much more difficulty. Allah has provided a wind at our backs tonight. Now it is time to see how well we row together. Aziza, count for us to give us the rhythm, just as we practiced. And be our eyes to guide us to our destination."

"ONE, two, three, four, ONE, two, three, four . . . ," Aziza called out in a low, clear voice, watching as the men fit their movements to her cadence. Soon the four paddles were slicing through the water in unison, propelling the small rubber craft onward with surprising speed.

A full moon rose above the mountain peaks. The men could see Aziza's face in the soft moonglow. Her eyes were cool and regal. Her high cheekbones and finely shaped nose presented the look of strong beauty. Her lips were full, promising warmth and a touch of the exotic. Reaching back, Aziza untied her hair, letting the movement of the raft and the wind cause it to swirl around her face, at once covering, then unveiling her eyes. All the while she continued calling softly, "ONE, two, three, four . . ." The men stroked the water's surface, keeping their eyes on Aziza and their thoughts to themselves.

3

Park ranger Carl Deeker lay quietly, staring at ceiling shadows broken by a narrow shaft of moonlight that leaked through the unwashed window above the bed.

Listening.

Deeker was a sound sleeper. After dinner he had read for a while before going to bed. But in the middle of the night he'd awakened. He'd heard something. What was it? Then it came again. The unmistakable sound of an outboard motor.

"Who do you suppose that is?" he muttered to himself. "No one is on the lake this time of night."

He continued staring at the darkened rafters.

Could be a lost fisherman, I suppose. Someone's out there, that's for sure.

He rolled over and reached for his wristwatch, holding it up until he could make out the time in the moonlight.

One-twenty.

Deeker sat up and rubbed his eyes, his ears keened for other unusual sounds. Throwing his feet over the side of the bed, he pulled on the pants he had earlier tossed over the back of the chair. Grabbing his jacket from a hook by the bed, he opened the cabin door and walked outside.

In the shadow of the porch overhang, he watched and waited.

The day before had been unusually warm for September, busy with loads of tourists making the cross-lake journey crowded onto commercial passenger boats. Nothing unusual. Maybe more visitors than normal for this late in the season, but otherwise just another summer's day at Goat's Head. People disembarking, spending anywhere from a few minutes to a few hours on shore, then returning to the vessels and back to civilization.

Ranger Deeker lectured each group about the flora and fauna of the forest, encouraging them to take lots of pictures but no souvenirs, answering silly questions, and sending them on their way with a friendly wave. Visitors always took pictures of one another in front of the large Rotary Club emblem honoring members of the worldwide service organization from both Canada and the United States. And they asked the inevitable question: "Why is there a Rotary emblem way out here in the wilderness?" The visitors' center and the emblem had been placed through private donations, Deeker told them, as a symbol of goodwill and peace between the two nations.

The afternoon had been warm, but it had cooled considerably since then. A stiff breeze clawed at the collar of his uniform jacket, reminding him that he was still in the north woods and not in sunny Arizona, where he liked to spend his winters.

He kept his attention on the lake.

Nothing. No sound of a motor. Nothing moving either.

Wide awake now and fully curious, Deeker reached back through the door for his boots. Balancing against the porch railing, he pulled on one boot, then the other. He stepped off the porch and headed down the path that led to the passenger boat dock about two hundred yards away.

Halfway to the dock, he stopped, straining to hear anything out of the ordinary.

Thought I heard something.

He took another few steps forward, then stopped abruptly.

Out of the darkness, moving rapidly toward the shore in the direction of the dock, was a low, dark shape.

A raft. Must have had some engine trouble. Or maybe they ran out of gas. Must be at least two of them rowing, maybe more, as fast as they're moving.

He continued down the trail, then hesitated, remembering he'd left his flashlight on the lampstand by his bed.

The moon is out. I won't need a flashlight tonight.

Deeker resumed his stroll. He was still a hundred yards from the dock when the raft ran onto the gravel beach at Goat's Head.

Aziza leaped out, rope in hand, holding the raft steady until the men could disembark. They went to work quickly, without a word. Akmed helped Aziza pull the raft up onto the beach. Just as they had rehearsed many times before, each person became responsible for specific parts of the equipment. Knapsacks, rope, sleeping bags, automatic weapons, bags of grenades and plastics. All five worked swiftly, cool perspiration from their efforts at rowing and unloading supplies running in tiny rivulets down their faces.

"What's going on here?"

Startled, they looked up to see the outline of a man standing slightly above them in a clearing where the pebbly beach gave way to the forest.

"Who are you?" the stranger called out again.

Dark shadows from the tall dock timbers kept the raft partially hidden. The group watched warily as the man, apparently alone, walked toward them, trying to get a better look.

Akmed's mind raced.

We must have awakened a ranger. Does he have any idea what we are doing?

He looked around quickly.

The guns were on the rocks near one of the pilings, out of the stranger's line of vision. Everything else looked innocent enough.

"We were headed up the lake to go camping and fishing when our motor stopped," Akmed called out. "We tried to get it going again, but haven't succeeded. We aren't sure what the matter is. Plenty of gas. But something's wrong. Where are we, anyway?"

"Goat's Head Ranger Station," Deeker answered, well out onto the beach now and walking straight toward the men. "I'm Ranger Carl Deeker. Glad to meet you. You boys are out kinda late, aren't you?"

As Deeker came toward him, Akmed tensed.

Behind the ranger, a shadowy figure emerged from beneath the boat dock.

"Ranger Deeker?"

Deeker slipped on the gravel as he turned, startled at hearing his name called from behind him—and doubly surprised that it was not a man's voice.

Aziza walked toward him slowly. His eyes widened as she brushed back her hair and her face became visible in the moonlight.

She's beautiful!

"Ranger Deeker, my name is Aziza."

He remained spellbound as she smiled, continuing to close the distance between them until she was only a step away.

"Don't worry," she said, "we won't be here long."

He looked into her eyes. They were as cold as they were beautiful. A sudden twinge of danger flashed across his mind. Before he could react, she stepped closer until her body pressed against his. Her smile faded, lips parting slightly, and her eyes locked with his as she slipped a long, thin blade under his rib cage, slicing cleanly into the left ventricle of his heart. He gasped as she pulled the knife clear and with her free hand pushed him off balance. He fell backward, groping at the wound as he rolled onto his side.

"Why?" he asked, coughing. A long groan came involuntarily from his lips as the pain quickly reached an unbearable crescendo. Curling into a fetal position, he looked up at the woman.

"What are you people doing here?"

Blood spread between his fingers, staining his jacket and dripping onto the gravel beach. His final question remained unanswered, lost in the swelling strains of another cricket symphony. Carl Deeker, veteran park ranger, would not be going to Arizona this winter.

4

For a long moment, no one moved. Each person stared silently at the body on the ground. Then Akmed walked to where the ranger lay, knelt down, and felt for the man's pulse.

"He's dead."

Mousa shuffled nervously, letting out a sigh.

"Come," Akmed commanded, his voice filled with urgency. "Help me wrap him in the tent canvas. Quickly, before his blood stains the beach. And be quiet! There may be someone else around here. He can't be left or we'll be followed. We must take the body with us. We'll dispose of it somewhere along the trail."

Listening to Akmed, Aziza was struck with an absurd awareness of dissimilar pronouns. *How quickly we change our thinking from "him" to "it,"* she mused. A sudden wave of nausea swept through her. Taking a few steps to the lake's edge, she threw up.

Meanwhile, Akmed and Ihab spread the canvas they had intended for later use as a shelter. They dragged Deeker onto it, then wrapped it around his still form.

"There's blood on these rocks," said Mamdouh, on his knees now with a flashlight, carefully examining the killing area.

"Get some lake water and take care of it," ordered Akmed. "There must be no trace of our presence here tonight. We've wasted precious time as it is. Let's gather up our things and be off."

The five set about shouldering the gear, according to their assignments. The two brothers, Mousa and Mamdouh, punctured the raft in several places until the air was expended. They folded the bulky remains as best they could between them in order to carry it into the forest. Nothing could be left behind.

Akmed and Ihab picked up the canvas-wrapped body. They wrestled it up from the beach and then up the steps leading past the Rotary International Peace Park Memorial. From there they spotted the trail leading inland, away from the lakeshore.

Aziza paused in front of the Peace Memorial, adjusting the straps on her heavy pack. There was enough moonlight for her to read the motto printed alongside the Rotary emblem: *Is it the TRUTH? Is it FAIR to all concerned? Will it build GOODWILL and BETTER FRIENDSHIPS? Will it be BENEFICIAL to all concerned?* She stared at the words.

"You did what you had to do, Aziza," said Akmed, observing the miserable look on her face. He had seen such looks before on faces in Gaza and in the Old City. "Our brothers at home will be proud when they hear of your heroism."

Heroism?

She reached for her Thermos and opened it, rinsing her mouth before drinking two short swallows of water to help settle her unstable stomach.

I was prepared from the start to kill on this mission. Even to be killed. But not tonight. Not the minute we crossed into America. This is not a good omen. Besides, how much heroism is there in killing an unarmed man?

Aziza cleared her throat.

There will be more killing before we're done. We ourselves will surely be in the number of those falling in death.

With a final look around, she joined the others as they trudged uphill into the difficult and rugged mountains of Montana's Glacier National Park.

The remainder of the night passed uneventfully. Aziza and the men were all in superb condition, having spent the summer working out at various health clubs in Toronto. Long daily jogs through the city's many beautiful parks had built their stamina and hardened their bodies. Still, given the steepness of the trail and the unexpected burden of the ranger's body, progress was slow. On several occasions they stopped to rest and regain their strength. There was little conversation. Talking required energy and every ounce was needed for what lay ahead.

Early in the morning, as dawn's first light began to penetrate the forest, the team veered off the trail. Deep amid the thick foliage beneath the towering evergreens, they covered the boat's remains with tree limbs and underbrush. Mousa and Mamdouh prepared a shallow grave and rolled the ranger's body from its canvas blanket.

As the two men stopped to catch their breath, Akmed used his foot to push the remains of their mission's first enemy kill into the grave. Aziza felt a hollow sadness well up in her heart. Still troubled by her feelings, she turned away as the others threw dirt on the lifeless form and then spread rocks and dead branches over the red dirt. Standing a short distance away, Aziza overheard the men agreeing among themselves that thirty meters was far enough off the trail so that no one would ever find the body.

Thirty meters? She wasn't sure that was far enough, but she held her tongue. What was done was done.

Akmed walked over and stood beside her, reading her thoughts as he touched her shoulder. He spoke softly, but firmly.

"There will be more, Aziza. Many more. This one is only the first. You did what you had to do. You are a true soldier. You knew this would be your duty when you volunteered."

She stared at the ground, moving the dirt with her toe in a circular fashion. *Yes. But that was a long time ago. And far away.*

"Allah has honored you with first blood. I am proud of you," Akmed continued reassuringly, watching her carefully.

Actually he had questioned the wisdom of bringing an untested woman on a mission of such great importance. His superiors, however, had insisted. A woman was essential, and she must be beautiful. Americans were easily swayed by feminine beauty. Such beauty would be a vital asset. Now it seemed their wisdom had been confirmed. Aziza was indeed temptingly beautiful, and she had acted swiftly and skillfully in order to save them.

They made their way back to the trail, doing their best to leave no trace of having been there. Free of the extra burden, they reorganized their packs while devouring small loaves of bread and cheese purchased fresh the morning before in Lethbridge. At about 7:45, they headed out again. A steady pace would be necessary if they were to reach their American rendezvous on schedule.

—᷉—

Forty-eight hours later, dense clouds lay low over Glacier National Park's high mountain country. Most visitors chose to remain inside Many Glacier Lodge, huddled around the huge fireplace, warming their hands with steaming cups of coffee and hot chocolate and commiserating with each other about the coming end of the vacation season. Winter did not seem far off today. It was too cold and wet for hiking any of the trails. Through the large windows, they watched raindrops disappear into the dark surface of Swiftcurrent Lake. Even with the downpour, this was still one of the most beautiful spots on earth.

Outside in the public parking area, a solitary figure, hunched against the pouring rain, wandered among the scores of vehicles sporting license plates from several states and provinces. He was dressed in hiking boots and pants that were caked with mud, obviously in need of laundering. He pulled the water-repellent parka up around his ears, slouching forward to keep the rain out of his face, while carefully checking each license plate as he walked past.

He turned his face away as a charter bus passed, its driver downshifting and braking as he prepared to turn right at the highway entrance.

And then he saw it.

Glancing around to be sure there was no one nearby, the man stepped over a chuckhole filled with rainwater and made his way to a 1997 Chevy van. He looked around again, then reached under the rear bumper and carefully ran his fingers along the surface until he felt the tape. Peeling it away, he retrieved a set of keys from their hiding place. With one he unlocked the door and slid wearily inside. He inserted the other key in the ignition and turned it over. The motor started up instantly, the gas gauge showing nearly full. Slowly he backed out of the parking stall and drove away in the same direction as the charter bus.

Three miles east of the lodge, he turned off the highway onto a road that was, in actuality, little more than a set of tire tracks through the tall grass. When he came to a stop, four muddy, rain-soaked people moved out of the brush and surrounded the vehicle. Wearily they pushed their packs through the side door opening and climbed in after. The driver and two of the men crawled underneath the gear and the tarp and lay on their backs, shivering from the cold dampness.

The remaining man climbed behind the wheel while the woman closed the side door, then pulled herself up onto the passenger seat. They each watched a side mirror while backing the van through the undergrowth and out onto the highway. According to the information they had been given, they would come to another ranger station a few miles down the road, this one part of Montana's Glacier Park system.

Fifteen minutes later, the van rolled to a stop in front of a small hut. A female ranger was sitting inside reading a paperback novel. The driver acknowledged her with a smile and held up the Glacier Park tourist pass that had been left on the seat. She returned the smile and waved the van through, not wanting to get wet for the sake of examining the ticket's date validity. Few people ever tried to cheat the system anyway. As the van pulled away, she quickly resumed her reading.

Had she been Ranger George McClintock, she might have taken note that the couple was of Middle Eastern heritage. And no doubt she would have noticed that the van had California license plates. But like Ranger McClintock before her, she would not have seen the other three passengers lying motionless in the back with their automatic weapons and bags of explosives.

As the rain continued to fall, the van sped on toward its destination.

Team number one was safely in the U.S.

5

Friday, 9 September, local time 1845
Baytown, California

Jeremy Cain was eleven years old when his family had moved to California, and he'd never quite gotten over it. Back in Washington, where they'd come from, Gramma and Papa Cain had lived about fifteen minutes across town, and Gramma and Papa Stevens were over in Spokane, about a five-hour drive away. Every year when he was a boy, they had spent the holidays with the grandparents—Thanksgiving at one house and Christmas at the other. Usually the cousins were all there too, and they always had great fun together.

But after the Cains moved to California, it seemed like they never saw anybody. There had been a few visits from the relatives, of course, but it wasn't the same. Six years later, he still missed sitting with the extended family around the holiday dinner table, holding hands while they listened to Papa give thanks to the Lord for His many blessings, and then digging in to all the turkey, dressing, mashed potatoes, brown gravy, yams, apple salad with walnuts, and hot rolls a boy could eat. And, of course, they always finished with a big slice of pumpkin pie with whipped cream on top.

He still remembered the Thanksgiving when he had carried his new baby sister up to Papa and Gramma Stevens's front door for the first time. He was so proud. He'd held her up to Gramma and she had taken Jessica in her arms while Papa looked over her shoulder, beaming with proud delight at their very first granddaughter. Somehow Jeremy had felt that he was a big part of it all. He was included. Secure. Important. That's how he'd felt. Like a big brother ought to feel.

But after they moved to Baytown, he felt like he'd been cut loose from all his moorings. Going into sixth grade—and then junior high—had to be the worst time of all to move, especially if your dad was a pastor. Once the other kids found out, they teased him mercilessly about being "the preacher's kid," and several of the more streetwise boys seemed to make it their life's mission to try to corrupt him.

By the time he entered his teen years, he had made some friends at school and in the youth group at Calvary Church, and he had proven himself on the basketball court, which earned him acceptance with the jocks and some of the girls. When he got to high school, he started working out on weights every day and by his seventeenth birthday, he was six feet two inches tall and weighed in at 178 pounds of lean, hard muscle. Every summer, the California sun shaded his body a darker tan and bleached his hair an even lighter blond.

As his senior year got under way, however, life was not going at all smoothly for Jeremy Cain. It was difficult and becoming more so every day. He looked good on the outside, but inside things were happening. Bad things. And Jeremy did not know what to do about them.

The first blow came when his girlfriend, Aletha, broke up with him during the summer. That was a real downer. Aletha was bright, beautiful, and popular—last year's homecoming queen—and being seen with her had really meant something. Status. Acceptance.

As if that weren't enough, his position as starting point guard on the Macarthur High School basketball team looked more like a question mark than an exclamation point. After working hard to make the team the past two years, and then turning in excellent performances, he should have been secure his senior year. Coach Riley had as much as said so. But Jim Burnett, a junior transfer from a big school in Fresno, was making a bid for the same spot this year, and he was good. Very good. Practice would not officially begin for another couple of months, not until after football was over, but the guys on the team got together on their own to play several times a week, and Burnett had been turning some heads with his ball handling and his ability to drive the lane.

Pressure. Jeremy felt a lot of it. Actually, he could not remember a time when he hadn't. Life was filled with pressure. Demands. Responsibilities. Deadlines. Up to now, he had been able to stuff it. He wasn't sure just how or where. Maybe it was in some inner room. His dad always talked about the importance of keeping one's "inner rooms" clear and clean. Maybe that's where Jeremy stuffed things. Only this time he couldn't find a room to stuff it in. They were all full. Finding a way to release the pressure was becoming critical.

Jeremy had first tried beer when he was a freshman. It tasted pretty bad. It was on a dare anyway, so there wasn't much to it. The next time was during his sophomore year out at the lake with a bunch of the guys. That day he downed a couple of cans. It left him with a weird sort of high he had never experienced before.

Later on, again on a dare, he smoked a joint with a buddy. The feeling of not being totally in control made him apprehensive. His parents, of course, were strongly against any experimenting with drugs. He wasn't sure about all the bad things drugs might do to you, but he did possess a healthy fear of their addictive power.

There were plenty of opportunities for experimentation, but Jeremy steered clear of them. And as far as smoking was concerned, that seemed stupid, period. He was outspoken on the subject and had a real thing about keeping his body free from its ill effects. He resented when others smoked around him and was quick to tell them so.

But when things had come to a head this past summer, Jeremy determined he had to do something to relieve the pressure he felt. He was tense a good deal of the time. Anxious. Most of all, he was angry. With Aletha. With Jim Burnett. With Coach Riley. With his father. With . . . well, who knows? But mostly he was angry with himself. The anger burned inside him like a furnace.

After he and Aletha stopped seeing each other, Jeremy chose what appeared to be the quickest, cheapest, and safest release, the one offering the easiest and fastest results. He remembered the buzz he had felt before when he'd had a couple of beers, so he started drinking. At first, not being in control bothered him. Then one night he got totally blitzed. Fortunately, he was at his friend Geoff's house, so he just stayed overnight and avoided being caught by his parents. With Geoff, he soon stepped up to smoking marijuana, and he made his first buy in July. In his mind, that was somehow different than smoking cigarettes, and it didn't take long before he was using pot regularly. By the time school opened in September, Jeremy was well into a downhill slide.

His grades had been okay last year. He was not a great student, but he was no dummy either. He figured he'd go on to college somewhere, and maybe there would be a basketball scholarship if he had a really good season. But the way things were going in his life lately, he didn't much care. A sinkhole had opened inside him. He felt empty. Lonely. Distant. He could not talk about it with anyone. The more he tried to fill the emptiness, the bigger the hole grew.

Jeremy knew he was slipping. He knew he needed help. But where does a preacher's kid go for help? He wasn't going to talk to his dad about anything. He was too busy with people from the church anyway, and besides, he was part of the problem. Jeremy had tested the water a couple of times, but his dad had been too preoccupied. In fact, for the past year, both of his parents were really out of it. They hardly talked to each other, much less to him or Jessica.

If the other pastors' kids knew what was going on, they would tell their parents and that would be that. Coach Riley would kick him off the team if he confided in him. If he went to the principal, he would probably be expelled from school. There was nowhere to go for help. So his slide continued, undetected by those closest to him.

One night, later in the summer, Jeremy went with some church kids to McDonalds for burgers and shakes. Afterward, everyone went to The Castle to play miniature golf and Jeremy ended up with Allison Orwell as his partner. Allison's father, Dr. Sidney Orwell, was the top orthopedic surgeon in Baytown and until recently had served on the board of elders at Calvary Church. Her mother sang in the choir. Jeremy and Allison putted around the course, laughed a lot, and genuinely had fun. Of course they weren't strangers, having been in Sunday school and youth group together for the past six years. Still, that night at The Castle had been different. Jeremy thought Allison had noticed it, too.

A few days later, he had called her and asked her out to a movie.

It felt good when she said yes.

Tonight was the big night, their first official date. Jeremy was on his way to Allison's house, and then they were picking up Geoff and Sarah on the way to the movie theater.

Geoff was fast becoming Jeremy's closest friend. Geoff's dad was also a member of the church board, but Jeremy didn't like him very much. He was too egotistical. Hardly ever smiled. Maybe that's the way attorneys are. Besides, he was overweight and Jeremy couldn't understand how someone could let himself go like that. Geoff and his dad didn't get along all that well, either, and Geoff had pretty much stopped going to church when he turned sixteen.

"Church is for losers," he had told Jeremy one day. "I know your dad is in the church business and all—and he's a cool enough guy, but I'm sorry. I mean, hey, get a life, Jeremy. There's just too much to do, too many things to experience, and too short a time to do it all in. Loosen up, man. You and I could have some really good times if we wanted to."

Jeremy wanted to.

And tonight was one of those nights.

6

Jeremy was dressed in a blue pullover, jeans, and Nikes when he rang Allison's doorbell. It was nearly seven o'clock

"Hi, Jeremy." Mrs. Orwell smiled as she opened the door. "Come on in. I'll get her for you. She's out back feeding the dog."

"Thank you, Mrs. Orwell."

He stood in the entry while she went to find Allison. It was an impressive house. From where he stood, he could see lots of wood paneling. Jeremy liked wood paneling. A mahogany hall table stood against the wall by the door. A small mirror in a wood frame with gold-leaf detail hung just above it. It looked expensive. His eyes wandered along the hallway. It all looked expensive. One wall was lined with pictures of boots and shoes. A blue velvet shoe. A brown boot. A purple spangle boot. A pink velvet shoe. Shoes worn by women a hundred years ago.

Why would anyone hang up pictures of old shoes? Strange.

Allison came around the corner. "Hi, Jeremy. Sorry you had to wait. Tango was hungry."

"I didn't know you had a dog."

"Seven years. Tango's a beagle. And she's *so* sweet. I just love her."

Jeremy opened the door just as Mrs. Orwell reappeared.

"Honey, remember your father and I have a fund-raising dinner for the hospital tonight. When that's finished, we've been invited to the Hatfield's for a reception. We won't get in until after midnight. What time do you plan to be home?"

Allison looked at Jeremy.

"We're picking up Geoff and Sarah, Mrs. Orwell. We figured we'd take in a movie and maybe go for something to eat afterwards. What time should I have Allison back?"

Mrs. Orwell smiled and put her hand on his shoulder. "I'd like her home by midnight."

"No problem."

"If you are going to be later than that, please call me. I'll keep my cell phone on. Okay?"

"Okay, Mom, I will." Allison gave her mother a kiss on the cheek. "Bye, Mom."

"Bye, dear. Bye, Jeremy. Have fun."

Jeremy followed Allison through the doorway and down the porch steps. She was wearing denim walking shorts and a white short-sleeve cotton knit top. Her skin was bronzed from the summer sun. Jeremy knew Allison loved the outdoors and was an excellent swimmer. Her brown hair was thick and long, past her shoulders. He opened the passenger door. As she stepped in, he noticed her silver ear hoops with dangling blue colored drops. *She's tall, too,* Jeremy decided, closing the door and walking around to the driver's side. *Maybe five-eight? It's funny how you can be in the same youth group all your life and not really notice someone.*

"What are we seeing?" Allison asked, as they drove away.

"I don't know. We'll wait to see what's playing."

Three stop signs and a signal light later, they saw Geoff and Sarah sitting on a corner bus stop bench, just south of Sarah's house. Geoff was in jeans, shoes with no socks, and a yellow shirt open part way down the front. Sarah, who was sixteen but could pass for eighteen or nineteen, was dressed in short shorts and a light orange cotton top, buttoned down the front, with long sleeves pushed up to the elbow. Her well-developed figure was often a topic of conversation in the boys' locker room, and she wasn't shy about putting her curves on display. When they saw Jeremy's car approaching, Geoff and Sarah stood up and stepped off the curb, each carrying a brown paper bag.

"Hey," greeted Geoff, sliding into the backseat. "Let's party."

"Hi, Allison," smiled Sarah. "Haven't seen you in a while." She and Allison both attended Macarthur but didn't have any classes together.

"What's in the bags?" asked Jeremy, as he turned left onto Sonora Drive. It was about a mile to the Galaxy Theater.

"What else?" exclaimed Geoff, reaching into the bag and lifting out a six-pack of beer.

"Where did you get that?"

"Never mind, ol' buddy. We got it. That's what's important." Geoff took an opener from his pocket. "You can never start a party too early, I always say."

Jeremy heard the cap pop off as Geoff opened the first beer. He handed it to Sarah. A second bottle was passed over the seat to Allison.

"No thanks, Geoff. We're almost to the theater."

"Here, Jeremy. Down the hatch." Geoff was laughing.

Jeremy suddenly felt awkward. He glanced over at Allison. She was watching to see what he would do.

"Not now. There's plenty of time later. Right now we have to pick a movie. What do you guys want to see?"

They pulled into the cinema parking lot. Geoff and Jeremy put the beer in the trunk of the car. They walked toward the box office, reading the marquee descriptions of movie titles and show times.

"How about *Thornton's Country*?" Jeremy said. "It starts in fifteen minutes and it's PG-13."

"Sounds good to me," Allison said.

"Whatever," Geoff said with a shrug.

"Yeah, that's fine," Sarah added.

They purchased four tickets and went inside. After the tickets had been torn by the usher, they stood in line for popcorn.

"Let's see *The Torn Edge*," suggested Geoff as they moved closer to the counter.

"But we bought tickets for *Thornton's Country*," said Allison.

"So? It doesn't matter. Once you're inside, nobody ever checks. We can take in any flick we want. I want to see *The Torn Edge*. I hear it's really good."

"Well, I've heard it's got lots of sex and violence. Some of it is supposed to be pretty explicit."

"Like I said, Allison. I've heard it's really good."

When their turn came, they ordered two large popcorns and two large Cokes. Sarah grabbed four straws and a stack of napkins, while Jeremy and Geoff picked up the popcorn buckets and Cokes. As they moved away from the counter, Allison reached for a handful of popcorn and turned away from Geoff and Sarah for a moment.

"Jeremy," she whispered.

"Hmmm?"

"I really don't want to go to *The Torn Edge*. Can't we see *Thornton's Country* instead, like we planned?"

Jeremy looked at her. He could tell by the look on her face that she was troubled.

"No problem. Hey, Geoff. We want to see *Thornton's Country*. If you want to see the other flick, we'll meet you here later."

"Aw, come on, you guys."

"There's only a ten minute difference in starting times, so the flicks will be over about the same time. All right? Then we can get something to eat."

"Okay. But you're making a bad choice here. I mean, really. This is a four-star job."

"We'll see you guys later," said Sarah, taking Geoff by the arm. "Hurry, Geoff. We don't want to miss the beginning."

The two couples parted.

"I'm sorry, Jeremy. I hope you don't mind not going to that other film."

"It's okay. I'm having a good time just being with you."

"It was nice of you to say 'we' just now, instead of blaming it on me. I'm kind of embarrassed. Are you sure you're okay about this?"

"Sure." Jeremy felt good. As luck would have it, he had stumbled into the right pronoun for once in his life.

The first preview was running as they found their seats.

—∾—

After the movies, the two couples drove to a nearby café for burgers and fries. Later they cruised the main streets of Baytown. It was warm, so they drove with the windows rolled down. The breeze blowing through their hair felt wonderful, and the beer was in the backseat again. It seemed like a great way to top off their meal.

Allison had accepted a bottle from Geoff after they left the café. Jeremy noticed that she put it to her lips a couple of times, but she didn't actually drink very much. He got the feeling it made her uncomfortable. Most of the beer was still in her bottle by the time the others were digging into the second six-pack.

After a few turns up and down the main drag, they parked on a dark side street near the Macarthur High School campus.

"Come on, guys," exclaimed Sarah, reaching for the door handle. "Let's go out to the football field."

They scrambled out of the car, scooped up the remaining bottles of beer, and ran toward the field. Jeremy was feeling light-headed, his first telltale sign of losing control. He knew he shouldn't. The caution light went on in his brain, but he kept on running.

They fell in a heap together at the center of the field, right on the fifty yard line. Sarah's laugh was louder than normal.

"Shhh," Geoff admonished with a hiss.

"Keep it down, Sarah. We don't want to get caught out here. Especially with this beer."

"Then let's drink it up," said Sarah defiantly, already giving evidence of having consumed more than enough. She reached for the opener and held bottles out to the others. "Come on. We're on the fifty yard line. Think about it. We'll be sitting in those bleachers over there next Friday watching a stupid football game. But we'll be remembering tonight."

Bottles clinked. Laughter filled the warm night air. Jeremy hesitated for a second, then took another bottle and joined the others. In the back of his mind he noted that Allison was still holding her first bottle. At least he thought it was her first. He thought he had better slow down, but soon all that remained were empties.

The four lay on the grass at midfield, looking up at the starry night.

"There's the Big Dipper," said Geoff, pointing off in the distance.

"Where's the little one?" Allison asked.

"Who cares?" said Sarah, turning until her arm was across Geoff's chest. Jeremy watched as she brushed her lips over Geoff's.

"You taste like lipstick and beer," Geoff laughed. He put his arms around her and drew her close. They kissed again.

7

Before long, it turned quiet on the football field. Geoff and Sarah were obviously engrossed in each other. Jeremy turned his attention to Allison. She sat cross-legged, across from him, drawing patterns in the grass with her finger. He struggled to focus clearly. Was she just being quiet? sad? or what? Maybe she was waiting for him to make a move. He couldn't tell. He reached for her. She hesitated at first, then scooted closer until his arm went around her. He really was feeling light-headed as he bent to kiss her. Their lips touched tentatively. Hers felt cool.

Encouraged, he drew her closer. His hand dropped to her leg.

She pushed his hand back, twisting away at the same time.

"Stop, Jeremy," she whispered. "That's enough."

Stunned, Jeremy sat back, staring at Allison. *What is this?*

She got to her feet and walked away.

Jeremy glanced over at Geoff and Sarah. They were locked in each other's arms, oblivious to anything else that might be happening.

He pushed to his feet, swaying slightly as he followed after Allison. She was standing just across the sideline, near where the home bench would be.

That's significant, Jeremy, a little voice inside his head whispered. Jeremy paid no attention. He'd gotten pretty good at ignoring his conscience.

"What's wrong?" His words slurred slightly as he came up to her.

She looked up. He saw that she was crying.

"Hey, I'm sorry. I didn't mean to do anything to upset you."

"You're drunk."

"Pardon me?" he said.

"You're drunk!"

Allison's blunt accusation sank in slowly.

"Wait a minute. I've only had . . . maybe three beers tonight."

"You've had four. That I counted."

"That you counted? You counted?" he repeated.

"Yes, I counted."

"Who do you think you are?" Jeremy's voice raised angrily. "My father?"

No answer. She brushed at the tears with her hand.

"Well?"

"Give me the car keys."

"What?"

"The keys. Give them to me."

"Hey, wait a minute. It's my car. These are my keys. I'm not giving them to you or anybody else for that matter."

"Jeremy, give me the keys or I'll walk home. I'm not getting in a car with a drunk driver!"

He peered at her in the moonlit shadows. The tears had caused her eye makeup to run. But she was not shaking or sobbing. She was not emotionally out of control. What was the look on her face? Disappointment? She extended her hand toward him, palm up. Without a word, he reached into his pocket, pulled out the keys, handed them over, then turned abruptly and walked back to the others.

Geoff and Sarah were sitting close together now, holding hands.

"You guys ready?" Jeremy asked.

"Sure. Hey, what time is it?"

Jeremy held his watch up close.

"It's past midnight."

Geoff and Sarah stood and started walking away, still holding hands.

"Wait. Help me pick up the bottles."

"Oh, right! Like, hey, man, who cares about the bottles? Let some bozo groundskeeper pick them up on Monday."

Jeremy flashed Geoff an angry look, but said nothing. Suddenly he didn't like Geoff very much. He was acting too much like his old man. He started putting the bottles back into the grocery bags.

"Chill out, man," Geoff responded gruffly. "Come on, Sarah. Let's give Mr. Clean here a hand."

"Where's Allison?" asked Sarah, wiping at her nose with her forearm.

"Over by the car," answered Jeremy. "Geoff, get those two over there. They're the last ones."

When they got to the car, Allison was sitting behind the wheel, looking straight ahead.

Everyone was quiet on the way home.

Geoff and Sarah got out at the corner near Sarah's house. They dumped the bags of bottles into a garbage can chained to the bus stop bench. Allison pulled away from the curb and continued driving toward her house. Jeremy leaned against the door, glaring out the side window. Once in a while she glanced over at him. He did not look at her.

"Jeremy, why are you so angry?"

Her question startled him. He struggled with his thoughts, trying to find a suitable response.

"I don't know. What makes you think I'm angry?"

No answer.

Allison slowed the car and pulled to a stop in front of her house. She shut off the engine.

They sat in silence.

"Do you want me to drive you home?" she asked.

"No."

"I don't think you should be driving in your condition."

"Stop judging me!" Jeremy snapped.

Silence.

"I'm not judging you, Jeremy. I care about you. A lot, in fact. Sometimes I think I care about you more than you do yourself."

More silence.

"What do you mean?" he asked at last.

"I mean, I want to know. Why are you so angry? I've been around you in the youth group for a long time. What I saw tonight is not the Jeremy that I used to know. You're different. You're angry about something. It frightens me. I didn't know you drank like this. I tried being cool tonight. But it's not me. I don't even like the stuff. And I hate seeing you drunk. It seems like such a waste."

Jeremy didn't respond. For a second, Allison thought he had fallen asleep. She leaned closer. His eyes suddenly burned into hers. *Surprise.*

"I was disappointed earlier," she continued when she saw that he was awake. She spoke quietly, evenly, but with conviction. "I mean with Geoff and Sarah. What they did made me sad. First of all, buying tickets for one movie and going to another. Maybe it's nothing, but to me it was dishonest. Next, the booze was illegal because we're all under age. You know what your dad says? He says we become tomorrow what we feed our minds and bodies today. I've decided he's right. Don't you think he's right?"

Jeremy sat up straighter. "I think you *are* my dad," he muttered.

"Why do you keep saying that I'm your dad? You said that before, too."

"Because you sound just like him when you preach," the slightest trace of a grin formed on Jeremy's face.

"I'm *not* preaching!" Allison laughed, slapping him gently on the shoulder. "I'm just concerned about you, that's all. Talk to me, Jeremy. What's making you so uptight that you have to drown it in all this alcohol?"

Silence. A long silence.

Why am *I so uptight? That's the big question, isn't it? How many answers is she ready for? Because my world is falling apart? Because I don't feel accepted? Because I hate being a preacher's kid? Because I've had to change my life so that Dad could "answer God's call"? Because the church people take everything he has to give and there's nothing left for me? Because my old man doesn't know who I am? Even Mom doesn't care. She just suffers alone. Well, I miss her, too.*

Jeremy felt the "inner furnace" flare suddenly at the thought.

How could God ever allow this? Maybe if we hadn't come here in the first place, all this might never have happened!

He opened his eyes. He hadn't realized that he'd squeezed them shut until that moment. Allison was looking at him. Waiting.

"I guess I'm not ready to talk about it," he said, shifting his legs and reaching across the seat to take her hand. "Not yet, anyway. You know something? You are the first person to ask. No one else ever has. No one. So thanks for that. But I think right now the best thing for me is to go home."

Jeremy pressed her hand gently.

"If I haven't blown our relationship completely tonight, I'd like to ask you out again," he said. "Next time, just you and me. No *Torn Edge* movies. No beer. No Geoff and Sarah. Maybe I'll be ready to talk then. Give me another chance?"

Allison stared out the window and didn't reply.

Jeremy thought about how he'd handled things the past few months. There wasn't much to be proud of. It wasn't the way he'd been brought up. He suddenly felt ashamed. He was acting like a hypocrite and that was a word he really hated. He had let Geoff control the evening. Even Sarah was more in charge than he had been. He was embarrassed. Humiliated. And angry. Why was he so angry? Maybe it would help to talk about it. Later.

"Allison, the truth is I don't really know much about anything right now." He hesitated. "I know that I like you."

Both of them laughed at that.

She leaned over, resting her hand on his shoulder and kissed him on the cheek. He sat perfectly still and looked into her eyes. They glistened, promising something more than he could fathom at the moment. Just what he wasn't sure. He got out of the car, walked around and opened the door for her. They stood close for just a moment. Then without a word, she started up the sidewalk.

"Jeremy?" She paused at the porch steps and turned toward him. "Be careful driving the rest of the way, okay?"

He waved and grinned.

"And what you asked about? With all the conditions you mentioned a moment ago? The answer is yes. Call me."

She ran up the steps and disappeared into the house.

He thought about Allison the rest of the way home.

And he smiled.

For the first time in a long time he felt . . . almost peaceful.

Peaceful, that is, until he reached home. As he drove the car into the driveway, he bounced the front left wheel off the pavement and onto the grass, breaking off a sprinkler head.

Oh, great. He backed onto the pavement and shut off the ignition. Heaving a huge sigh, one filled with spent emotion, he opened the car door and squinted at his watch under the dome light.

One-fifteen.

Carefully balancing himself, he got out of the car and instinctively locked the door. He was glad to have made it home safely and he looked forward to hitting the sack. He felt queasy.

He tried to close the car door quietly, but when it shut it sounded much louder than it should. He walked toward the house, tripping as he came around the corner of the garage. Catching himself before he fell, he looked up to gauge how much farther it was to the porch.

That's when he saw his father sitting in the shadows on the stone bench near the door.

8

9 SEPTEMBER, LOCAL TIME 1912
BOOTH BAY, MAINE

Mohammed Ibn Ahmer cast off the last line and jumped on board. He made his way quickly to the wheel of the twenty-four-foot cabin cruiser. Both large twin outboard motors gurgled to life at the first press of the ignition button. Carefully, and with a practiced eye, he guided the boat between the two larger vessels moored on either side and pulled away from the dock. He glanced at a man who was tying down a sailboat a few feet away, but the man didn't look up. Seeing a young, barefoot girl, dressed in shorts and a windbreaker, standing near the boat's single mast, Mohammed waved. The girl smiled and waved back.

Where do young families get the money for a boat like that?

Moving the throttle forward slowly, Mohammed turned his attention to the task of getting safely beyond the last of the small boats anchored around him. Most sailors were off the sea for the day. The only other vessel going out was the *Bay Lady,* carrying a load of tourists, hoping to catch the sunset and see the seals playing off the tiny island that divided the center of the bay.

Good. The fewer boats around the better.

Clearing the breakwater, Mohammed opened the throttle. The engines surged and the boat shot across the darkening surface of the water. The steady beat of choppy seas passing underneath vibrated through his feet and ankles. Clutching the wheel firmly, he bent his knees against the shock of the waves. Hundreds of colorful lobster markers bobbed up and down on white-capped waves as the westerly evening breeze began to increase in intensity. As the last of the sun disappeared behind trees lining the far shore, the early evening air took on a chilly bite.

Pulling his jacket tightly around his neck, Mohammed reached for the fur-lined gloves he had stashed in the cubby. Balancing the wheel with his knee, he slipped on the right one, then the left. Bracing himself against the captain's chair, his eyes darted back and forth, scanning the seascape. No other vessels were visible. The red beacon from the lighthouse on the point gave off its intermittent warning. Mohammed felt his pulse quicken with a first twinge of excitement.

Then he headed straight out to sea.

—∞—

The *Achille Larissa* took its name from a city of one hundred thousand citizens, located in the eastern Thessalonica region of Greece. For the last several days, the rusty old freighter had plowed through heavy, North Atlantic seas on its way to New York harbor. The captain and his small crew were tired. Rough weather made long crossings like these seem even longer. Only two crew members were on duty in the engine room. The others were sleeping in their bunks. On the bridge, Captain Nicholas Rotis checked the navigational instruments and peered into the night. Stars were no longer visible. A fog bank had settled on the water, making long-range visual sightings impossible.

"Go to half," Rotis ordered the ship's first mate.

"Half speed, cap'n," came the hoarse, deep-throated reply.

The freighter settled deeper into the ocean swells. For a full five minutes no one said a word. Both men kept an eye on the instruments, occasionally looking up to peer into the blackness of the night that enveloped them.

"Quarter speed," the captain said abruptly. "We have to be close now."

"Quarter speed, cap'n."

"Slow her till we're almost dead in the water, then hold her steady, while I go below."

No one was fooling first mate George Theophilous. He'd known about the three mysterious passengers ever since they came on board. He was curious, but knew better than to ask.

The last night the *Larissa* had been docked in the seedy port city of Piraeus, he had been standing in the shadows on the upper deck, having a cigarette when they arrived. They drove up together in a dark-colored automobile. It had barely come to a stop when the three jumped out, opened the trunk, and began removing baggage. There was a minute or two of indistinguishable conversation with the driver who remained unseen in the car. Then as quietly as it had come, the car pulled away and disappeared into the night, leaving the three men standing alone on the dock.

They'd made their way onto the main deck, each carrying a large waterproof duffel bag. The bags had looked heavy. Theophilous was certain they contained more than a change of clothing. He'd been about to call out when Captain Rotis had suddenly materialized in the darkness. Theophilous had stayed back out of sight while Rotis carried on a brief conversation with the men, then stepped to one side as they passed and disappeared below.

Theophilous had seen the men, only twice since then, both times in the late evening. They stood together near the starboard rail, smoking and talking quietly. He had not been able to make out their conversation, but he was sure they were not Greeks. The few words he had heard were not in his native tongue. Another language, possibly Arabic, but he hadn't been close enough to tell for sure.

The *Achille Larissa* rolled slowly as Theophilous kept her headed into the cold wind. Dampness from the fog beaded up, trailing in tiny rivulets across the cabin windows. He reached over to switch on the wipers.

Just then an object dropped away from the vessel on the starboard side.

"What the—," Theophilous exclaimed, leaning forward for a better look. Then he cursed. "A raft. They've dropped a raft." He peered past the window wipers, trying to get a better look. For a moment, the upper part of a man's torso was visible, then disappeared.

"One thing for sure," he said out loud to himself, "whoever these guys are, if they try getting off the ship in these seas they've got to be crazy—or dangerous. Or both."

Glancing at the chart in front of him, he estimated their position about eleven miles off the coast of Maine. Theophilous shook his head. "That's a long way to row your boat."

Below deck the starboard cargo door was partially open. The wind seemed even stronger here as the three men stood near the opening, making last-minute checks of their gear. The raft was a dark blob on the surface below, straining and bucking against its tether like some wild denizen of the deep. A rope ladder was dropped over the side. The distance was only a few short meters from the lower deck to the water and easily traversable under normal circumstances. But the wind and choppy seas made it more treacherous tonight.

Captain Rotis stepped forward. Each man shook his hand solemnly. The last man passed him an envelope which he stuffed inside his jacket. Padding to the doorway on swim fins, the first man attached a length of safety line to the tether ring, grasped the ladder tightly, and began his descent toward the raft.

Looking down, he tried to gauge his position in relation to the bouncing raft. With about one meter to go, and directly above it, he turned loose of the ladder and dropped. In that same instant the raft slammed against the ship and twisted away. The man landed against the side of the raft with one leg and disappeared into the sea.

Captain Rotis balanced himself with a handhold and leaned forward, straining to see what was happening. Out of the corner of his eye, he saw the others standing in the doorway. Neither of them made a sound. They appeared completely stoic, with no visible emotion, as they watched their companion resurface and struggle to reach the raft. His hand came out of the water, grasping for the line that was threaded through rings around its slippery sides. With a huge effort he pulled himself up and over, falling into the raft face first. He lay there for several seconds, gasping for breath. Then he rolled over and looked up. As the raft banged against the ship again, he reached up and slipped the line through the ladder's lowest rung, holding it taut and as steady as possible. The second man had already started down. In a few seconds, he was safely aboard the raft and unhooking his line.

At their signal, the remaining member of the trio attached the three water-sealed duffel bags to the tether line and watched as, one by one, they dropped toward the raft. The men below quickly gathered them in. Then the third man followed, dropping into the raft without incident.

They waved to the captain as one of the men produced a knife from his belt and cut the tether line. Captain Rotis pulled it in quickly, dropping it in a puddle of seawater on the cargo deck. Next, he dragged the soggy rope ladder back through the opening and pressed the button that powered the cargo door. As the door closed, a final glance outside revealed only the dark turbulence of the sea. All traces of his passengers were gone.

Captain Rotis touched the envelope tucked away inside his jacket and turned to go above deck.

—ꟽ—

Mohammed Ibn Ahmer kept his eye on the compass, occasionally taking a quick look at the navigational chart clipped to the board in front of him. The cold had turned bitter now and he wished that he could dig out an extra sweater.

He had put one on board, but he could not leave the wheel long enough to get it. The fog made visibility nearly zero. Every bit of his attention was focused on the task. In spite of the cold, a damp sweat was forming on his brow.

This is like looking for a small rock in the desert. Let's hope their signal device is working.

He flipped the small switch to an emergency radio channel. And waited.

I should be near them.

Nothing.

Mohammed maintained a steady course heading out to sea, but he cut the throttle back to half speed. The waves ran high and the fog was low here, but not all the way down to the surface. Visibility had improved to about fifty meters, and Mohammed stared intently into the darkness.

The radio crackled and Ahmer heard a steady *beep . . . beep . . . beep . . .*

Then silence.

As Mohammed peered again into the black night, the beeping was repeated. He answered with three clicks on his radio and waited.

Silence.

Finally, he heard *beep . . . beep . . .*

Then more silence.

They had heard. Mohammed knew they would not risk another transmission. They wanted to be located, but not by the Coast Guard. Five minutes later, Mohammed saw a light flash low against the sea, disappear, then reappear once more. It was starboard at about two o'clock. The cruiser churned through the swells toward where the light had last been seen.

There it is again!

Mohammed smiled, partly from elation, partly from relief.

Allah be praised! This is a good sign.

He flashed a signal in return.

Minutes later, he backed the throttle to near idle, just strong enough to hold the cruiser steady into the wind, and tossed a line toward the bobbing raft. The increased rolling motion threw him off balance. He missed, cursing as he fell to one knee. Retrieving the line now soaked with seawater, he coiled it and heaved it once again. This time it fell directly across the center of the raft. Cold hands reached out, grabbed it quickly, and slipped it through the anchor eye.

Mohammed held the cruiser steady, powering forward as slowly as possible as hand-over-hand the three pulled the raft closer. It seemed to Mohammed that it was taking an uncomfortably long time for them to come alongside, but he knew they were just being careful not to bang into the cruiser's outboard motors. No one wanted to capsize.

At last a hand reached over the side of the larger craft and one of the men pulled himself on board. Without a word he turned to assist the others, who balanced themselves as best they could while passing the duffel bags up to their teammate. Then, quickly, all three were aboard the cruiser and two of them were leaning back over the side to slash the rubber raft with knives. Satisfied that their task was complete, they cut the line. The sinking raft disappeared from sight.

Squatting down in puddles of water, they shivered with cold, gasping for breath as Mohammed Ibn Ahmer turned the cruiser about and headed for shore.

"Welcome, my friends," he said, looking back over his shoulder. "And congratulations. You have done well. Leave the bags where they are. They will be fine. Go below and you'll find towels to dry with and a fresh set of clothes for each of you. There are sleeping bags as well. If you need to lie down or simply wish to get warm again, use them. Go quickly. You've earned a comfortable journey the rest of the way to the enemy's stronghold."

9

From his sitting room window, Jim Brainard watched the light bobbing steadily nearer along the surface of the bay.

On nights when he couldn't sleep, Brainard often slipped out of bed, put on his robe and slippers, and shuffled into the next room. From his vantage point on top of McKnown Hill, he had the best of all worlds. Hill House was his pride and joy.

After working thirty-three years as a civil engineer for the City of Philadelphia, he and Middie had packed their things and moved "down east." There were no children and both of their parents had long since passed away. However, Jim and Middie Brainard both looked and acted the part of grandparents. Through the years, their snowy white hair and warm smiles caused the children of many a family to think of them as surrogate grandparents. Now, in retirement, they had each other and continued to share the rare, special gift of mutual love and respect that had carried them through all their years.

After searching for just the right spot, they had invested their life savings in Hill House, a rustic old place overlooking Booth Bay's harbor. It was a decision that turned out handsomely. Middie decorated the guest rooms in a colonial motif, each with a slightly different color scheme and thematic touch. Jim made certain that the heating, lighting, and plumbing continued to function and that all the bills were paid.

Many new friends from the community had come to the grand opening of Hill House, partly out of curiosity and partly because it was the only thing happening in Booth Bay on the last weekend in April. Champagne and New England cheeses were plentiful, along with ample amounts of punch and coffee. Walking through the well-appointed rooms or sitting in the spacious parlor, everyone agreed that they liked what had been done to the old place. Before the Brainards came, the house had fallen into disrepair, becoming an eyesore in an otherwise quaintly attractive seaside town. Now Hill House was once again something in which the whole community could take pride. And they did.

It was not long before the bed-and-breakfast was full, with a waiting list of people who wanted to stay there on vacation or for a romantic weekend away from the city. That first summer and fall, Hill House guests fell in love with their hosts. Amazingly, so did the locals, which is not the sort of thing Mainers normally do right away. But there was a winsome quality about this happy couple. They were genuine. They had not moved to Booth Bay to take so much as to give.

But then Middie had been diagnosed with cancer.

Surgery followed. Then radiation. But nine months later, Jim, with his customary tenderness and dignity, had laid Middie to rest in the community cemetery. He shed no public tears, shared none of his grief. As he stood by Middie's flower-bedecked coffin for a final solitary minute, a slightly quizzical look crossed his face, as though he still could not believe what had happened. Then he had shaken his head sadly, turned, and walked away. He had purchased Middie's burial plot and the one next to it only two days earlier. It was the one thing he and Middie had not taken care of before. They had come to Booth Bay to live, not to die.

Jim continued to operate Hill House, but with Middie gone he no longer served breakfast to the guests in the cheery kitchen overlooking the bay. He still had Rosa, though, the housemaid who had worked for the Brainards ever since they had opened the inn.

As the summer season began to wane and the number of guests declined, Jim gradually became more reclusive. At first, no one in town was concerned. Their customary reserve constrained them from "butting in" to a man's private grief. Most were not sure how to respond to sickness and sorrow. It made them uncomfortable. Soon it was easier just not to think about Jim struggling in the depths of his loneliness and loss. The few occasions when he attended mass at Our Lady Queen of Peace, or when folks would see him in town at the market, they would murmur their greetings and be on their way.

Now and again, Jim would be seen at the Harbor Inn, which had long been his and Middie's favorite place to dine. He always ate alone, with a book or newspaper on the table by his plate. He was polite. He smiled. He spoke when spoken to. But no one remembered hearing him laugh after Middie was gone.

During daylight hours, the view from the Hill House sitting room was nothing short of spectacular. Jim watched boats and people come and go around the docks at the bottom of the hill. His favorite window commanded a clear, unobstructed view of the bay all the way to the open sea. During the summer, fresh breezes blew through the screened opening, stroking his face with loving, seductive caresses that reminded him of younger days and the touch of Middie's hand on his cheek. When early autumn's crisp brush strokes emblazoned Booth Bay's canvas with hews of red, yellow, bronze, and green, Jim Brainard closed the window but maintained his daily vigil. He was contented, in a sad sort of way. It's just that all of this was meant to be shared.

At night, the magnificent bay became a black hole, befitting his feelings of loss and emptiness. The nights that he could not sleep he spent staring into the darkness. Sometimes he tried to read. Newspapers. Magazines. Books. Anything. But before long his mind wandered and he set the reading material aside. The small television in the corner near the ice machine remained dark. Inevitably, he came back to the black hole. The abyss. And the wearisome wait for dawn.

The light out on the bay was closer now.

After a while, Jim was able to discern the dark outline of a boat maneuvering through the maze of pleasure craft and sailing vessels. He listened as the sound of the outboard motors diminished and the boat slid silently into its place at the dock.

It's that Greek fella. Jim peered through the window as a man jumped from the boat onto the dock, reaching back as someone else handed him a line. *It must be him. He said he'd be late, but I thought he surely meant before midnight.*

He looked at the grandfather clock across the room. It read 2:20.

Jim Brainard's first encounter with Nicolas Hondros, "that Greek fella," had been several weeks before, when Hondros and his wife, Akilina, had come to Hill House for a night's stay. Before they checked out the next morning, they had inquired about renting a couple of rooms for a week's stay, beginning on September 11. When Jim commented on the date, Hondros had explained that a friend of his would be visiting from France and the two of them were planning to do some fishing, along with a couple of coworkers who would be driving up from Boston. The week of the eleventh was the only time they could all get together.

Hondros was small framed, dark skinned, and dressed well but casually, with expensive-looking shoes. Jim thought he looked Middle Eastern, or maybe Italian. He hadn't worked in the city all those years without becoming somewhat of an expert at ethnic distinctions. When he found out the man was Greek, it made sense. But the most memorable thing about Nicolas Hondros was that he paid for the rooms in advance, with fourteen $100 bills.

Just as Jim started to turn from the window, his eye caught further movement. He looked back at the boat. There were others on board. One. There's another. And a third man. Three all together plus the Greek. These must be the fishing buddies he was talking about. They were standing on the dock now, passing something between them. Ah, yes, cigarettes. Their backs were turned to the stiff breeze and away from Hill House. In the diffused light from a nearby street lamp, he watched the men pick up three large duffel bags and walk to a nearby car. A Cadillac. *Must be the Greek's car.* The four got in, the headlights came on, and the car pulled slowly away from the dock. As it started up the incline toward Hill House, Jim Brainard turned from the window and shuffled wearily back to his room. He would register his guests in the morning. He closed the door and climbed into bed, oblivious to the implications of what he had just witnessed.

Team number two was safely in the United States.

10

10 SEPTEMBER, LOCAL TIME 0125
BAYTOWN, CALIFORNIA

Jeremy stopped, startled by the silhouette of his father sitting there on the porch. For a long moment they just looked at each other. Jeremy's mind raced through a kaleidoscopic pattern jammed with emotional bits and pieces. He desperately wished he could turn and walk away, avoiding the inevitable confrontation. But his feet would not respond. He could not move.

The moon cast eerie shadows on his father's face. He looked sad, angry, tired—an ominous mix of emotions. He got up slowly from the bench.

"You're late, Jeremy," he said quietly, breaking the tense silence between them.

"I know," Jeremy mumbled, dropping his gaze to the sidewalk.

If I get any closer, he's going to know I've been drinking. I smell like a brewery.

"I'm sorry. The time got away from me."

Did I slur my words? Oh man, what's the best thing to do here?

"Come inside, son. I'll make us some coffee."

He knows.

Jeremy's anxiety heightened as he put one leaden foot forward, then the other.

Whatever you do, don't weave!

He attempted to focus on the front door, avoiding his father's steady gaze. He blinked several times to clear the blurriness from his vision, but it was hard. Although it wasn't the first time he'd had a few beers, Jeremy was not an experienced drinker. He thought the effects would have begun to wear off by now, but the amount he had consumed tonight was near his personal best, and he was still under the influence.

Try to be cool.

Unfortunately, his attempt to look cool was of such a quality that it would have landed him in the backseat of a patrol car if he had been pulled over.

His father's eyes never left him, even as he walked to the door and opened it for his son. Standing back, he waited for Jeremy to enter. Jeremy grasped the doorjamb for balance as he stepped up and in. In the entry, as he turned left toward the kitchen, the floor seemed to move a bit. With a feeling of relief, he reached the table and sat down heavily. His father busied himself with the coffeemaker, his back to the room and to Jeremy. So far, nothing more had been said between them.

For a long moment after the coffeemaker had begun to hiss and gurgle, John Cain stood hunched over the countertop. Slowly, he turned and came to the table, sitting down across from Jeremy.

The long silence between them continued, interrupted only by the sound of burbling water.

How long does it take to make coffee? And how long before he asks me the question?

John shifted in his chair. "You've been drinking."

Well, so much for timing. And no questions either. Just a matter-of-fact statement.

"Yes, I have," Jeremy answered, in as defiant a tone as he could muster.

A long pause.

"I thought you were going to a movie and then coming home."

"That's what we did."

"We?"

"Yeah, Geoff and I."

Pause.

"We went by and picked up Allison. And Sarah, too," Jeremy continued, adjusting the facts of his story slightly in an effort to make them more palatable to his father. "We went to the movie and afterward we had a couple of beers. Then we took the girls home and here I am."

Jeremy looked up, returning his father's steady gaze.

John pushed back his chair and went to the counter. He took two mugs from the cupboard above the coffeemaker, lifted the pot, and poured. Returning to the table with a cup in each hand, he held one out to Jeremy. Jeremy took it, but said nothing. The heat emanating through the ceramic surface warmed his hands. Lifting it to his mouth, he sipped at the hot, black liquid.

"Where did you go after the movie?"

"Just around. We drove around town for a while."

"The movie must have been over by nine-thirty. Four hours is a long time to just drive around town, don't you think?"

No answer.

"So I'm asking you again, Son. Where did you go after the movie?"

Jeremy scowled over the coffee cup. "What is this, Dad, the Inquisition or something? Hey, we drove around awhile and then stopped by the ball field."

"At your school?"

"Yeah. Then we dropped the girls off and here I am."

John looked steadily into his son's eyes.

"I didn't know there was a game tonight."

Jeremy locked eyes with his father's, but he couldn't hold it. He dropped his gaze to the table, slowly turning the coffee cup in his hands.

"So I take it that there was no game. What were you doing at the school at this time of night?"

"Look, what do you want me to say?" Jeremy's voice raised in defensiveness. "That we took the girls out on the field, jumped out of our clothes, and had sex? Is that what you want to hear? Well, we didn't. We had a few beers. We got back in the car and everybody went home. That was it. Now I'm tired of this. I just want to go to bed. Okay?"

Jeremy started to stand. His father reached a hand across the table, pushing him back.

"I'm not done talking to you, Jeremy," John said, his voice tinged with anger.

"Well, I'm done talking to you, Dad." Jeremy spit the words out, glaring defiantly at his father as he stood again. This time, John made no attempt to stop him. Jeremy started toward his room.

"Come here and sit down."

No answer. He continued walking away.

"Jeremy!"

He kept moving, feeling as vulnerable as a duelist stepping away from his opponent, all the while wondering if the other person would turn and shoot before ending their allotted paces. His steps quickened as he turned down the hall and into his room. Slamming the door behind him, he dropped down on the edge of the bed, brushing away tears of frustration with a clenched fist.

He swore angrily as he kicked a shoe into the corner. It was a word no one was ever permitted to use in the Cain household.

So he said it again.

—w—

John sat staring at the kitchen table, the coffee cup untouched and cold, and wondered how his world had gotten so out of control. The house was quiet again. It felt empty. Only an occasional night sound brought on by the changing temperature. He looked across the family room and through the patio door. Pale moonlight shimmered on the pool.

I guess the only good thing about tonight is that we didn't wake up the girls.

He felt old. Much older than his forty-four years. His thoughts moved from Jeremy to the breakfast meeting scheduled with the church board a few short hours from now. It was not a meeting he looked forward to. Then he still had some sermon preparation to complete before Sunday's services. Oh, yes, there was also the Hollister and Sanderson wedding. Saturday afternoon. He'd almost forgotten about that.

Early Monday morning, he would be counting noses at San Francisco International, gathering everyone for ticket and passport presentation at the departure counter as he and twenty-four other passengers boarded a flight to Los Angeles. From there they would take a transfer bus from domestic arrivals to international departures and board a KLM jet for a nonstop flight to Amsterdam. The group would overnight at the Krasnapolsky Hotel on Dam Square. John liked the Krasnapolsky. It was a great hotel in the old European tradition. The following day, at noon, they would be back at Schiphol Airport for another KLM flight, this one to Israel.

He knew the routine well. This would be his sixth trip to the Holy Land, and the fifth time he'd led a group there. It had been awhile since the last time, though. The perpetual fighting between Israel and the Palestinians had kept him away. But now, thanks to the two women featured on last week's *Time* and *Newsweek* covers, everything looked as good as it had in years. In a couple of weeks they would be signing a Permanent Agreement. Borders were open again. Tourism was coming back on line. Groups of pilgrims were returning to the sacred sites.

On previous journeys, the last-minute preparations had added to the excitement. Not this time. Esther had decided she did not want to go. John disliked taking long trips like this without her. He had tried talking her into it, thinking that the time away might help them both. But she was adamant and had grown angry, accusing him of manipulating her. She didn't want to go and that was that.

So John had decided to take Jessica instead. He and Esther had always planned for the children to see that part of the world. Jeremy had gone on the last trip. Jessica would miss two weeks of school, but she was an excellent student. John had talked it over with Esther and with Jessica's principal, and the three of them had agreed it would be very educational—the experience of her twelve-year-old lifetime.

John had been pleasantly surprised at Esther's willingness to let Jessica miss school and accompany him on the journey. Still he felt a gnawing depression. Esther remained locked in her despair over Jenny. Oh, everyone had been sympathetic. It was not your fault, they said. It could happen to anyone, they said. You must get on with your life, they said. And of course they meant well. But, John could see that the more people pressed their sympathy and concern on Esther, the more she retreated into herself.

He'd made arrangements for her to see a counselor with whom they were both acquainted. She had gone once, but after that she refused to return. No explanation. Just adamant refusal.

The last time John and Esther had made love was more than five months ago. She had not refused him, but she had not responded either. Lovemaking after the accident had been hard for them both. The last time had been a disaster, and they had not attempted since. As married couples sometimes do, they sensed their relationship was paper thin and fragile. Clinging to a tiny thread. They both seemed frozen by fear of what might happen if that slender thread was accidentally broken.

Tonight, John wished that this trip had not been scheduled. He had almost cancelled it a month ago. However, so many from the church were planning to go that he finally determined to just go through with it. Letting Jessica see Israel through her child eyes was added incentive. But now, on top of everything else, there was Jeremy. John had been increasingly concerned with Jeremy's attitude and behavior in recent months. Tonight's episode brought it to a head.

What's going on, God? Why are so many bad things happening to us? Where did we go wrong?

John pushed away from the table and walked into the family room. He stood looking out through the patio door. Moonlight shimmered incandescently on the surface of the pool. This had always been one of John's favorite night scenes. At least it used to be. He peered through the glass, recalling happier times. Memories leaped and played like phosphorescent dancers on the water.

He thought about the last night he had truly felt happiness.

It seemed like a long time ago.

11

The phone rang, interrupting a heated discussion swirling around the board room table regarding Calvary Church's current financial shortfall and what to do about it. John Cain had been listening for the past hour to what seemed to him more like a symposium on establishing past blame rather than dealing with the present problem.

"Hello."

"Hello, dear. How's the meeting going?"

"Well, I guess you could say we're moving along," he answered quietly, turning his chair away from the others while at the same time smiling at Ken Ralsten, who looked at him questioningly. "It's my wife," John mouthed silently. Ken frowned and turned back to the discussion.

"When will you be home?"

"Not soon enough."

"When?"

"Before we began, everyone agreed to be out early, not later than ten o'clock. So probably by ten-thirty or eleven."

"Have you eaten?"

"No. Nothing all day. Didn't have a chance. The staff meeting took most of the morning. I've had counseling appointments the rest of the day right up to the beginning of the finance committee. Straight from there to the board meeting. I tried catching up on paperwork during the noon hour."

"Hungry?"

"Is the pope Catholic?"

"Good. I'll have something for you when you get home. Okay?"

"Sure, great. I'll call before I leave."

John smiled as he hung up the phone, took a weary breath, and turned back to the debate.

At 11:10, John came through the door and dropped his briefcase on the entry floor. The pungent smell of food from the kitchen reminded him of just how hungry he really was. Esther met him with a glass of juice in each hand. He took one from her and their glasses clinked.

"Well, what a nice way to be welcomed home."

Their lips touched in greeting.

"My man deserves it after the day he's put in. Come over to the table and sit down. Here, let me have your jacket. It's time for you to relax, Rev."

John handed his jacket to Esther. She disappeared for a moment. He could hear her removing hangers from the closet. When she came back, he looked at her again. She was wearing an all white, two-piece rib knit lounging outfit that he had never seen before. Her brown hair was tied back casually in a ponytail.

"Unless I miss my guess, you've been shopping today."

"How could you ever tell?" she smiled, pirouetting gracefully, glass in hand. "Do you like?"

"I do like. In fact, my love, you are ravishing tonight. What's the occasion? Did I forget our anniversary?"

"No occasion. Just us. That's occasion enough, isn't it?"

"Absolutely," John replied, downing the remainder of his juice, suddenly not nearly so weary as he had felt an hour ago. "Are the kids tucked away in bed?"

"We have no kids. Just us."

"Are you serious?"

"Yes. I traded them off for a night alone with you. Bob and Joyce took Jenny and Jessica. Jeremy is spending the night at Geoff's house." Esther moved closer. Her gray-green eyes sparkled. He caught the light scent of perfume. "Is that okay, fella?"

"Fantastic. I just wish I'd been here two hours ago."

"Two hours ago, I wasn't ready for you," she replied, turning to the oven. "Go sit down. You've been feeding souls all day. I'll be with you in a minute bearing nourishment for your starving body."

John walked over to the table and started to sit down.

"Not there, love," Esther reprimanded coyly. "In the dining room."

John went into the dining room. The table was laid with two place settings, one at the end and the other close at hand on the right. The only light came from two candles at the center of the table. He was still standing, admiring the ambience, when Esther came in carrying two plates with baked potatoes, a green vegetable, and generous portions of filet mignon.

It was after midnight when they finished dinner, lingering over small portions of gelato. They sat, talking, holding hands, taking what nourishment they needed now just from being together in the flickering candlelight.

"Let's go out by the pool," John suggested. "It's still warm."

They took their glasses outside and sat at the pool's edge. Shoes had long since been discarded. Esther was barefoot. John pulled off his socks and they dangled their feet in the warm water.

"You were right. It is still warm out."

Esther stood to her feet, setting her cup on the patio table.

"What are you doing?" asked John as he watched.

"I'm going for a swim."

A moment later she stood poised at the side of the pool, bathed in the soft glow of moonlight. Then she dove gracefully into the water.

Soon they were swimming together, laughing and splashing like small children without any cares in the world.

And then they were in each other's arms.

—m—

Memories of love.

But not tonight.

Not any night, it seemed.

Life has been too hard. And love too hurtful.

Neither of them had been in the pool since that beautiful night together.

Not after what happened the next afternoon.

Now there was only pain where once had lived passion and delight. John stared at the shadow at the bottom of the pool, the familiar apparition.

His beloved ghost.

Slowly he turned away from the door.

Entering quietly into the bedroom, he slid under the covers so as not to wake Esther. His body ached with weariness. His spirit had fallen into a dark hole. Again. Each time it happened, the hole seemed deeper than before. After a long while, he drifted into a fitful sleep.

—m—

In the shadows of the bedroom, Esther's face was turned to the wall.

She did not move, but she had heard it all.

The loud voices in the kitchen, the heavy footsteps, the slamming door, the curse twice spoken by her son in anger. And, much later, her husband's entry into their room and their bed.

She heard everything.
But she remained silent.
Her eyes were open and dry.

12

9 SEPTEMBER, LOCAL TIME 2305
EILAT, ISRAEL

A full moon serenaded the Sinai desert with its ancient hymn of light, illuminating a landscape as stark and unyielding as the moon itself. A silver symphony, improvising its way through rugged hills, dancing across the Gulf of Aqaba, striking a chord of unearthly solitude on its journey across fabled Petra—a desert reminder of civilizations long past. On the far shore, the city lights of Aqaba, Jordan, flickered dimly. A span of darkness brief enough to surprise first-time visitors to the area separated their lackluster specter from the luminescence of Eilat, Israel's southernmost resort community.

Eilat's hotels, ranging from modest to magnificent, shone in the night. Lesser lights dotted the surrounding hillsides, glowing through curtained windows from look-alike cinder block houses. Even at this late hour, children laughed and played freely in the streets. No one seemed in a hurry to go home. Tonight everybody felt safe.

In ancient times, this place was known as Ezion-geber. Moses and the children of Israel had stopped here when there was little more than a drinking well and some palm groves. Later, Solomon developed copper and iron mines a few miles to the north. Ezion-geber became the terminal port for Solomon's renowned trading fleet, sailing to and from Ophir and Arabia. It was a center of business, not pleasure. But that was then.

Tonight, music and dancing could be heard in the hotel district as lovers and tourists returned to their temporary dwelling places. Eilat's gravelly beach, crowded with sunbathers during the day and looking ever so much like the Italian Riviera, was empty now, its only sound that of boats rubbing against the wooden pilings. At an outdoor food stand, a group of young people sat on wooden benches around a table cluttered with watermelon rinds and empty soda cans. They were dressed casually in T-shirts and shorts, except for one young man wearing a soldier's uniform. Their conversation in Hebrew was punctuated by occasional loud bursts of laughter.

On a beautiful night, Eilat's guests were enjoying a much needed respite from life's realities. Some were already back in their rooms, planning for tomorrow's cruise on one of the small passenger vessels that would take them a few miles out to sea, serving lunch along with Israel's finest wines, followed by a swim in the Red Sea and a leisurely return to Eilat in the afternoon sun.

Eilat. Relaxed. Captivating. Fun-loving.

And tonight, a doorway to danger.

—∿∿—

Several kilometers away, at a top secret defense intelligence center, satellite watchers sat hunched over pages of data routinely gathered and evaluated on a nightly basis. According to their log, the only activity that night along the coastal road from southeastern Israel and the Egyptian Sinai consisted of normal border crossings. Seven trucks, thirteen cars, six four-wheelers battered from their frequent use of Sinai roads, and three buses loaded with tourists, one group from Japan, another from France, a third from the United States.

These intrepid travelers were bent on completing a grueling, daylong roundtrip to Saint Katarina's Monastery, at the base of Mount Sinai. Tradition holds this to be the place where God met Moses and the Israelites on their wilderness journey, giving them the Ten Commandments, etched by Yahweh's own finger on tablets of Sinai stone.

Even the occasional camel rider was pinpointed by the silent spy cylinder high above in the heavens. These Bedouin wanderers, who recognize no borders between nations, served as regular fixtures throughout the Middle East landscape. On this night for example, when last marked by satellite photo, four such tribesmen and their camels were observed establishing a night camp in a deep wadi, approximately six kilometers west of Eilat on the Israeli side of the border. This was a common sighting. Nothing unusual. Nomads traversed their invisible wilderness highways every day, making their way across the desert in the timeless fashion of their ancestors. More than likely, this group would be on the move again before dawn. In fact, night travel was often preferred due to the extreme heat experienced during the day.

And so by early evening, all border crossings had been closed as the nation of Israel drew its curtains and locked its doors for the night.

The border guards standing at the Taba Crossing leading into the Egyptian-held Sinai noticed nothing out of the ordinary. Likewise the watchman at Eilat's popular Underwater Observatory. He was much closer to the wadi, but he was distracted by repeated attempts to get his balky cigarette lighter to work. The occupants of an army jeep moving rapidly north toward the city from the border crossing on Highway 90 noticed nothing unusual. They were off duty and anxious to get home and go to bed.

Israeli patrol boats drifted lazily along the dividing line between the portion of the Aqaba belonging to Israel and the remainder claimed by Jordan. Beneath the surface, underwater electronic surveillance was fully operational and set to signal against any sneak attack.

In the morning, new satellite photos would show four camels still tethered in the wadi west of Eilat. Perhaps the specialist examining the pictures would wonder where their Bedouin owners had gone.

Perhaps, but probably not.

Yes, Israel's curtains were drawn, her doors locked. The alarm system had been turned on.

But it would not make any difference.

The enemy was already in the house.

—∞—

Yazib Dudori and his three team members knew all about Israel's alarm system. Well, maybe not everything, but enough to believe they could avoid detection if they were willing to work at it. And their willingness was never in doubt.

For six months, they had trained for this assignment. It was the toughest and the most important that they and their teammates had ever been given. It was one thing to try to slip undetected across the vast borders of the United States, as others had been assigned to do. It was something else again to slip into Israel.

Israel's security was the finest of any nation's, due in part to the diminutive size of its land mass, but also because of their sophisticated, ultramodern, advance-warning equipment and the highly trained and motivated personnel whose business it was to guard her borders. The recognition that any one of her neighbors would just as soon push every last Jew into the sea was enough added incentive to maintain the necessary vigilance. But no system is ever perfect. A hole can always be found if one looks diligently enough.

Yazib swelled with pride at the realization that he had been chosen by the

Council to lead a major strike force into enemy-occupied territory—territory that he believed, by every historical and divine right, belonged to him and his countrymen. The task was full of danger. He understood that this adventure might not only be his greatest, it could also be his last. If so, he was ready. He was totally committed. His actions would be memorable enough to ensure his place among the elite freedom fighters. Of that, he was certain.

—w—

A little more than two years before, on May 12, Yazib and three others had staged a daring early morning escape from the Gaza Central Prison. A lingering embarrassment to the Israeli prison authorities. The fugitives had not been missed until the duty officer began his routine 6:00 A.M. head count of the nearly seven hundred prisoners crowded into the huge fortified police station that also served as the Israel Defense Forces (IDF) headquarters in Gaza.

When the officer reached Cell No. 1 in the Security Wing, which housed members of terrorist organizations, he noticed something was awry. A head count revealed that four of the twenty-five prisoners were missing. A further search of the cell showed that the bars over the window had been sawed through with files. Yazib and his cohorts had climbed through the window, jumped down into the inner courtyard, cut through the barbed wire barrier, and climbed over the wall right on to the main street of Gaza, which at that early morning hour was already busy with people on their way to work. No one turned them in.

Once the alarm was sounded, the IDF set in motion an immediate and sweeping search. Navy ships stopped fishing boats already out on the water and forbade others to leave shore. Army troops joined the Border Police in combing through the local citrus groves. Shin Bet, Israel's General Security Services, questioned all its sources in an effort to discover where the fugitives might be headed. All to no avail.

One of the four escapees was captured three days later, but he would say nothing about the intentions or the whereabouts of the others. As days turned into weeks, the authorities assumed the remaining fugitives were sitting tight in their hideouts or would try to get to Egypt. In actuality, they had already been smuggled from the area. These hard-core members of the Palestinian Islamic Jihad, a terrorist organization operating mainly in the Palestinian-Israeli arena, had been chosen as the ones best suited for an act of terror that would cause the world to cry, "Enough," and force the hated Jewish usurpers to their knees. It would be their moment of glory.

The three escapees still at large were Yazib Dudori, Imad Safti, and Fathi Adahlah. All were under the age of twenty-three and each was a callous killer. Acting in the name of their ideals, they had been operating as a band of assassins throughout the Gaza Strip since they were teenagers. None of the three had formal military training, but all had undergone arrest and interrogation and had not broken.

Initially, even their Palestinian brothers viewed them as reckless fanatics, motivated by ambition and childish bravura. But overnight their daring escape—the stuff of myth and legend—rekindled the *jihad* spirit in the minds of thousands of Palestinian youngsters who were hungry for glory and national identity.

Imad Safti and Fathi Adahlah, while they were students at Gaza's Islamic University, had been deeply involved in a philosophical war between the highly activist religious faction and the less intense—but far more popular—nationalist organization. The Israelis had welcomed the rivalry between these two groups as an impediment to the PLO. That is, until the friction got out of hand. Eventually, a lecturer at the University was stabbed and killed. A few weeks later, a member of Safti's family was shot by a PLO supporter. The offense? Lighting a cigarette in a taxicab during the fast of Ramadan.

Then one day Imad and Fathi were worked over by goons from the Islamic Congress—the front organization of the religious faction. They subsequently decided to sever relations with the group, having reached the conclusion that the Congress was more interested in settling scores with the PLO than in working against the Israeli occupation. Besides, they were angry about their treatment at the hands of the IC's goon squad. Together with several close friends, they joined with a clandestine force, the Islamic Jihad, which had split from the Islamic Congress.

Jihad leaders called on the radical, cold-eyed Pasha Bashera to take the place of the captured terrorist as the fourth member of the strike force. With her bronze skin, dark eyes, and short cut hair, she was attractive, if not beautiful, but her reputation for courage and resourcefulness in the face of danger was growing among her zealous "born-again Muslim" companions. She was wanted by the Israeli police for the slaying of two Jewish taxi drivers in Tel Aviv and an Israeli Arab from the village of Abu Ghosh, just west of Jerusalem. In each case, the murder had been committed in cold blood and in broad daylight with dozens of people nearby. The killer's identity was confirmed by witnesses, making Pasha the subject of a national all-points bulletin.

Even before turning to terrorism, Pasha had been well known in the area as the daughter of one of the leading Fatah figures in the Gaza Strip. From childhood, she had refused to remain compliant or passive toward Jewish injustice. Before she was twelve, she was already joining with some of the older boys in rock-throwing escapades against armed soldiers. When her father was arrested and their home blown apart with explosives as an example to other Arabs, she vowed never to forget. From that time, she devoted her life to the destruction of the evil occupiers of her homeland. Her father promoted Fatah policy by holding anti-Israeli demonstrations as acts of protest. Pasha, however, believed such demonstrations were a sign of squeamishness. There was no substitute for violent action. Filled with hatred and schooled in violence, she was primed in every way for this assignment.

Islamic Jihad's ultimate aim continued to be a call to arms against Israel. They made the fight against the occupation a central doctrine. Israel's defeat was the condition for an Islamic revival and a return to religious values. The Jihad numbered only a few hundred activists, organized into cells of five to seven members. Unlike other militant Islamic groups, they went to great lengths to remain anonymous and secretive. Men were ordered not to grow beards and to forgo wearing the *jalabiya*, a long cotton or linen robe worn by traditionalist Muslims. Of course, these practices were looked on with disfavor by traditionalists who viewed them as overt violations of the explicit commands of the Prophet Muhammad.

Though not in the mainstream of Islamic thought and practice, the Jihad represented a new kind of order. Through the years, they successfully brought together a hard core of angry young fundamentalists, fed by religious fervor, who were ready to use terrorism as a tool for determining the future of the world.

Now, their finest hour was only days away.

Defeat would soon give way to a victory never before imagined possible.

Soon the world would kneel.

Soon the challenger would be crowned as champion.

13

The tight-knit group huddled tensely together, listening for a word from their leader. Yazib Dudori ran his tongue over dry lips, peering from behind a large boulder about twenty meters from the highway. An army jeep was approaching carrying four soldiers, two in front and two in back. The driver's weapon was stowed by the gearshift. The others held rifles on their laps. Over the roar of the jeep engine, a portable radio blared, tuned to the army's popular 1000 AM station, playing loud pop music behind the voice of a female singer.

To his right, Yazib checked out the Underwater Observatory one last time. No one seemed to be about. The soldiers in the jeep were well off in the distance now, headed into town. A glance at the wrong time in the rearview mirror? It was a chance they had to take.

Now.

"Run. Don't stop until you reach the sea!"

The four sprinted from behind the boulder, covering the remaining distance to the road in a matter of seconds. They no longer wore the garb of Bedouins. Those props had been buried in the desert about a half mile from the camels. The team had changed into dark boots, black cotton pants and shirts, and black masks covering their faces. Black waterproof shoulder packs carried the rest of their equipment.

Running out in the open made them feel as if they were completely naked. Out in the open, anything could happen. If they were spotted, it was over. The echo of their boots as they crossed the highway pavement rang like thunder in their ears. Then it was gravel grinding underfoot like rocks in a bucket. Finally, they scrambled across a grassy strip and dropped, out of breath, into the shadows of a children's playground slide.

"Quiet," rasped Yazib, under his breath.

Chests heaving, hearts pounding, they huddled in the darkness, holding their breath, listening to the night sounds. Remaining perfectly still, they waited. A minute passed. Then another. Their breathing was nearly back to normal when Yazib stood to his feet, a tense smile on his face.

"So far, so good. Now let's get ready for a swim."

They moved a short distance apart and quickly began undressing.

—⁓—

Of all the steps required for them to make it to the staging area, the pros and cons of this next one had evoked as much debate as any during their planning sessions. They had pored over maps and spent hours discussing every possible option for moving undetected from their hiding place into Eilat and beyond. The way they finally agreed upon, that offered the best chance of success, had been suggested by Pasha Bashera. She was an excellent swimmer. So was Fathi Adahlah. Both had grown up swimming in the Mediterranean, diving off rocks with their playmates and seeing who could swim the farthest out to sea and back. Imad Safti was only a fair swimmer. Yazib Dudori was the least proficient of all.

"Let's get to the public beach near the Observatory," Pasha said, pointing to its location on the map. "We'll be well inside their electronic detection systems. From there we simply swim across to the main beach and walk into town."

It would be a long swim for Yazib and Imad, but Pasha and Fathi had gone that distance and beyond many times. The water would be cold, but not so cold as to make it impossible without wet suits. Though they would not be carrying weapons with them, the additional weight of wet suits and oxygen tanks was a major concern and appeared prohibitive, because the last six kilometers of their journey to Eilat would be over rough terrain and on foot. At the same time, the possibility of being discovered while swimming on the surface was too high. They could not permit that to happen.

Once again, Pasha came up with the solution.

"It doesn't matter how much time we take once we're in the water," she observed. "We'll have plenty of oxygen. Just as long as we get there before the sun comes up."

The others laughed, imagining the specter of the four of them suddenly rising from the sea in front of a beach filled with foreign tourists and Jewish sunbathers. They were beginning to like this new member of their group, even if she was a woman. Her reputation was impeccable. And she seemed able to do anything the men could do.

"We'll take two small tanks and four lightweight wet suits. When we swim,

Yazib and Imad can wear the tanks." She looked at them and grinned. "It will give you more confidence underwater. Fathi and I will stay close to each of you and breathe off of your systems. It should be easy. We'll carry just enough weight to keep us under. When we get close enough to shore to stand on the bottom, we'll take off the gear. We can either swim back out and sink the tanks or put them in our packs, walk up to the beach, get dressed, meet our contact, and be on our way."

Each man sat listening. Thinking.

"It will be easy," Pasha repeated with a winning smile. "We'll practice with the tank a few times after we get the equipment. I know we can do it. It is the best way. No one will suspect."

In the end they had all agreed. It was the best way.

—

Now they huddled under the slide, scanning the darkness. Listening for unusual sounds, anything that would indicate discovery.

Nothing.

Pasha checked Yazib's scuba gear one last time. Then she felt the weights around her waist, glancing at Fathi Adahlah as she did. He had just finished the same exercise with Imad.

He nodded.

She smiled and returned the gesture.

"Are we ready?" Yazib whispered.

All heads nodded affirmatively.

"Then let's do it."

The moon had moved away from them now, shining more from west to east. Once again, the feeling of exposure gripped them as they stepped from the dark shadows of the children's slide and made their way into the moonlit waters.

Careful. Careful. Be quiet. Don't splash the water.

They moved slowly into the sea, feeling vulnerable, feeling the chill of the cold water rising against their bodies. A few yards out, Yazib crouched low. The others did the same. They continued forward in their stooped positions, exposing as little of themselves as possible. In the distance, they could hear the faint sounds of music carried across the water.

Then the sea covered them.

Yazib took the lead. Pasha hooked her left hand through his belt. They had practiced this before. It was simple enough. Yazib swam awkwardly, but possessed a strong stroke and a good kick. The fins helped. Pasha moved her right hand in a full stroke and let him do the rest. They would not look back. It was up to Imad and Fathi to keep up.

They swam steadily through the darkness.

After about thirty minutes, Yazib felt his hand brush against seaweed rising from the floor of the bay. He stroked slightly upward. The water's color gradually turned from inky black to deep blue.

Okay, time to go up for a look.

Yazib and Pasha swam to the surface and took a quick look around.

Eilat's lights were directly ahead. The beach was only eighty or ninety meters away. Where were the others? Just then, two dark round objects broke the surface a short way away. Success.

Yazib saw the docking area in the distance. There were boats. It would be a good place to come out of the sea. Lots of shadows—but possibly some people, too. He continued looking for a safer spot. Then he saw where they should go. Away from the dock there was an open stretch of beach. In a few more hours it would be filled with people, but it appeared empty now. Yazib motioned to the others.

Just under the water's surface they swam for shore. A few meters away, it was shallow enough to stand on the slippery, rocky bottom. Their heads were all that showed above the surface of the water as they removed the scuba gear and wet suits. They had decided earlier to sink all the gear, keeping only a single waterproof pack in which they had placed their last changes of clothes and two towels. Pasha and Fathi tied the gear and the weights together. Swimming well away from the shore, they released their package and watched as it sank into the darkness. Diving, they swam silently and unseen toward the beach.

Near the shore, they came up for air. They were close enough to stand on the sea bottom once again. Pasha strained to see where Yazib and Imad had gone. They were nowhere to be seen. Then she noticed a hand waving from beneath another children's slide in a sandbox play area. She motioned to Fathi that she had seen the others.

Thankfully for us these Jews and their children like to play.

The pair glided through the water until at last they stepped out of the sea and onto Eilat's public beach.

Yazib and Imad had finished changing by the time the others ducked under the metal slide. They passed the towels and turned away to watch the beach in either direction. Working swiftly, Pasha and Fathi stripped off their wet underclothing and began drying themselves with the damp towels. Pasha shivered, feeling the effects of the cold water and wishing the towels were not already wet. She was conscious of her nakedness and the close proximity of the three men around her, but she went on with the task, keeping herself covered as best she could. There was a moment when she sensed Yazib looking at her. Turning away, she lowered her eyes, drying as rapidly as possible and hiding the smile that started to form on her lips. Yazib *was* interested in her. Good.

After pulling on dry undergarments, jeans, and a tank top, and slipping sandals onto her bare feet, Pasha ran the towel through her dark hair again.

The air feels warmer now. My hair will soon be dry. I am about to walk through town, looking like just another dark-skinned Jew woman on vacation. Incredible.

Pasha proceeded to stuff the towels and wet clothing into the remaining backpack, now caked with sand.

"Let's go. Slow and casual," said Yazib, in a low voice, edged with excitement. Pasha wondered if part of his excitement had to do with her.

Yazib and Pasha made their way across the sand, stepping over a low concrete divider and onto the frontage street. They held hands, keeping their heads close like two young lovers out for a stroll. Imad and Fathi walked on the opposite side of the street, following at a distance. The street was dark and deserted.

They approached an outdoor food stand. Wooden benches, pushed in at different angles, surrounded two tables with red and white table covers. A nearby garbage bin overflowed with melon rinds, soda cans, and flies. Another bin, half full but attracting just as many flies, stood next to it. The food stand was closed for the night, and there was no one around. Yazib dropped the backpack into the second garbage bin, covering it with overflow from the other receptacle.

"With a little luck, the collectors will throw it away without even noticing it," he said softly, wiping his hands on his jeans.

They moved on up the street. For the first time tonight, Pasha felt herself beginning to relax.

As they strolled along the boat channel, past the King Solomon Hotel, she gaped at its modernistic sandstone contours stretching upward into the night sky. Outdoor lighting gave the ultramodern facility the look of a sheik's palace.

Yazib glanced at his watch.

"It is nearly one-thirty. Most of the guests must already have turned in."

"Wouldn't it be nice to spend a night in that hotel? A clean pool, a hot bath, a soft bed?" Pasha mused, scanning the hotel entrance and nodding toward the enormous swimming pool shimmering under the outdoor lights. "Our enemies do know how to live."

With a long look, Pasha and Yazib gathered in the beauty of the architecture, digesting what had just been said. Then Pasha let her thoughts return to their reason for being here.

She had never been to Eilat before tonight. But according to instructions, the house at which they would meet their contact should be only two or three blocks from here. They had succeeded in crossing the open desert and swimming the Red Sea. Their enemies were none the wiser. The most difficult part of getting to the staging sight appeared to be over.

Islamic Jihad's third and final piece to the most sophisticated, daring, and deadly operation since the glorious martyr's triumph known the world over simply as "9/11" was in place.

As they stood admiring the scene, Pasha glanced away from the hotel and back along the street.

That was when she saw the police car headed toward them.

14

10 SEPTEMBER, LOCAL TIME 0750
BAYTOWN, CALIFORNIA

John set the carton of donuts and basket of fruit on the conference table. Yesterday he had promised Cary that he would be responsible to bring something for the fellows to eat. Out of force of habit he scanned the room, verifying its readiness for the meeting. Twelve chairs, covered in well-worn dark leather, surrounded the mahogany table.

Cary Johnson, the church's business administrator, walked behind each chair, placing agenda sheets on the table at each spot. He had already retrieved paper plates and napkins from the small counter/sink/storage area at the far side of the room, and had placed them at the end of the table nearest the door. The sounds and smell of coffee-in-the-making filled John's nostrils. He needed a cup of coffee. Moving to the wall, he straightened one of the several pictures hanging there. There were pictures of former pastors and families, as well as framed photographs of past board members and people engaged in various church activities.

The picture that was crooked was one of the Reverend William Jaspers, his wife, Betty, and their two sons, Mike and Cole. John stepped back for a better look, and as he did, he wondered what it would feel like to be framed and photographed as the most recent "former pastor."

Will anyone care if my picture is hanging crooked? Probably not.

He turned toward the door as voices in the hall signaled the arrival of the first elders. A moment later, Jerry North strolled in.

"Hi, Pastor." With a big grin on his face, Jerry extended his hand. "How are you this bright, sunny morning?"

Jerry was always warm and gregarious. Dressed in an open-collar, multicolored shirt, blue jeans, and bright white tennis shoes, he never seemed to change. His comfortable attire reflected the inner spirit of a man at peace with himself, his God, and the world. This morning, however, Jerry seemed even more effusive than usual. Almost too much so, John thought.

"I'm fine, Jerry. And you?"

"How could anyone be anything other than terrific on a morning like this? Just look at that day outside, would you?"

John turned his gaze to the large windows at the opposite end of the room. Immediately beyond the windows, a drip irrigation system watered the flowering atrium. A variety of birds had made it their sanctuary, fluttering in and out with ease. It was a tranquil picture, providing a calming effect on discussions that at times needed scenes of tranquility to help soothe the savage beast—or beasts, as the case might be.

John greeted Harold Cawston next, the youngest member of the board. His father, George, had served four terms and was working on a fifth when he became ill with cancer. Harold had been recruited by congregational vote to finish his father's term of office. George still came to worship services as often as he could, but the cancer treatments and his failing health had made it more difficult the last few months. John was going to miss him when the time came. He had been, in many ways, like a second father.

Mike Dewbar and Scott Peping were golfing pals, each possessing a handicap of under ten. On any other Saturday, they would be playing by this time, and they seemed a little bent out of shape at the idea of a board meeting as they came through the door. John noted their golfing togs, however, and decided they were not planning to miss their day in the sun. Their tee time would just be later than usual.

Ken Ralsten, one of Baytown's leading attorneys, walked in and went straight for the coffeepot. The circles under his eyes seemed darker than usual this morning. John wondered if he and Geoff were having relationship problems similar to those he and Jeremy were encountering. Maybe Ken was up late last night, too.

I'd like to ask, but if they are doing fine it will tip my hand that things are not what they should be at my house. Ken is not my most favorite person in the world anyway.

David Bolling and Dennis Lanier finished out the number expected for the meeting. David owned his own marketing consulting business and Dennis was Baytown's city manager. David was outgoing, personable, and very likable, though John sometimes wondered just how deep his commitment to the church and spiritual things was. He always seemed more at ease dealing with business topics than spiritual ones. His work also required him to travel a great deal, which probably did not help.

Dennis was thirty-seven, thoughtful, able to see the big picture instantly. After Sidney Orwell had asked not to be considered for another term, Dennis had seemed the logical successor. He and Barbara had enrolled their two children in Calvary Christian School this year. It had been a big decision. They faced a good deal of pressure to place them in public school because of his visibility in the community. But after much prayer and discussion, they had made the choice and it appeared to be the right one for their children.

Seven men.

The perfect number.

At least that was the idea expressed in Bible numerology. Six was the number of imperfect man. Seven that of divine perfection. Seven men had been chosen to serve the early church in the book of Acts. So it stood to reason that seven men should serve the church in Baytown. Or so it seemed to those older and wiser heads of yesteryear who had established Calvary's constitution and bylaws.

For a few minutes, small talk ensued.

"Do you have season tickets for the Niners again this year, Jerry?"

"Yeah. Their last preseason game is with Seattle this Sunday at the Stick."

"It's being televised locally, isn't it?"

"Channel Five has all the games, home and away, this year."

"How about Ken and Elizabeth's Hawaii vacation? Ken never got to the golf course."

"Hey, listen, Ken, if *we* had been there . . ."

"Do you think we'll get a break in the drought this winter?"

"I don't know, have you heard any long-range predictions?"

"When do you leave for Israel, John?"

"Monday? Terrific. Hope you have a good trip."

"Are you looking forward to this one? Or does it get old after a while?"

"How many times is this for you?"

"This will make six, but the experience never seems to get old."

Coffee was poured. Donuts, banana bread, and fruit were distributed. Each man finally moved toward his usual place at the table. When all were seated, their heads bowed for prayer, almost in unison. Harold took his turn leading in prayer, asking God's blessing on the meeting.

The minutes of the previous meeting were unanimously approved.

The latest financial report was reviewed and received.

Receipt of the minutes of other church committees was duly noted.

Next came a review of the quarterly calendar of church events.

"There is one correction," David Bolling said. "The date of our next meeting was changed and both dates are still in the calendar."

"Move to correct."

"Second."

"Received as corrected."

For about twenty minutes, housekeeping matters preoccupied the attention of the group. They were necessary exercises in the parliamentary process, but not anyone's favorite reason for board meetings. Clearly, everyone was anxious for this to be a short meeting.

New church members were noted, twenty-three in the most recent class. Also noted were thirteen people transferred to the inactive list. Five had moved from the area to other communities in California. One had been transferred by her company to Ohio. The remaining seven were attending other churches in the area.

For a large church like Calvary, with more than thirteen hundred adult members plus youth and children, this seemed normal enough. It did bother John, though, that seven of Calvary's members were now attending other churches. It was hard not to take such moves personally, feeling somehow that he had failed where these people were concerned. Intellectually, he knew it was unrealistic to believe that Calvary Church would be able to meet everyone's needs and desires. He also understood that he was not alone in responsibility for the welfare of the church family. Still, it bothered him.

It also disturbed him that the majority of new members were transfers from other churches and not new converts. It was his feeling that the church merry-go-round did little to grow the kingdom of God and often simply moved people and their problems from one church body to another.

But John had not prepared for what was about to follow.

Ken settled back in his chair, staring seriously at the table. He locked his hands together, slowly twirling his thumbs.

"Pastor," he began, pausing before continuing.

Uh-oh. I hate it when this happens.

John looked in Ken's direction. *Whenever he calls me "Pastor" instead of John, I know I'm in trouble. And when he twirls his thumbs and gives me his dramatic "lawyer's pause," I start feeling defensive before he even opens his mouth.*

"Pastor," Ken repeated again, clearing his voice. By now, everyone had turned toward him, waiting. "Doesn't it seem a bit ominous to you that seven of our good members are now attending other churches in Baytown? I've checked the member records from the last six months and we have a total of thirty-two Calvary members who have left us for other congregations. When we add these seven, it makes thirty-nine. Now I understand that some have moved away from Baytown. But most of these folks are still right here. Can you shed some light on what could possibly be behind this?"

John gazed steadily at a neutral point in the center of the table, preparing his response.

Be careful, fella. There's an edge to Ken's voice this morning. He's come loaded for bear. And he's probably got a little buckshot reserved in case he misses the first time.

"It always hurts when good people leave to attend another church, Ken. At least it always hurts me. Some go for good reasons. They're the ones who talk it over with me first. Most of the time it has to do with opportunities to serve they feel they will never get here. And there are other reasons. Jack and Julie Stevens, for example, have transferred to Faith Church because their son is the new pastor there. We can hardly fault them for wanting to be supportive of their son in his first pastorate, now can we? Unfortunately, some have left because they don't like the style of our worship. And I know two of the families on this list feel the church is getting too big. They want something smaller. We've tried to encourage them into some of the home small groups that meet in their area, but so far, we've not been successful."

"Thirty-nine fine members," Ken said again, as though he had not heard John's response. Then he lifted his gaze and directed it toward John.

"How many more are on the way out, Pastor? Do you know?"

It was silent around the conference table. The only sounds were the stirring of bodies on leather seats. Harold, Mike, and Scott looked at Ken, puzzled at what they were hearing, wondering where he was headed. David and Dennis leaned forward, waiting for John's reaction. Obviously, Ken had discussed this with them beforehand. Jerry glanced nervously at John, then proceeded to stare out the window. Cary sat quietly, waiting. Tension had suddenly gripped the meeting.

"I'm not sure what you're getting at, Ken. It's a little hard to read the minds of each church member. Help me understand where you're going with this."

John remembered a quote he had read recently: *When you swim in the ocean, you get attacked by sharks and guppies. Don't worry about the guppies.*

Through the years, like any pastor, John had taken his share of negative criticism. He had learned to field it while it was happening as well as anyone. It was always later, when he was alone, that he would give way to the hurt that tore at the fragile nature of his inner being.

Outwardly, as the group absorbed the stillness in the room, he remained calm and casual, displaying his most confident pastor's smile. Inwardly, the alarm he had learned to recognize through years of experience was sounding again, and a voice kept repeating, "*Trouble, John . . . shark attack!*"

Ken? A shark? He started thinking about all the "lawyer as shark" jokes he had ever heard. The inner tension subsided momentarily as he attempted to replace criticism with unspoken humor. Then he reminded himself that this was no joke.

"Where I'm going with this, Pastor," answered Ken, "is to a conclusion that appears rather obvious to me and to some of the rest of us. Something is amiss here. I've been receiving a lot of complaints recently. Some folks don't like the stuff we're singing on Sunday mornings. Too much with the hymns, not enough upbeat music. And I hate to be the bearer of bad news, John . . ."

Yes, I'll bet you do.

". . . but more than a few complaints have been coming in to some of us about the quality of our pulpit."

John knew Ken wasn't talking about the furniture. He remained silent, glancing around the table at the others.

Harold was the first to speak.

"Ken, you know that people complain from time to time about anything and everything. They even grouse about us once in a while. I certainly haven't heard anything negative about John's preaching. Personally, I don't think he has ever done a better job than recently. I can't believe what you are saying is representative input."

Scott and Mike nodded in agreement.

David and Dennis kept their eyes on John and said nothing.

Jerry stirred nervously, staring down at the table.

"It's out there, I'm telling you," Ken answered. "Not that I believe what is being said is true, you understand. No, I never said that. It is probably not justified."

Probably? thought John.

"But I feel it is my duty as an elder to call it to everyone's attention in this room," Ken continued, "including yours, Pastor. If people are not happy with the pulpit, attendance drops. When attendance drops, giving drops. When giving drops . . . well, you've seen the financial report. We're headed for trouble if we don't do something."

If it's not justified, why didn't you try to disarm the criticism?

"What do you recommend we do, Ken?" asked John quietly. "Do you have something specific in mind that you wanted to bring before the board this morning?"

Ken's eyes locked on John. The look was sober and unyielding.

"All I'm saying is what has been said. I know you carry a heavy load, Pastor. I know your time is taken up with a lot of things. And I know it has not been easy for you since . . . well, since you and Esther . . . well, you know. I'm sure all this has affected the whole family. Including Jeremy and Jessica."

How much do you know about what's going on in my family?

"Now here you are, going off to Israel. You'll be gone for two weeks. This is a critical time for the church, John. I'm not sure you ought to be leaving right now. Who knows what will happen? Maybe you should be staying closer to home. I know a little about the importance of adequate preparation before addressing a jury. Perhaps a little more time in the study would help."

A jury? Our congregation is a jury? And who am I? The defendant?

"But we've approved these group trips that John makes to Israel," Scott interjected. "They've become a kind of teaching and relationship-building experience that John does with the congregation. I went on one myself a few years ago. Surely you can't be serious, Ken."

Ken shrugged, resuming the slow, circling thumb motion, and returned his gaze to the tabletop.

The remainder of the meeting was completed by dodging through the strained feelings that were now everywhere present. The threatening implications in Ken's comments had caused a pall to settle on the group. It was difficult to talk or think about anything else.

Outside, birds sang and the sun shown brightly. Inside, a cloud had settled over the conference table. Deep inside, John did his best to control his feelings. He spoke in soft tones. He did not dare to think about or say what he truly felt. Hurt smoldered, ready to flare instantly if fueled with the high-octane anger he was doing his best to contain.

—∞—

Later, John sat alone in his study. Louvered window shades kept most of the daylight out. In the room's diffused light, his eyes wandered across book-lined walls. Each book was catalogued and accessible through a card reference system that enabled John to quickly locate any volume by subject, title, or author. He had personally hired a professional librarian to set up the system some years ago.

A pained smile crossed his face as he stared at the shelves housing a variety of Bible commentaries. When preparing to preach from a particular section of the Scriptures, John had, over the years, made a habit of perusing catalogs and bookstores. He normally purchased three or four, sometimes up to a dozen of those books he felt were the best. They were the tools of his craft. He pored over their contents as he studied through Bible passages, endeavoring to let the relevance of the Scriptures speak through him to the minds and souls of those who attended Calvary Church each week.

Once, a woman with little appreciation for books of any kind had suggested that the hundreds of volumes should be arranged according to the colors of the covers. It would add to the decor of the room, she said, which in her opinion could use a good deal of help. John had politely thanked her for her interest and the creative idea. When she had gone, he laughed out loud. Then he went to find Cary to tell him what the woman had said.

Now, John sat staring.

Maybe she was on to something after all.

He proceeded to boot up the computer on his desk. In moments, it displayed an array of options. John opened the "Letters" folder and double-clicked. After requesting a new file, he began writing:

> Calvary Church Board of Deacons and
> Calvary Church Family
> 4455 21st Avenue N.E.
> Baytown, California
>
> Dear Friends:
>
> After much prayer and careful consideration, I am submitting my resignation as senior pastor of Calvary Church, to be effective at a date to be mutually determined by the board and myself.
>
> It has been my joyful opportunity to serve this wonderful church during the past twelve years. I shall always be grateful, both to God and to you for this privilege. I have been to the best of my ability a faithful and honorable shepherd. In that regard let me urge you to . . .

"Join with others in following my example, brothers, and take note of those who live according to the pattern we gave you."
— Philippians 3:17

The love Esther and I hold for each and every one of you remains so strong that stepping away is filled with deep emotion. Since answering God's call to Calvary Church, I have enjoyed a long tenure of ministry among you. While much remains to be accomplished, it will be done under the leadership of another. It is time for us to go, in the same spirit of obedience in which we came.

Rest assured that as our Lord entrusts us with new responsibilities in another part of His harvest, no other ministry and no one else can ever take your place in our hearts.

Humbly yours,
John Cain

When it was finished, John read through it again. Then he guided the arrow to the shutdown icon. The screen went blank.

That's it. It's time. There's nothing about me that's not burned out. When I get home from Israel, I'll mail a copy to each board member. So much for twelve years of faithful ministry. I guess it's really over.

15

10 SEPTEMBER, LOCAL TIME 1730
BAYTOWN, CALIFORNIA

John slouched in one of the patio chairs and stared listlessly at the pool sweep, following its aimless meandering. The aftermath of the board meeting had left him despondent. His mind replayed Ken's accusing words and stinging tone. He saw David and Dennis's knowing looks and Jerry's outright cowardliness. That hurt. He had thought better of Jerry, but . . .

After a few minutes, the hum of the filtering system stopped and the sweep settled to the bottom. Complete silence prevailed, broken only by the cooing of a dove perched somewhere high overhead in the black pine tree. Slowly his thoughts came back to the moment, that incredibly tragic moment that had shattered all their lives—right here in this place.

The pool sweep is only a machine.

John's rational mind knew that. Yet each time he saw it, its image degenerated into the familiar apparition that constantly lurked in the back rooms of his mind. For more than a year now, it had haunted him.

His beloved ghost.

And each time he relived again what had happened here.

—w—

"Ball?"

Her eighteen-month-old eyes sparkled at the sight of the ball, all pink and blue and white. It was her favorite. And it was outside on the patio, beyond the screen door.

She looked at it for a while, her face pressed against the mesh-screen surface. Finally she stood on her tiptoes, placing a pudgy hand against the metal frame for balance. With her other hand, she reached as high as she could, until her fingers touched the shiny, brass, half-moon latch. She had watched her mother do it before. Many times. It looked easy. It was easy. She pulled down, the latch released, and the pressure of her hand against the door frame pushed it back.

As she waddled through the opening, bright sunlight caressed her face with a warm welcome. Smiling, she looked up and lifted both hands in a child's salute to the sky as she walked across the patio toward her ball. Bending over, her outstretched hands almost captured the prize, until her foot accidentally pushed it out of reach. She hesitated, watching it roll away.

As quickly as her unreliable feet would take her, she ambled toward the ball again, bending once more to pick it up. But the feet she tried so hard to control betrayed her again. This time the ball rolled to the edge of the pool and fell over onto the thermal cover that floated on the water's surface.

She stopped at the water's edge, gazing at the ball. Carefully she bent forward . . . slowly . . . slowly . . . she stretched out her hand . . . until she touched it.

"Ball."

She teetered there, bare toes curling around the tile coping along the side of the pool. A happy, innocent smile spread across her face.

"Ball?"

Esther looked up from her casserole preparations for the evening meal. Had she heard something? The stereo played soothingly in the background. A piano concerto by Mozart, the music she loved the best. She believed that by filling the background of their home with beautiful sounds, they would work their way into the infancy of Jennifer's musical taste buds. Esther had even played Mozart while she was pregnant. Her doctor told her that an unborn child is quite aware of voices and sounds. She wanted Jennifer, her last child, to love the very best of everything.

"Jenny?"

Esther listened for the toddler's answer.

"Jenny," she called again.

There was no response.

Esther put the mixing spoon down. Only a moment ago Jenny had wandered past, outstretched hands brushing against her mother's skirt, heading in the direction of her room. Esther passed through the living room and turned down the hall. The door to Jenny's room was open. Her toys were scattered about, a teddy bear turned upside down on its head.

"Jenny, where are you?"

From somewhere deep within, an anxious tremor alerted all her maternal instincts.

Something is wrong!

Esther turned abruptly and ran back down the hall.

Through the living room.

Past the kitchen.

Into the family room.

A doll lay twisted in pretzel fashion near John's chair. Her initial fear became a steel sword in her stomach as she looked across the family room. The screen was ajar. Running to the door, she pushed it open all the way and stepped outside.

A quick look. Relief!

Oh, thank God. She's not out here either.

"Jenny!"

No response.

Then her eye caught something on the pool cover near the deep end.

Jenny's ball.

In the same instant she noticed fresh water formed on top of the cover.

Jenny!

She ran to the pool's edge and lifted the cover.

What she saw slammed the breath from her body and turned her heart into stone. Esther's peaceful, happy world imploded.

Frantically kicking off her shoes, she threw back the corner of the cover and dove in. With one hand she gathered up Jenny's still form, frantically clawing her way to the surface. Gasping for air, she lifted her baby from the water and carried her toward the house.

"Oh, Jenny. No. Please, God. No. Jenny. Jenny. Jenny."

With her free hand, Esther flung open the door and rushed inside, placing Jenny's dripping body on the carpeted floor. For a moment she nearly despaired beyond the ability to function. Then, hands trembling, she dialed 9-1-1, hysterically crying into the telephone as she gave the person on duty their address. Bending over Jennifer's body she breathed into her mouth, trying to remember the CPR technique she had learned several years earlier at a clinic sponsored by the local fire department. She felt awkward, inadequate, as she worked desperately to resuscitate the tiny little form beneath her. A growing sense of hopelessness crowded its way into her mind until she wanted to scream.

Am I doing it right? Come on, Jenny. Oh, God, help me, please! Please . . . Jenny! . . .

The rescue team found them there, Esther's tears bathing the tiny girl's pale, silent face. Gently they pulled her away.

This was the scene that would forever be embedded in John's mind, its jagged edges unsmoothed by time. Arriving at home. The fire engine and ambulance, lights flashing, blocking the driveway—his driveway. Rushing into the front hallway. Calling Esther's name. And then the family room—Esther slumped on the couch, a vacant stare on her drawn, pale face. Two men in blue uniforms kneeling on the floor. Oxygen equipment. A medical bag. The patio screen door ajar. Tiny little bare feet protruding from beneath one of the men in blue. Even after all these months, the shock and sadness hit him full force, as if he were entering the room for the first time.

"Oh, Lord, no. Not Jenny. Not our beautiful little Jenny."

Invisible hands ripped at his stomach, then hammered his body beyond feeling. The room swayed as one of the men rose, a look of sadness in his eyes.

"I'm sorry," he said. "The little girl is gone."

John heard a low moan begin to build from the direction of the couch. It increased in volume until it became an elongated, piercing wail. He looked at Esther. Then at Jenny.

His voice stricken with disbelief and pain, he choked out the words:

"What happened?"

—∾—

John shifted his weight in the lounge chair as his thoughts proceeded—as they always did—to the day of the memorial service. It was the following Saturday. One o'clock. The service had been held outside, in the sunlight and fresh air that Jenny had loved with so much innocent exuberance. John later heard estimates that about seven hundred people had attended. A large crowd for such a little girl, but this was the Cain's daughter and so everyone who could be there was there.

John and Esther sat huddled together in front of the tiny, white coffin. Sixteen-year-old Jeremy and eleven-year-old Jessica stood behind them, hands on their parents' shoulders. Terri White, Calvary Church's minister to children, offered the eulogy.

"Jennifer has been like a flower to us all. Her innocence, her childlike love of living, was blossoming before our very eyes. There were never any strangers in her world. I remember seeing her walk down the hallway last Sunday, hanging onto Esther's finger."

Her voice broke as she brushed tears from her eyes with a small, white handkerchief.

"I said, 'Hi, Jennifer, honey, what do you say today?' She broke away from her

mother and ran the rest of the way to me. 'Jesus loves me,' was her answer as she threw herself into my arms."

Sniffles were heard here and there throughout the gathering of people. Men, as well as women, were wiping their eyes and staring off into the distance.

"All of us today know just how true that is," Terri continued. "Little Jenny has found the One who loves her more than we can ever know. She is looking down upon us in this moment of our grief, safe in the loving arms of Jesus."

Terri continued talking a few minutes more, giving words of solace to the little children who were there, watching and listening, clutched in the loving arms of parents. Mothers and fathers silently, even guiltily, thanked God that this was not a wake for their child. John stared at a spot just beyond the box with its precious treasure. In the grass, a tiny frog croaked and hopped on its erratic journey toward taller grass a short distance away.

Jennifer would be glad you came. She'd call you "fog" and take you home in her pocket.

John drew back from his reverie in time to hear Terri speaking directly to his family.

"This is a period of sadness for us all, but especially for John and Esther, Jeremy and Jessica. None of us can truly say that we understand your sorrow. Nor can we ever hope to answer all the 'why' questions that must lurk in your hearts. But be assured of our love for each one of you. Our prayers are with you. Even if we don't do it well at times, be certain of this, we care and we'll be here for you."

Turning to the large, somber gathering, she asked them to join her in praying the Lord's Prayer. And the words that have brought comfort and hope to millions of Christian believers in every sort of crisis and circumstance were uttered in unison once again.

Our Father in heaven,
hallowed be your name,
your kingdom come,
your will be done
on earth as it is in heaven.
Give us today our daily
bread.
Forgive us our debts,
as we also have forgiven
our debtors.

And lead us not into
temptation,
but deliver us from the evil
one.
For yours is the kingdom
and the power
and the glory
forever.
Amen.

—∞—

John continued staring at the object resting on the bottom of the swimming pool. The dove flew from the tree and was gone.

How often must I relive this? Will life ever be normal again?

Anger stirred in his belly. And bitterness. Unspoken grief rolled silently down the dark side of pain. Fists at his side clenched tightly, opening, then closing again. Finally, tears filled his eyes and spilled down his cheeks. Today had been one more in a long series of depressing, tragic days that seemed to pile up in his life, one upon the other, until he could no longer see over them.

Turning away from his beloved ghost, the Reverend John Cain, creative dispenser of divine inspiration, tireless shepherd of God's flock, unending provider of faith for today and hope for tomorrow, shuffled toward the screen door.

Numb.

Weary.

Broken.

Defeated.

PART TWO

Therefore, in the shadow of Islam, it is possible for all followers of different religions to live in peace and with security over their person, property, and rights. In the absence of Islam, discord takes form, oppression and destruction are rampant, and wars and battles take place.

—from the Hamas Charter, Article Six

When faith is lost there is no security nor life for
he who does not revive religion;
And whoever is satisfied with life without religion
then he would have let annihilation be his
partner.

—Muhammad Iqbal
Muslim poet

Peacemakers who sow in peace
raise a harvest of righteousness.

—The Holy Bible
James 3:18

16

Sunday, 11 September, local time 0930
Baytown, California

Calvary Church held three services every Sunday morning. The early service was generally the smallest, with about two hundred in attendance. The 9:30 service was the largest of the day. Six or seven hundred people normally were present, in addition to the choir and musicians. It was also the service that would be seen live on local television. A volunteer crew with a three-camera setup, produced this special outreach each week. Then at 11:00, another four to five hundred gathered for the final service of the day.

From the platform, John had a commanding view of the sanctuary. As the second service got under way, he noticed Mike Dewbar and Scott Peping seated together with their wives. John thought these two couples would be great ad models for a health club—all four were glowing with end-of-summer tans and sun-bleached hair representing more than a few hours beside swimming pools and at the beach with their children. Mike saw John looking in their direction and gave him an encouraging wink.

Jerry North was sitting with Teresa, but well back in the sanctuary, far from their usual seats near the front on the left. Given the tenor of yesterday's board meeting, John wondered what was running through Jerry's mind. Normally outgoing and affable, he had seemed distant and uncomfortable when they passed in the hallway between services.

Well, so what? The die is cast. I won't need to worry about any of this much longer.

About ten minutes into the service, as the last hymn neared completion, John noticed an attractive Arab-looking couple that he had also seen in the early service. They were sitting next to the Heidens, and for a moment, John's mind wandered to this nice young couple, who had shown a real eagerness to get involved at the church. He didn't know the Heidens very well, but then they were new to Calvary Church, having started to attend regularly about three months ago. He remembered that they were from up north, either Oregon or Washington.

Her name is Sherri. What is his? Bill? Or is it Phil? Yes, Phil, I think.

She was obviously very pregnant. John made a mental note to check on whether they had been contacted by Calvary's Young Marrieds' volunteer follow-up staff. He knew how important connecting with others could be after moving to new surroundings.

His gaze returned to the couple seated next to them.

Arabic. I'm sure of it.

John had spent too much time in the Middle East not to see the traits etched in their facial features. Sculptured noses, dark eyes, olive skin.

I wonder what their background is? Christian, probably. It isn't likely that Muslims would be here for one service, much less two. Maybe they are products of a Christian mission or something. What do you suppose prompted them to attend the service again?

John's attention returned to the final words of the hymn. He drew his thoughts together, momentarily forgetting the pair that had piqued his curiosity. The last phrase was sung, and sounds of the organ filled the church. The television camera zoomed in on his face as John stepped forward to lead in the pastoral prayer.

The prayer was followed with a worship chorus sung by the congregation and choir together. Next, an announcement concerning Calvary's annual men's retreat. It was scheduled to get under way with a golf tournament the day following Pastor Cain's return from Israel. Guests were acknowledged. Everyone was encouraged to stand, greet one another, and welcome new friends to the church.

—∞—

The Heidens turned and spoke to the couple standing beside Phil.

"Hi. I'm Phil. This is my wife, Sherri."

"Good morning," the handsome strangers responded with a smile. They shook hands.

"My name is Akmed and this is Aziza, my wife."

"We're pleased to meet you."

"Have you been here a long time in this church?" Akmed inquired as people around them chatted noisily.

"Not long. What's it been now, Sherri?"

"Nearly three months. We're pretty new. I haven't noticed you before. Is this your first visit?"

"Yes. We are from Canada. Actually, we're on our honeymoon."

"Congratulations," Sherri whispered, squeezing Aziza's hand as they sat down. She turned her attention back to the platform where the soloist stood ready as the introductory strains of a music background poured through the sound system. A few minutes later, Pastor Cain was preaching. The Heidens quickly became absorbed in the message. They loved the teaching emphasis and admired the skill with which Pastor Cain was able to relate Bible passages to present-day living. He was a great teaching pastor.

—∞—

John felt the weariness of the day inching along his body as the third service got under way. He had long since discovered that the farther into the morning he went, the harder it was to stay focused. His energy faded and his mind wandered. He flashed back briefly to early yesterday and the kitchen incident with Jeremy. It seemed longer than just a few hours ago. They had not seen one another to talk since then. Yesterday, Jeremy had still been asleep when John left for the breakfast meeting with the board. By the time he'd returned, Jeremy was gone, and their paths had not crossed all day. A painful heaviness stirred in John as thoughts of his son crowded into his mind.

This is such a crucial time in his life. What is going to become of him? And Esther. I can't imagine what hurts and bitterness are still hidden inside her. What is all of this doing to us?

After Jenny's funeral, Esther had continued functioning each day in robot-like fashion. Cleaning house. Doing laundry. Spending hours alone by the window, a faraway look in her eyes. Reading occasionally. Mostly staring. It was the quiet between them that got to John. It was not the spiritual quiet that exists comfortably between two contented lovers. This quiet was abnormal. Dangerous. They didn't seem able to share anything deeper than surface talk anymore.

His eyes skimmed across the third congregation of the day. There she was, sitting near the back with Jessica at her side. Jeremy had not been at either of the first two services. A quick scan confirmed that he was not in this one either. John's heart sank further.

Then his eyes fell on the Arabic-looking couple. This time they were sitting directly behind Ken Ralsten's family.

They're here again. I wonder what's going on with them?

John was puzzled. He determined not to let them get away without speaking to them.

How long has it been since someone has attended all three morning services, listening to the same message in each one?

He smiled to himself.

This may be a first!

Soon the soloist was standing and the taped orchestration had begun. Fingering the cover of the Bible in his lap, John forced himself to focus once more on the message he was about to give.

Thirty-two minutes later, he was standing at the main door, shaking hands and greeting people as they exited.

"Good morning to you."

"Good morning." The olive-skinned couple smiled pleasantly as John extended his hand.

"Welcome to Calvary Church. Glad you could be with us today," John said. "Your names are . . . ?" His voice trailed off as he waited for their response.

"I am Akmed. This is my wife, Aziza."

"I'm delighted. I couldn't help noticing you this morning. You are a very attractive couple. But what motivated you to attend all three services today? Either you really enjoyed them or there must be some other reason. People don't normally stay with us through them all."

Akmed and Aziza had been fearful that this would happen. The possibility of such a query had been discussed in the team's planning meetings, but no better alternative had been suggested. Firsthand knowledge was critical to their success. They needed to understand the Sunday morning routine of activities. What does the building layout look like? How many exits are there? How many services and which one do most people attend? What sort of security is in place? Scores of tactical questions required firsthand observation.

"Pastor, Aziza and I have never been to a Christian service of worship before today. We are Muslims. But we are curious about the Christian religion. This is our first trip away from our families and so we took advantage to come here. I hope this is all right?"

"It's more than all right," John replied warmly. "We are happy to welcome you. Where is your home?"

"Our parents came from Lebanon to Canada when we were very small," Akmed lied. "We grew up in Toronto and met each other there. Recently, we married and are on our honeymoon."

"Congratulations. How long will you be here in California?"

"We start our return journey this afternoon."

"I hope you left your address so that I can send you our thanks for being our guests today."

"Thank you, Pastor. It would not be appropriate. Our families are very strict and for us to receive mail from a Christian church would not be looked upon with favor. I thank you just the same."

"I understand. You are welcome. We will pray that you have a safe journey and a long, happy life together. It has been a pleasure to meet you both."

Akmed extended his hand to John once again, shaking it firmly. His eyes locked onto John's.

"One day perhaps we will see each other again."

17

MONDAY, 12 SEPTEMBER, LOCAL TIME 0450
BAYTOWN, CALIFORNIA

The alarm kept on buzzing until John reached over, shut it off, and turned on the bed lamp with one motion. He lay back against the pillow, rubbing sleep from his eyes while trying to remember why he had set the alarm for this unholy hour. Finally his mind clicked in.

Israel. I'm leaving for Israel today.

As his thoughts began falling together, John felt movement beside him.

"I guess it's time to rise and shine."

A stifled groan came from beneath the neighboring pillow. Her voice was muffled. "I'll make sure Jessica is awake."

John got out of bed and shuffled toward the bathroom. Thirty minutes later he was showered, shaved, and dressed for the day. John always traveled in casual clothes. Comfortable slacks, open shirt, definitely no tie. Today, a light jacket to ward off the early morning chill.

He heard Esther's and Jessica's muffled voices coming from Jessica's room. Jeremy had decided to stay over at Geoff's house. He and John had said their good-byes the evening before. As he went out the door, Jeremy shook his hand. John gave Jeremy a brief hug, but felt him quickly pull away. He knew things were not right, but they would just have to wait for now.

John examined the single piece of luggage he would be taking. Esther had selected and packed most of John's things on Saturday. She was so skilled at coordinating and packing clothing that John rarely removed anything from his suitcase until he was ready to wear it—and typically it required no ironing. This made travel much easier. One case that contained all he needed, prepared with such skill that it would be two weeks exactly before he reached for the final change of clothes. By that time he would be on his way home. No fuss. No need to decide what to wear. He could concentrate on the people in the group and the details of their travel. John liked the arrangement.

At 5:45, he loaded their suitcases into the trunk of the car. The girls were still wrapping things up inside when the delivery boy tossed the morning paper onto the driveway, and without a word continued peddling his bicycle along the street.

John bent down to pick it up. Sliding the rubber band from around the paper, he opened it, glancing at the front page.

PEACE TALKS CONTINUE TO GO FORWARD

Secretary of State Charles Freeman prepares to return home after three days of diplomatic efforts in the Middle East. Both the Israeli and Palestinian delegations are in agreement on the most important matters. Water rights are still to be determined, but discussions continue as details of the Permanent Agreement are hammered out. Barika Al-Kassem urged Hamas leaders and other rival groups in Gaza to join her in an orderly and peaceful resolution of differences with the PNA.

Great. Things seem to be moving along.

John's previous trips into the Middle East had helped him interpret news stories of this nature. Through decades of animosity, the Palestinians and Israel had been at each other's proverbial throats. It had been this way every time John had traveled to Israel. Israeli police and the military establishment did their best to kept a tight lid on things. But the macabre protest practice of martyr suicide bombings had intensified feelings of hatred between the two groups. That fact made this news even more wonderful. He was delighted that the impossible had seemingly become possible for that troubled land. He looked forward to being on the ground there once again.

His scanned the headlines on the rest of the page.

FIVE VEHICLE PILE-UP ON BAY BRIDGE

The upper deck of the Bay Bridge was closed for two hours yesterday after a truck overturned, colliding with four automobiles. . . .

WASTE-REDUCTION PACT SHOULD RESULT IN CLEAN BAY

The city of Palo Alto announced Saturday that it will require additional audits from some companies as part of ongoing efforts to clean up . . .

Turning to the inside section, he glanced through the editorial page and was skimming a book review of Richard Paul Evans's latest novel when Esther and Jessica came through the doorway. Jessica was talking a mile a minute, her enthusiasm bubbling over with the anticipation of adventure. Esther checked to make certain the door was locked behind them. She walked with slow deliberateness to the car, almost as if each step was a huge effort. Her face looked drawn. Though it felt like they hardly talked anymore, John sensed she was not looking forward to their being gone.

He laid the partially opened paper on the garage counter where she would be sure to find it upon her return. He didn't see the small article in the lower right-hand column of page three.

MISSING PARK RANGER'S BODY FOUND

Glacier Park Ranger Carl Deeker's shallow grave was discovered on Sunday. Deeker had been missing for more than three days. Bloodhounds led searchers to the remote wilderness site. The cause of death was a knife wound at the hand of an unknown assailant. Authorities are awaiting the results of an autopsy. An outboard motor and the remains of a rubber raft were found nearby. Authorities said the motive was unclear, but illegal entry into the country by persons unknown is a possibility. There are no known suspects, but the investigation continues. Concern that terrorists may have entered the United States from Canada is being assessed by the Office of Homeland Security, and the FBI has joined the investigation.

John backed the car out of the garage and turned south on Jefferson, heading for the freeway.

18

12 SEPTEMBER, LOCAL TIME 0600
SAN FRANCISCO INTERNATIONAL AIRPORT

On the way to the airport, Jessica leaned over the seat back in an arms-beneath-the-chin position, talking mostly to her mother. Esther was quiet, smiling at her daughter, nodding her head occasionally in motherly agreement. Jessica's conversation was basically one-way and nonstop. For once John was grateful. At least her voice filled what otherwise would have been an awkward silence.

He glanced over at Esther now and then, while at the same time keeping an eye on the brake lights of cars in front of them. Traffic was heavy, sandwiching them on either side as well as front and back, in the fast-slow-stop-go rhythm familiar to California commuters. As they crossed the long, low San Mateo Bridge, the early morning light revealed an uneven chop on the bay, its gray surface whipped by stiff breezes.

Esther did not seem sullen. Withdrawn was probably a better word. Did Jessica sense the growing rift between him and her mother? Of course they had never spoken of such a thing. But he felt the void this morning. Did Jessica feel it, too? Could that be why she was chattering so?

John tightened his grip on the wheel. Esther glanced over at him, a thin smile threatening to erase the serious look on her face. Her hand moved toward him, but the smile faded as quickly as it had come, replaced by the all-too-familiar sadness, like a dark veil covering a thousand unspoken emotions that John could only imagine. Her hand wavered slightly, then dropped back onto her lap.

Jessica was suddenly quiet. John glanced in the rearview mirror in time to see her eyes move slowly from her mother's face to his. She had noticed the movement of her mother's hand.

She's sharp, he thought guiltily. *She knows something is not right. I wonder what's going on inside her little head? Maybe the next two weeks together will give us a chance to talk. But what will I tell her? Lord, have I made another mistake? Should I have left her at home? If she starts asking questions, what answers can I give her? I don't have any that satisfy myself, much less a twelve-year-old.*

Then as suddenly as she had grown silent, Jessica jump-started her one-way conversation by rattling off trivia facts she had accumulated on her own in preparation for the journey. The rest of the way to the airport was filled with an amazingly accurate geography lesson on a land that she had never before seen.

John was impressed.

—ᴍ—

While her father scooped up their luggage and stepped off the escalator, Jessica spied Edgar and Jill Anderson talking with Shad Coleman and Mary Callahan. Shad and Mary were both in their mid-thirties and served as lay leaders in Calvary's singles ministry. Jessica knew them a little bit. But the Andersons were two of her favorite people. She had been delighted when she learned that they were going. They were standing halfway between the ticket counter and the outer edge of the lobby, drinking coffee and laughing at something that had just been said.

Edgar looked up and waved.

"Hi, Pastor. Hi, Esther. And good morning, Jessica! Here, let me help you with that case, young lady." Edgar reached out to take Jessica's luggage.

"Thank you anyway, Mr. Anderson," she smiled. "Daddy says I have to carry whatever I packed. So, I guess I'd better get used to it."

Edgar laughed. "Oh, your daddy is one tough hombre, Jessica. But, I think he wouldn't mind if I took it over there and put it with the rest of ours." He pointed to a small pile of bags near the counter.

Jessica looked at her father. He nodded.

"Okay, Mr. Anderson. Thank you."

Edgar Anderson's hair was snowy white. His face reminded Jessica of a well-worn, leather punching bag, a physiological fact of life that was not entirely without substance.

Edgar had grown up on the streets of Oakland. He'd fought his way up through gang-infested alleyways, at the same time avoiding the neighborhood drug dealers under the watchful eye of his mother and her sister. Edgar never knew his father. His mother kept them in food and a place to call home by working downtown for a commercial janitorial service. She had night duty, so her sister kept an eye on Edgar.

He began working out at a neighborhood gym when he was thirteen. It was a city-sponsored boy's program, designed to give street kids something constructive to do with their time and energy. The rest was history. Golden gloves middleweight champion. First professional fight at age nineteen. A contender for the world middleweight championship at twenty-three. Almost at the top. Then on the night he fought for the title in Las Vegas, he suffered a torn retina in his left eye. End of boxing career.

Unlike many fighters, Edgar had carefully invested his career winnings. It was enough to get him out of Oakland and into a small but comfortable condominium in Baytown. Not long after that, Edgar met Jill at a Chamber of Commerce luncheon where he was the guest speaker. Before lunch was over, he had asked her to join him for dinner. She had agreed, on the condition that he would come with her to church the following Sunday.

Though Edgar had never been much of a churchgoer, he was motivated. Jill was attractive, intelligent, and had a smile that lit up the world. That first Sunday, he'd noticed a few other African-Americans scattered through the congregation. Not many. But, hey, this was the suburbs. The church was mostly white, with a smattering of upwardly mobile Mexican- and Asian-Americans. At first, he had felt uncomfortable. But he soon discovered that color didn't seem to matter much to these folks. They didn't make a fuss over his boxing background, either. They welcomed him for who he was. It felt great. Four months later, Edgar made a confession of his faith in Christ. Five months after that, he and Jill were married.

Now, three grown children and thirty-eight years later, sixty-three-year-old Edgar had taken early retirement from his position as Pacific Telephone's public relations director. Going to Israel with Pastor Cain had been a long-standing dream for both Edgar and Jill. This morning that dream was becoming a reality.

During the next half hour, others made their way up the escalator and over to the group. Luggage was checked, travelers were identified, and tickets validated. John asked Shad and Mary to make certain that each piece was checked and every carry-on item properly identified. They handed out rose-colored tags, watching as the others filled them out and attached them to their bags. This up-front work would make travel easier later on. Shad counted the number of checked luggage pieces as they passed through. Twenty-seven. He rechecked his figures just to be sure. Still twenty-seven.

Each person clutched their carry-on, ticket, and passport, as the group proceeded to the security checkpoint. The federalizing of airport security had not seemed to speed up the process at all. Either that or more people were traveling these days. It was taking a longer time than he thought it should. John counted again to make sure everyone was present. Twenty-three persons were scheduled for the tour, plus Jessica and John. Twenty-five altogether.

Wait. I only count twenty-four here.

John looked around. He recounted, just to be certain. Twenty-four.

Terrific! Who's missing?

He checked his watch.

Seven-ten. We start boarding in thirty minutes.

John ran through the names on his passenger list, checking faces in the animated group that stood nearby. Anderson, Edgar and Jill. Callahan, Mary. Cloud, Jerry and Susan. Coleman, Shad. Eiderman, Harold and Gisele. Hansen, Patricia. Micceli, Nick and Patricia.

All here so far.

Mitchel, Larry and Sandy. Smith, Adele. Sommers, Greg and Debbie. Taylor, Ruth. Thomas, Bob and Donna. Unruh, Evelyn. Watson, Dan and Phyllis. Wilson, Dan.

Wait. Unruh. I don't see Evelyn.

John checked over the group again. People kept moving, talking with each other, as well as to family members and well-wishers who had come to see them off, making it difficult to keep track.

Still no Evelyn.

"Has anyone seen Evelyn Unruh?"

The small crowd grew silent as they looked around, shaking their heads.

Everyone knew Evelyn. Small, petite, and seventy-seven. In fact, the others had been delighted when they'd heard that Evelyn would be traveling with them. She was lively. No, *feisty* was a better word. A widow for nine years, Evelyn was warm and caring and amazingly aware of everything happening around her. The world had not passed her by, her friends declared, jokingly. It couldn't catch her.

John glanced at his watch. *Seven-twenty.*

A worried look crossed his face. He turned to Esther.

"Honey, here's my cell phone. Will you try to call Evelyn? Her home number is here on the group listing. While you're doing that, I'll check with the group ticket counter. I'll just be a minute."

Esther took the phone and tapped in the number on the passenger list.

"Good morning, sir," smiled the lady in uniform. "Is there a problem?"

"At the moment we're missing one member of our group," John said, returning the attendant's smile, noting from her nameplate that her name was Geri. "Hopefully she'll be along any minute. Her name is Unruh. Evelyn Unruh."

"Is everyone else in your group accounted for?"

"Yes. We're all here but Evelyn. May I call you Geri?"

"Of course, Mr. Cain. You've a nice group of people traveling with you. But I'm sure they'll keep you busy keeping them all together. Most groups do."

John scanned the lobby, his angst continuing to build.

"Is this Mrs. Cain?" the attendant asked, not looking at anyone, but seeing the name on the travel list, *Cain, J.*

"No, Jessica is my daughter."

"How exciting for her to be on this trip with you. I hope you have a wonderful time together."

"Thank you. I'm sure we will."

"No one answers, John." Esther had come up behind him. "She must be on her way. I think her son, Donald, was planning to drive her to the airport. At least that's what Jill said. They had offered to bring her with them."

"Okay, hon," John responded, looking beyond her as he spoke, trying to will Evelyn Unruh into existence. "I hope nothing has happened to them."

"There you are, sir. I've marked the seat assignments by each name so you'll know where everyone is. Most of you are together in one section. Flight 311 leaves from Gate 23 at eight o'clock. In Los Angeles, you have a two-hour layover in which to connect with your next flight. You should have plenty of time for a comfortable transfer. Boarding will begin shortly, so you had best move along quickly."

"Thank you, Geri," John said. "And by the way, this is my wife, Esther."

"I'm pleased to meet you, Mrs. Cain. Are you taking some time off while your husband and daughter are away?"

Esther attempted a smile, caught off guard by the question. "I haven't decided yet. Just getting them out the door has been the main task. Maybe some quiet time at home."

"Best wishes to all of you. I hope this will be the best of times for each of you. In fact, I'll pray that that will be the case." The attendant smiled across the countertop.

Startled, John turned back.

"Are you a Christian, Geri?" he asked.

"I am," she replied, beaming. "Two years and four months old, as a matter of fact. And I'm guessing that you're a pastor and these are some of your flock?"

"Right you are," John smiled. "Thanks again, Geri, for your service . . . *and* your prayers. Maybe you can shoot one up for Mrs. Unruh."

"Already have. You run along now. When she arrives, she'll have to come this way and I'll personally see to it that she gets on board. Bye."

"All right then," John smiled as the people gathered around. "Time to head 'em up and move 'em out."

"What about Evelyn?" someone called out.

"One of the airline staff has volunteered to watch for her. The rest of us have to go along. Say your good-byes and let's go."

Hugs and kisses were exchanged and the group proceeded slowly through the security checkpoint. As the carry-on items moved through the X-ray machine and passengers proceeded one by one down the corridor, John pulled Esther aside. Jessica had already given her mother an excited child's hug and kiss. She was walking on ahead, hand in hand with Edgar. They were talking animatedly to each other.

"Will you be all right, hon?" John asked, taking her in his arms.

"Do I have a choice?"

"I guess not."

"I'll be okay. Don't worry about me. Just take care of yourself and Jessica. And everybody else, too," she added, "just like you always do."

John hesitated for a second, then replied, "Sure."

Silence.

"I wish you were going with us."

"We've been through this, John. I just don't want to go on this trip."

"I know. Still . . ."

Esther slowly pushed away. "John, you need to go."

John looked into her eyes. They were dry. The sadness was there, but no tears. Just the veil. It was there again. He felt an ache in his chest. Familiar pain. It was not his heart, of that he was certain. At least not his physical heart.

This is not a good good-bye. I should not be going. I'm—

"Good-bye, John. Have a nice trip. Be safe." Esther broke away and started toward the exit. Suddenly, she stopped, turned, and stared for a long moment at John. "Take good care of Jessica. And remember, my darling, I love you very much."

John returned her stare, at a loss for words.

Esther hasn't said "my darling" in . . . how long? John warmed at this sudden expression of affection and love. Then in a flash the warm feeling disappeared, replaced by a stab of apprehension.

"I love you, too," he took a step toward her, then hesitated, not quite knowing what to do.

She stood a moment longer, sad eyes gazing into John's. Then she turned and walked away. She did not look back.

John stood, rooted, watching until she disappeared around the corner.

"Sir. You need to hurry. Your group is through."

With a sigh, John tossed his carry-on at the conveyor belt and walked through the metal detector. No buzzers. But John didn't even notice. His mind was elsewhere. Jessica was ahead of him at the gate. Esther was on her way to the parking lot. Jeremy was probably on his way to class by now. *And where is Evelyn? For that matter, where am I?*

He slung his bag over his shoulder and ambled away from the checkpoint.

Just then, rounding the corner and rushing toward them, John saw Geri, the ticket attendant. On her arm was a wisp of an elderly woman, all ninety pounds of her chatting and smiling as though she had all the time in the world. In Geri's other hand was Evelyn's suitcase. Geri led Evelyn past the line and up to the security station.

"Hi, Pastor," Evelyn called out, waving with her free hand. "Isn't this just the nicest young lady? She told me she knew you and that she would take care of getting us together." Her suitcase and small carry-on were moving through the scanner. Geri told John to hand the suitcase to a flight attendant. It was too late to check it here. They would need to do that in Los Angeles. Evelyn Unruh said good-bye to her new young friend.

John waved to Geri, shooting her a grateful look. Then he took Evelyn by the arm. "Okay, young lady, enough chatting. We need to hurry or they'll be off to Israel without us. What happened? Nothing serious, I hope."

"It was all my fault, Pastor. About halfway here, I decided to get my passport out of my purse. Well, I looked and looked, but no passport. Then I remembered. I had laid it on the dresser so that I'd not forget to pick it up. Well, Donald just cut over that grassy sort of median in the freeway and we were headed home before I knew what was happening. We got my passport and made it back here just in time. I hope God and the State of California forgive Donald for driving like he did!"

"Good morning." The cabin hostess was smiling as they made their way along the ramp. "You two just made it. You are the last to board. Your seats are down this aisle."

A cheer went up from twenty-three of the passengers as Evelyn and John appeared in the cabin.

John sat down in an aisle seat next to Jessica.

The attendant helped Evelyn strap herself in as the plane began backing away from the terminal.

They were on their way.

—∾—

The dark-haired man folded his newspaper and placed it on the seat next to him. As he stood, his eyes followed the attractive woman walking toward the escalator. He had noticed her when she first arrived with her husband and daughter. From a distance, he had watched as their group gathered in preparation for their journey. He'd listened as they spoke of Tel Aviv, Bethlehem, and Jerusalem, familiar scenes crossing his mind at the mention of each name. Eventually, he had watched them disappear down the corridor toward their plane.

Now, as he headed across the lobby, he kept his eyes on the woman who by this time he was certain was the wife of the group leader.

All at once he found himself in the middle of another tour group that was making its way toward the departure gate.

"Excuse me, sir."

"Oh, pardon me. I wasn't watching where I was going."

He stepped around two women who were pulling their luggage-on-wheels behind them, and brushed up against a middle-aged man.

"Pardon me."

By the time he was able to extricate himself from the group and look to where he had last seen the woman walking, she was gone. He pursed his lips, hesitated, then walked outside and took out a cigarette and a book of matches. Exhaling smoke, he blew out the match, dropping it on the sidewalk. Casually, as if he had all day, the man moved along the walkway to a telephone booth.

Smoke curling from his mouth and nose, he entered ten numbers, waited, and then spoke quietly into the phone.

19

12 SEPTEMBER, LOCAL TIME 0805
NAPA, CALIFORNIA

Akmed el Hussein returned the phone receiver to its cradle. Turning, he looked at the others around the table.

"That was Ihab. They're on their way!"

A smile broke out on their faces. Mousa punched at Mamdouh with a clenched fist.

"How many are there?" asked Aziza.

"Twenty-five."

"The pastor? He and his wife have gone as well?"

"Not his wife. She stayed behind."

"Do we know why? She was supposed to be with him. Isn't that the information we received from Tel Aviv?"

"Yes. She must have changed her mind. According to our man in the tourist agency, she has gone on all their other trips."

"He should have known," Aziza frowned. "I don't like it when there are surprises." Her mind drifted back to Goat's Head and the park ranger. She wished that she could forget the look in the man's eyes, but she had not been able to.

"It does not matter, Aziza," said Akmed. "Actually, this may even be better."

"What do you mean?"

"He took someone else with him."

"Someone else? Who?"

Traces of an evil smile twisted across Akmed's face. "His little girl. She's twelve or thirteen."

A long silence.

Mousa chuckled. "Perhaps our people at home can find the girl a good husband while she visits. Wouldn't you like to have a fresh young American girl for a bride, Mamdouh? Eh?" Mousa pushed Mamdouh's shoulder again with his hand.

Mamdouh grinned, glancing at Aziza.

Aziza kept her eyes on the center of the table. She was not smiling. She hated it when men talked in demeaning ways about women. Even American women. It was a cultural thing not uncommon among her people, but she resented it. True, a wife had some status. But unmarried women and young girls were little more than chattel. The double standard between male and female was never more evident than within the community of her own people. On that, she felt, there could be no argument.

"All right," Akmed sat down in the lone remaining chair and leaned his elbows on the table. His fingers touched in prayerlike fashion. "Let's get back to work. We were discussing the church building. Aziza, continue with what you were telling us."

Aziza had no notes. She did not need them. Her memory was excellent, almost photographic. She closed her eyes, bringing back the scene, allowing the details to imprint vividly on her mental screen. Opening her eyes again, she glanced around the table.

"As I was saying, the building has a large lobby with restrooms on either side. An information area is located inside the main entrance. There appear to be four other exits, in addition to the main one. The others are smaller. Two doors instead of four. Inside, a hallway circles around all but the platform wall. Behind the platform there is a large, stained glass window. There are exits on either side of the platform. We think they go to a hallway, perhaps to some offices, but we don't know for sure. There are five doors leading from the lobby into the auditorium where the people gather to have their meetings. These inside doors and the platform exits will need to be secured with explosives immediately. Here's the way it looks."

With a felt pen and a napkin, Aziza drew a rough sketch of the building, pointing out the parking lot and its off-street entrances. Mousa and Mamdouh leaned forward for a closer look.

She glanced at Akmed. He nodded for her to continue.

"The auditorium is fairly large. That is where the infidels have their meetings. It seats maybe eight or nine hundred, but there are fewer than that at each session. There are normally three meetings on a Sunday morning, but we'll shorten their schedule a bit this week."

A ripple of laughter ran through the group and their heads nodded in knowing agreement.

"They hold what is called Sunday school for the children and young people. Even adults attend some of these smaller meetings. These are like school classes, held in rooms off the hallway on both the first and second floor. It appears to be mostly children in attendance at the time we will arrive. These we can let go?"

She looked questioningly at Akmed.

He shrugged his shoulders. "Whatever is Allah's will, Aziza. Repeat the plan we discussed on our return here yesterday."

Aziza paused, reaching for a half-filled glass of orange juice. The others sat quietly as she finished it off. With a corner of the napkin on which she had been drawing, she dabbed at her lips.

"Yes. Now here is the plan that Akmed proposes since having been at the site."

20

12 SEPTEMBER, LOCAL TIME 0850
BAYTOWN, CALIFORNIA

Esther turned the key and opened the door leading from the garage to the kitchen. The alarm system released a piercing warning signal. She stepped inside and reached for the alarm pad, tapping in the four-digit code to silence the alarm. The red light turned green.

Green. The color for "go." But, go where?

She walked through the kitchen to the center of the family room and stopped. The sound of her heart was like the rhythmic beat of a distant African drummer. She heard it and felt it as the oppressive quietness of the room suddenly smothered her with such heaviness that she took a step back. Her eyes were watery. Reaching out to regain her balance she was left breathless, staring at the walls. The ceiling. Was it her imagination? Or was the room actually getting smaller? Esther closed her eyes tightly, then opened them slowly. Her breathing was shallow, rapid. She felt exhausted, her entire body weak, as if she had just run a marathon race.

Dragging herself to the patio door, Esther fumbled with the latch, threw it open, and stumbled outside. For a long moment she stood still, gulping in fresh air, feeling as though her heart might take flight. And wouldn't that be a good thing, after all? At long last escaping this miserable flesh and blood prison that held it captive?

Moving first one foot, then the other, her steps short and unsteady, Esther slumped down on the nearest patio chair. Her brain was spinning. She leaned forward and placed her head between her knees. She remained there for a full minute while the beat of her heart returned to normal. Once the fear of fainting had dissipated, she raised herself to a sitting position and gazed across the pool to the flowers in the distance.

"What was that about?" Esther spoke the question out loud, needing to hear a human sound, even if it was only her own voice. The morning sun felt warm, but her body continued to shake with an inner coldness.

Maybe I am losing it. Maybe I'm certifiable after all. Oh, God. John is gone. I'm here alone. . . .

Esther felt a new sensation. One that was even more frightening. Waves of intense loneliness, familiar, but even more overpowering than usual, crashed relentlessly against the shifting sand of her delicate nervous system. Closing her eyes, she gripped the arms of the chair, her knuckles turning white as she forced herself to take deep breaths and willed the feeling to pass.

She opened her eyes again. Every nerve ending seemed to be tingling. Her hands were shaking so that she grasped one tightly with the other, pushing them between her legs, trying to settle herself down.

This is insane.

She thought about that for a moment.

Yes, maybe that's exactly what this is—insane!

After a few minutes, slowly, hesitantly, Esther got to her feet. She looked at the door. It was only a few steps away, but it seemed much farther. She was surprised when she took a step, however, to discover her limbs working quite well. Gathering in another deep breath, she walked to the door, opened it, and went inside. She looked at the walls and ceiling again. They were still right where they belonged.

It was my imagination, she thought grimly. *I must be cracking up.*

The intense feeling of loss and sadness was all-consuming now, draining her mind of its protective boundaries. She made her way across the family room, turned down the hall and into the master bedroom. Hesitating again, she moved past the bed, the dresser, and through the bathroom doorway. She stood in front of the sink for a full minute, staring at her image in the mirror.

You are a total failure, Esther. You know that, don't you? You are nothing like your namesake in the Bible. You are a coward. You've failed John. He deserves more. He'd be better off . . .

She stopped, brushing at a tear that had leaked out onto her cheek. But her thoughts kept on spinning.

Jeremy doesn't need me anymore . . . he's old enough . . . Jessica is with John . . . He will take care of her . . . I can't be trusted . . . I'm so sorry I lost you, Jenny . . . I didn't mean for it to happen . . . should have watched you more closely . . . should have been there for you . . . it's my fault . . . you were there alone . . .

Esther opened the medicine cabinet. Her hand came to rest on a white bottle on the top shelf, hidden behind a deodorant container and some hair spray. Pulling it out, she held it up, staring at the instruction label. Then she twisted the safety cap off and poured the entire contents out onto the counter. She sorted through the capsules. Then she poured a glass of water.

—w—

12 SEPTEMBER, LOCAL TIME 0910
WASHINGTON, D.C.

THE WHITE HOUSE
OFFICE OF THE HOMELAND SECURITY DIRECTOR
SENSITIVE

RE: NATIONAL PARK RANGER, CARL FREDERICK DEEKER.
AGE: 41.
FAMILY STATUS: UNMARRIED.
LENGTH OF SERVICE: TWELVE YEARS.
WORK PERFORMANCE RECORD: EXCELLENT.
REPORTED MISSING, WEDNESDAY, 07 SEPTEMBER.

BODY FOUND SUNDAY, 11 SEPTEMBER, APP 0900 MDT. APPROX TWO MILES FROM GOATS HEAD RANGER STATION INTO GLACIER NATIONAL PARK. AUTOPSY SHOWS DEATH CAUSED BY A SINGLE STAB WOUND. BODY LEFT IN SHALLOW GRAVE OFF TRAIL. MURDER WEAPON BELIEVED TO BE LONG, NARROW KNIFE. NOT RECOVERED. RAFT AND OUTBOARD MOTOR, CAMOUFLAGED WITH BRUSH AND TREE LIMBS, RECOVERED NEARBY. TAKEN TO FBI OFFICE, KALISPELL, MT.

MOTIVE FOR MURDER: UNDETERMINED. SUSPICION DEEKER SURPRISED UNSUBS ENTERING U.S. ILLEGALLY. RAFT RECOVERED IS NEW. TERRORIST INCURSION A DISTINCT POSSIBILITY. NUMBER OF UNSUBS UNKNOWN. EST: THREE OR FOUR MALE.

—w—

12 SEPTEMBER, LOCAL TIME 0935
LOS ANGELES

"Okay, gang, everybody out." John stood in the street beside the transfer bus as the passengers disembarked into the warm, midmorning sunshine.

"Are we all here now?" he asked, scanning the group with a practiced eye.

"That's debatable, John," quipped someone from the back. Several laughed.

"I'm glad your sense of humor is manifesting itself so soon, Dan," John responded, recognizing Dan Wilson's voice. "We'll all need ample doses of it before the day is over."

As the bus pulled away from the curb, John pointed to the terminal entrance. "We're going through that entry over there," John pointed. "Be sure you have all your carry-on items. We're not going to see this place again for a long time."

Some cheers went up.

"Follow me. Larry, would you and Sandy mind bringing up the rear? That way we won't lose anybody."

"Sure thing, John." The couple moved to the back edge of the group.

"Okay, everybody, more security checks and our next stop is KLM's departure area."

John looked at the clock high on the wall to his left. It was nearly ten o'clock. Flight 2 was scheduled to leave on time, at 11:30, according to the screen displaying arrival and departure times. He slowed, momentarily, to permit an elderly Asian couple to cross in front of him. The man was pushing a baggage cart. The woman walked a step or two behind. John smiled, nodded a greeting, then resumed his confident gait at the head of the group.

We're doing fine. No problems. Looking good. A few more minutes and we'll be ready to board.

21

12 SEPTEMBER, LOCAL TIME 0848
BOOTH BAY, MAINE

Good morning."

Rosa Posadas smiled as she stepped to one side of the hallway so the man could pass by. "Good morning, sir. Are you and your friends enjoying your stay?"

"Yes, very much, thank you. By the way, I want to thank you for the way you've been caring for our rooms. You do excellent work."

"Thank you, sir. I am happy you are pleased with our service."

"We are indeed. Have a good day."

"And you as well, sir."

The man moved on, disappearing down the stairs.

Nicholas Hondros and his three friends had turned out to be good guests. They were quiet and well-mannered, not at all demanding. Even Rosa was impressed. She'd seen all kinds during her years at Hill House.

All the rooms had been filled over the weekend, a late season surge. Today, however, only four were in use. One by an older man and his wife, who were leaving this morning. Another by a honeymooning French-Canadian couple from Toronto. And the two rooms occupied by the four male companions.

Rosa knocked on the door.

"Just a minute."

She heard voices speaking in low tones, footsteps, then the door opened.

"It's your maid service, sir. But you are busy. I can come back later."

The man glanced over his shoulder. Rosa saw two men behind him. One was seated in a chair near the window, the other standing by the bed.

"It's all right," he said. "Come in now. We were just leaving."

He opened the door wide. Two of the men reached for windbreakers hanging in the open closet and passed by Rosa at the doorway. The third man got to his feet slowly as he shuffled some papers into a leather case. Rosa busied herself with gathering up clean towels and bathroom supplies from her hallway cart. Out of the corner of her eye, she observed the man zip the case closed, carefully setting the built-in combination lock. He placed the case in the top drawer of the room's small writing desk, pausing for a moment, as if debating whether or not to leave it there. Then pushing the drawer shut, he turned and came toward Rosa.

He was dressed in casual shoes, jeans, and a blue sweater pulled over a sport shirt with an open collar. A handsome face. Dark hair. But it was his eyes that caused Rosa to look again. They were piercing, a deep brown, leaving her with the discomforting feeling of being looked *through*. He gave the appearance of a man very much in control. Still there was something else about him—a sense of mystery, perhaps. Or . . . danger?

Come on, Rosa. Get a grip. You've been watching too much television.

He brushed against her as he moved through the doorway.

"The room is fine today. Make up the beds and clean the bathroom. Don't worry about anything else. Can you do that?"

"Yes, certainly. If that is all you wish."

"That will be fine," he said quietly, now standing outside in the hallway. "Nothing else is necessary."

Turning away, the man walked to the stairs and disappeared from sight.

Rosa set the towels and washcloths down, then proceeded to open the window. A strong odor of tobacco permeated the room. Rosa did not smoke and hated the way the smell worked its way into the bedding, rugs, towels, even the wallpaper. As she stood by the window, letting fresh breezes blow gently into the room, she saw the men leaving Hill House and getting into their car. The man with the piercing eyes looked up at the window and saw her standing there. He paused for a moment with his hand on the front passenger side door, looking directly at her. Then he got in and closed the door. The car backed out of the parking stall and headed off in the direction of town.

Rosa returned to her task. As she put fresh linens on the bed, she thought more about the room's inhabitants. She was used to all kinds of people. After all, she'd grown up in New York City, where a woman needed to develop an instinct about strangers in order to survive. You had to look out for yourself in the city. There were good people there. But there were plenty of bad ones, too.

Rosa was not unattractive. Her dark, reddish brown hair had a tousled, windblown appearance that was natural. It framed dark eyes, a delicate nose, full lips, and cheeks that dimpled when she smiled. Her overall appearance was one of fitness and health. Two children had not diminished the appeal of a well-formed body. She hoped this would still be true after number three.

During her teen years, Rosa had been propositioned for sexual favors by many young and not-so-young men in the old neighborhood. Had it not been for her strong religious upbringing and the powerful sense of family her parents had instilled, she often wondered what might have happened to her. She was sure that her faith in God was part of what protected her. It had also been God who had brought Manuel into her life. Of that she was absolutely certain. She took pride in the fact that she had been a virgin when she joined Manuel in the marriage bed on their first night together as husband and wife. In her neighborhood, that was no small feat.

She had developed an acute sense of what was right and wrong, good and bad, safe and unsafe, during those earlier years. Maybe that was what she felt this morning—the same feeling she used to have when things were amiss in the old neighborhood. Her mother said it was an instinct that animals were given in order to survive their predators. It had served her well on more than a few occasions in the past. But she had not felt like this for years. Not since arriving in Booth Bay. Not like this.

Rosa stopped her work. Standing in the center of the room she stared at the drawer in the writing desk.

What do you suppose is so important that it requires the protection of a combination lock? Why would a man bring that sort of thing with him on his vacation? It could be business, of course. That's probably all it is. Some kind of business deal that these four men are involved in together.

Having processed that thought, Rosa glanced around the room one last time before leaving. She paused at the doorway, staring at the beds. She placed the soiled linens in the laundry bag and then came around to the farthest bed. Kneeling, she looked underneath.

They're still there.

Yesterday, while cleaning, Rosa's vacuum sweeper had bumped something under the bed. She had bent down to look. Usually there was nothing stored under any of the beds. She saw three long, waterproof bags, zipped and obviously locked, pushed up against the wall. Out of curiosity, she felt one of the bags. She could not make out the contents. She pulled on the end of one of them. It was heavy.

Rosa had also wondered about suitcases. More precisely, the lack of suitcases. The bureau drawers contained neatly folded shirts, socks, and underwear. Pants, sweaters, and jackets hung in the closet. Toiletries were carefully arranged in the bathroom.

But there were no suitcases.

And only one suitcase in Mr. Hondros's room.

One case for four men.

It seemed strange.

At first Rosa thought the bags under the bed must contain their clothing. However, her brief investigation seemed to rule out that possibility. Whatever the bags contained, it was almost certainly not clothing. But what? Normally, Rosa was not nosy. She respected the privacy of her guests. So what was eating at her this morning?

Rosa, you are being foolish. There is nothing here out of the ordinary. These are just four men on vacation. Leave them alone and hope that they give you a big tip. You can use it.

She stood up, walked back into the hall, and closed the door, turning the key in the lock. Gathering her things together, she moved down the hall to the honeymooners' room. She knocked while reaching for her key. She was sure the couple was not there, but she waited. As she entered the room, her mind was still on the men whose room she had just left.

One man in particular.

He is a handsome one, I'll say that. Very strong and athletic looking. And those piercing brown eyes.

Rosa chuckled to herself.

But no one is perfect.

She remembered the scar. His beard appeared to cover part of it, but not all. The scar ran across the cheek toward his ear.

Leaning down to get towels and washcloths, Rosa wondered how he had gotten it.

22

Mohammed Ibn Ahmer eased the rented Cadillac through Booth Bay's narrow streets until they reached Route 27. As they passed the Booth Bay Railway Museum, Mohammed informed the others that it contained a ridable miniature railroad, a turn-of-the-century barbershop, a bank, and a country store, as well as an antique auto museum.

Their lack of response ended his attempt to serve as tour host for the others. They drove on in silence. As they made their way through the wooded countryside, the others gazed out the car's ample side windows at the passing farmhouses, rivers, and saltwater inlets. America was a beautiful land.

Easing onto U.S. 1, they drove through Wiscasset and on to Bath, the former shipbuilding capital of Maine and one of the nation's busiest producers of navy ships. They stopped for breakfast near the Bath Iron Works. From the café, they had a good view of the towering cranes and other shipbuilding equipment. The gray overcast skies made the town's red brick buildings appear to be ancient fortresses of commerce. Monuments to the evils of capitalism and to America's military tentacles. Several appeared to be empty, apparently conquered at last by the passing of time and the death angel of economics.

After breakfast, the four men crossed over the Kennebec River, traveling west to I-95. The pace picked up now as they entered the multilane turnpike. Past Brunswick, the home of Bowdoin College, according to the road signs. Then Freeport, with its shopping outlets tempting tourists and locals alike. Finally, Portland, coastal Maine's largest commercial center, clinging precariously to the shores of Casco Bay. Past the Kennebunkport exit, the occupants of the Cadillac rode on in silence.

They crossed into New Hampshire at Portsmouth. A few minutes later, they passed by a sign welcoming them to Massachusetts.

"Well, my friends," sighed Marwan Dosha. "It won't be much longer. In a few short days we will bring them all to their knees. The Americans think they have beaten our brothers in Afganistan and Iraq. They think they are on the brink of peace between Israel and Palestine. They think their 'Homeland Security' will stop us from waging the battle. But here we are. They have not won the war. Our immortal heroes of 9/11 are cheering us on. They did not become martyrs in vain. Their courage made the enemy stagger. We will do more. I am confident of this. We will see victory. The Great Satan and its harlot offspring will be on their knees begging for mercy. Your brothers in prison will be set free. Your homeland will be yours once more. And you will be heroes of the revolution!"

The others gazed at him with an admiration akin to hero worship. Though he himself was not a Palestinian, he fought for the ideals of Hamas and Islamic Jihad. Dosha looked pleased, his face glowing at the thoughts of their adventure. He thrived best when living on the edge. His daring reputation inspired confidence in those with whom he worked. However, Marwan Dosha was no ideological fool. Just in case this or any other mission was not successful, he had established several private bank accounts in Switzerland and Brazil. These would provide him with a more than adequate and readily available income if things went badly. He had always been mindful of "back door" exits being available if required.

It never hurts to plan ahead, he thought, smiling to himself. *Just in case.*

The countryside was becoming more populous now as they drew closer to their destination. Quaint little villages rapidly gave way to a sprawling suburbia that embraced one and a half million households.

Finally, there it was.

The skyline of America's twentieth largest city.

Six hundred thousand souls.

Fifteen thousand people per square mile.

John Winthrop's Boston.

The perfect place for a holocaust.

23

12 SEPTEMBER, LOCAL TIME 1127
BOSTON

It was almost 11:30 as they drove past Logan Airport and entered the Ted Williams Tunnel that took them under Boston Harbor. Once through the tunnel, Mohammed expertly navigated the car along the crowded downtown streets, past Faneuil Hall Marketplace, eventually coming to Boston Common, the city's central park.

Statues, monuments, walkways, and benches were scattered throughout the grassy field. The Frog Pond, normally filled with splashing children on a warm summer's day, was peaceful and quiet. Working people on their lunch hour strolled along walkways or sat and talked on park benches. Tourists busily snapped pictures of the State House, its gold dome shining and visible for miles. A young couple stood on the steps of the tall-steepled Park Street Church, obviously absorbed in one another.

"That's the Old Granary Burying Ground," said Dosha, pointing to a fenced-in field of weathered tombstones adjacent to the old church. "A number of Americans who fought for their independence from Britain are buried there. Samuel Adams, John Hancock, Paul Revere. Some others, too."

Yusif and Safwat leaned forward for a better view. Mohammed looked at Marwan in surprise. "You have been here before?"

"Yes."

Mohammed waited for a further word of explanation. There was none. He turned his attention back to the traffic, wondering what else he did not know about Marwan Dosha.

Having circled the Boston Common, Mohammed turned onto Cambridge Street and followed it across Longfellow Bridge. Sunlight had finally broken through the clouds, transforming the Charles River into a watery carpet of royal blue. White sails filled by a light northwest breeze propelled sleek vessels across the river's surface. A white cabin cruiser, with a man and a woman visible on the upper deck, disappeared from view as it passed beneath the bridge.

"That's what we want," said Dosha, sitting forward, straining to catch another glimpse as the cruiser came into view on the other side. "Where is the best place to rent something like that?"

Mohammed turned right onto Commercial Street. "The Charlesgate Yacht Club is a short way ahead. We can check there. I dropped by a couple of weeks ago and they had three or four boats that would meet our needs. If what we want is not available, there are three other powerboat marinas on the river that I know about."

"All right," said Dosha, "here's what you must do. Take Yusif. Check out the boats. Tell them that you want to take your girlfriends out for the weekend. You want to do some cruising and fishing. Rent it for the week, beginning Saturday afternoon. When we are ready, you will take the boat upriver a ways and drop anchor. You'll wait there until I give you the signal. When it comes, you will position yourselves and be ready to do the deed. Whatever way the wind is blowing, head into it. When you are finished, leave the boat and drive north to Canada. We have friends in Montreal who will see that you are returned home safely."

"What about you and Safwat?" asked Mohammed.

Safwat was quiet, his eyes narrowing in concentration as he listened for the details of his assignment.

"Safwat will purchase a token on the MBTA Red Line. He'll begin at Alewife and work his way to Braintree. At each station, just before the door closes he will leave a small 'gift.' From the last station, he will drive a rental car we will leave nearby to New York City. The safe house address is back at the room in my case."

"And you, Marwan. What about you?"

"I will accept the most challenging of all roles. I will negotiate with the enemy powers that be. But before I do this, I will provide a little demonstration for our 'clients.' Hopefully they will see their situation as intolerable and be willing to meet our terms. If not—" Dosha raised his eyebrows and smiled, "—then you will carry out your tasks and the infidels will die."

No one spoke for the rest of the way, until the Cadillac pulled into the yacht club marina.

24

12 SEPTEMBER, LOCAL TIME 1510
BAYTOWN, CALIFORNIA

Esther squinted against the brightness. Where was she? Her mind was a blank. She stared up at the ceiling as the room gradually slowed its swirling. The wispy remains of a spiderweb in the corner continued moving back and forth, given life by a soft breeze. Esther turned her face, surprised yet relieved to see the familiar outline of her own living room. She was lying on the sofa.

Her gaze returned to the spiderweb.

How long has it been since I've cleaned this room?

She couldn't remember.

And, if I am in my own living room, where is that breeze coming from?

After pondering that question for what seemed a more than adequate amount of time, she gave up. Then, she heard the soft sound of the air conditioner.

It comes on automatically. It must be warm outside. What time is it?

She moved her arm upward until her watch came into view. *Three-ten. Jeremy! He will be home soon. I need to get up.*

Esther rolled to one side and dropped from the sofa onto the carpet. Her head felt ready to explode. The pain was excruciating. Both hands came up as she tried getting to her knees.

"Oh, my—"

A wave of nausea churned upward from her stomach. She covered her mouth with her hand and tried to get to her feet. She couldn't seem to do it. She began crawling toward the hall on her hands and knees.

I'm going to be sick. The kid's bathroom. It's closer.

Banging her shoulder against the doorjamb, she kept moving forward until she reached the porcelain fixture. At that precise moment, her stomach erupted. She continued throwing up until nothing but dry heaves remained, leaving her body soaked in perspiration. *What is making me so sick?*

She clung to the bowl, waiting for her insides to settle down. She heard a key in the front door. And then she remembered.

He's home!

Disoriented and weak, Esther frantically searched for the flush handle. She felt it finally and pulled, but her hand slipped and banged against the bowl, dropping to the floor. She reached for it again.

I can't let him see me like this.

"Mom? Mom! What's the matter?"

The voice was close by. Esther turned away from the toilet and looked up. Jeremy was standing in the bathroom doorway.

"Are you all right? What's the matter?"

He dropped his book pack in the hall, stepping over her and stooping down. Seeing the contents in the toilet, he grimaced, reached over and pulled the flush handle down. Esther gave him a wan smile.

"I'm sick."

"I can see that. What's the matter with you? How long have you been this way?"

"That's a good question. I'm not sure I know the answer." Esther's words slurred. "Help me up, okay? Can you help me walk to the bedroom?"

"I can do better than that," Jeremy answered.

One arm circled around her back as he grasped her tiny waist. His other arm went under her legs. Jeremy effortlessly lifted his mother off the bathroom floor. She closed her eyes as the carrying motion sent another wave of nausea through her. This one wasn't as bad, though. Not like the others. Her head sagged against Jeremy's shoulder, her arm brushing the bedroom door. Jeremy handled her gently but firmly, as if he thought she might break. Maybe she already had.

When did you get to be so strong, Jeremy?

Carefully, he laid his mother on the bed. Adjusting a pillow under her head, he stood there wondering what to do next. Her eyes were closed, but she was breathing regularly.

"Jeremy?" Her lips formed his name slowly, the retched taste of bile in her mouth causing her to grimace.

"I'm here, Mom. What should I do? Call a doctor or something? Maybe 9-1-1?"

"No, no, don't. Please. I'll be fine. I just got a little upset, that's all."

"A *little* upset?" Jeremy's look was one of alarm, thinking of how he had just found his mother in the bathroom.

"Would you get me a glass of water, please?" Esther's lips and tongue felt thick and dry as she struggled to form the words.

"Sure, Mom. Just a sec." He started toward the master bathroom.

Suddenly Esther remembered the pills. Were they still there? *Did I take them all? Where is the bottle?*

"Jeremy, don't use our bathroom," she said desperately, struggling to sit up. "Get it from yours."

But it was too late.

25

12 September, local time 2055
KLM Flight 2, Enroute to Amsterdam

John looked over at his seatmate. He was glad that she had finally settled in. Earlier she had been in the aisles, carrying on nonstop conversations with others in the tour group. Laughing, excited, happy, and twelve years old. She related easily with adults—not in the obnoxious way of a child striving for attention, but naturally, spontaneously, with bright-eyed enthusiasm that drew people of all ages into her circle.

She had even made friends with one of the airline attendants, a blue-eyed, fair-skinned, blonde woman from Rotterdam named Sanne. As he watched the cabin crew working the aisles after dinner, it occurred to John that all the flight attendants, men and women, had blue eyes, fair skin, and blond hair.

He enjoyed the Dutch. They were, generally speaking, very pleasant and accommodating. To him they represented the quality of confident determination that declares no matter how hard it gets, it will never be too hard. We will overcome. Even their national language was difficult. The Dutch themselves jokingly agreed that it was too hard even for them to learn. However, in the tradition of many Europeans, they then proceeded to learn not only their own, but three or four other languages as well. Thankfully, one of those was English, the world's universal business language.

On another visit to Europe, while attending a luncheon near Bern, Switzerland, John had been introduced to the Swiss minister of defense. In the course of the meal, the subject of bilingualism had become the topic of table conversation.

"Look around this room, John," the minister had said. "I know almost every person here and I can tell you they all speak four or five languages fluently. Of course, locally, we speak mostly Deutsche as you know. What you may not know is, the Deutsche we speak is not the same as what we write. Throw in some French and Italian and you can see it all becomes very complicated. But one thing I can say to you with absolute certainty. When it is time to get serious about business and it becomes imperative that we are understood, we speak English."

"Lucky for us Americans," John had replied, grateful and at the same time a bit envious of such impressive language proficiency among so many.

John looked out the cabin window. By now he guessed they were somewhere over northern Canada. A heavy cloud layer enveloped the tundra and lakes of an inhospitable wilderness far below. Though the terrain was eclipsed from view, John knew that this bleakest of all landscapes had already begun freezing over, even though winter's severest lashing was still a long way off.

The aisles were filling with passengers making their way to restrooms as the flight attendants finished their cleanup duties. The dinner service had been excellent as always, in the best Dutch tradition. A movie was scheduled to show in a few minutes. Jessica was ready. Her earphones were already in each ear and she was listening to the Western music channel, something John did not think she ever did at home.

"Daddy," she said, looking up at him as she peeled an earphone away from her ear. "What does a cowboy get when he plays his tape deck backwards?"

"I don't know. What?"

"He gets his girlfriend back, his pickup back, his dog back . . ."

John chuckled. "That's a good one, sweetheart. An old one, too. You hear that on your down-home channel there?"

"Yup," she answered with a grin and her best cowgirl drawl. She crossed her legs and leaned back in the seat.

John took a small New Testament out of his pocket. As he sat back, Jessica pulled the earphones down around her neck. Her finger pressed down on the volume control.

"Daddy, will you read to me, please?"

"Okay, hon. What'll it be? Anything special?"

"No. I just want to hear you read," she replied, pushing her small airline pillow against him and snuggling her head on his arm. "You pick out something."

"Well, why don't we do what normally we would not do. Let's just open it up and read whatever comes. Okay?"

"Sure."

John placed the New Testament on the foldout tray. The well-worn binding let the pages fall open easily. He picked it up and began reading.

"That day when evening came, he said to his disciples, 'Let us go over to the other side.' Leaving the crowd behind, they took him along, just as he was, in the boat. There were also other boats with him. A furious squall came up, and the waves broke over the boat, so that it was nearly swamped. Jesus was in the stern, sleeping on a cushion. The disciples woke him and said to him, 'Teacher, don't you care if we drown?'"

John looked down at Jessica. Her eyes were closed. She was smiling.

"He got up, rebuked the wind and said to the waves, 'Quiet! Be still!' Then the wind died down and it was completely calm.

"He said to his disciples, 'Why are you so afraid? Do you still have no faith?'

"They were terrified and asked each other, 'Who is this? Even the wind and the waves obey him!'"

He closed the New Testament and dropped it beside him in the seat, looking again at the precious cargo leaning against him. He smiled, shaking his head.

Jesus may be awake, sweetheart. But you're not.

Adjusting her pillow slightly, John sank back into his seat, stretching his legs as far as he could, while musing over what he had just read.

He had been too busy making sure everyone was taken care of to think about other things. That in itself had been a welcome relief. Now, however, for the first time since leaving San Francisco, John's mind began revisiting the reality that was his life. His thoughts were disconnected, yet held together by an invisible cord. They roamed across the screen of his soul as random, unconnected scenes, broken now and then by some capricious hand on the channel selector before they could form any logical sequence.

The resignation letter, tucked away in his office. Ken Ralsten's veiled insinuations at Saturday's board meeting. Yesterday's services. The Arab couple that attended all three services. Jeremy's anger. Esther's look of sadness at the airport. "*Remember, my darling, I love you very much.*" A small cloud of apprehension surfaced once more. Her words, her tone—almost like some kind of pronouncement. Had it merely been the finality of the moment? Or something else . . . ?

When the storms were the wildest, Jesus was in the boat with his disciples. Isn't he supposed to be in my boat, too? That's what I tell our people at home. Well, God, if you really are in my boat, it would be nice to hear from you. I've been pointing people to you for years. So, where are you when I need you? I'm not sure anymore about much of anything, except it feels like I'm touching bottom. How much worse can things be?

John looked down at Jessica's sleeping form.

I do know one thing, little lady. I love you!

He closed his eyes.

The familiar ache returned.

The one that came each time he looked into a clear, sparkling pool of water.

The foreboding shadow that kept haunting him. It was there again.

His beloved ghost!

—~—

From across the aisle, Edgar was watching the face of his pastor. He knew there was something important on his mind. More than just responsibility for their group. There was something else that was eating away at him. Even though John was sleeping, it was easy to see the tension in his face. He looked unrested. Troubled. Edgar knew that John constantly carried with him the secrets and burdens of others. That in itself was enough to wear a good man down.

But this was different.

Edgar wasn't sure, but he thought he might know.

And what he thought gave him genuine concern.

He loved this man and the "Mrs." He loved their children, too.

The cabin suddenly darkened as the evening movie flashed up on the screen.

He closed his eyes.

He was not watching.

He was not sleeping.

Edgar was praying.

26

TUESDAY, 13 SEPTEMBER, LOCAL TIME 1005
TEL AVIV, ISRAEL

The phone rang four times before Aryeh Shamrir picked up the receiver.

"Yes?" he said, twisting a cigarette beneath his fingers in the ashtray. "How many? Yes. Twenty-five. Yes . . . yes. Our man will meet them when they arrive. All right. Thank you."

Aryeh pulled open the left-hand drawer in his desk, ran his fingers quickly across the file tabs, withdrew a form with the words *Group Arrival* printed across the top in Hebrew, and directly underneath, *Cain/Barak.* The next few minutes were spent filling in the blank spaces. This completed David Barak's guide packet. Tomorrow afternoon he would take it with him to meet John Cain's tour group at the airport.

Aryeh knew that David had worked with Reverend Cain twice before. David liked the man and was looking forward to serving as the Cain group's professional guide during their sojourn in the country. Aryeh's pen flew over the empty spaces and when he had finished, he attached a listing of the names of Israel's latest anticipated guests from California.

Adnan Dakkad sat across the office, near the door. He had overheard every word of the telephone conversation. His understanding of spoken Hebrew was adequate. Enough for him to know that this was the call for which he'd been waiting.

The old man turned a page in the international edition of *Time.* He had been unable to decipher the details describing the cover story. It was written in English, the language of the Great Satan. There was no escaping the power of the pictures, however, and their message served up a mystical adrenaline to his gaunt, aged body. They were done in full color. He especially liked the cover scene, captured in film only a few days earlier by a photo journalist. It was the Gaza Strip.

In the foreground, two young boys and a girl who could not have yet reached her teenage years, armed only with stones, stood near the northern security border. With fists jabbing the air, they faced two well-armed Israeli soldiers. Behind the soldiers sat an armored tank. A building burned in the background. Rocks lay scattered across the street between them.

The peace negotiations had initially caught the Islamic Resistance movement off guard. As a result, things had been quiet for some weeks now, while their leaders determined what action to take. After many extended and heated arguments, they had rejected the so-called Permanent Agreement that was about to be signed into law.

Yesterday, major rioting had broken out at several points along the border, signaling a breakdown in the ability of the Palestinian residents to govern themselves peacefully. Defiance was the unwritten motif in the picture. It was there. Anyone could see it. And as Adnan studied the picture, his tired old eyes flickered with an ancient flame.

"Adnan."

He looked up at Aryeh Shamrir, his occasional employer. Shamrir was used to seeing the old man sitting near the door. During the past six months, he had become a normal part of the room's sparse but functional fittings of steel-framed desks and stiff-backed chairs, computers, and telephones. A few travel posters were tacked to the walls and the single open window let in noise, light, and automobile fumes from the outside.

Dakkad came to the office three times a week to sweep the floor, wipe off counters and desks, and empty the garbage. For this he received a few shekels. Occasionally, Shamrir also used him as a messenger. Dakkad knew the city well and had proven his willingness and ability to follow orders when given a task. He was a harmless old man who had lived out his best days. His ready smile, revealing several missing teeth, had a disarming quality about it. The few teeth that had somehow managed to cling to his gums were stained yellowish brown from a lifetime of tobacco use. Shamrir doubted they had ever felt the hand of a dentist.

Dakkad knew that Shamrir had checked him out with local authorities. That was fairly routine, one of the indignities of living as an Arab national in the occupied land of their birth. Adnan Dakkad was originally from Nazareth, had survived all the wars between 1948 and the present, and was now an old man, living alone in a tiny hole-in-the-wall apartment in a poor Arab sector of Tel Aviv.

Until his failing eyesight made it impossible to continue, he had driven a taxi, primarily in Jerusalem, but also in Tel Aviv. Now he survived any way he could, mostly picking up odd jobs here and there. He had no criminal record. He always proved faithful to the task and never failed to complete an assignment, whether it was sweeping the office floor, going out for soft drinks for Shamrir's small staff, or carrying messages around the busy downtown streets.

The man who had held this part-time job before him had suddenly taken ill. A day or two later Dakkad had shown up, indicating that he had heard there was work available. When Shamrir asked how he knew of the opening, Dakkad simply shrugged his shoulders and smiled his toothless best. A simple soul, he was one of many poor old castaways, living out their last years as best they could in the land of their birth. Besides, Shamrir never gave the old man an assignment that could be security sensitive. After all, this was only a travel agency.

But there were a few things Shamrir did not know about Adnan Dakkad. Of that Dakkad was certain. Shamrir had no inkling of Dakkad's longtime connections in the dark alleys of the Old City. He was unaware that in earlier years Dakkad had been involved in a series of terrorist incidents in Israel, including the 1972 massacre of passengers at the Ben Gurion airport, where twenty-six people were murdered and seventy-six others were wounded by the Japanese Red Army, strange bedfellows of the PLO.

In that mission, Dakkad had served as a contact courier between the PLO and the Red Army. There was never any mention of his name or his connections with either group. He had been too far down the ladder of importance to merit such visibility. Dakkad was always careful never to verbalize his political views. If he had been asked, Shamrir would have expressed serious doubts that the old man had any. That was the way Dakkad wanted it. And that's the way it was.

"Adnan, come here."

Dakkad smiled his winning, gap-toothed smile, bringing an entirely new set of wrinkles to his wizened, bronzed face. He put the issue of *Time* down on the small wooden table in front of him and slowly stood to his feet.

"I want you to hand deliver this to David Barak. You remember David. He was here yesterday, getting ready for a group of Americans who are arriving tomorrow."

The old man put his hands on the counter between them. Still smiling, he nodded his head.

"Yes," answered Dakkad. "I remember him well."

Shamrir wondered just how well the old man remembered anything, but gave no indication that such a thought had crossed his mind. After all, a little dignity might be one of this ancient Arab's few remaining possessions.

"I need you to take this to him. It was not ready when he came by on Sunday. He will need it in order to meet the group when they arrive at Lod tomorrow. He and his wife will be having lunch at one o'clock at the Espresso Kapali on Dizengoff Square. Go there and see that he gets this. All right?"

Dakkad nodded and smiled. "It is not a problem. Consider it as good as in his hand." Turning, he shuffled toward the door.

As the old man disappeared into the hallway, Shamrir shook his head, lit a cigarette, and returned to his desk.

—w—

A block away, Adnan Dakkad motioned to a young Arab man who was smoking a cigarette in front of a doorway. He handed him the papers and the man disappeared inside. Three minutes later, he reappeared, returning the original plus one copy of each page to Dakkad.

Dakkad stuffed the copies inside his shirt and continued along Frishman to Dizengoff. There he turned right and made his way toward the square. Cars moved in and out, horns honking, buses belching their way through the center of town. Pedestrians strolling along the sidewalks eyed the merchandise displayed in store windows.

Dakkad saw Espresso Kapali across the street. He stood for a moment, squinting into the bright sunlight for some sign of David Barak. Most of the customers were sitting outside rather than inside, enjoying the pleasant weather. Every table was full, with a few people standing around, soft drinks in hand, waiting for others to leave. It had been like this ever since the truce had been declared.

Two young men and a woman, in military uniforms and with automatic weapons slung casually over their shoulders, stood near the door. They looked so young, like children. But the old man knew these "children" to be dangerous warriors, like their fathers before them. He continued watching them. They appeared to be normal security. Dakkar decided they might even be in line for a table and dismissed them from his mind. Espresso Kapali was a popular place, especially with the young.

He had seen the man he was looking for only once before, but the Jewish guide should be easy enough to spot again. Brown hair, tanned, medium build, narrow-rimmed glasses shaped in the latest modern design. Dakkad took a few steps forward, then paused again, his eyes darting from table to table.

There.

Under the awning.

David Barak was leaning back in his chair, legs stretched full length under the small table. The blue sport shirt with a large white fish imprinted on it was the same one Dakkad had seen him wearing on Sunday. Only today he had on white shorts and Nike running shoes. His glasses were the type that darkened outdoors, shielding his eyes from the sun's glare.

Across from him sat an attractive young Jewish woman, fair-skinned, with short black hair, wearing a white blouse and khaki shorts.

Probably French. Maybe German or Russian. Who knows? These Jews come from everywhere in the world to take our land from us.

Crossing the street, Dakkad approached slowly, then stopped while still a short distance separated them. He waited patiently for Barak to look his way. After a few moments, he caught the man's eye. When he was sure he had been seen, he raised his hand in greeting, at the same time, revealing the paper he held. Barak nodded, saying something to the woman, whom Dakkad assumed was his wife or girlfriend, as he rose from the table. Reaching for his glass, he downed its remaining contents in a single swallow and began angling his way toward Dakkad, through the jumble of tables and customers.

Dakkad stayed out in the open, obviously alone. Of course there was nothing for anyone to be afraid of. He was an old man, much too frail to be mistaken for someone dangerous. Besides, Barak had been notified that he was coming. Still, due to the rash of suicide bombers in recent years, Tel Aviv was filled with nervous citizens, ever vigilant when bridging the racial and political barriers between Jew and Arab, even on a main avenue in the middle of the day.

"You are Mr. Barak, yes?"

"Yes. And you are from the travel agency," the guide responded, his tone indicating a statement instead of an inquiry.

"That is correct, Mr. Barak." Dakkad bowed his head ever so slightly. "I have the good fortune to bring you these important papers so that you may proceed with entertaining your guests from America."

Dakkad handed the forms to the handsome young Jew whom he guessed to be in his early thirties. Barak flipped through them quickly, then looked up.

"Thank you. These are what I need."

Dakkad waited, smiling his gap-toothed smile.

Barak reached into his pocket.

"Here, old man. Your job is finished now. Go home and take the rest of the day off." He handed him some shekels.

"*Shokran,*" said Dakkad, nodding his head respectfully as he took the money. "*Ma-ah-salameh.*"

"*Shalom,*" Barak replied, turning to go back to his companion, who sat at their table, watching.

—∾—

Adnan Dakkad continued walking west, away from the square and down a narrow street in the direction of the sea. In the middle of the second block, he turned into a small Tabak store. Inside the shop a lone customer waited for the proprietor to finish ringing up his purchases.

Dakkad smiled a silent greeting, nodding to his old friend behind the counter. They had known one another ever since the attack on the Israeli farm collective at Ma'alot in 1974. It had been a huge success. Twenty-seven dead, one hundred thirty-four wounded. For weeks Dakkad and the store owner had remained in hiding together while the IDS scoured the countryside, looking for two terrorists believed to have escaped in the confusion of the aftermath. They were never discovered.

Dakkad said nothing. He squeezed between the crush of tables, display cases, and wall shelves filled with pipes, tobacco, and cigarettes, fingering several items while he waited for the other customer to leave. When the store owner looked up, Dakkad gave him a knowing glance. The man lowered his eyes and nodded imperceptibly.

Dakkad moved to the rear of the little shop and pushed through a curtained doorway into the storeowner's small living quarters. The single room was tiny and stuffy, reeking with a combination of lingering body odor and tobacco smoke. A small, dirty sink was fastened to the wall in one corner. Pita bread, some food tins, and a bottle of water were piled together on top of a tiny cooking stove. Flies zipped through the air toward the old man, exploring his face before settling down in helicopter fashion on their pita bread landing pad.

His eye followed a dark cord that protruded from the near wall, snaking its way along the floor until it disappeared under a pile of carelessly strewn newspapers. Reaching under the papers, Dakkad found a black rotary telephone. Checking for the dial tone, he cranked in numbers that had been memorized months earlier. He could hear the phone ringing.

Once, twice.

He hung up.

Waited for a moment.

Redialed.

Once, twice, three times.

"Hello," answered a dull-sounding voice.

Dakkad's heart was beating rapidly. This was his great moment. A contribution, perhaps his final one, to the Intifada. The culmination of months of careful placement and patient undercover work. He wet his lips with his tongue.

"Twenty-five birds arrive at the store tomorrow. Some male. Some female. One smaller than the others, but all are healthy." *There are twenty-five in the group, including one small child.*

"How much will they go for?" the voice asked. *What time will they arrive?*

"Five-fifty each, as late as the store stays open. You will need to sign the invoice," Dakkad answered. *They will come at five-fifty in the afternoon. The list of passenger names will be at the drop site.*

He heard the phone click at the other end. Then the dial tone.

He returned the receiver to its cradle, spreading the newspapers over the phone again, in more or less the same manner in which he had found them. He pushed his way past the curtain and walked back into the store. Dakkad picked out a pouch of tobacco and a packet of cigarette papers and went to the counter. Like many of his peers, he preferred rolling his own to smoking ready-made. He enjoyed the ritual of forming the cigarette with his own hands. He was also able to maintain his habit for less money this way. He passed the appropriate amount across to the storeowner, together with the copies of the group itinerary and traveler's names. Someone else would pick them up shortly.

"*Naharak sae'id,*" he said to his old friend as he headed out into the sultry afternoon air.

Adnan Dakkad had no idea what the result of his telephone call and the hard-copy drop would be. He was only a small piece in a much larger puzzle. Small, but important. At least for now he *felt* important. He knew that he had done his job and that he had done it well.

His part was over.

The Intifada, however, was not.

Far from it.

No matter what others believed.

It was just beginning.

27

13 September, local time 1530
Eilat, Israel

The old one promises that twenty-five birds will arrive at the store tomorrow." *Our contact confirms that the group of twenty-five persons we have been anticipating will arrive at Lod on Wednesday.*

"They are to be gathered up and prepared for resale at the first opportunity." *We will keep track of them the rest of the week. They are to be taken on Sunday.*

The voice that had spoken to Adnan Dakkad was now filling the ear of Yazib Dudori. As the instruction came across in low, guttural tones, Yazib felt the anticipation growing. *This is it. Everything has come down to this moment. Mankind is about to feel the heel print of the forces of liberation. I am a part of something that is about to shake the world. It is really happening.*

"We are ready to receive delivery," said Yazib reassuringly.

The phone line went dead.

Yazib looked at the others. They had not been outside the safe house since their arrival in Eilat early Sunday morning. He looked across the room at Pasha, and for an instant he mentally relived their narrowly averted crisis. . . .

—w—

It seemed to them that Eilat's King Solomon Palace Hotel was grand beyond measure. They had become used to cold prison cells, spartan training camps, and traveling by camel across the hot, dry desert. This hotel rose from Israel's sands like a pyramid of Egypt. Stately and beautiful. Overwhelming. They stood together silently on the steps, letting its luxury feed their starving senses.

Then Pasha turned to say something to Yazib. Whatever she had planned to say, the words remained forever frozen in her throat. Coming toward them along the narrow street she saw the police car. Yazib did not. There was no time to run and no place to hide. They had foolishly permitted themselves to be caught out in the open at a late hour. In a few seconds, they would be discovered and their mission would be lost!

Pasha threw herself into Yazib's arms, kissing him hard and long. A very surprised Yazib caught himself, then put his arms around her, relishing the response of his own emotions to her unexpected passion.

The car slowed. From eyes that feigned closure, Pasha saw the policeman laughing as he looked their way. He nudged his partner, saying something as he pointed in their direction. The other officer leaned forward for a better look. Then the car rolled past.

They remained locked in each other's embrace for a long moment. Pasha gave herself to the warm response of Yazib's lips and the strength of his arms as he gathered her to himself. When at last they broke free, Pasha found herself gazing into Yazib's smiling eyes. That was when he saw her worried face. She turned slightly to look at the street behind him. In the corner of his eye, he caught sight of the retreating police car. His mind raced to catch up with his emotions. The vulnerability of their circumstance stunned him, draining his face of its color.

"The police," Pasha whispered. "I did not know what else to do."

Her face was only inches from his. He felt her rapid breathing, her heart beating.

Yazib cleared his throat as they drew back from each other. The picture of young lovers, they moved off the steps and began walking away from the hotel. He looked across the street for Imad and Fathi. They were invisible in the darkness.

"You did well, Pasha. Because of your quick thinking, we're still operational."

"I am sorry if I surprised you."

Yazib smiled. They were away from the lights now, walking along a narrow section of the street. The fear they had felt was rapidly receding. He turned to Pasha.

"It was a pleasant surprise."

Pasha pushed his arm gently.

"I knew you had not seen the police car. It was all I could think to do. It was my duty," she added demurely.

She heard Yazib's quiet laughter and felt her face grow crimson in the darkness.

—m—

"We are in business," Yazib exclaimed as he put the telephone down. Excitement was written on his face.

The others did not move. There was a strange silence. They stared at the phone. Then at each other.

Pasha was the first to let go. "It's happening then. It's really happening at last," she said. Her voice was full of feeling.

Smiles broke out quickly, then laughter, as they jumped up and pounded one another with exuberant congratulations. They were where they should be, doing what they had been called to do.

"Blessed be Allah!" Fathi said reverently. "Truly, he will be with us now!"

"What is our next step?" Imad asked as he pulled back a corner of the curtain that covered the window and peered outside. They had been cooped up in this little cinder block hovel for two days. He was ready to get on with it.

"Relax, Imad. We must wait here awhile longer." Yazib saw the disappointment in his eyes. He didn't blame him, really. The waiting was the hardest part. "We will move out tomorrow morning."

"Morning?" Fathi repeated in surprise. "Not at night with the cover of darkness?"

"No, Fathi," Yazib answered. "In the morning. We will not crawl like snakes to our strike point. We will cross enemy territory in style. In broad daylight."

"Are you serious?"

"Never more so. I spoke with our host this morning before he went to work. It is all arranged. Early on Wednesday morning we shall be on our way."

Smiles all around again as they looked at each other. Yazib was enjoying his little secret. In the last few weeks the group had become as one. Their trust in each other was rock solid. They were even beginning to think alike.

"If you are pulling our leg, Yazib, you will ride a camel all the way!" declared Fathi, pounding the table for emphasis.

"Backwards!" Pasha added, laughing as she said it.

The others agreed, offering mock threats of demeaning punishment to the man who was their leader.

"Enough, enough," said Yazib, holding up his hands in surrender. "You will see soon enough that I am a man of my word. Now, let's eat and get some rest. We have a long week ahead of us."

In another time and place, an observer to this scene might have described a group of college students preparing to amaze their campus friends and the school administration with the ultimate prank of the year.

But these young people, made immune to the consequences of their actions by the poison of life's empty promises, were not college students.

And their mission was not a prank.

28

13 SEPTEMBER, LOCAL TIME 1523
AMSTERDAM

Seasoned travelers aboard KLM Flight 2 felt the precise moment that the plane's descent began. The nearly imperceptible movement somewhere over the North Sea could not be seen, only felt. In fact, outside it was impossible to see anything.

As the jumbo jet broke through the last thick cloud layer, passengers strained to catch a glimpse of God's green earth, thereby being reassured that they were not far from where all mankind belonged. In John's opinion at least, that would be with both feet firmly planted on the ground.

A breathtaking patchwork of green fields rose to meet them like a gigantic front lawn. Hours before, they had been lifted above the golden hills of San Francisco, then again over America's dry Southwest desert. Here, an emerald carpet awaited their descent. Exclamations could be heard throughout the plane. First timers leaned across the laps of friends to snap their memory photos. Amsterdam. The Netherlands. The moment they first touched down. This was Europe.

Dutch natives returning home from their overseas holiday watched with jaded amusement. They had seen this before. Many times. They loved their homeland and were proud of its history and their accomplishments.

But, oh, how the sun shone in California!

Through the long winter months ahead, they would not forget.

Schiphol Airport's expansive gray buildings flashed by the windows. Then came the sound of rubber touching runway. The long-awaited, reassuring *thumpity-thump* of tires reaching out to grip the cold tarmac. The engines screamed like mighty eagles, announcing another successful return to the grip of earth's gravity. Passengers clapped and cheered spontaneously throughout the plane. What for? *Don't they realize they are only partway through one of the two most dangerous moments in flying?* Still, as the plane slowed and finally turned toward the main terminal, John had to admit that they were about to survive yet another flight in one piece.

Gradually he released his white-knuckle grip on the arms of the seat. Loosening the seat belt, he smiled at Jessica, then looked around to see that the rest of his group was all right. Everyone appeared to be fine, excited, laughing. He wondered what they would say if they knew the agony he went through every time he took off or landed in an airplane. John had never given Esther even a hint of the anxiety that was a customary part of his flying experience, even after all his years of traveling. He knew his feelings were pathological. He had read numerous articles that attempted to reassure air travelers in matters of safety and survival. He had prayed for relief from this abnormal fear.

All to no avail.

The airliner lumbered into the disembarking zone, finally coming to a complete stop. Outwardly, John appeared calm and pleasant. But as he joked a bit with Edgar and Jill, waved to the Micellis and smiled at Shad and Mary, he suddenly became aware that he was angry. When he realized it, he was startled.

Why am I angry, for goodness sake?

He decided it must have something to do with his fear of flying, piled on top of all the other things that were haywire in his life.

It isn't fair. None of this is fair. Not Esther. Not Jeremy. Certainly not Jenny. Not the church . . . and not this bizarre fear of flying. Why doesn't God ever do something?

Mentally, he did what he had done so often of late. He shrugged the anger off, gathering up his and Jessica's things as he did, and prepared for the familiar aisle surge as people jostled one another and apologized their way off the plane. It always seemed to work itself out, although John sometimes wondered where the anger went after one of his "emotional shrugs." He had no idea. He knew it was not healthy to stuff anger like this so much of the time. He also knew that he'd been doing it quite a bit lately.

Oh, well. What's one more unanswered prayer?

29

13 SEPTEMBER, LOCAL TIME 2000
AMSTERDAM

People started pushing away from the table at eight o'clock, confessing amazement at how much they had eaten after so many hours of "just sitting on the plane."

Once passport control had been cleared, the bus transfer had gone smoothly. John was grateful. He remembered another time in this same airport when his chartered bus had failed to come at all. He had ultimately moved his group into the city by train. Even then, the closest point they had been able to reach was more than half a mile from their hotel. John found a taxi driver who spoke English, who in turn called for help from some of his friends. It probably took a taxi or two more than was really needed to haul their luggage and a few of the older travelers the rest of the way. But he had not argued. Business is business. The rest of his group had decided to walk the final lap since it was not raining and it wasn't all that far. Like most vacationing travelers, they were prepared for the unexpected and chalked it up as another "great story to tell when we get back home."

This time, checking in at the Krasnapolsky had been both pleasant and efficient. It was one of Amsterdam's finest and best-known hotels, and they knew how travelers wished to be handled. Keys were handed out promptly. Luggage immediately began disappearing from the lobby as bellmen came and went.

Following a short trip upstairs to find their rooms and freshen up, "the troops," as John often referred to them, had assembled in the dining room for dinner. Most had testified to not being hungry until they saw the attractive table settings, smiling servers, and deliciously tempting food. Their enthusiasm heightened with the visible reminder that this was not airline food, and it was not being served on plastic dishes. Several courses and a delightful Dutch dessert later, they were all stuffed. Dinner was washed down with the guest's choice of a cup of steaming, black coffee or English tea.

They left the table in groups of two or three. John discouraged anyone from going out alone, especially at night. There was always the chance of being pickpocketed or mugged in the popular tourist areas. But even more at issue was the chance of getting lost. Some were tired. Especially the travelers who were up in years. Even the Eidermans had decided to call it a night.

"I think we're going to bed." Harold and Gisele came over to where John and Jessica were sitting. "It's been great so far. You've done a good job arranging all of this and keeping us together today. And this place is wonderful. But I think we'll join the old folks and hit the sack."

"Thanks, Harold. I hope you have a good night's rest. Breakfast is in this room from seven to eight-thirty. Come down whenever you wish."

"What are you going to do now, Pastor?" asked Gisele.

John looked over at Jessica.

"What do you think, hon? Should we go for a little walk?"

"Sure, Daddy!" Jessica's tired eyes lit up at the thought. "I'm ready if you are."

"Everyone is on their own this evening. I think some are going out. Maybe we'll see somebody we know on the street. I'm sure no one will stay out very late, though. They'll want to get in early tonight. We should, too, so let's go. Let's take in a little of Amsterdam."

John wiped his mouth with his napkin and pushed back his chair. Jessica followed suit. Only Evelyn Unruh and Dan and Phyllis Watson were still at the table, sipping tea and admiring the room's exquisitely blended appointments, all done in tasteful shades of green. The intricate skylight roof promised sunlight at breakfast time, unless of course it was raining instead, as was often the case in Amsterdam.

John took Jessica's hand as they walked up the steps from the dining room into the small lobby. "Wait here. I'll go up and get our coats and umbrella, just in case."

In a few minutes he was back. Jessica slipped into her jacket as they made their way outdoors. They started across the large stone-paved area known as Dam Square. The shadowy outline of the old cathedral loomed directly in front of them, easily seen in the semidarkness. John paused for a moment to get his bearings. They wandered across the square and picked up the pace along the "Walking Street."

Shops lined either side of the wide pedestrian way. Anything, it seemed, was for sale. Stereos, clothes, tourist trinkets, pizza, magazines, embroidery, and shoes, wooden and otherwise. Dark, narrow doorways opened off the street into mysterious, hole-in-the-wall nightclubs from which loud, pulsating music could be heard.

They stopped in a souvenir store where Jessica purchased several small, inexpensive pins shaped like wooden shoes and Dutch windmills. She'd been saving her money for this trip, part of which she had budgeted for gifts to take home to her friends and classmates. This was her first chance to spend some of that money. Some picture postcards and a small, white doily for her mother. John stood by, watching with interest and a little amusement. Jessica was a very independent young lady, busily using up her final preteen year.

After a while, they strolled into a residential area filled with old hotels and apartments. The row houses were narrow and tall, throwing long shadows across the sidewalk. John thought they were headed in the general direction of the hotel, although he was not certain exactly where it was located. Dark, watery canals lined each street, crossable every so often by traversing a narrow footbridge. In the darkness they all began looking very much alike.

"Can we take a boat ride on the canals, Daddy?"

"Tomorrow, if we have time. Otherwise we'll be sure to do it on the way home. We'll be stopping over here when we return," he promised as they turned the corner. "There is one thing that I definitely want you to see tomorrow. It's the house in which a young Jewish girl lived, during World War II. Her name was Anne Frank. She was about your age when she lived here."

"I've read about her. Our history teacher told us about her. She died during the war, didn't she?"

"Yes, she did. It's all very sad, but I want you to see her home. She was a brave young girl."

Jessica squeezed John's hand in what he took as an expression of appreciation. He looked down at his daughter, but she was not looking at him. Instead she was staring straight ahead. He let his line of sight follow hers and saw what had captured her attention.

Directly ahead, in a large window, Jessica's attention had been drawn to the figure of a scantily clad woman who looked like a department store mannequin. Only this was no mannequin. She was very real and dressed only in the briefest of revealing undergarments. Little was left to the imagination. The young woman was dancing slowly, sensuously, her body swaying to sounds of music that only she could hear. Outside the window, a young Japanese family, obviously tourists like John and Jessica, were talking and laughing among themselves before moving on along the street. Though John had not been here before, he had often heard of Amsterdam's red light district. Now he feared he had stumbled into it.

As they came nearer, he saw that there were other windows with other young women, similarly clad in undergarments or revealing lingerie, some sitting in chairs, others dancing by themselves, smiling provocatively at potential customers outside along the sidewalks. A few doors down, three young men were making hand signs to one of the women. Two of them jovially pushed their companion forward, pointing at him to the woman inside. She motioned to the young man, who disappeared through the door accompanied by shouts of encouragement from his friends. The others strolled on, laughing, and lighting cigarettes.

"What is she doing, Daddy?" whispered Jessica, staring at the young girl in the window.

John grimaced as Jessica pulled at his hand, signaling him to stop. *Wouldn't you know it. Our first night in Amsterdam and I walk my daughter straight into the heart of the red light district! Now what do I do?*

John looked around the corner. Ahead were still more windows with still more attractive young women on display. There would be no getting out of this without an explanation of some kind.

John had never personally talked to Jessica about sex. Her mother had done that, alerting her to the changes that were soon to overtake her young body. Three months ago, Esther had informed John that Jessica's menstrual cycle had begun. She assured him that Jessica knew how to take care of herself, should it be necessary while they were gone. He certainly hoped that Esther's confidence was well founded.

John remembered reading somewhere that since the turn of the century, better health and nutrition habits had lowered the average age of sexual maturity. He had been surprised that the onset of menstruation in young girls was dropping at an average rate of three months with each passing decade. The urges that once arrived at fourteen were starting to hit children at twelve. He had observed that his daughter had recently taken a fresh interest in boys as being something other than the enemy. But he was unsure as to exactly what sexual ground the two women in his life had covered in their "little talks."

John also knew that young people on the whole these days were far more advanced in their knowledge of sexual matters than he and Esther had been at that age. It was frightening, really. Jerry Anchor, Calvary's youth pastor, had recently shared with the staff that, by the time kids reached fifteen, a quarter of the girls and a third of the boys had become sexually active. John had been stunned at that figure.

Still, he knew that some junior-high-age Baytown children had already been experimenting with sex. He also knew that many young people in high school, including some in the church youth group, had been initiated into the world of sexual irresponsibility. It was like a huge tidal wave. There seemed to be no holding it back.

Now as he looked down at Jessica, her hand still holding tightly to his, a lump rose in his throat. He blinked back a sudden moistness that rimmed his eyes. He looked first at Jessica, then at the young woman in the window. Then back at Jessica again. John swallowed as he squeezed her hand.

"Jessica, honey," he began, hesitantly, not knowing exactly whether or not he wanted to hear a *yes* or a *no* to his question. "Do you know what the word *prostitute* means?"

"Sure, Daddy. Everyone knows that. It's someone who sells their body for money." Her answer was matter-of-fact and direct.

Well, so much for innocence.

She looked up into John's eyes, inquiringly. "Is that what she is doing?" she asked, turning her gaze back to the window.

"Yes, sweetheart. That's what she is doing."

They stood together silently. The woman in the window kept her eyes on them until at last she stopped her slow, sensuous gyrations and sat down in a chair, still facing them. She smiled.

Jessica smiled back, her hand coming up in a timid greeting.

"But she's so beautiful," said Jessica.

The young woman lifted her hand in acknowledgment.

"Yes, she is," John agreed. "At least for now."

"What do you mean?"

"I mean, after a few years in this business, she'll be all used up. Drugs and disease are always a danger to someone like her."

"You mean like AIDS and stuff?"

"Yes, that's what I mean. And how will she find a husband who will want her after a life like this? Will she have children? If she does, what will they think if they find out what their mother does? Even without marriage, unwanted pregnancy is always a possibility. For anybody really, but especially someone like her. She may go through several abortions before many years have passed. Do you understand about abortions, honey?"

"Yes," Jessica replied, a touch of sadness in her voice.

John waited.

Jessica added no further comment.

Slowly they backed away from the window. Other windows to be navigated were still ahead, but John could see that Jessica seemed taken by this young girl. Some kind of emotional connection had been made between them. John wanted to move on, but for some reason he hesitated.

"Why is she doing this?" Jessica persisted, her words tinged with a plaintive tone that caused John to look down at her again. There was a tear on her cheek.

He searched desperately for something wise to say, but nothing came.

"I don't know, sweetheart. Money, I guess. It is sad, but it's the way she makes her living."

A long silence wrapped itself around them.

"I wish I could tell her about Jesus," Jessica said at last, almost reverently, as she stared at the window. "She needs to know about him."

The girl ignored them now, polishing her nails. John put his hand on Jessica's shoulder as they walked away in the direction of the hotel.

"You could never tell that young girl about Jesus," he said, "because you don't speak her language."

In more ways than one.

"But," he continued, "there are some Christian missionaries that work among people in this area. I know of at least one missionary family that has been here for years. They live somewhere nearby and share Christ with prostitutes and drug addicts and others who live in this part of the city. Perhaps they'll have a chance to speak with her."

Jessica did not answer. They walked the rest of the way in silence. John grew more and more concerned. He knew he should not have let them wander into that area. It was safe enough. Lots of tourists and families wandered through just to see it for themselves. But this was different. This was Jessica.

After several blocks they came out onto Dam Square. Crossing over the cobblestone pavement, they entered the hotel. John glanced up at the clock in the lobby.

10:30.

Shad and Mary were sitting on a sofa on the other side of the lobby. They were drinking sodas and chatting gaily between themselves. John nodded and smiled. They waved back.

"Time for bed, honey," he said, guiding Jessica toward the elevator.

Jessica still said nothing.

His concern continued to rise.

Once they were in their room, John encouraged Jessica to take a shower.

"You'll feel better and sleep a lot more soundly," he promised.

A few minutes later, he heard the steady sound of running water coming from the bathroom. John eased himself onto the only chair in the room, leaned back, propped his feet on the end of one of the beds, and closed his eyes. They burned from lack of sleep. Tiredness gripped his back and limbs like a vise. Even his neck felt stiff and tense. He thought about the shower and how glad he'd be to get in it himself.

Before long, Jessica came out of the bathroom wearing the robe her mother had packed, and her hair wrapped in a towel.

"Your eyes say, 'I'm sleepy,'" John said fondly, pulling his feet down from the bed.

Jessica smiled. It was a familiar phrase from her father, one that she had heard often as a small child just before bedtime.

"Daddy?" Jessica was standing in the middle of the room. "I've been thinking."

John waited.

"You know that girl we saw?"

He nodded, waiting for her to continue.

"I'm going to pray for her every day while we're on this trip." Jessica hesitated, then continued. "Like what she is doing must really break her parents' hearts, don't you think?"

John felt the lump gathering. She looked so tiny and so vulnerable standing there. And yet so mature. He fought back the wetness in his eyes.

This girl is mine. My only little girl. John felt deeply moved. *And she's growing up, there's no doubt about that.*

"Yes," he replied, his voice husky with emotion. "Yes, I am sure her parents are very sad. They couldn't help but be."

Jessica came over to him, putting her arms around his neck.

"Daddy, thanks for bringing me on this trip," she said, suddenly changing the subject. "I'm so excited. I can't wait to get to Israel. It's so much fun being with you. Just you and me."

She thought for a moment.

"And twenty-three others, of course," she added, laughing. "But you know what I mean. Mother and Jeremy are not here. Sorry. I don't mean that like it sounded. It would be great fun to have them both here, but it's the first time you and I have ever done anything like this. All by ourselves, I mean."

She hugged him as hard as she could. Then, as if she could read his thoughts, she exclaimed, "I feel so . . . so grown up."

"Okay, little Miss Grown-Up, why don't you turn in and get some sleep," John replied, pushing her gently in the direction of the beds.

John went into the bathroom and turned on the shower. In the mirror, he saw Jessica reflected through the partially open door. She was kneeling beside her bed. He shook his head and reached for the toothpaste.

What did we ever do to get her? Maybe I need to let up on God a little and give him some credit for this one.

"Daddy?" John heard her calling, as he unbuttoned his shirt. "Daddy!"

He poked his head through the doorway.

"What's the problem?"

She was standing by the bed with an exasperated look on her face, hands on hips.

"How in the world do you get into this thing?" she asked, helplessly.

Jessica had discovered the wonderful mystery of European bed making that challenges every first-time visitor to the continent. The custom of tucking the sheet sides into the bed had long since reached America, too, but this was Jessica's first big trip.

John chuckled as he came into the room and helped her pull it all apart and then remake it the American way. He had never learned how to do it any differently.

30

WEDNESDAY, 14 SEPTEMBER, LOCAL TIME 0846
AMSTERDAM

The next morning, most of the group awoke early, ate breakfast in the sumptuous hotel dining room, and went sightseeing around Amsterdam. They were not scheduled to leave for the airport until eleven, so there was time to walk, shop, take a canal boat ride, or a boat tour of Amsterdam's busy harbor.

John and Jessica were up early, too. John knew that this morning would likely be their last opportunity to be alone together. Once they arrived in Israel, John would need to concentrate on the needs of the group as a whole, and private father and daughter times would be harder to come by.

After last night's unanticipated detour through the red light district, John was more determined than ever for Jessica to visit the house of Anne Frank.

"I want you to see that not all of Holland is like the area we were in last night," he said. "And not all of Holland's young women work behind glass windows. There are some really wonderful people here, Jessica. They have a great history. Many of the finest artists of the world were born here. People like Rembrandt and Van Gogh. I wish the Rijksmuseum was open this early. Some of the world's most valuable paintings are displayed there. But we'll just have to do that another time."

The air was brisk and the two left damp footprints in the sidewalk's early morning dew as they walked along picturesque, tree-lined streets that were showing the first signs of autumn color. Along the Jordaan District's canals, fresh flowers graced the window boxes and porch planters of the narrow, brick houses jammed side by side on each block.

"The Dutch are a courageous people, too. That's another reason I want us to visit Anne Frank's home."

They walked along Raadhuisstraat, following the directions given by the hotel concierge. John had visited the site once before and knew it was not too far. But he also recalled that it was not well marked and could easily be missed by a stranger to the area. Sure enough, they walked too far and had to double back. Finally, a short distance away, at Prinsengracht 203, John saw the small marker identifying the Anne Frank House.

The door was closed, but a sign gave the hours during which the house was open to the public. John looked at his watch, then tried the door. It opened onto a small landing at the bottom of a narrow, steep flight of stairs. They were greeted by a middle-aged lady sitting behind a small ticket window.

"That will be 9.50 Euro. I will take U.S. also," she said, glancing at Jessica.

As they walked up the steps, Jessica whispered, "We didn't say anything, Daddy. How did she know we're Americans?"

John chuckled. "I don't know, sweetheart. We must stick out somehow. Europeans are used to identifying accents. They can tell the minute we open our mouths. Maybe this morning it was the style of our clothes. I know. I'll bet she saw the American flag sticking out of your nose."

Jessica swatted his arm, grinning, obviously in a good mood after a full night's rest. Her smile went away, however, replaced by a sober, reflective mood, when they reached the top of the stairs and saw the hidden room where the Frank family had lived.

"Was she really just a year older than me?" Jessica asked.

"Mm-hmm," John replied quietly. "Can you imagine our family having to hide in a space like this?"

Each room in the apartment was small. A sparsely outfitted kitchen. Tiny bedrooms. A sitting area. Very plain. There were museum-style photographs hung on the walls, depicting vignettes of life and local events during the Nazi occupation of World War II. Family pictures were scattered here and there and the story of the Franks' hiding was told on placards attached to otherwise bare walls. Included were numerous comments from Anne's famous diaries.

They walked from room to room, John watching silently as Jessica touched a table, a lamp, a book. He sensed the totality of her absorption. She was transfixed by it all. He knew that she was there. With Anne. Imagining how it must have been to be in hiding for more than two years. Never able to leave these rooms. No playmates. No running in the rain or splashing in puddles. No school plays, no recess, no sitting in the sun, sharing lunches, talking to friends that she would get to see again tomorrow.

"Do you think Anne was a Christian?" Jessica asked as they walked along the cobblestone streets on their way back to the Krasnapolsky.

"I don't think so, hon," John answered. "She was Jewish. From her writings, though, it appears that she loved God very much. And we know he loved her. She was a courageous young girl, that's for sure."

They walked with hands tucked inside coat pockets for warmth. The streets and sidewalks were noisier and busier now. Smells of fresh bread wafted from a nearby doorway. Lace curtains were pulled back on an upstairs window, a woman's face appearing briefly as she checked the day outside. John paused to allow Jessica to step ahead of him when a pile of refuse that had been pushed up against the wall of a building partially blocked the narrow sidewalk.

"I'm glad I don't have to do that," said Jessica, after a long silence.

"Do what?"

"What Anne Frank had to do."

Her hand reached for his, seeking its warmth and reassurance. For a moment, John was moved by a sense of profound peacefulness. All seemed well with the world. Strange. He had not felt like this in a long time.

"I'm glad, too," he said.

The sky was overcast, threatening rain. Their breath rose in thin wisps in the autumn chill as they strolled together back to the hotel.

31

14 SEPTEMBER, LOCAL TIME 0815
WASHINGTON, D.C.

THE WHITE HOUSE
OFFICE OF THE NATIONAL SECURITY DIRECTOR
SENSITIVE

MOSSAD REPORTS POSSIBLE TERRORIST ACTIVITIES PLANNED SOMEWHERE INSIDE USA. EXACT LOCATION OR TYPE OF ACTIVITY UNKNOWN.

INTERNET CHATTER UP. AN IMMINENT MAJOR ISLAMIC JIHAD EFFORT TO HUMILIATE USA IS RUMORED UNDER WAY. OBJECTIVE: PRESSURE ISRAEL TO PULL BACK FROM SIGNING PERMANENT AGREEMENT WITH PNA. SOMETHING TO ATTRACT MAJOR MEDIA AND FURTHER HOLY WAR OBJECTIVES. ARAFAT MAY BE POSSIBLE TARGET. UNVERIFIED NUCLEAR CONNECTION TO IRAN, SYRIA, OR LIBYA.

FBI INDICATES SOME KNOWN SLEEPER GROUPS IN CANADA AND USA MAY BE AWAKENING. HOMELAND SECURITY WILL DETERMINE OPTIONS AND CONTINGENCIES.

QUALITY INFORMATION SOURCE: HIGH.

CURRENT TERRORIST ALERT: GUARDED (BLUE).

14 SEPTEMBER, LOCAL TIME 1745
BEN GURION INTERNATIONAL AIRPORT, ISRAEL

KLM Flight 312 touched the runway with such finesse that, at first, John did not think they were on the ground. Then came the familiar *thumpity-thump* of tires rolling rapidly over the runway's paved surface, followed by engines screaming in protest as the pilot reversed power and began to apply the brakes. John grimaced at the clapping and cheering of the relieved masses over another safe, normal landing. He did not join the festivities.

Fifteen minutes later, they were pushing their way through the crowd that milled about the Lod reception area, caught up in a kaleidoscopic sea of faces and colorful clothing. It was a scene that never ceased to stir John's soul.

Eight or ten French-speaking Africans, resplendent in their national dress, crowded around their leader, pointing at a map that obviously had them confused. Into an adjacent concourse a large jet had just disgorged a crowd of poorly dressed men, women, and children. As everyone converged on the passport control area, John listened out of one ear until he identified their language. The men and boys all wore yarmulke skullcaps and appeared very happy to be in this humid place. John decided they must be part of the increasing number of Russian Jewish immigrants that were coming to Israel in the hope of a better life.

John motioned to his group to stay together amid the crush of people and resigned himself to wait. Several dispassionate government workers in small booths systematically dealt with the onslaught of new arrivals, opening passports and examining them quickly. The agents glanced up at each carrier, back at the photo, and then hand-stamped the document. One by one, red, green, blue, and brown passports each received the same treatment as Israel's latest pilgrims gained entrance to the Holy Land. But it was hard to think of it as holy at this particular moment.

John thought the noise, on a scale of one to ten, should rate at least a nine. He looked at his fellow travelers from Calvary Church. They had queued in two lines, with faces ranging from serious to apprehensive to open excitement, all the while clutching their passports protectively. Soon they were swallowed up in the stream of humanity, moving forward an inch at a time, eyes turning first in one direction and then another, trying to take in everything at once.

John saw David Barak standing a short distance beyond the passport control area. He waved to indicate that he had seen him. Tousled, sandy-colored hair, skin darkened from hours in the hot sun spent on several of Israel's numerous archaeological digs, David was wearing sunglasses, a brown shirt, walking shorts, and well-worn tennis shoes. Looking a trifle bored as usual, David lifted his hand in response.

John knew better than to be fooled by their guide's sleepy appearance. David was a brilliant young man, a skilled leader, and very patient toward those with whom he worked. In the next several days, he would draw on a lifetime of experience in his homeland along with his educational background in Middle East history, a subject in which he had been a top student and now served as an adjunct professor at Tel Aviv University. For these reasons, John had requested his services for the third straight time.

John knew that David would expose the members of the group to an unsurpassed breadth and depth of knowledge about the land of Abraham, Isaac, and Jacob. He wanted them to feel both the modern and ancient heartbeats of a people whose heritage and stories stretched for centuries across the scroll of human history. In the days ahead, he would work alongside David to bring additional insight and understanding to the group from the New Testament events surrounding the coming of Jesus Christ to this land and to the world. John felt a fresh wave of excitement just being here again.

Greg and Debbie Sommers were the first of the group to reach a control desk. John pointed toward David Barak and asked them to wait with him. Then he stood between the two lines as each person handed their passport to the uniformed immigration agent, reminding them not to permit the stamp of Israel on their passport.

The Israelis were used to this request, understanding that if the passport holder traveled to any predominantly Muslim country after being in Israel, they might be refused entrance with an Israeli stamp on their passport. In spite of recent peace accords and progress in the Palestinian/Israeli dialogue, even countries immediately surrounding Israel would summarily reject the passport and the carrier, as part of the Arab world's refusal to formally recognize Israel's existence as a nation. Though it was difficult for many non-Muslims to comprehend, Islamic nations from as far away as Malaysia and Indonesia considered themselves technically to be at war with Israel.

Instead of a stamp in their passport, travelers would receive a piece of paper with an entrance permit stamped on it. John knew from experience that this practice must be scrupulously adhered to. When John's turn finally came, the agent tucked the entrance permit inside John's blue U.S. passport, welcomed him to Israel, and continued to process the next person in line.

John slipped his passport into the travel pouch on his belt and walked to where David Barak stood bantering with the rest of the group. Jessica, as promised, had stayed close to Edgar and Jill Anderson.

"Shalom, John," said David. "You decided to bring some nice people with you this time."

"Shalom, David," John answered. "I always bring nice people."

They hugged one another warmly. On John's previous sojourns in which David had been his professional guide, the two men had developed a strong mutual relationship of trust and respect.

"Your luggage is coming in over there right now." David pointed to a rotating carousel that was receiving bags and boxes from a conveyor belt. The men stepped forward to retrieve the group's bags, stacking and counting until all were accounted for.

"Follow me to the bus," David said, heading for the exit.

"I'm surprised there is no baggage check," Nick Micelli commented as they hurried to catch up with David's rapid strides.

"No need," John replied. "We did all that in Amsterdam. Remember the way they examined us and our things there? They are even more stringent than in the States. They do that with all flights into Israel. Don't worry, though. You'll get a chance at a real baggage check when we leave. They'll go through your socks and shorts one by one."

As they passed through the exit door, the afternoon's lingering heat and humidity quickly enveloped them. The bus driver was already placing their luggage into the underbelly of the bus. All of John's group were first-time guests in Israel. Even though they had been promised comfortable transportation, several were surprised as they boarded the sleek and modern Mercedes bus. Inside, the air conditioner's cool airflow was greeted with enthusiasm.

In a few minutes everyone was on board and the luggage had been expertly stowed. As the driver guided the bus away from others parked nearby, David took the microphone in his hand and stood in the door well.

"Shalom," he said, looking at the eager faces all turned to him with looks of anticipation.

"Shalom," the group responded in unison.

"Welcome to Israel. I hope you are all rested and ready to go to work."

He was greeted with groans from those who were beginning to feel the effects of the long journey's jet lag and a lack of sleep.

"No? You don't want to go out dancing tonight? Did you hear that groan, Amal? Already they complain about being tired. Wait until we are through with them," he teased, his sleepy eyes twinkling, as he memorized the name tags on the shirts and blouses of those nearest him.

"By the way, this is Amal. He is an Arab and the best driver in all Israel." The driver smiled and waved as he maneuvered the bus out of the terminal area and onto the main road.

"My name is David Barak. You may call me David. I am Jewish," he continued, his English clear and distinct, more American in accent than British. "And, of course, I am the best guide in all of Israel." His captive audience cheered and clapped their hands as David bowed in mock humility.

"During the next few days, you will be seeing so much history of the Bible before your very eyes. I promise you the experience of a lifetime. You are fortunate to have a pastor who will take the time and make the effort to bring you to our land. We have worked together before. He is a fine man."

Another round of applause and a few whistles were heard as John raised both hands in the symbolic prizefighter's victory signal.

"Well, now that we have established how wonderful we are, I am sure you will show me during the next few days just how wonderful you all are. But enough of that. Look around you." The group turned their attention to the large open windows and the vistas outside. "We are leaving Lod, which is our international airport for the entire country of Israel. I happen to know you have three such airports in the Bay Area. For us one is enough. But anything worth doing, you Americans always think is worth overdoing."

The group laughed, feeling a rush of pride at the comparison and, at the same time, recognizing the truthful irony in David's comment.

"Have you been to California?" someone asked from the back.

"Yes, of course. I graduated from UCLA. And four years ago, I spent a summer in the Bay Area. My brother lives in Redwood City and teaches at Stanford."

Everyone began to relax as John had known they would once David joined them. And in that strange way for which American travelers are known throughout the world, they gathered David into their confidence. They had decided he was a friend who could be trusted.

John leaned back in his seat. Jessica sat next to him, her eyes fastened on the dark, handsome tour guide, listening intently as he shared introductory facts about Israel, pointing out landmarks along the way. As they turned onto the main highway heading northwest toward the city, the sun was giving way to a magnificent orange glow that outlined the darkening, tree-covered hills.

Israel. I love this land. John let his mind wander as David continued to narrate their trip into Tel Aviv. He rested his eyes, which were gritty from lack of sleep, and his mind raced across ten time zones in an instant. A rush of mixed feelings suddenly made him uneasy. The pangs of guilt. Were they real or only imagined? He did not know. Uncertainty. About the future. About the letter of resignation stored in his computer. Silently, he prayed, *Lord, watch over Esther and Jeremy. Keep them safe in your arms.*

Soon the bus entered the outskirts of Tel Aviv. David continued answering questions as the first lights of evening began dotting the city's landscape.

—≈—

After dinner, John volunteered to take everyone for a walk. All but the Mitchels and Gisele Eiderman decided to go. The Mitchels said they were too tired and Harold indicated that Gisele was feeling a bit of traveler's upset. She had remained in their room during the dinner hour. Nothing serious. She had taken something to settle her stomach and wanted to be ready for tomorrow.

David Barak returned to his home on the north side of the city. This would be the last evening with his wife and children for a week. After tonight he would stay with the group until they arrived in Jerusalem.

"Is it safe?"

John looked at Ruth Taylor, who had asked the question. Single, thirty-five, and about forty pounds overweight, Ruth had already been complaining about the heat. Perspiration dotted her forehead, even though the hotel's temperature was comfortably controlled by a modern air-conditioning system.

"Sure it's safe. And by now it should be a little cooler outside, too," John assured her.

"Come on, Ruth, the walk will do you good. Tel Aviv awaits."

They fanned out along the wide, waterfront promenade. The white sand beach, stretching along the western edge of the city, was empty now. John explained that before sunrise tomorrow, its daily evolution would get under way. First a group of hardy old-timers would gather to swim and exercise. Later as the sun came out, so would the local *poseurs on parade,* turning the beach into a sort of Israeli Copacabana. By afternoon, the sand would be dotted with folks playing Israeli beach tennis, a popular game known as *matkot.* Finally, as evening approached, fishing would take over as people tossed their lines at the sunset and enjoyed the glorious colors of sky and sea.

The lights from hotels, some with familiar American names such as Hilton, Sheraton, and Ramada, ran together along the beach in true resortlike fashion. Surrounded by myriad Euro-Middle Eastern accommodations of varying quality, these bulwarks of American hospitality gave a further feeling of familiarity to this strange, yet fascinating city. The Mediterranean Sea remained hidden under a blanket of darkness, speckled with pinpoints of starlight, and a not-quite-full moon rising behind them in the east.

Turning away from the beachfront, the group strolled along a narrow connecting street, past a small Tabak shop. An old Arab, who appeared to be the proprietor, was outside closing up for the evening. John greeted him as he walked by. The man stared for a moment, nodded, then returned to his task.

The street was not well lit, but after a few blocks it opened up on the nightlife of Dizengoff Square. A burst of neon signs. The cacophonous sounds of music. A large circular fountain spouting garishly in the glow of multicolored lights. John explained that the fountain had been designed by Ya'acov Agam, a leading Israeli artist, whose prior claim to fame was the paint job on the Dan Hotel. Most of the group agreed that he had missed his calling and should go back to painting hotels. Drink shops, ice cream stands. A McDavid's. Even after their hotel dinner, a few McDonald's enthusiasts wanted to try it out. So much for weaning themselves away from the West.

People were everywhere. Attractive young girls in short skirts and shorter shorts. Boys wearing jeans, sandals with no socks, and shirts unbuttoned halfway down the front. Young men and women in uniform, automatic weapons slung over their shoulders. Everything looked so casual, so chaotic, so different from what they were used to. As the tour group walked across the square, John reminded them of an earlier conversation.

"You see now that what I told you back home is true. In Haifa, they work. In Jerusalem, they pray. But here in Tel Aviv, they dance. David is a bit more blunt about it. He says that the best part of Jerusalem's nightlife is the road to Tel Aviv."

At last John spied the small café he had been looking for.

"Let's go over there," he said, pointing to the sidewalk tables. Several were empty. "Grab those tables before they fill up again. We'll scoot everyone together and the sodas are on me!"

The waiter and waitress helped them push tables and chairs together, then took their orders.

"Have you been here before, John?" someone asked as they sat, drinking sodas, eating ice cream, and enjoying the convivial atmosphere of nighttime in Tel Aviv.

"No, not to this specific café. But when I mentioned to David that we might go for a walk, he suggested this place. I guess he and his wife came here for lunch yesterday."

The lighthearted banter continued. John sensed that his "troops" were beginning to relax, settling in to the constant milling of people around them, calling out to one another above the amplified sounds of pop songs sung in Hebrew, soaking up the exotic sensation of being a world away from everything familiar. He glanced at Jessica. Her eyes danced with excitement, her face aglow as she took everything in. He smiled and released a deep, contented sigh.

This is a good thing.

—~—

A short distance away, standing in the garish light of the fountain, an olive-skinned man in blue jeans and a wrinkled button-down shirt glanced at a list of names in his hand. His gaze returned to the sandy-haired man seated next to the young girl, and the cluster of Americans around him. He had studied the group long enough to recognize the leader, even without the help of a photo. Folding the sheet of paper, he slipped it into his shirt pocket and walked slowly away from the fountain, glancing both ways before crossing the street.

He had tailed them at a distance from the hotel. He knew they would be returning there shortly. He knew what time they would have breakfast in the morning, what bus they would be traveling in, what sites they would visit, and where they would be sleeping tomorrow night. The papers the old man had copied and left with the Tabak shop proprietor told it all. He knew everything he needed to know.

Pausing long enough to light a cigarette and inhale deeply, he released the smoke casually while surveying the group one last time. Then he turned and walked into the darkness.

PART THREE

As long as Islam does not take its rightful place in the world arena, everything will continue to change for the worse. The goal of the Islamic Resistance Movement therefore is to conquer evil, break its will, and annihilate it so that truth may prevail, so that the country may return to its rightful place, and so that the call may be broadcast over the Minarets proclaiming the Islamic state. And aid is sought from Allah.

—from the Hamas Charter
Article Nine

And did not Allah check one set of people by means of another, the earth would indeed be full of mischief: But Allah is full of bounty to all the worlds.

—The Qur'an
Sura 2: Baqara:251

For God so loved the world that he gave his one and only Son, that whoever believes in him shall not perish but have eternal life.

—The Holy Bible
John 3:16

32

FRIDAY, 16 SEPTEMBER, LOCAL TIME 2045
BAYTOWN, CALIFORNIA

The night was warm. Not a breath of air was stirring as evening shadows crept across the flower garden and onto the surface of the pool.

Esther and Jeremy sat across from each other at the patio table. The only sounds were those of birds singing farewell songs in preparation for their annual journey south. Two partially empty iced tea glasses left damp rings on the table. Esther stared off toward the pine tree as Jeremy twisted his glass, rolling the bottom edge back and forth along the tabletop.

Three days had past since he had found his mother on the bathroom floor—and found the empty sleeping pill bottle.

Over her protests, he had called 9-1-1. Within minutes, an emergency medical team had arrived at their door. Esther underwent an examination and was pronounced out of immediate danger. Her stomach had already, on its own initiative, purged the major portion of the medication from her system. She did not remember how many pills she had swallowed, but it obviously had not been enough to do what she had set out to do. The dosage had made her violently ill, but no longer threatened her life.

By the time the paramedics were finished, she had appeared relatively calm and rational, and Jeremy volunteered to watch her for the next forty-eight hours. The paramedics team recommended that she see both her own physician and a psychiatrist as soon as possible. Then they filled out their report and left.

This all happened on Monday afternoon, the day that John and Jessica left for Amsterdam. The rest of the week passed uneventfully, but without much conversation between mother and son. Jeremy stayed home from school on Tuesday to keep an eye on Esther, but after a day of sitting around while she went through the motions of keeping house, sat in the family room leafing aimlessly through a women's magazine with the cooking channel on in the background, and then napped for several hours, he was more than ready to return to his usual routine. Dinners consisted of microwave meals or sandwiches, but they were eaten mostly in silence. In the evenings, they sat out back until it was time for bed. Jeremy did his homework at the patio table, but Esther just sat.

Tonight, with no homework assigned for the weekend, Jeremy drank the last of his iced tea and watched his mother stare off into the gathering twilight. His stomach churned as he tried to muster the courage to ask the questions that had been burning in his mind all week.

What is happening to us? To our family? How could Mom try to kill herself?

He could hardly bring himself to think those awful words.

Dad is off with Jessica, halfway around the world. I'm still not sure if I should have tried to call him. But even if I did reach him, what could he do?

And what about Mom? Maybe it was an accident. Well, it could be, couldn't it? Why would she want to kill herself? Oh, God, I can't believe this is happening. What am I supposed to do?

Jeremy kept his eyes on the glass, rolling it back and forth, back and forth, back and forth. Finally, he glanced up at Esther. *What do you suppose she's thinking about right now?*

"Mom?"

Esther didn't move. He began to wonder if she had even heard him. At last she shifted her gaze and looked at him.

"Yes?" she answered softly.

"Mom—" Jeremy hesitated, wanting to talk, wanting to question, not knowing quite where to begin. Finally, taking a deep breath he plunged ahead. "This is the fourth day now. You've seen the doctor. You've even been to see the shrink. But I don't really have a clue as to what's going on inside your head. You haven't talked to *me* yet."

He paused to catch his breath, working to keep his voice steady amid rising emotions. He did not want to upset her. He was nervous about this. *Hey, this is Mom!*

The glass shook in his hand.

"What's with you anyway?" he continued. "I need to know if you're okay. I don't know if I did the right thing by not calling Dad. I'm afraid to go to sleep at night. I get up and come into your bedroom . . . just to be sure you're still there. I don't . . . I don't know what to think."

Her gaze was steady as she looked across the table. When she answered, her voice was quiet, matter-of-fact.

"Jeremy, I am so sorry to have put you through this. I want to tell you that it was all an accident—that somehow I blanked out and lost track of how many pills I had taken." She paused and looked away.

"That's what I want to tell you," she said finally, "but it wouldn't be true."

Jeremy kept his eyes on his mother and remained silent. He didn't know what else to do.

Esther twisted the end of her blouse, her left hand clutching at the material, moving it back and forth, tightening, then loosening it with her fingers. With her other hand she brushed back a loose strand of hair as she stared down at her lap.

"These last few days, I've thought a lot about what has been happening, Jeremy. About what I did. When I went to see Dr. Benton, he sat across from me just like you are now and asked what I believed had happened." Esther paused before fixing her gaze on Jeremy. "I told him that I tried to take my life."

Jeremy could not move. He wanted to, but he couldn't.

"I'm sorry."

He heard his mother's voice but he was numb, not certain that he was even breathing. His hands came together, though he didn't remember moving them that way, fingers intertwining as he rubbed one thumb against another.

"I've no right to ask this, Jeremy, but I will. I need to. Can you forgive me?"

He looked away. The words caught in his throat.

"How . . . how could you . . . ?" Jeremy's question died in midsentence.

Esther sat quietly, her demeanor perfectly composed, as calm as the evening around them.

That wasn't what stopped his question.

It was the look in her eyes.

Worn down. Drained. The stark pain and sadness drew him to a place he had never been before. Not with his mother. Not with anyone.

Esther held Jeremy's gaze steadily for what seemed like forever, then looked away to the swimming pool. Jeremy suddenly realized he'd been holding his breath. He released it gradually. The sun's last rays danced on the water's surface. It was clear. Clean. The only thing disturbing its perfection was the dark outline of the sweep at the bottom of the pool. Even that was still. It ran only during the morning hours.

He turned back to his mother.

She continued staring at the pool. He could feel her drifting. She was out there. Somewhere. But where? In the water?

He followed her gaze back to the pool.

And then the answer hit with a force that took his breath away.

"It's Jenny," he whispered. "It's Jenny, isn't it?"

He felt the silence between them.

Esther nodded slowly, her gaze fixed on the memory of so much pleasure, so much pain. Her thoughts wrapped around the little person who haunted this watery grave.

"Sometimes when your dad doesn't know I'm close by, I find him out here talking to that pool sweep. I've heard him call it his 'beloved ghost.' When I see him here . . . like that . . . when I hear him talking . . . to her . . . I can hardly stand it. I feel like dying myself. I've never been able to talk to him about what happened. Not like this. Or to anyone else for that matter. You are the first.

"I feel so responsible for Jenny. I brought her into the world. And then I let her die. I've hated myself for not being here. For not protecting her. I've been angry with God for taking her instead of me, so much so that I haven't been able to really pray for a long time. The other night when I overheard you and your father arguing, it seemed like the last remnant of our family was tearing itself apart. I felt myself slipping. I just kept going down. The sadness, the pain, just got to be too much. So when Dad and Jessica left . . . well . . . I did it."

Jeremy's mind was reeling. This was his mother! It was her voice, her words, but maybe not. He wanted to think it was a dream—a nightmare—but it was all too real.

How could this have happened? She's always been there. For everybody. The family rock. Jeremy had never thought of her in any other way. She was just . . . Mom. She was always there. *That's how it's supposed to be, isn't it? But now . . . now what?* Life had suddenly changed. Where his mother was concerned, life would never return to the way it had been.

He was suddenly aware of her fragility. Her delicateness. This was not simply his mother. She was a piece of rare porcelain, perched on the edge of a chair, in danger of falling and shattering. This was a woman he had never seen before. Not like this, anyway. His mother was the safe one, the one everybody counted on. Took for granted. This woman across the table was a stranger he did not really know. A stranger haunted by guilt, needing forgiveness. His forgiveness.

Jeremy got to his feet and came to her. Taking her hands in his, he gently lifted her from the chair until she was standing, looking into his face.

His arms went around her.

Silently she responded, her body folding into his, her arms encircling her son.

They held each other that way for a long time.

A tear fell onto her cheek. Then another. A crack in the dam. A reservoir of hurt and anger and guilt had begun its release. Soon, indescribable waves of emotion rose and fell between them.

The day's last ray of sunlight had ceased to exist.

But the first ray of hope for tomorrow had already dawned.

33

16 SEPTEMBER, LOCAL TIME 1830
AYELET HASHAHAR, ISRAEL

Jessica turned the hair dryer off, shaking her long hair loose with a flip of the brush. Its chestnut highlights glistened in the late afternoon sunlight streaming through the small window to her left. Her green eyes sparkled as she turned to her father. "What a terrific day, Dad. And getting baptized in the Jordan was a real trip!"

John smiled, wondering what Jesus' response to that descriptive statement might be, but said nothing. *She is beautiful. Looks more like Esther every day.*

"What time is dinner?" she asked.

He checked his wristwatch.

"In about half an hour."

"Then let's go for a walk. I want to see what this place looks like in the daylight."

"I'm tired, sweetheart. Don't you ever wear down?"

John had been amazed at Jessica's stamina. Since leaving California, she had seemed ready for anything. Because Jessica had never been on an extended trip like this, and with only adult companionship surrounding her, John had wondered at the outset how it would work. He had long since stopped worrying. She always had gotten along with adults. This trip was turning out to be no exception.

The group had molded into a family within a couple of days. Age extremes were represented by Evelyn Unruh, in her seventies, and Jessica, who had celebrated her twelfth birthday in July. Everyone was careful to watch out for them both, making certain that they were included in all the activities. John was continually impressed by how people who traveled together would close ranks, set aside differences, and become friends. This group was one of the best at this he had seen.

They had been kept busy since their arrival earlier in the week. Thursday had begun in the urban sprawl of Tel Aviv. The highlight had been time spent in the ancient community of Old Jaffa, known in Hebrew as *Yafo*. The Greeks called it Joppa, and that's the way it is found in the Bible. The prophet Jonah had set sail from here on his great adventure. The apostle Peter had stayed in Joppa, at a tanner's house, where God spoke to him in a vision.

Everyone enjoyed the restored alleyways and gardens around the port. It was delightful to wander through the artists' quarter. For hours they mingled with other tourists, wandering aimlessly through little shops, eating ice cream and drinking sodas with the locals at sidewalk tables outside the tiny cafés.

In Netanya, north of the city, they watched skilled craftsmen cut and polish a seemingly endless supply of beautiful diamonds. A few miles farther up the coastal highway, they tramped around the seaside archaeological site of Caesarea, Judea's Roman capital for almost six hundred years. After lunch, they drove through the seaport of Haifa. In Akko, cameras whirred and clicked incessantly, trying to capture the picturesque Old City with its minarets and domes and subterranean Crusader City.

Hot and tired, but still enthusiastic, they investigated Tel Megiddo, a major city in Solomon's time, and best known today as Armageddon, the biblical symbol for earth's last great battle. A few miles across the valley, late in the afternoon, their bus crept along Nazareth's noisy, narrow streets. The skyline of this predominantly Arab town was dominated by a large building looking like a misplaced lighthouse. The Basilica of the Annunciation contained a rare collection of murals depicting Mary and the Baby Jesus, donated by Roman Catholic groups from around the world.

The sun was setting behind their bus by the time they crested the final hill and first caught sight of the Sea of Galilee. Some thought it breathtaking. A few were disappointed to discover it was really only a large lake, approximately eleven miles long and five miles wide, with the Golan hills rising sharply from the eastern shore. After inching their way through traffic in Tiberius, they drove north to their lodgings for the following two nights, the kibbutz at Ayelet Hashahar.

Friday had also been a full day of travel by bus. A trip to the artist colony at Safed and a visit to that community's small but quaint wooden synagogue. David Barak had grown up here. It was his mother's hometown. As a child, he had attended this synagogue. John knew that David felt at home here, walking through the streets, now and then greeting an occasional acquaintance.

They traveled north to Air yet Shimon, a short way from Medulla and the Israel-Lebanon border. From there they turned east, climbing the Golan

Heights. David reported that some places in these hills were still unsafe, littered with undetonated land mines. It had been from this vantage point that Syrian troops had at one time shelled the communities and farms in the valley below. They were ultimately driven back in a bloody battle with the Israeli army and volunteers whose homes and families were in the valley. In the years that followed their occupation, some of the more desolate Golan areas had been settled by Israelis who planted numerous vineyards and orchards.

Following an afternoon rest stop at an alligator farm not far from Jordan's border, they drove past banana plantations and fishing villages until arriving at a point along the Jordan River, a short distance south of the lake. Here, John and the group joined other Christian pilgrims in a water baptismal service. And then they were back in their rooms at the kibbutz, changing clothes and drying their hair. Jessica, still full of energy, was urging John to go with her on a walk around the kibbutz.

"Come on, Daddy," Jessica pleaded, pulling at his hand. "The walk will do you good. You need the exercise."

"That's probably true," John acknowledged reluctantly. He rolled over, sat on the edge of the bed and began lacing up his tennis shoes. With a weary sigh, he grinned. "Okay, squirt, let's hit the trail."

Jessica skipped across the room, pulled the screen door open, and rushed out into the sultry afternoon. The smell of freshly mown grass greeted them along the path. This was their second and final night at Ayalet Hashahar. They strolled, hand in hand, beneath the trees and alongside the various buildings that formed the kibbutz centrum. Farm animals, crops, exotic birds, and a major tourist trade had allowed Ayelet Hashahar to grow into a large and very lucrative community.

"Why do all these people live out here?" asked Jessica as they walked along the perimeter road encircling the kibbutz. Outside the roadway, a heavy mesh and barbed wire fence marked the border. Beyond the fence, unidentified intruders were likely to be shot. The kibbutz's location was far enough north that one year, while John and Esther were visiting, they had heard artillery shells exploding a few miles away, inside Lebanon.

"A kibbutz is a community of people who live together on the basis of sharing ownership and responsibilities, sweetheart. Unlike what you see back home, here there is not always a direct connection between work and wages. In other words, the type of work they do does not determine what their paycheck looks like."

"How do they live then? Don't they have to pay bills or something?"

"Sure they do. But it's like an extended family here. Suppose your grandparents and cousins all decided to come to California and live in our house."

"Wow, that would be fun! But it would be crowded, too, huh?"

"Yes, it would. So we'd have to build on to the house or find more property. But if we did that, we could share responsibilities. See that man over there?" John pointed to a man with streaks of gray in his hair, riding a lawn mower in front of a long, two-story building. "His job is mowing all the lawns here. While he's doing that, someone else does the washing and ironing."

"I'll take his job," Jessica said, watching the man turn the mower to take another swath. "I hate ironing."

"Each family has its own apartment. Sometimes all the children live together in separate quarters."

"They don't live with their parents?"

"Not always. But they visit regularly. And often they eat together or have play days with their mother and father. There's really no right or wrong way to do all this. That's just the way it is here at this kibbutz. They grow up viewing all who live here as their extended family."

"Then how do they support themselves?"

"Almost every kibbutz has at least one factory. Some have three or four. Farming is important, too. David says that the kibbutzim supplies over half of all the country's agricultural produce. In the case of this particular kibbutz, tourism is one of the main ways they make their living."

They walked past the dairy section with its barns and animals. The odor coming from the freshly churned earth and the faded red barn caused Jessica to wrinkle up her nose.

"Boy, that smells yucky!" she exclaimed.

"You don't like the fresh country air?"

"I'm a city girl, Daddy. I can do without this. Yuk!"

John laughed.

"Are you about ready to head back? Let's go see if dinner is ready. I'm hungry."

"Me, too. But, do we have to eat that kosher stuff again? We did that last night."

"No, we can eat from the other menu tonight. You'll like it better."

They walked along the narrow roadway, listening to the sounds of birds in the trees. The man on the mower could be heard in the distance. Warm humid air tugged at their clothing and beads of perspiration trickled down John's nose. As they crossed over to the dining area, he noted that several new buses had joined theirs in the parking lot.

It was going to be another busy night for the kibbutz at Ayelet Hashahar.

—ᴡ—

A small bronzed man with a long, thin nose and a yarmulke perched precariously on top of his thinning hair dialed a number and placed the receiver to his ear. Picking up the cigarette he had set on the shelf under the pay phone, he inhaled deeply while listening to the rings.

Once, twice.

Hang up.

Wait.

Redial.

Once, twice, three times.

"Aywah?" answered the dull-sounding voice at the other end of the line.

The man spoke softly, his head tucked down, a hand covering his mouth. If those nearby could have heard him, they would have been surprised. The man with the yarmulke did not carry on his conversation in Hebrew or English. Instead, he spoke quietly into the telephone in Arabic.

"The shipment is on time." *The California pastor and his group are keeping to the schedule we were originally given.* "All the birds will be alive and well and will be delivered tomorrow as promised." *The group is still numerically the same as predicted.* "Be sure to have someone ready to receive them." *The special operations team must be ready.*

"Understood," the voice responded.

Click. The line went dead.

Putting the receiver back, he drew deeply on the cigarette, flicked it onto the marble tile, ground it beneath his shoe, and kicked it under the phone out of sight. He started toward the exit, stopping long enough to pick up an international issue of *Newsweek,* flipping through its pages before returning it to the table. Then he casually continued toward the exit.

He was reaching for the door just as a young girl and a man opened it from outside. They smiled and stepped back, the girl holding the door.

"Please." The man motioned to the one wearing the yarmulke.

"Todah," the man thanked the American.

"Afwan," the girl answered with a smile.

For an instant the man hesitated, stunned at the girl's polite acknowledgment, while at the same moment recognizing who these two were. He glared at the girl, opening his mouth to say something but unable to think what his response should be.

"I am sorry," the man spoke up. "It is my daughter's first visit to your country. She is learning Hebrew phrases and also some Arabic words. It is hard sometimes to remember which is which."

Looking at Jessica, John chuckled. "You startled this man, Jessica, by saying, 'you are welcome' in Arabic instead of Hebrew."

"Oh, I'm sorry," Jessica apologized, embarrassed as she noticed others in the lobby starting to look their way.

The man with the yarmulke also saw that others were watching with growing amusement. Without a word, he strode through the doorway and didn't look back.

"Oh, Daddy, I feel terrible. I offended him."

"Don't worry, sweetheart. He'll get over it."

—∞—

16 SEPTEMBER, LOCAL TIME 2000
WASHINGTON, D.C.

THE WHITE HOUSE
OFFICE OF THE NATIONAL SECURITY ADVISOR
SENSITIVE

RE: PARK RANGER CARL DEEKER MURDER.

UPDATE: FBI AND LOCAL AUTHORITIES INVESTIGATION CONFIRMS RAFT AND MOTOR SOLD BY TORONTO DEALER. CUSTOMER PAID WITH CASH. NO PHYSICAL DESCRIPTION OF CUSTOMER AVAILABLE.

WATERTON PARK RANGER RECALLS MAN AND WOMAN ENTERING PARK EVENING, 06 SEPTEMBER, WITH RAFT ON TOP OF VAN. RAFT FITS DESCRIPTION. VEHICLE CARRIED PROVINCE OF ONTARIO PLATES.

A PARK SEARCH HAS NOT TURNED UP THE VAN OR UNSUBS FITTING THE COUPLE'S DESCRIPTION. NO ONE REMEMBERS SEEING THEM AT CAMP SITES OR MOTELS. A PARK RANGER HAS PROVIDED

DETAILED DESCRIPTIONS. AGE: TWENTIES. NATIONALITY: MIDDLE EASTERN. ARTIST SKETCH BEING PREPARED BY RCMP. WILL FORWARD. FBI, MOSSAD, AND INTERPOL COOPERATING. PICTURES OF KNOWN TERRORISTS ARE BEING MADE AVAILABLE TO RCMP AND TO PARK RANGER FOR POSSIBLE ID.

34

16 SEPTEMBER, LOCAL TIME 1310
BOOTH BAY, MAINE

Rosa Posadas glanced around the room one last time. Everything was as it should be, ready for the next guests. She checked her watch. Ten after one. She was running late. The downstairs room with the family from New Jersey had taken her longer to clean than normal. It looked like the children had eaten chocolate ice cream in bed. A pair of small hands had cleaned themselves on the wallpaper, while another pair chose the carpet in the corner. Rosa wondered what the family home must look like.

She moved her cart along the hall to the next doorway. All that remained for the day were the two rooms occupied by the four male friends. This was to be their last night. She had been surprised by how neatly they had kept each room throughout the week of their occupancy. Her experience with other male-only guests had been quite the opposite. She knocked and listened, but there was no answer.

She knocked again, this time a little louder.

Still no answer.

They must be out again.

The men had gone fishing on their rented boat two or three times since they arrived.

They must not be very good at it, though.

Rosa inserted the key, opened the door, and entered. *They never bring anything back. At least nothing I have seen.*

"Maid service," she called out.

Nothing.

As usual, the room was in order, but there was a heavy smell of stale smoke. She opened the windows and emptied both ashtrays into the garbage basket. Fresh air and a thorough spraying of room freshener was her first line of defense in any room that smokers had occupied the night before.

What is it about this room? Something keeps feeling out of place. But what?

Rosa stopped in front of the closet and looked around again.

Smells. That's it.

She went into the bathroom, picked up the used towels and washcloths and stuffed them in the towel bag on her cart in front of the door. Gathering together the replacements, she returned to the bathroom and hung them on the wall rods. All the while she continued thinking about smells. When she had finished wiping down the shower and damp mopping the tile floor, her mind was made up. Rosa opened the closet door. No clothes bags. No luggage except for the canvas bags that were probably still under the bed.

No fishing poles. No tackle boxes or gear of any kind. And no fishy smells!

Rosa had grown up with fishermen in her family. She could fly cast as well as most men. She joined her husband, Manuel, and the boys on Saturday morning fishing jaunts whenever her schedule permitted. One thing she was certain about when it came to fishing were the smells. The smell of the catch on a person's hands and clothes lingers. It isn't long before it spreads from the clothing into a room.

She always knew when Manuel or the boys had been fishing, whether or not she had been told they were going. When they returned, she knew exactly what they'd been up to. And she always opened the windows and sprayed air freshener to eliminate the fishy odors.

No equipment. And no smells. That's what is missing here.

Rosa's curiosity had finally gotten the best of her. It was more than curiosity now. It had become suspicion. No clothes bags, only small shaving kits. *Now that I think of it, those kits are all look-alikes, too, as if they were bought in the same store. But Mr. Hondros said that they had not been together like this in years. In fact, he said that they came here from different places.* Yet even the canvas bags she had seen under the bed looked alike, as near as she could tell.

Hondros. That's a Greek name. The man from Canada is French. That's what Mr. Brainard said. But is he really?

She went to the door and checked the hallway, listening for sounds of movement on the floor below or on the stairway at the end of the hall. Nothing. Turning back into the room, she went around to the side of the bed nearest the window and knelt down. Lifting the dust skirt surrounding it, she peered into the semidarkness underneath. There they were. Pushed up against the wall under the head of the bed. Just like before.

Rosa dropped the dust skirt and sat back on her heels. Inordinate curiosity regarding other people's things did not normally disturb her work ethic. So why was this different?

Something doesn't add up. If they aren't fishing, then just what are they doing?

It was hard for her to believe what she was thinking. But suddenly she made up her mind. Rosa trusted her intuition. It was a sixth sense that rarely ever led her astray. And that sixth sense was now urging her on.

She lifted the dust skirt and reached underneath, stretching as far as she could. Her hand touched the nearest bag. Rosa ran her hands along its surface until she came to a handle. She grasped it and pulled. The bag was heavy, but it moved. Bracing her other hand against the bed frame, she pulled it toward her until it slid out from under the bed. Rosa stared at it, feeling guilty, her heart pounding with the knowledge that she was breaking a house rule. Never meddle with a guest's personal items.

The bag was black. A heavy waterproof coating made for a slick surface. A combination padlock was in place to keep out prying hands and eyes. She tried to feel the contents. With both hands, Rosa pushed and squeezed at the stiff outer shell of the bag. It felt as if there were several boxes inside. One seemed to be open. She pushed some more against the outer surface of the bag, feeling for what was inside. Small, cylindrical items were attached in place in the box.

Fishing poles? No. They are too large and too heavy. Then what?

Rosa continued to feel the contents. All at once, her mouth went dry. She ran her hand along the thin, round objects, with growing apprehension.

These feel like . . .

One of the objects took shape as Rosa pressed down on the canvas cover.

This feels like . . . like a gun!

Rosa gasped. Her hand jerked off the bag as if from a hot stove.

These men are not hunters either. So why would they have guns?

Leaning over the bag, she examined the lock. Seeing there was nothing she could do with it, she let it fall back against the bag. Then with both hands, she molded the shape of the bag around the contents as best she could.

Not just one. There are several. And they don't feel like ordinary guns, either.

Her heart pounded beneath her uniform. *These are different. Yes, these are like in the movies! Could these men be criminals . . . or worse! What if . . .*

Her total concentration on the black canvas bag, the open door behind her was momentarily forgotten.

What happened next took place so rapidly, there was no time even to cry out. A sudden awareness of someone with her in the room. The smell of tobacco. A hand pressed down over her mouth. She fell backward, her hands and arms flailing the air as she tried to regain control, to recover her balance. It was too late. Her eyes locked onto the cold stare of the man who lived in this room. The man with the scar on his cheek. A searing pain at the base of her neck.

No . . .

Rosa dropped limply to the floor.

35

16 September, local time 1057
150 km north of Eilat, Israel

The truck rolled along Highway 90, slowing as it neared Ketura Junction. Just before the split, the driver saw a military jeep parked at a slight angle in the northbound lane. Two soldiers were standing by the vehicle, facing the oncoming traffic. A third watched impassively from behind the steering wheel. One of the soldiers held up his hand and motioned the driver over, using his automatic rifle as a pointer.

Reaching back between the seats, the driver pounded three times on the wall between the cab and the cargo hold. His forearm muscles flexed nervously as he came to a stop.

"*Sabah-al-kheir,*" the young Israeli soldier greeted the truck driver in Arabic. In his hand was a small writing pad, together with a list of vehicle licenses that deserved special attention. "What is your destination?"

"My next stop is Ein Bokek. Then on to Masada and Bethlehem."

"What are you carrying?"

"I have pottery and glassware from Eilat."

"Pull over and shut off the engine."

The driver carefully maneuvered the truck onto the road's edge under the watchful eye of the soldiers. He shut off the motor.

"Get out and open the doors in back."

The driver opened the door. There was no breeze and the heat was sweltering, though it was still an hour before noontime. The sun's rays baked the huge stones and rising cliffs on the left, while beating down incessantly on the salt-flat wasteland along the right side of the road. At 386 meters below sea level, the lowest point on earth was living up to its reputation for being painfully hot. Even desert creatures were seeking cooler refuge under rocks and in the occasional cave.

The driver jumped down from the cab, feigning boredom as he removed the padlock and chain and swung open the doors to the rear of the truck. The security checkpoint had been routinely set up today for all trucks moving along the Dead Sea's western shoreline. It was not done every day along this road because truck traffic was normally light. Tomorrow these same soldiers would be on duty checking the flow of trucks crossing the Allenby Bridge, in and out of Jordan.

One of the soldiers came around to the back and looked in. A hand cart was strapped to wooden slats that ran the length of the inside wall. A stack of dirty packing blankets were piled carelessly to one side. Halfway forward, cardboard boxes and wooden crates were stacked on top of each other and tied into place.

"Pottery and glassware, you say?"

"*Ay-wah,*" answered the driver. With unusual politeness, he asked, "Do you wish to look inside the boxes?"

The soldier squinted into the back of the truck, now a suffocating oven. The last thing he wanted to do was climb up there and open those boxes. He hated this kind of duty, even in the Galilee region where it was more temperate and beautiful girls were never far away. But here at this time of the year it was pure torture. Wanting to get this over with, he motioned to the Arab.

"Let me see this crate and that box back there."

The driver climbed up onto the truck bed and handed down the box that had been pointed out. The soldier pulled out his knife and attacked the box, making quick work of it. As he did, the driver wrestled the larger wooden crate over to the door's edge.

"I have nothing to open this with," he said, sweat running down into his shirt.

The soldier used his knife once more, pushing it under the lid at the corners. With a few prying twists, the cover gave way. He looked inside, ran his hand through the loose Styrofoam packing, and stepped back. There was nothing unusual here. He scrutinized the driver. Nothing in his mannerisms suggested anything but the usual passive frustration of being subjected to an inspection that he could do nothing about.

Now the part he really hated.

Gun in hand, he climbed up into the oven-like interior, randomly lifting a few of the boxes as best he could, checking their weight. They all appeared to weigh about the same as the one he had opened. Three other wooden crates were tied to one side. He thought about opening them, too, then, decided against it. He did not want to find anything. Getting this inspection over with had become the goal. He peered over the tops of the boxes. They were stacked solidly, to about chin height, all the way forward.

Satisfied, he turned back to the driver, who sat in the door entrance, feet dangling outside, smoking a cigarette. Sweat poured off both their faces and ran in rivulets under their shirts and trousers. The soldier motioned with his hand. Both men jumped down from the truck.

"Open the hood."

Used to this sort of request, the driver pulled the release and lifted the hood. Contraband, including both weapons and drugs were sometimes found taped behind an engine block, in the oil pan, behind hubcaps, or inside tires. It was one of the reasons trucks in this country often looked so stripped down. It made them easier to inspect. The soldier leaned forward for a look around the engine. Then, stepping back, he motioned for the hood to be dropped in place.

"Let me see your manifest."

The driver walked around to the cab and withdrew a clipboard containing the appropriate manifests and bills of lading indicating drops at the three locations he had mentioned earlier. The soldier flipped through the paperwork, by now disinterested in the whole task. He was already convinced that the truck carried nothing illegal. He wrote some notes down on his pad, then handed the clipboard back to the driver.

"You can go."

The soldier motioned to two cars and a tour bus that had slowed their approach, stepping out of the way as they drove past.

"*Shokran,*" the driver responded. He walked to the back of the truck and slammed the rear doors, slipped the chain through the handles, and snapped the padlock into place. Nodding to the soldier, he stepped up into the truck cab. "Don't you wish you had my job now and could get in out of this sun?"

The soldier said nothing in return. It was too hot to engage in roadside repartee. The Arab started the engine, slowly moving the truck back into the northbound lane. He grinned at the soldiers and waved. One gave him a half wave in return. The truck roared away, kicking up dust as it pulled off the shoulder and back onto the paved roadway.

Reaching back between the seats, he hit the wall four times.

—ɯ—

The human cargo was accustomed to the darkness by now. It was the heat that had become unbearable. The feeling of the truck rolling along the highway was their only relief. The four of them had sat, motionless, cramped against the forward wall of the truck during the inspection, fearful of making any sound. Pasha's left leg was in such severe pain from cramping that she wanted to cry. As the truck bounced along, they did their best to change positions. They had soaked through their clothing and were sitting in puddles of perspiration.

"Broad daylight, you said," muttered Fathi, the darkness hiding his scowl.

"So what are you complaining about?" Yazib answered back with a chuckle. "It is broad daylight. We are in Israel. Soon we will be taking cool showers and having a nice lunch. What more could we ask for?"

"We could ask for our camels back," Fathi answered.

"No thank you, Fathi. My backside has only recently gotten over that ride," said Pasha, rubbing the cramp in her leg as best she could.

Laughter, mostly relief at not having been discovered at the checkpoint, followed her assessment of their previous week's journey across the Negev. No one disagreed.

They rode on in the stifling darkness, unable to see that the truck was encountering increasing traffic as it moved northward—mostly weekenders from Jerusalem, along with several tour buses bound for Eilat. As the truck passed by Sodom and the Dead Sea Works Ltd. plant, the sea itself was in clear view, the sun casting a glaring sheen across its surface, but only the driver could enjoy the view. They passed Newe Zohar's messy jumble of new and old buildings, situated at the Highway 31 junction that led away from the sea into the Hatrurim Hills and on to Arad. A kilometer and a half further, the driver reached back and pounded the wall three times. Then he turned off the highway and into the parking lot of Ein Bokek's Salt Sea Hotel & Spa.

The main lot in front of the four-story hotel was about half full. In a few hours, most of the remaining spaces would be filled. The crowd today would be typically international in its composition, with guests from as far away as Australia, Great Britain, Germany, Scandinavia, and the United States.

They came to experience the sensation of floating in the Dead Sea, sunning on its sandy beaches, and taking prescribed treatments for a variety of ailments. They came because Dead Sea water contains twenty times as much bromine—a component of many nerve relaxants—as regular seawater, and its extremely high magnesium and iodine content counteracts skin allergies, opens bronchial passages, and is touted as beneficial for glandular functions. Other hopefuls came seeking treatment for rheumatism and arthritis.

The truck lumbered across the lot toward the back of the building. The driver looked around carefully before stopping near the service entrance. He shut off the engine, nervously scanning the area for unusual signs of danger, then reached back and knocked on the truck wall four times. Sliding out from under the wheel, he jumped down onto the sun-cracked pavement and walked around to the back of the truck, glancing about one last time before removing the padlock and chain from the doors and releasing the latch. Then he strode quickly to a hotel door marked Employees Only.

The door was opened by a man wearing a light blue suit. The driver nodded to the man and disappeared inside. The man in the suit went to the truck. Opening the door, he saw three dripping, bedraggled men and a woman facing him.

"Which one of you is Yazib?"

Yazib raised his hand.

"Quickly, through that door over there," he ordered, handing Yazib a piece of paper and a key.

"Once inside, follow this map to the elevator. Your room is at the end of the hall on the fourth floor. Hurry. Try to avoid being seen!"

The shock of jumping from the truck bed to the pavement sent stabs of pain through Yazib's feet and legs. He could see the others had experienced the same debilitation from their ride. But they did as they were told and moments later were inside the hotel. Yazib held the penciled diagram up to the light, then looked around.

"This way," he said, pointing to an open door that led into a narrow passageway. They jogged along the passage until coming to another door. It opened onto a small concrete landing and a stairway. Halfway up, another landing, then more steps and another door. Cracking it open, Yazib could see a hall leading to the main lobby area. He studied the map again. Halfway down the hall and to the left were the two elevators that serviced the upper floors. When the lobby looked like it was clear, he opened the door and they entered the hall. At the corner they turned toward the elevators. They were only a short distance from the registration desk, but out of the clerk's line of vision.

Yazib pushed the button, uttering an involuntary sigh of relief as the door of one elevator opened immediately. They entered quickly and pushed the fourth-floor button. The doors started to close.

"Wait!"

Startled, they stepped back as a young girl about ten years old slipped between the doors. Her bathing suit was dripping beneath the towel draped over her shoulders. She looked up and smiled, then punched the third-floor button.

"Hi," she said in English, with an Aussie accent. She surveyed the four of them as the elevator rose, noticing their soaked appearance. "Did you go swimming with your clothes on?"

The door opened before they could respond. The girl stepped out, turned and waved. "G'day."

The door closed. The four looked at each other, then burst into laughter. On the next floor they exited the elevator and hurried down the hall to the right. Yazib checked numbers on the wall signs until he found 424.

At the door, he quickly inserted the key. They pushed their way into the room and an instant later the door was securely shut and locked. Exhausted, the four dropped into chairs and onto the beds. An atmosphere of released tension filled the air. They looked at each other, no one saying a word.

"We made it," Imad sighed, breaking the silence at last.

"Yes," agreed Yazib. "We made it. Allah be praised. We are at the strike point!"

Pasha stretched out on the bed, totally spent. Yazib could not help but notice how her damp blouse clung to the curves of her body. Sandals kicked off to the side of the bed, her brown feet looked delicate and feminine. She looked good in jeans, too. Her Western-style apparel would be quite unacceptable to many in their fundamentalist Islamic culture, but here it was necessary. Eyes closed, her lightly bronzed face streaked with dirt and sweat seemed alluring somehow, delicately defined by her dark hair and the stark white of the pillow.

No beauty in the classic Arabic style, Yazib mused, *but she is a woman created to evoke great desire in a man.*

Her eyes opened.

She saw Yazib looking at her.

Out of the corner of her eye, she also saw the other two standing near the window, watching the delivery truck pull away from the service entrance and disappear around the corner of the hotel.

She turned her gaze back to Yazib.

He was still watching her.

Pasha smiled wearily.

Yazib looked away.

"Come, Pasha, get up. You are first into the shower. We want to take one as well, so hurry. I am very hot and sweaty."

"I can see that," Pasha said, getting up from the bed.

36

16 September, local time 1230
Eilat, Israel

The two young windsurfers shot across the water on their sleek projectiles, a stiff breeze filling the sails as they headed back to shore. They were still some distance from the beach when the wind shifted suddenly. Before the one surfer could adjust, he was pulled off balance and blown on a collision course toward his companion. Shouting a warning, he veered past, barely avoiding a direct hit.

Both surfers hit the water hard. They came up at the same time, signaling to each other that they were okay. The young man was only a short distance from his bright red sail, now floating limply on the surface of the water. The woman's board continued to skitter across the water before finally turning on its side and coming to a stop. She dove under the surface and began swimming toward it.

As she swam, she saw something unusual and definitely out of place directly beneath her. Immediately, she rose to the surface.

"Dan! Come here."

"Are you okay, Sheila?"

"I'm fine. But come over here. I want you to see something."

She treaded water, waiting as he paddled his board over to her.

"What is it?"

"There's something down there. It looks like diving gear. Come take a look."

Dan and Sheila were both expert swimmers. They dove together, slicing beneath the clear blue sea.

When they broke the surface again, they were tugging at four wet suits, two tanks, and several body weights, tied together and abandoned to the sea. The idea that perfectly good scuba gear would be abandoned to the sea was unusual enough. That it was discovered directly off Israel's southernmost shore was a matter of grave concern.

Twenty minutes later, the equipment was on the beach in front of the

Neptune Hotel, next to the two rented surfing boards. A small crowd gathered around Sheila, asking questions and staring curiously at the equipment. Dan ran to call the police.

Before long, several officers from Eilat's tough, security-conscious police force had surrounded the mysterious scuba equipment that lay drying in the afternoon sun. One of them began questioning the two Israeli teenagers who had made the startling discovery.

37

16 September, local time 2230
Booth Bay, Maine

She heard voices. They seemed close, yet far away. Was it a radio?

Where am I? And why is it so dark? A moment ago, the sun had been shining through the window.

Then it all came back.

Hill House. The man with the scar. The bag beneath the bed.

I have to get out of here!

Rosa tried to sit up, but for some reason she could not.

She tried to call for help. But no sound came out.

Then she realized why it was dark.

—∾—

Across the room, the desk had been pulled away from the wall. One of the three men surrounding it glanced over at Rosa, who was lying on the bed.

"She's awake," he said, watching her struggle, then settle back.

"How much did you give her?"

"Not very much."

"She's been out for six hours."

"So? She had a nice nap."

The other man chuckled.

"Pay attention here, you two. We're almost finished."

On the desk lay an assortment of containers and rags—and a disassembled AK-47.

A cloth lay stretched over the carpet. On the cloth were three other AK-47s, together with an assortment of ammunition, grenades, knives, and handguns. Everything had been freshly cleaned and wiped down.

The woman on the bed moved again.

"Should we take the blindfold off?"

"In a minute. Finish putting this together."

"What's her name again? Rita?"

"Rosa. She said her name was Rosa."

"There. We're done. It's ready to go. As soon as the rooms are prepared, we can leave."

"Wait."

The others looked up from their task.

"Rosa was curious. She wanted to see what was in the bags. Take it off."

Yusif walked over to the bed. He hesitated, taking in the attractive, helpless form in front of him. Her feet were bound at the ankles and her wrists were tied behind her back. A wide piece of adhesive tape ran from ear to ear over her mouth. Yusif pulled the blindfold over her head.

—∞—

For a moment the light was blinding. Rosa squinted against its sudden brightness.

It's like this in the early morning, when I go to the kitchen and turn on the light to make coffee for Manuel.

A man's face hovered over her. She wanted it to be Manuel's. It wasn't.

She shut her eyes again, desperately wanting the face to go away.

When she opened them again, it was gone.

She felt like laughing from sheer relief. Or crying.

It's a dream. A nightmare. Wake up, Rosa.

She turned her head.

Now there were two faces. No, three.

Oh, God. It's not a dream. It's real!

"Good evening, Rosa." The man with the scar stepped forward. He noted with satisfaction the fear in her dark eyes. "Yes, it's evening."

He glanced at his watch.

"Actually, it's ten-thirty. You've had quite a nap," he continued speaking softly. She watched his eyes. They were without expression, hooded, like those of a cobra. "I know you must be uncomfortable. I am sorry. You will not have to endure this much longer, I assure you."

A flicker of hope.

"I wish you had not been so curious, Rosa. You've done such a good job of caring for our rooms. But you are not a woman easily fooled. You knew we had not caught any fish this week, didn't you? What else did you notice, Rosa? Did it occur to you that our shaving kits were all alike? I think so. I spoke to Mohammed about that. He did not believe anyone would notice. But he was wrong, wasn't he? His mistake was in underestimating the powers of observation of someone such as you."

The man moved closer, hands in his pockets.

"So you wondered just what we were doing here. And you discovered the bags beneath our bed. Rosa, Rosa. A woman of your intelligence and beauty should be doing something other than cleaning rooms, don't you think?"

He smiled.

This man. There is something about him. His smile? The scar? No. It is the eyes. Brown. Deep and piercing. He doesn't look at you. He looks through you!

Though the room was warm a chill ran down Rosa's back.

"Take a look, Rosa," the man continued, motioning with his hand. "You wanted to know what was in the bags. Well, here it is."

Rosa turned her head until she could see the cloth on the carpet. Her eyes grew wide as she looked at the guns and grenades. There were knives and ammunition clips. And several odd-shaped stainless steel containers. She turned her eyes back to the man with the scar. He saw the questioning look.

"Let me introduce myself. My name is Dosha. Marwan Dosha. Maybe you have heard of me? Then again, maybe not. Perhaps you remember reading of last year's bombing in Florence, Italy? or the attack last April on the infidel Jews in the London synagogue? Ah, yes. I see you do recall that one. May I introduce you to Yusif Shemuda and Safwat Najjir? They can describe those events to you in great detail, actually. They were the leaders of those particular strikes.

"Why are we here? I know you must be wondering. Can you understand that necessity demands it of us? Allah requires it as well. You see, Rosa, the world as it is today is how the infidels have shaped it. They have left us with only two choices. Either we must submit to the way this world is, which means Islam will die, or we can strike back and conquer and reconstruct the world as true Islam requires."

Dosha leaned over Rosa, gently running his fingers across her forehead, brushing back tousled strands of reddish brown hair. Rosa closed her eyes at his touch.

A gentle man. Please, God, let him be gentle. Make him turn me loose now. Please . . .

When he withdrew his hand, she opened her eyes.

"That's why we are here, Rosa. Allah has called us to build a new world. But first the old one must be destroyed. East and the West are both alike. They are our enemies. Communism crumbles today because of Allah's judgment. Liberalism and socialism and democracy must fall as well. We do not operate within the rules of the world as it now exists. We reject those rules. We are warriors in a holy war that can end only when total victory has been achieved.

"Some of your people know this already and have come over to us. There are more Muslims in your country than Methodists. Did you know that? What about you, Rosa? You are both beautiful and intelligent. Is it possible that you would come to our aid? Would you be willing to help us destroy the enemies of Allah?"

Rosa tensed as Dosha reached for her again, sliding his hand past her ear and along the curve of her throat. At the collar of her blouse, his fingers touched a thin gold necklace, last year's anniversary gift from Manuel.

"What is this?" Dosha proceeded to pull it free, revealing the small gold cross attached to the necklace.

In her mind, she heard the words he spoke the night Manuel gave it to her. *"A token of my love for you and of God's love for us, Rosa."* It was the most eloquent expression that Rosa had ever known him to utter. She often thought of the tenderness with which he had placed it around her neck. And how later they had made love.

Rosa never took it off after that night. Whenever she touched it, whether at home or work or at play with the children, she could feel Manuel's gentle hands on her neck. She could see again the look of total devotion in his eyes. She was the luckiest woman alive. No, not lucky. Blessed. Manuel was a gift from God.

Dosha's face hardened.

"Ah, Rosa, too bad. It is as I thought. You are one of them."

He gripped the gold cross and yanked it toward him. Rosa's neck whipped and then fell back as the necklace broke free.

"You are an infidel, Rosa. You are the enemy of Allah."

The others watched, nostrils flaring their approval of the passionate fanaticism in Dosha's voice. Any last doubts they may have harbored about their team leader were quickly evaporating. He was not Islamic Jihad. But he was one of them!

Rosa turned away, her mind gripped by equal parts of terror and anger.

Dosha flung the necklace across the room. Reaching over, he turned her face toward him again. His fingers pressed hard against her cheekbones. Rosa didn't blink, and this time she didn't look away. A fierce combination of hurt and anger blazed in her eyes as she stared back at the terrorist leader.

Oh, God, I know it's wrong to hate. But he is going to take it all away from me. I can feel it. Lord, how can you expect me not to hate these men?

The three men's attention was momentarily diverted as Mohammed Ibn Ahmer returned to the room. He smiled grimly at the fiery connection between Dosha and the cleaning woman.

"How many others in the house tonight?" asked Dosha, never taking his eyes off Rosa, who now stared resolutely at the ceiling, listening as the men talked.

"Only two other rooms are occupied," replied Ibn Ahmer. "A young couple is at the other end of our hallway in the room nearest the stairs. An older couple is on the second floor. And, of course, the old man is on the first floor in his room as usual. Everyone appears to have settled in for the night. There was no one around when I came up from the reading room."

"Safwat. Put everything back in the bags," Dosha ordered. "Then take them to the car. Use the fire exit stairs. And be quiet. Yusif, write a note to Mr. Brainard explaining that we had to leave early in the morning rather than at the expected time. Mohammed, you will help me check our rooms. Make certain nothing is left behind. Wipe for fingerprints. We have been careful to touch only certain areas, but make sure nothing can easily be traced to us."

Rosa watched helplessly from the bed as the men set about their tasks.

By 11:15 they were finished. Yusif returned from delivering the note.

"The old man is prowling around downstairs," he said, a worried look on this face.

"What's his problem?" asked Dosha.

"He says that Rosa, the cleaning woman, is missing." He glanced over at Rosa, who listened intently from her prone position on the bed. "According to the old man, she did not return home this afternoon. He asked if I had seen her. I told him, no, not since yesterday. He wanted to know if our rooms had been cleaned. I said, yes, she must have been here because the rooms had been cleaned today. I guess the woman's husband came by looking for her. They have reported to the police. It won't be long before they show up asking questions."

A tear fell from Rosa's eye. Manuel had been in the house looking for her. *So close, Manuel. You were so close and did not know it!*

"It is time for us to go. If we stay longer, this woman's curiosity may get us all in trouble," said Dosha. "Yusif, go down and keep the old man occupied while Safwat and Mohammed take our friend here to the car. There is not room in the trunk. Put her on the floor, behind the front seats. And make certain there are no police lurking about.

"Give them five minutes, Yusif. Then go out the front door. Once Yusif is at the car, you two come back up the fire escape. We will all go downstairs together, say good-bye, and be on our way. If he asks, tell the old man that some unexpected business has arisen. Tell him that I have to catch an early morning plane to Chicago and that this requires us to go into the city tonight."

Yusif nodded and left the room.

Safwat picked Rosa up and slung her over his shoulder like a sack of grain, gripping her legs with his arms. Mohammed opened the door, looked both ways, and then made for the window that opened onto the fire escape at the end of the hall. It faced out onto the back side of the inn. The window released easily and Mohammed stepped through the opening onto the small landing. Quickly he removed the globe from the landing light and unscrewed the bulb. Dark shadows were all that remained along the narrow, weathered staircase. Safwat passed Rosa through the open window to Mohammed and followed after her. Because he was the larger of the two men, Safwat took Rosa back from his partner, threw her over his shoulder again and started down the steps.

In a matter of minutes, Rosa was lying facedown on the floor of the rented Cadillac. Yusif slid into the backseat, his feet pressed up against her face. Five more minutes passed before the others reappeared, crowding into the car. Mohammed backed out of the parking stall and started down the hill, on their way north toward Highway 27. About three miles beyond the city limits, Dosha touched Mohammed's arm, motioning for him to slow down. Where the highway dipped sharply, a solitary street lamp identified a side road leading into the wooded hills. Houses here were far apart. They turned into an area lined by a dense profusion of trees and underbrush.

About a half mile further, the car lights picked up a dirt road going off to the left. Mohammed steered off the highway onto the bumpy, narrow side road, the car scraping bottom now and then while limbs and branches brushed against the sides of the vehicle. It looked to be an abandoned logging road or a right-of-way used by hunters during deer season. There were some tracks, but they did not look fresh. It was hard to tell in the uneven light as they bounced along, but Dosha doubted anyone had been through here in weeks.

"Stop," ordered Dosha. "Shut off the motor. Lights out, too."

They sat for a moment without moving. All that could be heard were the endless night sounds of crickets and frogs. Rosa stirred beneath the feet of the two men in back.

Dosha opened the door and got out. The others followed, peering at their leader in the darkness. The light of a full moon filtered through tree branches and tall undergrowth, revealing a small clearing off to their right.

"Take her over there."

Safwat grabbed at the back of her skirt, dragging her out of the car. Her face banged painfully against the doorjamb, with no way to protect herself. By now, her wrists had been tied behind her back for so long her hands were numb. But pain shot through her neck and shoulders with every move of her body.

Safwat carried her to the clearing and dumped her unceremoniously on the ground. She uttered a muffled cry as her shoulder banged against a rock. Safwat had torn her skirt, dragging her from the car. It fell open now, showing a large bruise on her thigh, apparent even in the dim moonlight.

Dosha looked around the clearing and the darkened area beyond. Perfect. There was no one anywhere near this remote spot. Nor would there be any time soon. He turned again, looking down at Rosa. Without warning, he reached down and ripped away the adhesive tape that had covered her mouth for nearly eleven hours. Her eyes clenched shut involuntarily and she cried out with pain. When the intensity subsided and she was able to open her eyes again, salty tears fell onto her checks.

The four men stood around her. Dosha placed a cigarette between his lips and reached in his pocket for a lighter. As the flint sparked and flared, Rosa saw enough to cause her heart to sink in hopelessness. Those eyes. Dark. Cold. Without feeling.

"Is there something you would like to say, Rosa?" asked Dosha. The others were smoking now as well.

She tried to moisten her lips with her tongue.

"Why . . . are you . . . doing this?" she gasped through swollen lips.

"Because, Rosa, you are in the way." The man with the scar smiled a thin, hard, joyless smile.

"You are in the way of our most glorious achievement. Do you remember the stainless steel containers that you saw in our room? Didn't you wonder what might be in them? Even a little bit? Well, I will tell you. They hold enough anthrax to wipe out the entire city of Boston."

Rosa's eyes grew wide in horror.

"Do you understand what that means? By this time next week, the world will have come face to face with the fearful judgment of Allah."

"But . . . why?" Rosa gasped in disbelief.

"Ours is a holy war, Rosa. Something you would never understand. It will end only when total victory has been achieved. We are not fighting so that we can be offered some token to appease us. We are fighting to destroy the enemies of Allah. In our lifetime we will see the conquest of the entire globe by the true faith!"

"You . . . are . . . all . . . mad," she whispered.

Dosha's gaze lingered on this defiant, helpless woman. A servant, but not servile. She knew she was beaten, but still she did not beg.

"Good-bye, Rosa."

He looked at the others and nodded.

"This infidel woman is my gift to you. Enjoy her. It may be a long time before you are able to have another. Take your time. I'll wait for you in the car. When you have finished with her, we will go on to complete our mission." Dosha drew deeply on his cigarette, then turned and strolled away from the clearing.

Rosa returned the stares of the other three men. Fear clawed at her throat like a wild animal. She had seen this look before. Years ago. When she was a young girl in the city.

"Please, don't do this. I've done nothing to you. I am married. I have two little boys. I am pregnant. You should not . . . please . . ."

Safwat knelt down beside her and pressed his damp mouth over her lips. His breath reeked of tobacco.

Rosa bit him as hard as she could.

He fell back, cursing, while the others laughed. Rosa struggled and twisted, her whole being charged with renewed energy, fueled by fear. Desperation stoked adrenaline as she struggled to get to her feet. Safwat stunned her with an open-handed blow to the side of her face, driving her back to the ground. Then he was on top of her. She felt him tearing at her clothes.

Oh, God. No. How can this be happening? Mama. I'm a good girl, Mama. Manuel. My darling. My babies. I love you . . . love. . . . Our Father . . . who art in heaven . . . forgive . . . as we forgive . . .

Leaning against the car door, Dosha listened with perverse satisfaction to the sounds coming from the clearing. His team would be ready after this. They would be grateful to him. They now understood how Dosha takes care of his own. Their trust in him would be complete. They would do anything he told them to do.

Power is sometimes gained with such small price tags.

38

SATURDAY, 17 SEPTEMBER, LOCAL TIME 0730
BOOTH BAY, MAINE

Marwan Dosha didn't know it, but he had just committed his first error.

He had allowed arrogance to interfere with his judgment.

Early the next morning, a battered, old pickup truck turned onto the Maine woods side road just as the sun's rim peeked over the forested hills.

"Look, Roy," Jim Stevens said, pushing in the clutch and coasting to a halt. "Someone was in here last night. See? They turned around right here."

He slapped at the steering wheel in frustration. "I'll bet they got the stuff I left out here last night!"

"Doesn't that beat all?" Roy Blanchard answered, yawning and rubbing his eyes. "What do they do? Just sit around somewhere, watching for you to start a new job so they can pick you clean?"

Jim put the truck in low gear and gunned the engine. They bounced along for another fifty feet or so into an open clearing before he slammed on the brake, almost putting Roy's nose into the windshield.

He had spent the day Friday hauling in lumber, bags of cement, and foundation forms in preparation for beginning the summer cottage project that he had put off until now. A family from up in Bangor had bought this property late last spring and hired Jim to build for them.

The thought of pilfering always angered him, but this time he was partly mad at himself. He had left the job site in a hurry the night before to make it back to town in time for a meeting, and in his haste he had left a small power generator on the far side of the meadow, along with the building materials and several cans of gasoline. He was certain that no one would have come up this way. But he'd been wrong and it made him angry. Someone had discovered where he was building on the very first day!

Jumping out of the pickup, he looked around.

There was the generator, right where he had left it.

The cans of gasoline were there. The lumber, too.

He shook his head.

Roy came around the front of the pickup and stood alongside Jim.

"They take anything that you can see?"

"Nope. Not a thing. Can you beat that? I wonder what they were doing in here."

"Maybe some local kids with a couple of six-packs."

"Yeah, maybe. Well, whatever. I know someone was in here. I'm positive that there were no other tracks here but mine yesterday."

"Well, your secret lane is no secret anymore. We'll just have to gather everything up tonight. Let's get to work."

Roy started around the pickup to get his tools. He glanced back at Jim and stopped. Jim was staring intently off through the trees.

"You see something?" asked Roy.

There was no answer as Jim walked slowly across the meadow.

"Hey, what is it?"

Roy followed as Jim headed toward a stand of tall pines. He had almost caught up with him when he saw what Jim had seen. Something white. A piece of cloth caught on a tree limb, on the opposite side of the clearing from where they had parked. Roy was only a few steps behind when Jim suddenly stopped. Roy looked up and saw what had frozen Jim in his tracks.

It was not just a piece of white cloth.

It was a woman's blouse.

A badly torn blouse that looked as if it had been tossed carelessly and remained caught on the low-hanging limb of a tree.

A bit further along, other pieces of clothing were scattered about.

"Something bad happened here, Roy. Something real bad." The grim look on Jim's face reinforced the apprehensiveness in his voice.

Roy's heart pounded out his response as they edged slowly into the underbrush. Abruptly, Roy caught his breath and gripped Jim's arm, pointing to the left.

Protruding from behind the trunk of a tree was a shock of disheveled, reddish brown hair. The face was turned down and away from where they were standing, but a slender arm and feminine hand confirmed their worst fears.

Walking around the tree, Jim bent down to look at her face.

"Oh, no!" Jim's gasp was followed by a curse. He looked up at Roy, his face an ashen gray.

"What?" asked Roy, staring at his friend.

"I know her!"

"You know her?" Roy repeated incredulously.

Jim nodded silently, gazing back at the face of the dead woman.

"Well?"

"It's Rosa Posadas. You know, Manuel Posadas's wife? We worked together on a job last winter." His voice choked. "They've got two kids."

The two stood silently together, the construction project totally forgotten. Roy reached down and picked up a piece of thin cord. It had been cut. There were obvious rope burns on her outstretched wrist.

Jim's eyes filled with tears.

With a grief-stricken cry, he smashed his fist against one of the trees. It remained unyielding and silent, its limbs extended over Rosa's battered body in regal sadness, as if it too felt the unbearable pain.

Had Marwan Dosha been there, he would have recognized his mistake immediately.

Soon every law enforcement agency in New England would be on the lookout for four Middle Eastern males in a silver Cadillac.

39

17 September 0915 local time
Baytown, California

Are you ready for a waffle?"

As Jeremy entered the kitchen, he was surprised to see his mother with a mixing bowl in her hand. She lifted the cover on the waffle iron and paused, waiting for his answer. It had been weeks since he had eaten anything but cold cereal or a piece of toast he prepared for himself.

She looked up and smiled.

"Well, what do you say?"

"I say, yes, I'd like a waffle. Thanks, Mom."

She proceeded to spoon the batter onto the heated surface. Jeremy stood by the counter and watched.

"I know," she said apologetically. "It's been awhile."

"How are you feeling?"

"I feel . . . ," she paused, placing the spoon down on the counter's tiled surface, "all dried up actually. I guess that would be the most honest way to put it. Like I've had everything squeezed out of me. Kind of like I look, huh?"

"No, Mom," Jeremy responded a bit too hastily, "you look great."

Esther cocked an eye knowingly.

"Well, actually," he said with a wry smile, "maybe not *great.* Maybe just—"

"Okay, okay. I get the message. And remember, Jeremy. The truth. We promised last night to tell each other the truth and nothing but from here on out. About everything. Always. Even if it hurts."

"Yeah, we did. Well, so much for white lies. The truth is, I've seen you look better. On the other hand, I've seen you look a lot worse, too."

"Thank you . . . I think. The truth is, I feel pretty yucky. No energy. Depression really seems to do a person in. But, you know something? There is one thing today that feels different. It's a good thing, too. You are the first person, outside of Dr. Benton, that I've been able to share my . . . the difficulty I've had accepting Jenny's death. I really regret dragging you through all of this, but I am more grateful to you for being here for me than you will ever know."

"That's what you said yesterday. What about Dad?"

Esther shook her head and looked away.

"I don't know. I know I should have, and at times I've wanted to desperately. But I haven't been able to. It's this awful, terrible guilt. In my mind I know Jenny's death was an accident. I didn't cause it. God knows, enough people have reassured me of that. Including your father." A tear fell onto the counter surface. "But it happened when I was here, Jeremy. I was the one who was supposed to be taking care of her. And I just haven't been able to get over that . . . at least not until now."

"And you and Dad haven't talked at all about this?"

Esther forced a half smile as she turned toward Jeremy. "We've tried. He's assured me that he knows it was not my fault. 'Accidents happen' and 'it will be all right.' You know?"

Jeremy grinned. "All the encouragement stuff, right? Dad should have his own Dear Abby column and make some real money."

"Jeremy, be nice."

"Yeah, well, it's hard sometimes to separate whether or not what he's saying comes from Dad the dad, or Dad the Rev."

Now it was Esther's turn to smile as she brushed back the tears. "I know. And I'm sure what he said was coming from Dad the dad—or, in my case, Dad the husband. But then I would see him out by the pool. And I knew down inside that it wasn't ever going to be *all right* again. I think he's tried. No, that's not fair. I know he's tried to understand where I've been with all of this, but I haven't given him much of a chance. Not him or anyone else, really. Not until this week. There's just been too much guilt. And anger. Mostly at myself. But I've been angry with God, too."

Esther opened the waffle maker and placed the waffle on Jeremy's plate.

He smothered it with syrup and stuffed the first bite into his mouth.

"Yeah, well, I understand that last part."

Esther wiped at the counter with the dishcloth.

"What do you mean?"

"I mean that I've got some big-time hang-ups where God is concerned, too."

For the next hour, Esther and Jeremy sat and talked. They talked about love, acceptance, and forgiveness. Especially forgiveness. At one point, she reached over and put her hand on his, caught up for the first time in a long time in someone else's struggle besides her own.

"Last night when I went to bed, I read Psalm 32. I read it at least a half-dozen times. In it, David talks about the burden of guilt he was feeling, the relief that confession brought, and the joy of forgiveness. He says, 'Then I acknowledged my sin to you and did not cover up my iniquity. I said, "I will confess my transgressions to the LORD"—and you forgave the guilt of my sin.'

"Those words are exactly what I've needed. I've carried a burden of guilt about Jenny for so long. But finally, really and truly confessing this to God . . . and to you, Son . . . has already brought a huge sense of relief. I'm not all the way there, but I'm getting closer. Closer to the forgiveness part, too. In my mind, I know God has forgiven me. He's even forgiven me for what I foolishly tried to do to myself. But I still have a ways to go to get it down into my heart. Be patient with me? And I do hope you forgive me, Jeremy. I need that so very much."

They were silent, each lost in their own thoughts for a moment. Then Jeremy said, "Well, okay then. Let me give you my verse, Mom. Because these last few days I've been doing some reading of my own." He reached for the Bible that was always on the counter near the telephone. Then he grinned. "I used to think you guys left this here just to put me under conviction or something."

He thumbed the pages until he found his place.

"Here it is. Ephesians 4:32. 'Be kind and compassionate to one another, forgiving each other, just as in Christ God forgave you.'"

Jeremy looked serious and the tone of his voice became soft and sincere. "I don't remember anyone ever needing my forgiveness before. Not really. Not like this. Of course I forgive you, Mom. The question is, will you forgive me for being so selfish and self-centered that I've not been here for you in all of this? The last few days I've been thinking about a lot of things. And one of them is how so much of my life up to now has been all about me and not anybody else."

They looked at each other and smiled. Then the tears started rolling down Esther's cheeks. She dabbed them with a napkin and laughed.

"For so long I haven't been able to cry. Now I can't seem to stop." She walked over to the counter and carried back a box of tissue. "Jeremy, do you know how strange it feels for a mother to be talking to her son like this?"

"Well, I know it's never happened to me before," he answered.

"I feel as though I've been pouring out my soul to a Father Confessor. And here it is my own son. I am so sorry that I've put you through all this. No mother wants to be remembered for her worst moments."

Jeremy covered his mother's smaller hand with his own. "It's okay, Mom. Don't start with the guilt thing again. You know what I'm going to remember most of all about this week? I'm going to remember that you trusted me enough to be real with me. A real person. Not just a role-playing mom. I guess for the first time in a long time . . . I feel kind of hopeful. You know?"

Esther nodded.

Yes, Son, I do know.

The house grew still around them. The events of the week had shaped a passage in life that would forever alter their relationship. Jeremy had been catapulted into an understanding of his mother that most children don't gain until their adult years—if even then. Esther was floating in a vulnerability that many mothers never permit themselves to feel with their children. Only time would reassure them as to whether or not this was good.

"Mom? One more thing."

"Yes?"

"Any chance I could have another waffle?"

With a playful slap at his hand, Esther got up from her chair.

"Some things never change, do they? Including your bottomless pit. By the way, young man, what's on your agenda today?"

"Well, I'm not exactly sure . . ."

Esther sensed the tentativeness in his voice and understood.

"Look, I'm fine. Really," she said. "You don't have to be worried about me today. I've got a ways to go before I'm my old self, but I'm past doing something stupid. Actually, I'd like a little quiet time on my own without you underfoot. God and I have some things we need to straighten out. Okay?"

"Okay, Mom. I think I'll give Allison a call. If she's home, I'll see if maybe she wants to go out for a while."

"Good idea. She's a nice girl."

"Yeah, I think so."

Jeremy picked up his dish and headed for the sink.

"Going to church tomorrow, Son?"

He offered up a guilty grin.

"I'll be there. Want to go with me?"

"I'd like that. Why don't you ask Allison? Maybe she'd like to sit with us?"

"Good idea. I'll check it out."

40

17 SEPTEMBER, LOCAL TIME 1400
BOOTH BAY, MAINE

By two o'clock in the afternoon, the local police had thoroughly scoured the area now marked off as a crime scene. Rosa's body had been taken to the funeral home and an autopsy had been scheduled.

Manuel was grief-stricken when a police officer, hat in hand, came to his door and broke the news. He had spent the night looking for Rosa. Now his worst fears were being realized.

Two small boys struggled to understand why their mother wasn't there.

"Where is Momma? Isn't she coming home? Why not? Is she hurt? Can we go to the hospital to see her? What do you mean, Momma's in heaven with Jesus? Will we ever see her again? Why didn't she tell us good-bye, Daddy?"

As word passed through the tight-knit community of Booth Bay, neighbors brought in food. Mrs. Cantor from next door took charge of the boys. Harriet Lawson, from the church, brought cookies and stayed to answer the phone.

Father Mike came to offer condolences and prayer. He promised that the congregation would offer special prayers for Rosa the next day. Manuel thanked him over and over. The priest and the carpenter both shed tears as they hugged each other tightly.

By four o'clock, the police had arrived at Hill House to question Rosa's employer. Jim Brainard brought out the guest registration records. The two officers flipped through the most recent cards, pausing as they noted that two rooms had been vacated the night before. One officer held the card up.

"Nicolas Hondros?" Jim read. "Yes, he and three other men spent the week here—said they were fishing. Hondros and these two came up from Boston. The other one said he was French-Canadian. From Toronto."

"Have they stayed here before, Mr. Brainard?"

"Hondros and his wife were here one night a few weeks ago. But not the others."

"Did they pay by credit card or check?"

"They paid cash. In fact, he gave me some extra, in case they needed something. Didn't want to take it back. I tried to reimburse them when they left."

"You saw them leave?"

"That's right. Sometime after eleven, it was. They said they had to leave early because the one fella had to catch a plane somewhere. An unexpected business situation."

"Did he say where he was going?"

Jim thought for a moment. "Chicago, I think he said. Yes, I'm sure of it. Chicago."

"Is there anything you can remember that was out of the ordinary about these men?"

"No, not so's you'd notice at any rate. I talked with the one fella earlier, after Manuel came by looking for Rosa. Asked him if he'd seen her today. He said no. Not since the day before. Said she'd been here, though. His room had been cleaned. Not that I thought for a minute that it wouldn't be. And her cleaning cart was put away where it always is. I checked after Manuel stopped by. Rosa is . . . was . . . as dependable as anybody you'd ever want to know. A real good worker." Jim paused, then added, "And a real good mother, too."

He looked at the two policemen.

"What in the name of heaven will Manuel and those two boys do? They'll be lost without her."

The officers nodded understandingly.

"She was pregnant, you know."

They looked at one another, then one of them pulled out a notepad. They didn't know. In his grief, Manuel had failed to mention it.

"Is there anything else before we look at the rooms these men occupied, Mr. Brainard? We'd also like to meet your other guests while we're at it."

Jim thought for a moment.

"Hondros, he said he was Greek. They were all Americans, except for the one. But . . ."

"But what?"

"Well, sir. They were all pretty dark-skinned, except one. And they all had dark hair."

"What are you saying?"

"I'm sayin', now that I think about it, they could have been Middle Eastern. You know, Arabs."

The policemen glanced at one another.

"Did you think of this before?" one of the officers asked.

"Well, maybe at first. But they were all Americans, except for the Canadian. And, well, I just figured their ancestry was Greek or Italian or French, like they said. I never was in favor of racial profiling. You know what I mean?"

"So you think they were Middle Eastern?" the officer with the notepad said. Jim shrugged.

"Maybe. I can't be sure. Maybe not."

"Did they arrive together?"

"No. Mr. Hondros came in with his wife the one night. Then when he came back, he was by himself. He had reserved two rooms for a week. Lucky for him, I had two rooms cancel at the last minute. I remember I got the cancellation the day he walked in. He rented a boat, too. It's that cabin cruiser right down there," he said, pointing out the window toward the dock in the distance. "The one over by the sailboat there that's got the twin masts."

"Do you remember the name of the family that canceled?"

"Yep. It's all right here." He thumbed through the register. "A Mr. and Mrs. Thomas Head. From Augusta. The address, phone number, everything. Right here."

The officers took down the information.

"Now, as I was tellin' you, this Hondros fella rented that boat down there. You asked if they arrived here together. Well, after this fella took the rooms, he told me he was goin' to pick up his friends in the boat. Said they were visiting down the coast a bit. He went out alone. Came back with the other three. Matter of fact, I saw 'em. About one or two in the morning. Couldn't sleep, so I happened to be up when they pulled in. I figured he had done just what he'd said. Now I'm beginnin' to wonder."

"What is it that you wonder, Mr. Brainard?"

"I'm wonderin' if he really did pick them up the way he said. If these fellas are Rosa's killers, maybe he picked 'em up offshore somewhere. Coulda' been from a ship out at sea, maybe. I read where there's been lots of folk comin' to America illegally lately, according to the papers. But they've been mostly Mexican and Chinese down south and out west. I don't know, though, maybe that's how these fellas got here. Could they be up to somethin' maybe?"

The officer continued writing. His partner sat quietly, studying Jim Brainard as the old man talked on. Finally he interrupted.

"Mr. Brainard, we'd appreciate it if you'd show us the rooms now. We may need to see them all, but let's start with the two these four men stayed in."

Jim fumbled through his keys until he found the right ones.

"This way, fellas," he said, heading for the staircase.

—ʍ—

By 6:30, the police had questioned the other guests, confirming Rosa's presence the day before. They learned that she habitually made top-floor guests her last stop of the day unless circumstances dictated otherwise. A team of experts checked the two upstairs rooms and found an unusual absence of fingerprints. Only a couple of smudges that were of no value. One clear thumbprint was finally picked up on the underside of a windowsill.

Jim stood in the doorway, watching, when an officer bent down and carefully lifted something up.

"You recognize this, Mr. Brainard?" He held it out as he walked across the room. "I found it over there in the corner. Almost missed it. It was down in the carpet tufts."

Jim swallowed. Tears welled up in his eyes.

"Mr. Brainard?"

"Yes. It belongs to Rosa. Manuel gave it to her on their anniversary. She was so proud of it that it was the first thing she showed me the next day when she came to work. I asked her to sit and have a cup of tea. We talked about Manuel and her boys and how happy she was. You could see it in her eyes. After that I never saw her without it around her neck."

The officer wrote something down. It seemed to Jim that they were always writing something down at odd moments.

"Mr. Brainard. Do you think you could identify these men?"

"Face to face? Absolutely."

"How about in a picture?"

"I think so, yes. Especially one of 'em. He has this scar on his face. Right here," Jim said, touching his cheek.

"And you think they're on their way to Boston?"

"That's what they said. At least as far as Logan. The one fella was supposed to be goin' on from there."

"Good enough." He turned to one of the other men. "Joe, I think it's time to call the FBI. This is a whale of a lot bigger than a local rape and murder. I'm sure of it. We've got good reason to believe that these four have committed a capital crime and that they may have fled across the state line. Kidnapping, rape, and murder. But maybe there's more. Mr. Brainard may also have given us a good idea. Perhaps these four are illegals. If they are, and if they're Arabs or whatever, then we'd better get the net out and drag 'em in. Make an appointment for Mr. Brainard to look at some pictures as soon as possible. Remember those guys started up all the 9/11 chaos by flying out of Portland. Maybe they're back here again."

"Okay, Les. I'm on my way."

They were all back in the Hill House reception area when Randle returned.

"The FBI is with us on this. They'll be contacting you later at the station, Les. I made an appointment for Mr. Brainard to look at pictures tonight in Portland."

"What time?"

"Eight o'clock."

"Will that work for you, sir?"

"Of course. I'll do whatever I can do. You fellas need to know I love that woman and Manuel. They're like my own. And I'm 'Grandpa' to those boys. Now that she's gone, they'll be devastated. This is such a tragedy. Will someone drive me?"

"Joe here will take you."

"Then let me get my jacket. I need to call my Sunday helper to see if she can come in tonight. Then I'll be ready. And can we stop at Manuel's house? I've got to see him before I leave."

41

17 SEPTEMBER, LOCAL TIME 1245
EIN BOKEK, ISRAEL

A cloud of steam escaped from the bathroom as Pasha emerged, wrapped from her shoulders to just above her knees, in a large white towel. The men in the room looked at her, stunned, as she walked over to the window and sat demurely in a chair. Crossing her legs, she tugged at the towel, tucking its edges underneath her at mid-thigh. Her hair was shiny black, still wet from the shower. She looked at the others and gave them an open-handed shrug.

"My clothes were soaked with grime and sweat," she said. "I washed them as best I could and now they're drying. Furthermore, I hope you will all do the same? You smell awful!"

The tension that her appearance had created broke as suddenly as it had come, laughter taking its place. Yazib nodded and headed for the bathroom.

A loud knock on the door froze everyone in place.

Yazib was closest. He peered through the peephole and then opened the door. The man in the light blue suit stepped inside. His eyes darted around the room, stopping with a disapproving look directed at Pasha.

"What is going on in here? Young woman, why are you sitting there half naked?"

"My name is Pasha and my clothes are drying. I am as modest as circumstances allow and my dress or the lack of it is none of your business!"

The man's mouth dropped open as though he could not imagine the insolence to which he had just been subjected. The others, equally startled by Pasha's defiant tone, quickly murmured their approval. She was one of them. A proven member of the team. And nothing untoward was going on.

Yazib stepped forward.

"You are our contact?"

The man's attention turned away from Pasha. For the moment.

"Yes. My name is Amir Yassim. I am the day clerk here at the hotel. This is an envelope with your instructions. If two of you will come with me, I have the equipment you will need locked in a storage area on the first floor."

Pasha scooted forward in the chair. "I'll go," she said sweetly, adjusting her towel, obviously taunting the clerk with her behavior.

The desk clerk's face deepened in color, from embarrassment or anger, or both. "No. It will take two *men* to carry the equipment back to this room."

"Imad, you and Fathi go with Mr. Yassim," ordered Yazib, doing his best not to smile. "Remain alert and try to be as discrete as possible."

The clerk opened the door, then turned, pointing his finger at Pasha. "Young woman, I do not approve of you or your conduct. I intend to include in my report what I have found here today."

Yazib moved closer to the clerk until their faces were only inches apart. "Mr. Yassim. What you have found here are four very hot and dirty soldiers of Islam. It is not always possible for us to conform to all the rules of the faith while we are on the front lines. But I assure you that we will cooperate with you completely. And we expect your cooperation in return."

Yazib's eyes were like flint.

"It would be very unwise of you to include derogatory statements directed at any member of this team," he continued, his voice hard and flat. "Our lives are on the line during this mission, my friend. Yours is not. At least not yet."

The clerk stepped backward through the door, pulling a handkerchief from his pocket and nervously wiping his mouth.

"My apologies. And I will see what I can do about getting all of you some fresh clothing."

He turned and walked down the hallway. Imad and Fathi went with him, one on either side. Yazib closed the door and turned toward Pasha.

"You were not very nice, Pasha," he chided. "We cannot afford to offend those who work with us."

"I know and I am sorry," she pouted, settling back in her chair as she contemplated her toes. "But I cannot stand such pompousness. It makes me ill."

Yazib did not respond.

She looked up. He was grinning. Pasha's face lit up with relief.

"I will take my shower now and hope that our friend will supply some larger towels for us to wear," Yazib mocked her. Pasha shot him a fiery look, but she couldn't keep the smile from her face.

"Good," she retorted. "You stink."

He went in the bathroom and started to close the door.

"Yazib."

He poked his head back into the room.

"Thank you."

His eyes locked with hers for a moment, and he thought about how lovely she looked sitting there, and how he wished they could have met in a different life than the one they were in.

He nodded and closed the door.

A moment later Pasha heard the shower running.

—~—

The clerk was true to his word, supplying a full set of clothing for each one. He also arranged for room service to send up a meal, which the four eagerly devoured before getting down to the business of the evening: checking each gun, grenade, and explosive device that Imad and Fathi had retrieved from the desk clerk's hiding place. The group worked well into the night making sure everything was ready for instant use and then repacked carefully. There would be no time for preparation and no margin for error once the strike was under way.

42

17 September, local time 2015
Portland, Maine

Jim Brainard had been feeling the drain of this dreadful day. The impact of Rosa's death was starting to sink in. Spending a few precious minutes with Manuel had been stressful and poignant, but necessary, though no words could assuage the bereaved husband's grief. During the ride to Portland with the police officer, there was little conversation. The grimness of their mission precluded much in the way of small talk. At 8:15, they pulled into a parking space in front of an obscure, gray building in downtown Portland. On the second floor, they were greeted and ushered into the brightly lit offices of the FBI.

They were ready for him, and once he was settled in it didn't take Jim long before he looked up and motioned one of the agents over.

"This is the man who called himself Nicolas Hondros," Jim said, pointing at the face of Mohammed Ibn Ahmer. "At least that's the name I knew him by."

"This is the man who rented two rooms from you a week ago?"

"One and the same."

"Are you sure?"

He studied the picture again, then looked up.

"Absolutely."

"All right. Thank you, Mr. Brainard. Please keep looking through these photos. Perhaps you will find the others as well."

Thirty minutes later, Jim looked up again and motioned excitedly to the agents.

"I've got another one," he said.

The agents gathered around to see.

"This one."

A sudden stillness enveloped the room.

Jim looked up, quizzically.

"Are you sure, Mr. Brainard?"

"I've never been more positive in my life," Jim assured the agent. "See the scar? It runs along his cheek and into the beard right here. Just like in the picture. That's the man. He's one of the four who have been staying at Hill House. Why? Who is he?"

The men threw glances of concern at each other.

Finally the Special Agent in Charge spoke up.

"His name is Marwan Dosha, Mr. Brainard. You have just identified one of the world's most wanted terrorists. This picture was taken when he was in prison. You're absolutely certain?"

Jim took a deep breath, then let it out slowly. He stared at the picture, nodding emphatically.

"And your Mr. Hondros has been under suspicion as a terrorist link ever since the Trade Center bombing in New York. We brought him in to talk after 9/11, but there has never been anything concrete. He's still on our watch list, but no one has been able to connect him. Then, a few days ago, he dropped out of sight. We lost him. Until now."

Jim tried to absorb what he was hearing.

Terrorists? At Hill House? Unbelievable!

"Steve, get word off to Washington. And contact Ellis in Boston. Have him cover Logan and every bus, train, and car rental in the area with these pictures. Hurry." The agent swore under his breath. "I can't believe this. They started for the Twin Towers right here in Portland. And now this. Mr. Brainard, keep looking. See if you can spot the other two."

Jim spent the next forty-five minutes sorting through the remaining pictures of known terrorists from around the world, but with no luck. He was unable to identify the others.

43

17 September, local time 1834
Ein Bokek, Israel

The Israel Tours bus came to a stop under the entry canopy of the Salt Sea Hotel & Spa around 6:30. The sun was low in the west, but as the passengers stepped down from the bus a blast of hot, desert air hit them. It didn't take long for the group to make their way through the front door and into the lobby area. A young employee in a white jacket moved among the weary travelers with a tray containing small glasses of fresh-squeezed orange juice. There was no lack of takers.

David Barak went straight to the registration desk where he spoke to the man in charge. After a brief exchange, the desk clerk stepped around the end of the counter and approached the group.

John thought him to be a bit overly effusive in his mannerisms.

"Good evening, Reverend," the man gushed. With a half bow, he held out his hand in greeting. John acknowledged the welcome, while silently reaffirming his disdain of limp handshakes.

"I am so glad to welcome you to our hotel. We have been looking forward to your arrival. As you see by my badge, my name is Amir Yassim. You may call me Amir. Whatever you need, sir, we will do our best to provide. I am at your service."

John smiled and thanked him politely.

"And this little girl is your daughter?"

"Yes. Jessica, meet Mr. Yassim."

"*Masa'al-kheir,*" said Jessica, with a smile.

"Ah, Jessica. How wonderful. You honor us. You have been in our land for only a few days and already you are speaking our language! It is a distinct pleasure to greet you."

Mr. Yassim began checking David's passenger list against his own. The others lounged about while watching the driver unload their bags. Still twenty-seven. None lost. Most were heavier than when they had started, however, doubling as hiding places for a growing accumulation of souvenirs purchased along the way.

"You can go swimming tonight if you wish," John told the group. "And tomorrow is a rest and recreation day. We'll not be leaving until late afternoon. This gives everyone an opportunity to sleep in, wash clothes, relax in the sun, or whatever. The idea is for us to arrive in Jerusalem at sunset tomorrow. It should be spectacular.

"Breakfast will be served from seven until nine-thirty at your leisure. Lunch time is twelve noon and we eat together. The bus will leave at four-thirty. Our rooms are only available to us until three, however. Then we have to be out. I would suggest a walk or a quiet time of reading between checkout and four-thirty. Also, don't forget that tomorrow is Sunday. We'll have a worship service by the seashore at nine-thirty. Any questions? Okay, you're on your own. See you at dinner. We'll be eating in the dining room. It's across the lobby through that far door."

Names were called, keys handed out, and the tourists disappeared into the elevators. Most were pleased to see that they would be staying on the fourth floor—the top floor, which held the promise of less noise and possibly even a good night's rest.

44

17 September, local time 1630
Baytown, California

Esther sat next to the window where she had spent so many hours since Jenny's death. A hummingbird darted in and out of the red hibiscus, striking a series of graceful poses in its never ending quest for nourishment. Esther loved hummingbirds. As she watched, her thoughts were with Jessica and John and the others.

I wonder how they're doing?

Absentmindedly, she picked up the Bible laying nearby. It fell open to the book of Job.

How many times have I read your words, Job? I used to dislike what you had to say. You seemed so depressing. Now I understand you so much more than I ever did before. Before all this, I read you from an intellectual point of view. But to really get hold of what you are saying, you must be read with feelings, not simply intellect. I apologize, Job. Maybe we can be friends after all. Sorry I gave you such a bad rap for so long.

Esther thumbed through the dog-eared pages, stopping to read again some of the underlined verses.

> For hardship does not spring from the soil,
> nor does trouble sprout from the ground.
> Yet man is born to trouble
> as surely as sparks fly upward.
> But if it were I, I would appeal to God;
> I would lay my cause before him. . . .
>
> Blessed is the man whom God corrects;
> so do not despise the discipline of the Almighty. . . .

> His wisdom is profound, his power is vast.
> Who has resisted him and come out unscathed? . . .
>
> Though he slay me, yet will I hope in him.

She stared out the window. The hummingbird was gone.

Gone, like my Jenny! But there is nothing I can do about it. Nowhere to look. No one else to turn to. Lord, help me, please. I know that she is gone and I still don't understand why. Were you angry with me? I've surely been angry with you.

Esther felt ashamed as she prayed.

Lord, I'm so sorry for my anger. I've blamed you for not being here when I needed you. Still, I know your wisdom to be so much more profound than mine. I have "resisted" and I've not come out "unscathed." Lord, forgive me. I hurt so very much. I need you to cleanse my mind and heart of this incredible, debilitating guilt. I've got to break out of this depression. Please help me to live again, Jesus. I really do want to live!

She continued her page-turning journey through Job. Several chapters were without underlined verses. Then she came to one she did not remember underlining. But there it was. And it was done with a different color marker than she remembered using.

> But he knows the way that I take;
> when he has tested me, I will come forth as gold.

Lord, I don't remember this verse being here. Did I mark it? Or was it John? Maybe you marked it for me. In any event, thank you for the reminder. I am so grateful that you know the way I take. By faith I am going to hold on to this as your promise to me. Lord, let the tests you take me through cause me to "come forth as gold."

She knelt in front of the window, tears flowing freely as she accepted the power of divine reconciliation into her mind and heart. It was not something of her own making. No, that she knew for certain. She was positive that at this very moment the Greater One was taking the initiative with the lesser. His touch was tender and warm to her weakened spirit. Her faith soared upward. All at once, an incredible lightness replaced the ever-present heaviness in her heart. She gasped. It was like bursting to the surface after being underwater too long. God was at work reconciling her to himself just as he had with Job, centuries earlier. But this wasn't simply an intellectual reconciling. It was like nothing she had ever experienced before.

She was kneeling before an altar, cradling a small child in her arms. She could feel the elfin heartbeat as she hugged this little body to her own with a mother's recognition. She basked in the child's winsome smile and sparkling eyes. Then the little one wriggled free and on tiny feet ambled innocently toward the altar. It was much taller than the child, so she stood beside it for a moment, running her hands over the rough stones.

Turning, she smiled and waved.

Esther started to reach for her. But she could not. She could only watch as, somehow, the child began climbing up the side of the altar. There were no handholds visible and Esther watched in amazement as the little girl made her way easily to the flat surface at the top.

She caught her breath as a man appeared on the side of the altar opposite her. Was he dark-skinned or light? It didn't seem to matter. What mattered was the way he looked at her. In some way an indescribable feeling of compassion transferred between them. Its diffusion was so real . . . like a physical touch. She could not speak. She could not move. There was nothing she could do.

Nothing at all.

The child was standing on top of the altar now, in front of the man, her back to Esther. They appeared to be talking to each other. Esther strained to listen, but couldn't hear what was being said. Slowly the child turned. Her eyes were dancing with delight. She lifted her hand and waved once more. Then she turned to the man standing beside the altar and lifted both her hands as high as she could. Those little hands stretched high above her head were such a familiar sight. Both the child and the man in white were laughing as he reached out to her. She ran to him and he lifted her ever so gently from the altar's surface.

And then they were gone.

Esther blinked.

Outside, the hummingbird was once again dancing in flight over the red hibiscus. It pirouetted to the window and for one brief moment it posed there, holding Esther's gaze.

And then it too was gone.

Nature's *Amen* to eternity's drama.

A holy moment.

One that Esther Cain would never forget.

She dabbed at her tears and looked up, smiling.

You were there with her all the time, weren't you? I should have known.

45

17 SEPTEMBER, LOCAL TIME 2130
NAPA, CALIFORNIA

Like the others embarked on this mission of terror, Akmed and his group worked into the early hours of the morning cleaning, oiling, checking, and double-checking their weapons. Strewn about the living room in semiorganized chaos were AK-47s, hand grenades, plastics, detonating devices, knives, pliers, wire cutters, a small hammer, screwdrivers, a miniature set of wrenches, and as many rounds of ammunition as they could carry.

There was little conversation. The business of the next few hours would be the most serious they had ever undertaken. And probably the last.

In the corner, a television had been turned on earlier in order to watch the news. Its volume was barely audible now and almost forgotten by those present in the room. It was the faint sound of a crowd cheering that caused Akmed to look up. A rerun of the day's earlier football contest between the University of California and Oregon State University was playing itself out on the screen. Halftime had just been reached and the teams were running off the field. California led 24-0. Akmed watched as a camera caught the players heading into the locker room. The door shut behind the last blue California jersey and the station cut away for a commercial break.

Akmed turned his thoughts back to what lay ahead. Like any team sequestered in the locker room at halftime, the young men and the woman in this room were getting ready. They were poised, trained, well-equipped, and primed. They were as seasoned as they could be. All that remained was for them to play out their part of the final half.

A sudden sadness came over him. Looking at the others busily checking and rechecking the tools of their trade, Akmed determined that there was one big difference between his team and the players on the television.

Win or lose, it was unlikely his team would be going home.

17 SEPTEMBER 2210 LOCAL TIME
BOSTON

The boat that Mohammed and Yusif had chartered earlier in the week was an eight-year-old, thirty-four-foot trawler. Mohammed had taken it out for a run, during which he'd been asked to confirm to the rental agent routine docking and navigational skills. He had checked out on all the boat's systems and electronics. Papers were signed under the name of Nicolas Hondros, and the $2000 charter fee for the week was paid in cash.

Darkness was setting in as the four men carried their gear on board. The anthrax canisters and weapons were quickly stored below in the stateroom. Safwat had shopped for provisions at a nearby supermarket. He stowed the perishables in the galley refrigerator.

At 9:30, Mohammed dropped the rental car at a long-term public parking lot near Logan Airport instead of returning it to the rental agency. If the police and the innkeeper somehow put two and two together and began looking for the men who had been driving this car, it would be awhile before they found it. He caught a shuttle, as if he were headed for the terminal to catch a flight. At the terminal, he went inside and waited until the bus moved on. Then he walked outside and hailed a cab. By 10:15, he was back at the boat slip. Lights were out and everyone had settled in by 11:00.

The last few hours had been busy.

Preparations were complete.

The cleaning woman named Rosa was already a fading memory.

They needed a good night's rest.

Tomorrow the strike would take place.

—w—

17 SEPTEMBER, LOCAL TIME 2215
WASHINGTON, D.C.

TO: DIRECTOR OF HOMELAND SECURITY
FROM: NSC NEW EAST / ASIA BUREAU
RE: MOSSAD INTELLIGENCE UPDATE
DATE: 17 SEPTEMBER 2215 EDT
GERMAN SOURCES BELIEVE AS MANY AS THREE LITERS OF

ANTHRAX SPORES—LABELED AS INDUSTRIAL CHEMICALS—MAY HAVE PASSED THROUGH A MUNICH EXPORTING HOUSE FOR SHIPMENT TO AN UNKNOWN DESTINATION. POSSIBLY ATHENS.

SOURCES IN LEBANON REPORT HAMAS AND THE ISLAMIC JIHAD GROUPS ARE GEARING FOR A NEW ATTACK—POSSIBLY IN EUROPE OR ISRAEL OR AMERICA. THIS OPERATION MAY ALREADY BE UNDER WAY. AS 24 SEPTEMBER SIGNING OF THE ISRAEL AND PNA PERMANENT AGREEMENT NEARS, MOSSAD BELIEVES TERRORIST ATTACK INSIDE ISRAEL OR USA IS LIKELY.

INTELLIGENCE DATA HAS BEEN PASSED TO INTERPOL, CIA, FBI. NSA AND THE PRESIDENT HAVE BEEN APPRISED OF A POTENTIAL "SITUATION" ON AMERICAN SOIL.

SOURCE QUALITY: HIGH.

---

17 SEPTEMBER, LOCAL TIME 2230
WASHINGTON, D.C.

TO: FBI, OFFICE OF THE DIRECTOR
FROM: COUNTERTERRORISM DIVISION
RE: MARWAN DOSHA; MOHAMMED IBN AHMER; TWO UNSUBS
DATE: 17 SEPTEMBER 2230 EDT
INCIDENT REPORT

FBI, PORTLAND, ME., REPORTS POSITIVE CIVILIAN ID OF 1] MARWAN DOSHA AND, 2] MOHAMMED IBN AHMER. WANTED FOR QUESTIONING RE MURDER OF ROSA POSADAS, BOOTH BAY, ME. BOTH MEN LINKED WITH MIDDLE EAST TERRORIST ORGS. TWO UNSUBS ARE REPORTED TO BE WITH THEM. ALL BELIEVED TO BE ISLAMIC EXTREMISTS. VERY DANGEROUS. POSSIBLE LOCATION: BOSTON, NYC, DC, OR CHICAGO. THE TWO NAMED SUSPECTS PLUS TWO UNSUBS ARE KNOWN TO HAVE STAYED IN BOOTH BAY, ME., AT A GUEST HOUSE FOR ONE WEEK. CHECKED OUT 09/17.

FBI OFFICES AND LOCAL AUTHORITIES IN BOSTON, NYC, AND CHICAGO HAVE RECEIVED DESCRIPTIONS AND/OR PICTURES OF SUSPECTS. AIRPORTS, TRAIN AND BUS STATIONS, AND CAR RENTAL AGENCIES ARE BEING NOTIFIED.

—∾—

18 SEPTEMBER, LOCAL TIME 0930
WASHINGTON, D.C.

TO: COUNTERTERRORISM DIVISION & RADICAL FUNDAMENTALIST UNIT

FROM: AGENT J. KESSLER, KALISPELL, MT.

RE: UNSUBS, UNKNOWN NUMBER; DOSHA/AHMER LINK

DATE: 18 SEPTEMBER 0930 MDT

INCIDENT REPORT

ACKNOWLEDGE NOTIFICATION RE M. DOSHA, MOHAMMED IBN AHMER AND TWO UNSUBS IN EASTERN USA. POSSIBLE LINK BETWEEN THEIR CASE AND MURDER OF GLACIER PARK RANGER ON 06 SEPTEMBER. BODY FOUND 08 SEPTEMBER. DEATH BY SINGLE STAB WOUND.

LEADS: RECOVERED RAFT AND OUTBOARD MOTOR. RAFT AND MOTOR TRACED TO TORONTO DEALER. PURCHASED WITH CASH BY CUSTOMER BELIEVED TO BE OF MIDDLE EASTERN DESCENT. A WATERTON PARK RANGER HAS DESCRIBED MIDDLE EASTERN MAN AND WOMAN ENTERING WATERTON PARK WITH THE RAFT ON BLUE MINIVAN. ONTARIO PLATES. VAN AND OCCUPANTS HAVE NOT BEEN LOCATED.

REQUEST EVALUATION LIKELIHOOD THE SUPRA INCIDENT IS CONNECTED WITH BOOTH BAY TERRORISTS ENTRY INTO USA.

RCMP CONTINUES SEARCH FOR MINIVAN. ARTIST DESCRIPTIONS OF THE TWO UNSUBS HAVE BEEN CREATED AND DISTRIBUTED TO OUR OFFICES IN ALL WESTERN STATES AND CANADIAN PROVINCES.

REQUEST PERMISSION TO CONTINUE LIAISON WITH RCMP.

The message from Kalispell's FBI office was received midmorning on Sunday. Helen Cartier put down her lukewarm cup of coffee and pulled the message, glancing at its contents. She knew that the division head, Gerald Lawford, had returned to Washington after speaking at a law enforcement convention in Atlanta on Saturday night. On Sunday mornings, he and his family usually attended services at Messiah Lutheran Church, near their suburban Virginia home.

Cartier looked at her watch.

She was not sure whether her boss would be sleeping or attending church.

She smiled.

Maybe he's doing both.

In any event, this could wait.

At least for a few hours.

She dropped the message in Lawford's priority folder and returned to the paperwork scattered across her desk.

PART FOUR

Allah is its Goal.
The Messenger is its Leader.
The Quran is its Constitution.
Jihad is its methodology, and
Death for the sake of Allah is its
most coveted desire.

—Motto of the Islamic Resistance Movement
Hamas

Of a truth ye are stronger [than they] because of the terror in their hearts, [sent] by Allah. This is because they are men devoid of understanding.

—The Qur'an
Sura 59: Hashr:13

If you hold to my teaching, you are really my disciples.
Then you will know the truth, and the truth will set you free.

—The Holy Bible
John 8:31–32

46

SUNDAY, 18 SEPTEMBER, LOCAL TIME 1000
BOSTON

Anthrax has been identified by Defense Department officials as their choice for the ideal biological weapon. It has the dubious distinction of being the granddaddy of biological weapons. Winston Churchill recognized its military possibilities as early as 1925.

In 1942, British researchers turned fiction into fact at the Porton Down Microbiological Research Establishment, by exploding the first anthrax bombs on a rocky outcrop of an island known as Gruinard, off the northwest coast of Scotland. When sheep tethered in concentric circles died within days, it was hailed as a great success. The following summer, a bomber dropped another anthrax bomb on the island. It has since been determined that anthrax spores can survive for well over fifty years. To this day, Gruinard remains contaminated and off-limits.

By 1944, American researchers at the Camp Detrick center for biological warfare research had produced five thousand anthrax bombs, and military strategists conceived a plan for their use to wipe out six German cities. This saturation bombing with anthrax never took place because the war ended. If the plan would have been carried out, the cities of Berlin, Hamburg, Frankfurt, Stuttgart, Aachen, and Wilhelmshaven would still be contaminated cemeteries today.

In the early 1960s, the United States military phased anthrax out of its arsenal of biological weapons, because it was discovered to lurk in the soil indefinitely, denying the target area to friend and foe alike.

In June 1979, stories leaked concerning a terrible accident at a secret biological weapons research facility in Sverdlovsk, Russia. Reports from this industrial city of about one and a half million people, located in the rolling hills of the Ural valley, 850 miles east of Moscow, posted the death toll at a thousand, with additional thousands injured by the dread disease of anthrax. Russia insisted that the anthrax outbreak was due to natural causes resulting from people having eaten contaminated meat. Experts, however, believed the reports of swift death had to do with inhalation anthrax, which kills within two or three days. Inhalation anthrax occurs only when some force propels it into the air, thus giving further credence to the story of a biological accident resulting from an explosion.

Following the demise of the Soviet Union, economics dictated the closure of the research and development center in Sverdlovsk and other similar institutions throughout the countryside of the former Soviet republics. Numerous scientists, skilled in their knowledge of biochemical warfare techniques, were displaced and forced to stand in bread lines. When it became obvious that their future was nonexistent in post-Cold War Russia, large numbers left for other countries where their services would be well reimbursed. Syria, Iran, Iraq, Egypt, Lebanon, and Libya were all bidders in the mad dash to acquire mass destruction weapons capable of annihilating hundreds of thousands of people at a time.

In a secret terrorist training camp in Lebanon's sun-baked Baaka Valley, Marwan Dosha, together with Yusif Shemuda and Safwat Najjir, had been schooled in the use of the deadly anthrax spores. Mohammed Ibn Ahmer had no training in biological warfare other than what he had gathered the last few days, listening and observing as the others rehearsed the steps they would be taking. He was an excellent boatman, however, and also knew Greater Boston better than the others. He was not expected to have to work with the special weapons, except as a last resort.

While everything hinged on whether or not world leaders would act on their ultimatum with immediate and all due seriousness, there was little doubt their demands would be rejected. They were confident they would use their biological weapons. It would be a necessary demonstration in order to bring the world to its knees. And they were ready. In fact, they would be disappointed if they didn't get the chance to display the power of mass destruction in their possession on this most glorious day in history!

At 8:30, they had split up. Yusif cast off the lines and hopped on board the chartered trawler. Mohammed expertly backed the boat away from its slip and into deeper water. Then he brought her about and headed slowly out into the Charles River.

Dosha and Najjir, each with a pack on their back, walked away from the slip until they reached Commercial Avenue. There they parted. Najjir went to check into a nearby hotel, while Dosha ordered a cab to take him into the heart of the city. At the corner of Charles and Beacon Streets, Dosha paid the driver and waited while he drove off. He looked at his watch. Ten o'clock. Seven on the West Coast, where he knew their team was getting ready to attack the unsuspecting California target. He also knew that the team in occupied Palestine was prepared as well.

He smiled. The climax was near. He was beginning to taste the excitement that always came to him just before turning unsuspecting enemies into victims of the *jihad.*

When he was growing up in the West Bank town of Ramalla, throwing rocks at Israeli tanks and soldiers was expected of boys his age. As he matured, his mind had been further inflamed with religious rhetoric by the mullahs' passionate calls to resistance. But now, years later, his *raison d'être* had surpassed a righteous call to destroy the enemies of Islam. Dosha had developed a taste for terror. And he was very good at what he did. A star. Number one. At least until Osama had come along. In his mind, he still was. Feared by the world. Admired by other young boys and men in his homeland who had never graduated beyond throwing stones. After this special operation was finished, there would be no question in the minds of the world's citizens. Marwan Dosha would definitely be number one. That was important!

He walked over to a park bench and sat down. Slipping the straps away from his shoulders, he placed the pack in his lap. Thirty or forty people, half of whom were children, were lounging or reading or playing in nearby Frog Pond.

Not so many, but enough for the demonstration.

He reached into the backpack and pulled out a PDA, made the connection, entered the prearranged code phrase, and pushed the send button. Then he waited.

One minute.

Two.

Dosha smiled. He saw the coded response appear on the handheld data assistant. First from Safwat in his hotel room. Then from Mohammed and Yusif.

Everyone is ready to begin.

Dosha leaned back, closing his eyes at the sudden rush of pleasure. He was about to signal the world that he was in control. He locked his hands behind his head as the soft September breeze played around his face.

Sounds of laughter filled the air as little children splashed their way in and out of Frog Pond. They did not want this glorious day to end.

But in a few short minutes, it would.

He looked around. Then he saw them.

Four adults. Five small children.

They will do fine. Like rats in a laboratory. Only better.

Two of the adults were men, sharing a blanket and a Sunday morning edition of the *Boston Globe.* One offered up a disgruntled groan while reading the box score of the Red Sox game.

Every April, Bostonians touch their beer steins together and declare this to be the year of the Bosox. Come September, true Sox fans sink into an undeniable "Fenway funk" at the realization that their team will again not make the playoffs. Recently, the Sox had come through for their fans, but this year . . .

The indefatigable sports fan rolled over onto his elbows, spreading the newspaper out flat on the blanket. He was now engrossed in a story about the preseason prospects of the New England Patriots, who were off to a shaky start in exhibition.

The other man skimmed the front section, including a page-three article about yesterday's rape and murder of a married woman in Booth Bay, Maine. She had two sons and a third child on the way. No motive was cited and no suspects had been identified. He glanced over at his own two children, splashing in the water at the edge of the pond. His wife was engrossed in conversation with her best friend. They were together. Safe. That's all that mattered today. He turned the page.

The two young mothers were facing each other yoga style, tracing imaginary lines through the grass with their fingers, engrossed in a discussion of what they were going to do this fall now that each of their youngest had joined the rest of their children in school. From where he was sitting on the park bench, Marwan Dosha couldn't hear their conversation, but he saw the blonde throw back her head in laughter while her dark-haired friend reached out a hand in mock protest over whatever had just been said.

Dosha stood up and strolled toward the tiny, tranquil gathering. As he drew near, the blonde woman squinted up at him, the sun hitting directly in her eyes. He smiled politely and she turned back to her friend, who was still talking.

Three or four steps more. Dosha appeared to fumble something, dropping it in the grass. Bending down, he picked it up and continued walking.

More sounds of laughter.

Life is good, isn't it?

If someone had looked in the grass where the dark-skinned man had stopped to pick up what he had dropped, they would have realized that he had not picked anything up. He had left something.

A tiny, three-inch stainless steel canister.

He was counting on the fact that no one would notice.

No one did.

Five minutes later, with a muted pop, it exploded.

A small aerosol-like spray cloud poofed into the air. The light breeze swept it toward the adults. They looked up, startled.

"What was that?" the dark-haired woman asked.

"You got me," the other replied.

They looked in the direction of the sound.

Meanwhile, dispersed by the soft September breeze, the tiny cloud floated toward the children.

—∾—

18 SEPTEMBER, LOCAL TIME 1000
BAYTOWN, CALIFORNIA

Nearly seven hundred people were singing the opening hymn in Calvary Church's second service as the 1997 Chevy van with California plates turned into the main parking lot. The three volunteer parking attendants had just finished their assignments and were walking up the steps to the church's main entrance when the van came to a stop in one of two remaining handicap parking spaces next to the north side entrance.

One of the volunteers stopped to look.

"Someone is late," he observed. "Think we should go help them?"

The others turned to check out the van.

"Naw, let's go in. Looks like there's a young person driving. They'll be okay. I want to find Debbie before the singing is over."

They needed no further encouragement. They enjoyed their ministry as parking attendants. Smiling. Helping people. Welcoming and giving directions to newcomers. But it always meant getting into the service after it started. With one last glance at the parked van, they hurried through the door.

Faint sounds of singing could be heard coming from the sanctuary as Akmed, Ihab, Mousa, and Aziza jumped out of the van. There was no one in sight. Good. Surprise was essential. The four scooped up bags and boxes and ran for the entrance. Mamdouh waited anxiously, transferring the rest of the supplies from the back of the van onto the pavement. Mousa and Ihab rushed back to the van and quickly gathered all but two of the remaining boxes in their arms. Mamdouh picked those up and followed after them. Exactly as they had rehearsed. Nothing left to chance.

They stacked their supplies along the inside wall of the empty hallway that encircled the sanctuary. Akmed and Aziza had earlier determined that there were four public entrances leading into the worship area, plus one on either side of the platform. Six altogether. Because there were only five of them and it would be physically impossible to begin the strike by covering all the doors, they had decided on a bold plan, full of surprise, deception, and trickery. No one had ever done what they were about to do, so they felt confident that shock and surprise would work to their advantage.

The singing had stopped. As the congregation stood for the pastoral prayer, the sounds of collective movement just beyond the door startled the terrorist team. For an instant they remained frozen. Then a woman's voice was heard guiding the congregation in prayer.

Beads of perspiration formed as they tore into one of the bags and drew out the freshly serviced and already loaded automatic weapons. Akmed's mind was racing. He remembered that in the services he and Aziza had attended, people sometimes moved toward the exits following a prayer. They needed to be in position before then.

"They are praying," he hissed to the others. "They stand and close their eyes for prayer while someone leads them. Get inside before they finish!"

Aziza peeked around the corner into the main lobby. It was completely deserted. "*Now!*" she whispered, leading the dash across the large, empty space. Their feet were silent on the thick carpet, but she was feeling more vulnerable than she had ever felt in her life.

In seconds, Aziza was at the far door. Akmed took up his position at the central entrance. Mousa was at the door nearest the weapons cache. Ihab and Mamdouh remained in their kneeling positions, busily arming the detonators and preparing plastic explosives. Neither man looked up.

Akmed threw a glance at Mousa, then at Aziza. Through small viewing windows in the doors they could see the congregation, still standing and focused in prayer.

"And, Lord," the woman was nearing her conclusion, "we especially pray for Pastor Cain and all those who are with them in Israel this morning. Watch over them. Keep them safe and free from danger . . ."

At that moment, a young boy came out of the restroom and walked straight up to Aziza. He looked to be six, or maybe seven years old. His huge brown eyes took her in from head to toe, and then fastened on the gun in her hand.

"Watcha doing, lady?"

Aziza stared at the lad, speechless. This was not part of the plan. Desperately, she looked over at Akmed, whose attention had been drawn in her direction by the sound of the boy's voice.

The lad continued to look up at Aziza, waiting for an answer.

"Are you a Sunday school teacher?" he asked, finally.

"*Yes*," Aziza whispered. "Now, go over there and sit down." She pointed to a folding chair against the wall.

"No. I have to go back to my mom and dad." Before she could react, the little boy pulled the door open, just enough to slip inside.

". . . and lead us not into temptation . . ." the congregation continued reciting the Lord's Prayer together.

Akmed nodded, reaching for the door. A moment later the three were inside.

". . . and deliver us from evil. For thine is the kingdom, and the power . . ."

They hid their weapons behind them, hugging the back wall as tightly as they could.

". . . and the glory forever. Amen."

There was a rustle as the congregation sat down.

The little boy tugged on his father's jacket. "Daddy, look. That woman over there? She's a Sunday school teacher. And she's got a gun."

The boy's father glanced in Aziza's direction, puzzled at what his son could be talking about. He did a double-take at the woman standing near the door, her back against the wall. She *was* holding a gun! Not just any gun. He recognized the AK-47 from his tour in the army.

"What the—"

A burst of gunfire directly behind him stopped him in midsentence. He dove for cover, instinctively pulling his wife and son down with him.

—⁂—

18 SEPTEMBER, LOCAL TIME 1545
THE DEAD SEA, ISRAEL

It seemed as if they had been over their plans at least fifty times, though twenty was probably a more accurate count. Their weapons had been checked and checked again. Tension ran high as Yazib looked at his watch. Five minutes had passed since he had looked at it the last time. The only sound was that of the room's air conditioner, providing them with one of the last vestiges of comfort that they would enjoy for some time. Maybe forever.

Pasha was nearest the door when the knock came.

She opened it.

Amir Yassim, the desk clerk, stepped inside. He gave Pasha a hard look of animosity, running his dark eyes up and down the white jacket, blouse, and light blue skirt that was the Salt Sea Hotel & Spa staff uniform for women personnel. He said nothing. Instead, he pushed past her and stood in front of Yazib.

"It is time."

Yazib held the desk clerk's gaze for a long moment. Then he turned to the others.

"This is it then. We are ready." He spoke to Yassim. "Where is the driver?"

"He has gone to start up their bus. It takes a little while for the air conditioner to bring the temperature down inside."

Brilliant. State the obvious.

"Their bags have been stored in the bus. The group is gathering in the lobby. They plan to leave on time," he continued.

"You have been a great help, Mr. Yassim," Yazib said as he guided the man to the door. "You had best return to your duties now. Thank you for your hospitality."

The clerk nodded. He stood still a moment longer, as if waiting for a tip. Seeing that none was offered and no further conversation was forthcoming, he licked his lips nervously, glancing over at Pasha one last time. Then he turned and left, closing the door behind him.

The four stood in a circle, silently holding out their hands until each touched the other. They might have been an American basketball team, ready to go out and do damage to their rival. Slowly they removed their hands and stepped back. Yazib smiled.

"*Allah u Akbar!* Go, Pasha. And hurry. We will soon follow."

47

18 September, local time 1005
Baytown, California

For one extraordinarily long moment, there was stunned stillness.

All eyes were drawn to a young dark-skinned man, dressed in a peach-colored sport shirt open at the neck, blue jeans, and tennis shoes. He held an automatic weapon in his hands.

In the next second, pandemonium broke out.

Screams. Frightened cries. Shouts of "What's going on?" and "What is this?" could be heard throughout the sanctuary. Some people jumped to their feet and pushed into the aisles, instinctively heading for the exits.

Another burst of gunfire, this time on the left side of the sanctuary.

Everyone froze in their tracks. Faces swiveled in the direction of the new sounds. A beautiful, dark-haired woman stood in front of the exit door, feet spread apart, holding a gun in front of her, looking very professional and very serious.

"Sit down, please," Akmed ordered. "If you remain in your seats, you will not be hurt. Do not worry. Soon you will all be released."

A man seated on the left front row jumped to his feet and bounded up the three platform steps, heading for the exit. He was almost at the door when Yazib calmly pointed his weapon and fired. Bullets thudded into the wall to the man's left. Others cut through his jacket. Staggering forward, he fell onto the platform floor.

Screams of horror erupted. An elderly woman sank between the pews in a faint.

"Silence!" roared Akmed.

Every eye became riveted on the young man in the center aisle with the AK-47. The man who had just shot Jake Lunder, the head usher.

"Understand this," Akmed spoke loudly, pausing to smile benignly at the people in the pews. "You will not be hurt unless you do something foolish. If you try to run, you will be shot. Even as I speak, the exit doors are being sealed with explosives. If anyone tries to come in or go out, it will mean their death and the death of others. Nothing is to be gained by foolhardy actions. Remain calm, do what you are told, and you will not be harmed."

Lowering his voice, he nodded at Crystal Abrams, the organist. "Now if you please, may we enjoy some music?"

Crystal did not move, paralyzed by the events unfolding in front of her.

"Play," Akmed motioned at her with his rifle. "We enjoy the organ music. It will help calm us all."

Slowly, Crystal sat forward and moved her hands to the organ keys, placing her feet on the pedals. Soft music began flowing from the large speakers overhead. Though the song was not familiar to their three unwelcome visitors, its meaning was not lost on the people of Calvary Church, who recognized the soothing strains of "It Is Well with My Soul."

On the far right, near the back, a well-dressed man stood to his feet.

"Sit down," Mousa commanded sharply. Akmed looked over in that direction.

The man remained on his feet, careful not to make any sudden move that could be wrongly interpreted by these strangers. His voice shook at first, becoming stronger as he directed each word to the man who was the apparent leader, standing in the center aisle.

"I do not know who you people are or what you want. But I am a doctor. The man you just shot is our friend, Jake Lunder. We know him. We know his family. He needs medical attention. You must let me go to him."

The congregation was still, their attention fixed on this new drama.

"Please," Dr. Orwell pleaded, hands extended outward, palms up.

Akmed directed his gaze at the man who had spoken out.

"What is your name?"

"Sidney Orwell."

"All right, Doctor Sidney Orwell, you may examine him. However, I can assure you that it is not necessary. He does not need your help."

Sidney Orwell touched his wife's shoulder reassuringly as he moved past her into the aisle. There were three center aisles that converged on the platform, in addition to the aisles at the far left and right of the auditorium. Pews were arranged in a manner that gave the appearance of a gentle crescent curve, with the floor sloping gradually toward the platform and pulpit. This design permitted everyone to participate with the awareness of others being present, while at the same time never losing sight of the pulpit, the communion table, and the choir.

Dr. Orwell hurried down the right center aisle and crossed over the open area between the front pews and the platform. He went up the steps and knelt beside Jake Lunder, feeling for a pulse. Then he turned Jake over and placed his ear against Jake's chest. Every eye strained to see some signal of hope. A groan went up as they saw Dr. Orwell shoulders slump. He brushed his fingers over Jake's eyes, closing them for the last time. Slowly he stood up and turned toward the congregation that waited for an official pronouncement of what they already knew in their hearts.

Dr. Orwell glared angrily at the young man with the gun, his voice passionate. "You were right. The man you shot . . . *in the back* . . . is dead!"

The collective exhalation was followed by soft sobs. Whispers of, "Oh, no," could be heard scattered through the sanctuary. Dr. Orwell scanned the crowd, looking for Thelma and Laura, Jake's wife and daughter. He was relieved that he did not see them there. It was strange, though. The Lunders were so faithful. They never missed church.

Unless one of them is sick.

Dr. Orwell's mind raced as he looked into the lenses of Calvary's three television cameras. They were positioned strategically, two on either side of the balcony and one on the main floor. He saw the red light illuminated on camera three. The 9:30 worship service, televised live each Sunday and fed by cable to a local Baytown station for immediate airing, was on the air right now. Those cameras were windows through which the viewing audience had to be seeing the crisis that was developing inside Calvary Church. A wave of relief swept over him. Help will surely be on the way. Then he tensed.

If Thelma and Laura are at home, sick . . . they may have watched this whole tragic affair. If that's the case, what must they be going through right now? Take care of them, Lord. And us, too.

—~—

Jeremy sat like a coiled spring on the edge of the pew, third row center, watching the astonishing events taking place around him. As Dr. Orwell started to leave the platform, Jeremy felt a movement to his left. He glanced over at Allison, instantly registering the concerned horror on her face. Allison's gaze was fixed on her father. As he walked across the front of the church, she leaned forward to call out. Jeremy, seeing what she intended to do, clutched at her arm and pulled her back.

Startled, Allison turned toward Jeremy. With a slight head motion, he signaled her to be quiet. Her body was tense against his arm, but she did not move. Her eyes followed her father to his seat. She saw her mother's worried look and tried catching her eye, but Helen Orwell was focused on her husband as he came up the aisle.

Jeremy glanced at Esther. Her face was pale, her eyes closed.

How will Mom handle this? Will this push her over the edge?

He started to put his hand out, then stopped. He saw her lips moving silently in prayer.

48

Emergency response operator Helen Garvez took the call at exactly 10:14.

"Hello, you've reached 9-1-1."

"Yes. I've been watching the telecast of the Baytown Calvary Church's worship service. I think something is wrong. There are people with guns in there and somebody has been shot! They need help."

"Your name, please?"

"Sylvia Wall."

"You say you're watching television?"

"Yes. I can't get out to church anymore, so I watch Calvary Church of Baytown. Their service comes on at nine-thirty every Sunday. But I just saw people with guns there. And they shot somebody!"

"Are you sure this is not a television movie you're watching?"

"No. It is a church service. I see it every Sunday. You've got to do something!" The caller's voice was becoming agitated.

"All right, Sylvia. Calm down. Do you know the church address?"

"I can't remember it exactly. They show it at the end of the program, though."

"We'll find it, Sylvia. The police will check it out immediately. You did say that someone has a gun?"

"Not just someone. I'm watching right now and it looks like two or three people with guns."

"Thank you, Sylvia. We'll check it out."

Helen turned to her coworker. "I've heard some strange ones, but this is right up there. I'm sending a policeman to a church because a woman thinks she sees somebody there with a gun. She says she's getting all this from her television set."

"God works in mysterious ways," the other operator chuckled, leaning forward in her chair to answer another call.

"Hello, you've reached 9-1-1."

"Yes. I know this will sound strange, but I've been watching Calvary Church's worship service on television. And I think something is wrong there. It looks like there are people with guns in the auditorium. I think somebody was just shot!"

The operator glanced over at her colleague. "Helen, I've got another one about the church."

But Helen didn't answer.

She was busy with another incoming call.

—w—

"Hey, Frank, turn on the tube, will you? Emergency dispatch is getting calls about some people with guns over at Calvary Church. They say they're watching it on television."

"What channel?"

"How should I know? They have a service on TV every Sunday, but I've never watched it. My kid goes to their school, though. It's that big church over on Twenty-first Street."

Sergeant Frank Castor waited momentarily for a picture to appear on the screen. Then starting at channel 2, he began flipping through the channels. Cartoons. News interviews. A rerun of yesterday's Cal–Oregon State game. MTV. More cartoons. He paused at Channel 17, KMAN, an independent, originating in Baytown. Their studios were only a few blocks away, on the top floor of the Burton Building.

"Here it is," he said, stepping back from the set.

Lieutenant Joe Randle got up from his desk and came around to stand beside Sergeant Castor. Their faces registered surprise that turned serious as they stared at the picture on the screen. It was Calvary Church all right. Randle remembered being there for a meeting that included all the school parents. There were so many that the church's sanctuary had to be used. He and Emily had sat over there on the right side about halfway back, where three teenagers were huddled at the moment. He noted the location mentally, while trying to discern what was going on.

The organ was playing.

A man was kneeling over someone on the platform.

Randle stepped forward and turned up the volume.

Someone was down on the floor. The other man, well-dressed in a suit and tie, was getting up now and facing the audience. The camera moved in on his face. It was flushed. He was obviously fighting to stay in control of his emotions. They heard him speaking to someone off camera.

"You were right. The man you shot . . . *in the back* . . . is dead!"

The man's face faded from view and was replaced by that of another man. Young. Good looking. Fade. A full room scene came up on the screen.

"Joe, look. That guy has an automatic. Looks like an AK-47."

Lieutenant Randle whirled around and poked his head through the open door. "Cindy. There's a guy over at Calvary Church with a gun. Looks as though he may have shot somebody already. APB our guys on patrol. For starters, I want every street closed off around that church!"

"Yes sir, got it." The dispatcher began relaying the lieutenant's orders over the police radio channel. "Anything else?"

Lieutenant Randle did not answer. He was staring at the television, motioning with his hand for quiet.

The camera shot revealed most of the sanctuary now. The two policemen could see at least three people, all holding automatic weapons. A fourth person was kneeling at one of the sanctuary doors, working with something.

Randle swore.

"See that guy? Over at the door? He's got to be sealing it off with explosives. Isn't that what it looks like to you?"

As Frank Castor watched, he shook his head.

"I wouldn't believe this if I wasn't standing right here watching."

He scanned the picture on the screen. The producer at the television studio was doing a fine job of mixing the camera shots to show as much of the activity at the church as possible. Now the cameras were zooming in on the faces of the gunmen.

"I don't know who's on those cameras," Castor said, "but they've got guts. I wonder if those characters know they're on 'Candid Camera'?"

"Do you see what I see, Frank?"

"What?"

"Look."

"They all look like—"

"Arabs!" Randle confirmed. "Come on."

They rushed for the door. "Cindy, you'd better contact the chief. And get ahold of the FBI in San Francisco. Ask for Duane Webber if he's there. I want their negotiating team out here, pronto. If they're not available, then get ahold of that guy with the Oakland PD. You know, the one who talked that woman with the baby off the Bay Bridge last week? Was his name Cole? Something like that."

"You want a negotiator?"

"I'm not sure yet. But I think we may have a group of terrorists holding a church full of people hostage, so stay alert."

The dispatcher looked up in astonishment.

"Terrorists?" she repeated. "In Baytown? Are you serious?"

The two policemen were already out the door.

—∞—

"Terrorists? Get out of here. At a church? You're pulling my leg, right?"

Police Chief Jim White leaned back in his chair and clasped his hands behind his head.

"Turn on the tube, Chief," Joe Randle said over the police radio as he and Frank Castor turned onto Second Avenue and sped across town. "You can see for yourself. At least we could five minutes ago at the station."

"Okay. Listen, I'll meet you there," Chief White said. "Should be with you in ten minutes. And don't turn on any sirens!"

49

18 SEPTEMBER, LOCAL TIME 1015
SAN FRANCISCO

Assistant news director Jody Ansel pushed through the main entrance of station KFOR on San Francisco's Stockton Street. The Hispanic security guard looked up from behind his desk, smiled in recognition, and turned back to the three black-and-white security monitors in front of him.

"Hi, Paulo," Jody waved as she passed by the ugly modern art statuary in the center of the lobby. She glanced up at the four Sony overhead monitors, all tuned to KFOR. The early NFL game was just getting under way. Jody thought that whoever had the clever idea of placing four monitors in the lobby entrance, all tuned to Channel 4, deserved an award.

Anything worth doing is worth overdoing.

She pushed the elevator button. As she waited, she noticed a stack of brochures announcing a fund-raiser for Oakland Children's Hospital. The event had taken place two weeks ago. She scooped up the brochures and a tattered copy of the weekly *Bay Guardian* as the elevator doors opened.

On the second floor, she stopped by her desk, depositing her purse in one of the drawers and dumping the newspaper and the out-of-date brochures in the wastebasket. She proceeded to the news desk and began sorting through the latest newspapers and bulletins from Reuters and the Associated Press. Her watch said 10:25, same as the clock on the wall. She was late, but it was Sunday.

Things were quiet in the newsroom. Across the room, Sally Duggan was trying to coax the coffeemaker into doing its thing. It had gotten especially stubborn of late. Copywriter Jerry Leighton was busy at his desk. She knew that Vern McNair was overseeing the control room on the third floor. Sunday morning's skeleton crew. Ninety minutes until the Channel 4 Noon Update.

Get with it, Jody.

Her phone rang. Once. Twice.

"Jody Ansel."

"Jody!" The excited voice fairly shouted her name. "This is Jim over at Daystar. Check out Channel 17. We're feeding live from Calvary Church in Baytown. They've got a hostage situation under way!"

"A what?" Jody lowered the phone and waved to get someone's attention. Sally looked up. "Sally, bring up Channel 17.

"What do you know about it, Jim?" Jody knew Jim Wilson on a casual basis. Daystar Cable had a contract for daily televised news updates by KFOR anchors. These news briefs were used on the various cable channels that were a part of the Daystar system.

"Just what you see."

"Thanks, Jim. Gotta run."

Sally was staring at the images coming on the monitor. She turned to look at Jody.

"Check the police calls. I'm going to run a crawl line." Jody dialed the control room intercom.

"I'm sending you a crawl line, Vern. It's hot. Get ready for a busy morning."

Jody fed the notice into the computer and sent it to the control room on the third floor. A few seconds later, the black crawl line appeared just below the green and white jerseys slugging it out back in Philadelphia, and made its way across the newsroom monitor screens.

THIS IS A SPECIAL CHANNEL 4 NEWS BULLETIN: UNCONFIRMED REPORTS INDICATE A HOSTAGE SITUATION MAY BE DEVELOPING AT THE CALVARY CHURCH IN THE SUBURBAN COMMUNITY OF BAYTOWN. SOURCES REPORT UNIDENTIFIED PERSONS ARMED WITH AUTOMATIC WEAPONS HOLDING CHURCH ATTENDEES HOSTAGE. STAY TUNED.

The crawl line was repeated three times.

Jody pulled her list of emergency home numbers out of the side drawer and began punching numbers as fast as her fingers could move.

But it *was* Sunday morning.

"You've reached the Foster residence. We can't come to the phone right now. At the beep, leave a message and we'll get back to you as soon as possible."

"Alice. This is Jody. We've got a hot one. A hostage situation at a church in Baytown. I need you in here." Alice Foster was KFOR's news director and Jody's immediate superior.

"Hello?" The familiar television voice of Tom Bernstein sounded hoarse and groggy this morning.

"Tom. This is Jody. Sorry. I know you were out late last night with the benefit at the St. Francis. But you've got to get in here now!"

"What's up?"

"A hostage situation. Some crazies are holding an entire congregation out in Baytown."

"Confirmed?"

"I'm watching it happen in front of me. Daystar is showing a live feed from inside the church."

"I'll be there in fifteen." The phone clicked. Jody checked the time again. She knew that Tom lived in Marin County. His commute across the Golden Gate Bridge would take twenty-five minutes on a good day.

"Sally, help me make some calls. We've got to get a crew going."

Jody called the home of George Mason, KFOR's corporate president. She knew that he and his family were vacationing in Hawaii, but she wanted her message to be on his voicemail. That way at least Mason would know she had thought of him.

Finally, the call to her least favorite person, Betty Filtcher, the station's senior vice president. Conniving. Conceited. Controlling. Ambition personified in a tight-lipped package of dyed hair and plastic surgery. Worse yet, she was bossy and inclined to bad decision making, Jody dreaded her interference if this thing really took off. But there was nothing she could do about it.

"Hello?"

"Hi, Betty. I'm glad I caught you." *Lie.* "We've got a story coming over Daystar. A hostage situation in a Baytown church. I thought you'd want to know." *You'll want to have both sets of claws right in the middle of it.* "The Masons are in Hawaii, so you're the senior person, Betty." *Wipe your chin, Betty. I can see you drooling over the prospect of being in charge.*

"I'm coming down as soon as I get dressed. Do you have confirmation?"

"I'm watching a direct feed from the church right now."

"What have you done so far?"

"I called Alice. Left a message. Tom is on his way. We're putting a crew together. As soon as we have one, I'll send them down the road. We should be on site in forty-five. Maybe sooner."

"Alice is spending the weekend with her kids in Mendocino. I don't know how to reach her. Push for sooner, Jody. I want us to be the first on site!"

"I'm workin' on it."

Jody put the phone down. "Such is life in media-land," she murmured to herself.

—w—

Monitoring the police scanner brought further confirmation that a big story was breaking.

Exactly twenty minutes from the time he had hung up the phone, Tom Bernstein burst into the newsroom. "Sally. Find somebody to park my car when you get a break, will you? Here's the keys. It's out front. Thanks. What's happening, Jody?"

"Channels 2, 5, 7, and 20 are all at crawl-line status. Nothing else. We were first up," she added smugly.

"Get me on the air. Maybe being first up to bat on this thing will help our ratings. God knows we could use some help."

Tom's shirt was open. He had not taken time to shave or put on a tie. He threw his jacket on the back of his desk chair and strode over to the update desk, a small cubicle designed for special bulletins and update reporting, located at the far end of the newsroom. He did not take time to put on makeup. Part of the station's economy crunch had forced the news personalities to take care of their own television makeup. He would do that later.

He glanced at a pink-colored script outlining the few details known at the moment. Jody had typed it herself. Spelling and punctuation were unimportant.

"Fifteen seconds."

Tom looked up and grinned. He nodded.

Jody had put on a headset and was acting as the floor director, taking her cues from Vern upstairs. She stood by the camera, her hand signals counting down.

Five, four, three, two, one . . .

"Good morning. This is Tom Bernstein with a special news bulletin from Channel 4's twenty-four-hour news desk. It has now been confirmed that at approximately ten o'clock this morning, the worshipers gathered at Baytown's Calvary Church had the quiet peacefulness of their church service shattered by gunfire. Just who the gunmen are and what they want is not known. Unconfirmed reports indicate that it is a group of Middle Eastern terrorists. They are currently holding the entire congregation hostage, a group estimated to be several hundred people.

"The pictures you are now seeing are live from the church's weekly service, normally seen on Channel 17. Police have surrounded the church. The FBI is responding as well. All streets leading into the area have been blocked off. If you have family or friends who may be in attendance at Calvary Church, please stand by. Law enforcement officials are requesting that you do not call the church or local police at this time. All lines must be kept open. Continue to watch this station for further information."

Yes!

Jody smiled at Tom.

This is one time KFOR is first with the news.

50

18 September, local time 1300
Boston

You've reached WBZ, Channel 4. How may I direct your call?"

"I'd like the newsroom, please," the slightly accented, male voice answered politely.

"One moment."

Thirty seconds later a male voice said, "Yeah. Newsroom."

"Listen very carefully," the voice instructed. "The people of Boston are in grave danger. If the reasonable demands of Islamic Jihad are not met, we will loose an epidemic of death in this city on a scale never before experienced anywhere in the world. I will present you with our demands in one hour. Be ready. And understand that this is not a prank."

"What are you trying to pull, fella, whoever you are? Don't you know it's a crime to make a hoax call like this? You can go to jail."

"This is no hoax. One hour."

"You can't expect me to believe you are serious!"

"To illustrate just how serious I am," the voice continued, "at around ten this morning, at the Boston Common, at least nine people were exposed to a lethal dose of inhalation anthrax. They will all die. There may be others. We are prepared to kill hundreds of thousands of others in the same way as these. The city itself will be left in irreparable desolation for decades. You will be contacted again in exactly one hour."

The line went dead.

—∾—

18 SEPTEMBER, LOCAL TIME 1330
BOSTON

The police unit came to a stop near the Joy Street steps. Both officers exited from the car and paused, looking around.

"Lots of people out today, Jim."

"Yeah. Where is this supposed to have happened?"

"Somewhere in the Common. That's what dispatch said. Some creep called Channel 4 and claimed nine people had been exposed to inhalation anthrax."

"What in the world is inhalation anthrax?"

"It's the stuff that NBC secretary got exposed to in a letter. And the post office people down in Washington."

"I used to think it was something you got from eating bad meat."

"I know. This has got to be somebody's bad joke. At least I hope so. You never really know for sure these days. Especially since those Arab fanatics up and declared war on us."

"Yeah, you're probably right. It's getting to be a crazy world, isn't it? Makes you wonder what it's going to be like for our grandkids someday. Well, as long as we're here, let's go see if we can find anybody that might know something."

They walked across Beacon Street and into downtown Boston's fifty-acre park, known simply as the Common. Making their way south and down toward the east end of Frog Pond, they stopped a family that looked like they were probably tourists.

"See anything unusual around here this morning?"

"No, sorry."

"Got a report there might be a sick person here."

"Not here, officers. Haven't seen anybody."

They moved on, circling the southern side of the concrete depression used as a children's wading pool in the summer and a skating rink in winter.

"Seen anyone who looked like they might be sick?" the officer asked a group of teenagers cutting across the park toward the Esplanade.

"No," they answered, giggling and shaking their heads as they pushed and shoved one another along playfully.

"Let's angle over to Charles Street and then back around. Okay?"

"Okay. Hey, wait. Over there. Didn't dispatch say nine people?"

He pointed to four adults standing near the west end of the pond. Just beyond were five small children, rolling in the grass and kicking a beach ball between them.

The policemen waved and called out, "Hello there."

"Hi."

"You folks seen anything strange around here? Anybody who looked like they might be sick?"

The woman with long, blonde hair looked curiously at the officers.

"As a matter of fact, there was something earlier this morning. It sounded sort of like a *pop.* Then there was this puffy cloud of stuff. Came from over there." The woman pointed to her right. "A little got on us, but no big deal. We just brushed it off. Why? Is there anything wrong?"

"Do your remember what time it was?"

"Around ten, I think."

"Do you feel okay, ma'am?"

"Well, actually, I do have a headache and my allergies are kicking up. I'm a little short of breath. Brian says he's not feeling too sharp either. We were just deciding to cut the afternoon short and go home. Why do you ask?"

"We had a report that we think is probably a crank, but we're just making sure. Someone claims to have exposed nine people to inhalation anthrax. We saw nine of you over here and so we came to check it out."

"Inhalation anthrax?" the younger-looking man repeated.

"Never heard of it. Wait a minute. Isn't that the stuff that was in the letters that closed down the Senate Building right after 9/11? Hey, are you saying you think that's what we saw?"

"I doubt it," replied the officer, "but if you keep feeling poorly, you might check with your doctor tomorrow. Sorry to have bothered you. Have a nice afternoon."

The two policemen walked away.

The adults finished putting their picnic stuff together.

About halfway between Frog Pond and Charles Street, the officers heard a commotion behind them.

Turning, they saw the youngest of the five children sitting on the path. The officers ran back.

"Now Jimmy says he's not feeling good," one of the women exclaimed, concern on her face.

One policeman knelt beside him and held the boy's hands. The other whipped out his radio transmitter. "Get a medical team to the Common. On the double. We're near the west end of Frog Pond. Child down. Breathing is labored. Two adults complaining of allergies and headaches. We're here responding to a call concerning possible exposure of civilians to anthrax."

Radio static.

Then a woman's voice.

"The EMT is on the way. ETA, four minutes."

—∾—

Mohammed Ibn Ahmer and Yusif Shemuda smoked cigarettes and drank mineral water, watching the shoreline as they drifted under the Harvard Bridge, which connects Cambridge to Boston along Massachusetts Avenue. A small PDA lay between them on a box. They heard the beep. A few seconds passed.

Safwat's code phrase appeared.

Yusif entered his response and waited.

Another message appeared on the PDA screen. What they had worked for and waited for and dreamed about was now a reality.

They looked at each other and smiled.

The strike had been launched.

51

18 SEPTEMBER, LOCAL TIME 1605
THE DEAD SEA, ISRAEL

Amal sat in the driver's seat of the orange and blue Israel Tours bus, out of the sun, while the engine idled and the air conditioner cooled the interior. It was "September hot" at the rim of the Dead Sea. He wasn't certain how hot, but knew it had to be over thirty degrees Celsius. He relaxed in the familiar manner of a veteran driver who was used to waiting for passengers to board.

He glanced down at the instrument panel, making certain the engine did not overheat. He hoped that David Barak and his group would not be too much longer. He had been reminded earlier that they wanted to arrive in Jerusalem at sunset. He looked forward to it. Leaving the heat here at 390 meters below sea level and climbing up to Jerusalem's hills, more than 700 meters above sea level, would be a cool and welcome relief. Sunset was also one of the city's most beautiful moments, a spectacle in which even the natives took delight.

Looking up again, he noticed a woman coming out from the shadows at the south end of the hotel and heading in his direction. She was dressed in a white jacket and light blue skirt, the uniform of a hotel employee. The only others on the lot were three elderly Japanese tourists, shuffling lethargically through the sweltering heat toward the lobby. This woman, however, seemed oblivious to the heat as she walked swiftly across the lot toward the area where the four buses were parked, each representing tourist groups currently in residence.

Because he was the only driver preparing to leave, he thought that she must want to speak with him. As the woman came nearer, Amal bent forward, pretending to be busy with something beneath the instrument panel. He acted as if he had not seen her and did not look up until she knocked.

Opening the door, Amal looked down inquisitively at the woman. *Very nice. I have not seen her before.*

"You are the driver for the Reverend Cain's tour group. Yes?" the woman queried in flawless Arabic.

"Yes, I am Amal, and this is the bus for his group."

"Please come with me. Your guide, Mr. Barak, wishes to speak with you."

Amal hesitated for a split second, then slid out from under the steering wheel. Stepping down and out of the bus, he turned to lock the door.

"Is there a problem?" he asked the woman, while he made sure the bus was secure.

"He did not say. Follow me."

The driver smiled as he happily obeyed the woman's instruction. He kept his eyes on the light blue skirt that came to the knee in Western style and hugged smoothly each graceful movement of her body. On her feet, she did not wear the customary sandals. Instead, she had on low-heeled dress shoes that accented her very attractive ankles.

"I have not seen you here before," Amal spoke as he tried to keep up with the woman.

"I am on duty at the desk this evening," she replied over her shoulder. "I have been sick for two days."

Friendly, too, Amal thought. Some of the women who worked behind hotel desks would not speak to mere bus drivers. *This one is not like the ones who get too much freedom and authority and begin thinking they are really somebody.*

He continued to admire the view she provided as they drew near the hotel building.

"Mr. Barak is waiting inside. We will go in here."

The woman walked up three concrete steps and inserted a key in a door marked "Exit Only/Use Front Entrance." Opening the door, she hesitated long enough for Amal to put a hand on it, before stepping through in front of him.

Inside, the light seemed dim in comparison to the brightness of the late afternoon sun. Amal saw a man about halfway down the hall, standing in front of an open door. The man looked away and then disappeared through the doorway. As they passed, Amal saw that it was a maid's room, with shelves stacked with towels and linens. The man inside had his back turned, hands on his hips, apparently checking inventory; or perhaps the condition in which the maids had left the room at the end of their shift. Anyway, it did not matter. Amal's attention had quickly returned to the woman in front of him.

—⁓—

As Pasha and the bus driver passed by the door of the maid's room, Imad turned and moved through the doorway, taking three quick steps that put him directly behind the driver.

Amal started to look over his shoulder.

It was too late.

Imad delivered an expert blow to the bus driver's neck. He dropped quickly and silently to the floor.

Imad and Pasha hurriedly dragged the limp body into the maid's room. Pasha shut the door and locked it from the inside. She removed the bus door key from the Amal's pocket and handed it to Imad.

"Will he live?" asked Pasha.

"I hit him with a simple spinal chop to the neck. He'll be out for a while. I did not kill him."

"He has seen my face."

"It does not matter.

"But he can identify me."

"It makes no difference. In a few hours all our faces will most likely be on the front page of the *Jerusalem Post* anyway," Imad grinned.

Pasha didn't like the sound of it, but said nothing more. Imad took a roll of tape from his pocket and secured Amal's hands and feet. He wrapped several strips of tape around his head, covering his mouth, but leaving room for him to breathe through his nose. A large stack of dirty towels and sheets lay piled in the far corner near a washing machine. Imad and Pasha scooped them back, dragged Amal over against the wall and covered him with the linens.

"It will be awhile before he is found," said Imad, reassuringly.

"I think we should kill him," Pasha declared emphatically.

"He's an Arab," Imad protested.

"He has sold his soul to the Jews," Pasha responded passionately, her eyes blazing. "He *works* for them. He takes their money. He kisses the hand of our enemy."

"Come on, Pasha. Enough. He is unimportant. Let's get out of here."

Reluctantly, Pasha backed away.

"We have bigger fish to catch," Imad reminded her. "We must focus our attention on them. The driver is only a pawn. He is of no consequence. We are after the king."

Pasha looked at Imad and with mock reprimand in her voice asked, "And what do you know about pawns and kings? Was the game of chess not forbidden in your house?"

Imad looked a bit sheepish. "I have watched a game or two in my youth. But how did you know I was describing the players on a chessboard?"

Now it was Pasha's turn to look smile ruefully.

"My brothers," she said, simply.

—∾—

"Just a minute."

David Barak was rinsing out his mouth in the sink when he heard the knock on the door. He pushed his toothbrush into the travel kit and tossed it on the bed, alongside his small bag. "Who is it?" he called, squeezing through the narrow space between the bed and a small writing desk.

"A message from Reverend Cain," the muffled voice answered.

David felt in his pocket for some tipping money. Then he opened the door and reached for the note. For a brief moment, his eyes widened in disbelief. The man standing in front of him did not hold a note. He held a handgun with a silencer attached.

Pffpht! Pffpht!

David was driven backward into the room by the force of the two lead projectiles tearing into his body. He staggered, clutching at his bleeding chest, then fell against the bed.

The hallway figure stepped inside the room.

In an instant, David knew.

He was helpless to defend himself.

The face behind the gun was cold, unmerciful.

David felt a sudden sadness.

Not me. Not now. Not like this.

The man elevated his gun slightly. David could see directly into the barrel opening.

Pffpht!

52

A few minutes before three, John and Jessica had entered the Salt Sea Hotel & Spa lobby, relieved to escape the shimmering heat, if only briefly. They had placed their luggage outside the door of their room. Hotel staff would gather all the group's luggage and, under Amal's supervision, place each piece in the bus baggage hold.

With nothing left to do, they strolled out to the pool. John dropped the appropriate change into a Coke machine and handed one of the cans to Jessica. They removed their shoes and sat beside the pool, dangling their bare feet and legs in the water. For the next hour, they sat and talked about everything they'd seen so far. The shade of the hotel building made the sweltering heat bearable. It was the first time in several days they'd had time alone, other than late at night in their room.

After a while, Jessica let her feet stay in the water as she lay back on the warm concrete. John knew she did not feel well. She had complained of an upset stomach. He sat quietly, watching as she appeared to doze off. Her color looked better than it had earlier. He was glad for that.

What a sweetheart. I'm so glad you came with me on this trip. We've gotten closer. I can feel it. You are truly God's gift.

John checked his watch. Four o'clock. He hated to rouse her, but it was time.

"Hey, kiddo. Let's go."

Her eyes opened and looked into his. She smiled wanly as she sat up, lifting her feet from the water.

"Are you feeling any better?"

"A little."

"Think you can take the bus ride?"

"I hope so."

"Okay then. Let's go gather up our gang. You can get a good night's rest in Jerusalem. You'll be ready to go tomorrow."

Everyone was in the lobby, ready to leave, when John and Jessica entered.

"Time to hit the trail, Pastor." Edgar slapped him on the shoulder as he walked by. "And I am ready, man! I think this place is too close to you know where."

"Daddy, I'm going to the restroom," Jessica whispered in his ear. "I'll be right back."

John nodded and faced the group as he wiped beads of perspiration from his face with a tissue.

"It is a little toasty today, isn't it?"

Groans filled the lobby.

"Well, we'll fix that. An air-conditioned bus ride will be just the ticket. By the time we arrive in Jerusalem, you will have forgotten all about Masada and Jericho and the Dead Sea. We'll be basking in the fresh, cool air of the Judean hills."

"Can't be too soon for me," complained Ruth Taylor. She was sprawled in a large chair that suited her ample frame.

"Reverend Cain?"

Mr. Yassim was walking toward him, a message memo in his hand.

"Yes?"

"Mr. Barak was looking for you about thirty minutes ago. He received an emergency call from his wife in Tel Aviv. Their son was hit by a car while riding his bicycle home from school. He was injured severely. The hotel loaned Mr. Barak a car and he has gone to be with his family."

Concern etched John's brow.

Expressions of alarm were mirrored on the faces of the rest of the group.

"Oh, no. We were out by the pool. Was the injury critical?"

"I am sorry. It sounded very serious. But we have no further information."

"Perhaps I should call their home."

"I suggest that you do it after you are in Jerusalem, Reverend Cain. Mr. Barak will not yet be in Tel Aviv and Mrs. Barak is at the hospital with her son," the clerk lied nervously. "He asked me to arrange for someone to take his place on your journey to Jerusalem."

"That will not be necessary. We can do quite nicely with our driver, Amal. I will serve as guide for this short period."

"Oh, no, Reverend Cain. The tour company would be upset if we sent you on without a proper guide. I have asked one of our employees to go with you. She is extremely competent. It will not inconvenience her, as she lives in Bethlehem."

"Amal is from there."

"Oh, really?" Yassim feigned surprise.

"Perhaps they will know each other."

"Yes, it is possible. Bethlehem is small." The clerk wiped perspiration from his face with a handkerchief. "Ah, here she comes now."

An attractive woman in a hotel uniform walked up and bowed her head in greeting. Yassim moved away as she introduced herself.

"How do you do, Reverend Cain. I am Pasha. I am sorry to learn of Mr. Barak's family difficulty. I trust that his son will recover very soon. In the meantime it will be my honor to attend to your needs on your journey to Jerusalem. I understand you wish to be there by sunset. Is that true?"

John nodded affirmatively, his mind still on David's crisis and the need to be at his family's side. His sudden departure was disconcerting.

"Then we must hurry. Please tell your people to board immediately. Your luggage is already in the bus and your driver is waiting. The bus is cool inside and comfortable. We can discuss Mr. Barak's situation as we travel. He has assured us that he will meet you tomorrow at your hotel. Or if that is not possible, the agency will send another guide to serve you. Shall we go?"

John pondered his circumstances for a moment. It was not like David to disappear without a word. But he probably had been so distraught that he didn't take the time to check the pool area.

"All right, everybody," John said in a loud voice. "Head 'em up and move 'em out. We're on our way."

People shuffled and struggled to their feet, gathering up cameras, carry-ons, and other miscellaneous possessions before exiting through the doorway.

"You will wait for me, please, Reverend Cain?" Pasha said to John. "I must get my handbag."

She disappeared around the corner. John walked over to the window, watching the group cross the parking lot and crowd into the bus, anxious to get out of the heat.

A moment later, the young woman reappeared.

"I'm sorry. Tell me your name again?" John asked. "I wasn't paying attention when we were introduced."

"It is all right. You are upset because of Mr. Barak's misfortune. My name is Pasha. You are ready?"

"I believe so."

"Then we shall go, yes?" She opened the lobby door.

"Yes," he said, his thoughts jumping from the group and their upcoming bus ride to David and his son in the hospital.

They were halfway across the parking lot when suddenly John stopped. "Oh, I almost forgot—"

He felt a sharp jab in his side.

"Keep walking, Reverend Cain." The woman's voice was no longer warm and friendly.

"But—"

"Walk!"

He looked at the woman who was now his interim guide. Her eyes were steely as she pushed him forward. His mouth dropped open as he saw the gun in her hand, then felt it again jabbing into his side.

"What is this?"

"Keep walking. Get into the bus. Quickly!"

John stepped up into the bus and knew at once that everything was wrong. A stranger was sitting behind the wheel.

"Where is Amal?"

Pasha pushed John forward and stepped in behind him. The door closed and the bus began to roll.

John looked around the group. They were stone silent, faces pale, terror etched into every pair of eyes. No exceptions. The front half-dozen rows of seats, normally the first to be filled, were empty except for two large canvas bags and two hostile-looking young men, both armed with AK-47s.

"What is the meaning of this? What are you doing?" Even as John's questions spilled out, he sensed that he already knew the dreaded answer. "What have you done with David and Amal?"

The bus pulled onto Highway 90 and headed north. Salt crystals, like monstrous snowflakes, jutted upward from the sea on the right. Just ahead, carved out of the Jordanian eastern shore, were man-made canals dug into the Lashon Peninsula. Filled by pumping stations located at Israel's Dead Sea Works and Jordan's Arabic Potash Corporation, these canals were the waterways that keep the southern portion of the Dead Sea from drying up altogether.

John remained standing in a hunched position near the front seat while scenes like these, normally items of interest that David Barak would point out, passed by unheralded.

"I asked what have you done with David and Amal?" John's voice was tinged with indignation and anger.

The man in the seat across the aisle leaned forward and gave him a vicious shove. John fell sideways across the front seat, his shoulder slamming painfully into the bottom of the window frame. The man was on him like a hawk, talons poised, ready for the kill.

"You will stop asking questions," he snarled, his face inches from John's.

John opened his mouth to respond.

The man hit him with a stinging blow that jarred John's teeth, cutting his lip. Blood trickled from the left side of his mouth.

"John Cain, it is important that you understand this. You are no longer in charge! You and your friends from America are now prisoners in a holy war. *Allah u akbar!* You have been honored by Allah to be a part of what he is doing in our world. You are a vital element in a battle that will ultimately bring the world to its knees in praise to Allah!"

The other man kept watch over the people huddled in the back two-thirds of the bus. He turned and whispered something to the first man, who looked at John.

"I am informed that there are only twenty-four people on board. Yet there were to be twenty-five. Who is missing?" asked the first man.

John remained silent, glaring at his questioner.

The man's hand suddenly shot forward. It held a handgun with a silencer attached. Pressing it up under John's jaw, his voice shook with anger. "Now tell me who is missing!"

"My . . . my daughter," John replied hesitantly.

"Where is she? Why is she not here?"

"She . . . was in the restroom. Not feeling well."

The man cursed and then hit John hard across the side of his face with the handgun. John fell unconscious against the seat. Frightened screams escaped the lips of the horrified onlookers.

"Shut up!" the other man roared, waving his weapon wildly. "Another outburst and you will regret it! Just sit back and keep your mouths shut. We have a long ride ahead. Do not talk at any time. Not even to the person beside you. And do not try any heroics. It will only end in getting people killed."

53

The bus rolled past Metzada Junction. Masada's cableway could be seen on the left, carrying passengers to and from the imposing mountaintop fortress. Evelyn Unruh stared out the side window at the site they had visited only two days before. A subconscious need to touch the familiar tore at her mind. Masada's story was as familiar as anything could be for now. She forced herself to think about it, to run as many details of it as she could through her mind in an effort to escape the frightfulness of their present situation.

She and the others had enjoyed their visit to the top of Masada, in spite of the heat. They had sipped bottled water almost constantly to avoid dehydration. Meandering through the ancient ruins, David had given them a lesson in Jewish history. He explained that the wilderness summit had first been fortified by Alexander Jannaeus. Later, around 43 BC, Herod the Great turned it into a formidable and luxurious palace refuge, completing the work about 35 BC. *Or was it 38? No, David had said 35 bc.*

Jewish zealots captured it, turning it into a refuge for themselves and their families in AD 70, at the time the Romans were putting down a Jewish insurrection and retaking Jerusalem. These zealots remained in control of Masada for three years. Ultimately, eight camps of Roman soldiers, totaling about fifteen thousand men under the command of Flavius Silva, laid siege against 967 men, women, and children atop Masada. Evelyn remembered the rock outlined border of the camps far below that she had viewed from on top.

The Romans had ultimately used Jewish slave labor to build a ramp of stone on the western side of the mount to reach the defenders who then determined to commit suicide rather than surrender. Choosing lots, ten were elected to the task of killing all the others, then nine of the ten killed themselves, leaving the lone survivor to set fire to the palace before killing himself. When the Romans finally stormed the complex, two women and five children who had survived by hiding were able to tell what had happened.

Looking up now, Evelyn recalled David Barak standing with them at the Tanner's Tower, next to Masada's Western Gate, reciting this ancient story. He told them that Masada had become a symbol for the modern state of Israel.

"Masada shall not fall again" is a clarion call to the hearts of modern Israelis, he had said.

She remembered seeing a group of schoolchildren visiting the site as a part of their curriculum, and watching a unit of the Israel Defense Forces hold a swearing-in ceremony atop the mountain fortress. Two Israeli jet fighters had screamed low over the site, waggling their wings in a grand salute to the men below. It had been an awesome experience, a dazzling composite of ancient and modern, burned indelibly into the minds of all who had witnessed it.

As the bus sped along, Evelyn gradually permitted her mind to reenter the present.

Is this real after all? Or is it only a bad dream?

Jerry Cloud and Shad Coleman were nearest to the gunmen. They gave each other knowing looks as they silently measured the distance and the odds. Eventually, each saw the other ease back in his seat. It was no use.

John stirred with a groan, pain shooting through his head. He pulled himself to an upright position. There was blood on his shirt. He felt for the cut near his left eye.

"Ah, Reverend Cain. I am pleased that you are once more with us."

The young man sat across the aisle, straddling both seats with his legs as he spoke.

"I was about to tell your friends here what is happening. Now you are available to listen as well. My name is Yazib Dudori. This lovely woman is one of my partners, Pasha Bashera. Over there is Fathi Adahlah and at the wheel, our expert driver, Imad Safti. We are one of the teams engaged in the greatest offensive battle ever mounted by our small group of oppressed Palestinian people."

"You cannot possibly get away with this," John protested.

"You are wrong, Reverend Cain. We can and we will," said Yazib. "You see, we not only possess you who ride with us in this bus. Others with whom we are working in this holy war offensive are right now preparing to turn your city of Boston into a field of the dead."

John felt his stomach churn. *They must have a nuclear bomb.*

Yazib moved closer, leaning over the seat as he spoke directly to John.

"We also have your wife and the congregation you left back home."

John's mouth dropped open. He stared at Yazib in total shock.

—∞—

Jessica emerged from the restroom and walked out to the center of the lobby. It was empty except for two people working at the hotel desk.

Where is everybody?

She went out the front door.

The bus is gone!

How can that be? Had they had gone off without her?

No. They wouldn't leave me behind.

Jessica walked the length of the building. From the corner she could see the rest of the parking area, but the familiar orange and blue bus was nowhere to be seen.

Mounting alarm was causing added upset to her already delicate system.

What should I do now?

She ran back through the entrance doors and crossed the lobby to the desk. Both clerks were working quietly on reservation forms for the final tour group of the day, due to arrive at any moment.

Jessica hesitated, her anxiety continuing to build.

"Excuse me."

"May I help you?" the man asked, looking up.

"Yes, I am Jessica Cain. My father is the leader of a tour group that has been staying here for the last two nights. I think they just left without me."

"Your group left without you?" the man repeated, staring at the girl. He came around the side of the desk and stopped in front of her. "How could such a thing happen?"

"I don't know. I wasn't feeling well, so I went to the restroom. When I came out, they were gone. But surely Daddy would have missed me. I sit in the seat next to his when we are on the bus." Jessica fought back tears that threatened to spill out onto her cheeks. "What should I do?"

She waited for something to happen. Anything. She tried acting as grown-up as she could. But this was different. This shouldn't be happening. She probably looked like some forlorn little waif. The desk clerk continued staring at her. She assumed that he was trying to decide how best to handle her situation.

After a long moment, the man put a reassuring hand on her shoulder, offering a toothy smile.

"Don't worry, my little friend. We live in a small country. They've probably missed you already and are turning back. In any event, it is no problem. I'm sure we have your father's itinerary here somewhere. I will personally call ahead and let them know you are safe and well, just in case they go all the way without you. Meanwhile, there is an extra room available. I will get the key and show you where you can wait. Don't worry. They will contact us before long, one way or another. Come with me."

"Maybe I could just wait out here in the lobby." Jessica didn't like this man. There was no particular reason. She just remembered that her father did not seem to like him either.

The clerk smiled.

"It is no trouble at all, Miss Cain. This unfortunate event should never have happened. But since it has, I will show you to a room and bring you something to drink. How would that be? Would you like a Coke? Or juice, perhaps? If you are not feeling well, it is not good for you to wait out here. This place will soon be full of travelers coming in for the night. You should have somewhere to lie down. By the time your father returns, you'll be feeling much better."

Reluctantly, not knowing what else to do, Jessica waited while the clerk checked through the registration listings for a vacancy. She watched as he reached underneath the counter and withdrew a key.

Motioning for her to follow, he headed across the lobby to the elevators.

Jessica was nervous, but tried not to show it. She walked behind him.

The elevator door opened and an elderly couple stepped out, dressed in swimsuits and conversing in a foreign language.

She followed the clerk into the elevator. He pushed the fourth-floor button.

"Thank you for helping me, Mr. . . . I've forgotten. What is your name?"

"Yassim. My name is Yassim."

The elevator door closed.

54

18 SEPTEMBER, LOCAL TIME 1035
BAYTOWN, CALIFORNIA

On this Sunday morning, the San Francisco regional office of the FBI was in the hands of two people. Doris Lander was the clerk on duty and Steve Jackson was carrying out one of his least favorite tasks, that of ACD—Agent on Complaint Duty.

"Hello, FBI."

"Yes, my name is Holanda Seers, and I want to talk to somebody 'bout my civil rights bein' violated."

"Ms. Seers, I'm the only agent on duty today. Would it be possible for you to call back tomorrow morning?"

"Hey, who do you think you are, Mr. FBI? I ain't got time to call you tomorrow. I gots to work tomorrow. Ain't got no cushy desk job, neither. Now I want to file a complaint. Are you gonna help me, or aren't you?"

"Well, Ms. Seers. I'm here to help if I can. But you'll have to wait one moment, please. I've got another call coming in. I'm putting you on hold and I'll be back as quickly as I can."

"Now you wait just a—"

Agent Jackson punched the hold button. Then, line two.

"Hello, FBI."

"Yes, my name is Dr. James Novell. I am prepared to present you with irrefutable data regarding an unauthorized landing of aliens near the university campus in Berkeley. It happened again last night."

"One moment, Dr. Novell." He put the second caller on hold and reached for the "nut box." Under *N* he found a 3x5 card. In the upper lefthand corner was the name *Novell, Dr. James.* Beneath the name was a San Francisco address and phone number. Handwritten dates and times indicated previous calls that had been taken by other complaint duty agents, along with instructions for dealing with Dr. Novell.

Jackson read the information, smiled, put the card down and punched the caller up again.

"Dr. Novell, are you ready with your information?"

"Yes, thank you, I am," was the polite reply.

"I need to record your statement, Dr. Novell."

"I understand. I've done this before, many times."

"All right, sir. When you hear the click, go ahead and begin."

He pushed the hold button again and chuckled as he thought about Dr. Novell reading his statement. He'd check back in ten minutes. If he was still reading, he'd put him on hold for another ten. If there was a dial tone, he would know the treatise had been delivered. At least for today.

"Now," Jackson said under his breath, "what shall I do with Ms. Holanda Seers and her civil rights?"

He was thinking of several options, none of which would be palatable to Ms. Seers or the FBI, when the phone rang again.

"Hello, FBI."

"Hi, Steve. It's Jim Cantor. How's complaint duty going?"

"Like a root canal, Jimbo. What's up?"

"You watching TV?"

"No, should I be?"

"Tune up Channel 4. They're running a news bulletin. Unconfirmed. Says a hostage situation is developing in a church in Baytown. Looks like it could be big time. Any word?"

"You're the first."

"Wait a minute. Bernstein's their anchor and he's just come on. Just a sec . . . okay, he's confirmed it. Better make some calls."

"Thanks, Jim."

Agent Jackson hung up the phone just as another line lit up.

"Hello, FBI."

"Yes sir. My name is Cindy Carlson. I'm with the Baytown Police. We may have a serious situation here. . . ."

He listened, asked a couple of questions, then assured Ms. Carlson he would be right on it. He thought about the people on hold. Dr. Novell would eventually run out of space aliens and hang up. Ms. Seers's civil rights would have to wait. He dialed Frank Lyons's number.

—w—

Some people complain about being on call. For Frank Lyons it was a way of life, twenty-four seven. Usually calls were of a general nature from the office. But when his SWAT team emergency number rang, he knew it meant trouble. He put down the Sunday *Chronicle* sports pages and reached for the phone.

"Get your boys to the garage, Frank."

"What's up?"

"It's the world's biggest something," Steve Jackson answered with a phrase often used by agents when there was no time for explanations or not enough information to give.

Lyons hung up, took a deep breath, and began calling his team leaders.

—✂—

Paul Danversen, Assistant Special Agent in Charge (ASAC) of the San Francisco office, returned Agent Jackson's call from the seaside resort community of Carmel, where he and his family were spending the weekend. As they conversed, he calculated the time it would take for someone to fly to nearby Monterey Airport, pick him up, and then fly back to San Francisco. Two hours, minimum. Probably longer. Paul would drive instead. Code 3. He could do it in an hour and forty and he was on his way. Jackson got the name and number of the hotel where they were staying and assured him that the department would send a car down in the afternoon for his family.

Next, Jackson dialed the cell phone number of Special Agent in Charge Duane Webber.

—✂—

"This is Webber."

Like most police work, much of what the FBI does is dull and routine. Big-time cases, the ones that really pump adrenaline into an agent's veins, are few and far between. But when they come, they generate excitement that draws the agents to danger like moths to a flame. This morning, as Duane Webber listened to Steve Jackson's account of the unfolding events, he sensed that just such a case was coming his way.

He stood alongside his neighbor's backyard pool, drying off with a towel as he cradled the cell phone to his ear. The Carringtons were in Hawaii for a month and they had invited the Webbers to use the pool in their absence. Duane had just finished swimming laps when his phone had begun to ring on the poolside table.

His raspy voice sounded raspier than usual when he got excited. And he was excited.

He looked up and waved as his wife came through the side gate and walked over to him.

"Get whoever is available out to Baytown ASAP," he continued. "Code 2. Fly them, if you have to. I want a team assembled on site in one hour."

Janice Webber stood next to her husband, watching and listening to the one-sided conversation as he plied his stock-in-trade. Duane turned his gaze to the exquisite features of the woman who was his one and only true love. Her olive-colored skin required absolutely no sun for her to look stunning in whatever she wore. At least that's the way Duane felt about it. And the white, one-piece swimsuit she had on this morning was no exception to the rule.

He winked, but his face was serious.

She smiled back, the knowing smile of a wife used to being stood up by a husband whose life was regulated, twenty-four seven, by a cell phone.

Webber listened as Agent Jackson informed him of some extraordinary luck. FBI pilot Sam Seitzman had the whirlybird in the air right now. Apparently, Seitzman's wife was down in Fresno, visiting her family. With nothing else to do, he had decided to check the helicopter out after a broken rotor blade had been replaced the day before.

"Get him over here. I'll be at Webster High School in twelve minutes. Have him pick me up on the football field. And tell him I don't want to be kept waiting. Thanks, Steve."

Webber pressed the cut-off button. Phone still in hand, he looked solemnly at his beloved and beautiful wife. How he loved this woman. His only regret was that they had not been able to produce any children.

"What is it, darling?"

"Terrorists in a church in Baytown. Can you believe it? In a church? They think they might be Arabs. Come on. Drive me over to Webster High. I'll change in the car."

—w—

Sergeant Frank Castor drove as fast as possible without using a siren. The streets were nearly empty, with the only real activity happening around Baytown Mall. It looked as if there was a pretty big sale going on today. More cars than usual in the parking lot for this time of day. A number of people were already headed toward the mall's main entrances.

Radio static and conversations between patrol units being called to the Calvary Church area filled the airwaves.

"Car 11."

"Eleven here, Cindy."

Her usually calm voice carried an edge of excitement.

"Special Agent Webber is on the phone from the FBI. He asked for the officer in charge. I told him Lieutenant Randle. He said, 'Great, let me talk to Joe.'"

"Okay, Cindy. Patch him through."

Castor lifted his eyebrows. "Joe? He called you Joe?"

Randle smiled.

"This is good. We're going to need this guy."

They were turning into the church parking lot when Duane Webber's raspy voice came through the car radio receiver.

"Hey, Joe. Good to hear your voice. How ya doin'?"

"Not so good this morning. A little while ago, I thought about taking some vacation time and getting out of town but I guess it's too late for that. It looks like we've got major trouble. A hostage situation. A church full of people being held by what we think is at least four heavily armed persons. So far we've seen three men and a woman."

"Seen them?" asked Webber. "How?"

"On television."

"Are you serious? This thing really is on TV?"

"Calvary Church televises one of its Sunday services live each week over Channel 17. We started getting calls from viewers and then turned it on ourselves. Looks like the real thing. May already be one victim. We're not sure about that."

"Sounds like we might be interested."

Randle paused. What would Chief White say if he took the lead in accepting the not-so-subtle invitation being offered by SAC Duane Webber. He was all too aware of the intense rivalry between law enforcement agencies. Each agency wants in and hopes to gobble up the glory. Jurisdiction was a line over which careers were won and lost. Politics. He hated the politics. Maybe that was why he'd been passed over before. But he also knew that if a terrorist incident was unfolding, the correct way to go was to the FBI. They had the real tools for this sort of thing. Then he thought about the people in the church.

"Get in here as quickly as you can," Randle said at last. "I think we can use the help."

"Okay, Joe. I'll get things moving. You sure about this?"

Randle wasn't certain whether Webber was asking about the situation or the request for help.

"I wish I wasn't, but yeah, I'm sure. We're pulling up to the church's front entrance right now. We're the first on scene. Nobody outside. Looks quiet. There's a blue van parked near a side entrance in a handicap zone."

"So?"

"So the side door is wide open and nobody's around it."

"All right, I'm on my way. Be careful."

"Count on it."

"Sounds like you know each other," Castor said, stopping the car directly in front of the main entrance to the church.

"Yeah, we do. Remember when White was named chief? About a month later he asked if I'd like to go to the FBI National Academy. He had an invitation and couldn't make it. The Department sent me to FBINA instead."

"Lucky man. You've got to be pretty special to get to take that in. How long were you there?"

"Ten weeks. That's where I met Webber."

They sat talking, looking for some sign of movement in the building. There was none.

Randle picked up the mike. "Cindy. We're in front of the church. Nothing going. What do you see? Are the cameras still on?"

"Yes. It looks like they're just standing around. The people who have guns that is. Everyone else is still sitting down."

Two black and whites turned into the parking lot and sped toward where the other officers were parked.

A uniformed officer jumped out of the first car and jogged around to where Castor and Randle sat sizing up the situation.

"All the streets leading in or out are shut down, Lieutenant. We've got the place locked down. Starting to divert the traffic coming for the eleven o'clock service."

"Thanks."

"What do we do now, sir?"

"Good question. For now we sit here and wait."

55

Eleven minutes and thirty seconds later, Duane Webber stepped out of his car and scanned the sky. Janice came around to where he stood, still in her swimsuit, but with a royal blue blouse covering her shoulders and tied loosely at the waist.

"There he is. Over there," said Janice, pointing at the skyline opposite the playing field. "He'll be here in a couple of minutes."

Duane glanced at his watch. "Not bad. Not twelve minutes, but not bad."

"You're the bad one," Janice chided him playfully, moving her arm around his waist. "How you can go from a wet swimsuit to a dry business suit, complete with tie, socks, and shoes, while driving down the road, I'll never know."

"I wasn't driving. You were," he responded with a chuckle.

"What do you suppose some of those people we passed thought you were doing?"

"It will give them something to talk about over Sunday supper."

Duane strapped on the Glock 22 .40-caliber semiautomatic pistol that was standard issue for all special agents these days. He dropped an extra fifteen-round ammunition clip into his pocket, then threw on his jacket as the helicopter settled down in front of them.

Duane gave Janice a quick kiss.

As he started to leave, she wrapped both arms around his neck and kissed him hard on the lips.

"You be careful, Duane Webber."

He saw the serious, worried look that had become a familiar trademark in moments like this. He knew it was different for her to send her husband off to work than for most women.

He nodded.

"Not to worry. I'll be home as soon as we're finished."

Janice waited by the car as he ducked beneath the helicopter's rotating blades and climbed on board. In seconds, the helicopter was off the ground and on its way. Looking down, Duane saw Janice still standing by the car as they swept across the football field and out over the bay.

They headed northeast. The San Mateo Bridge was below on the right, Oakland International Airport straight ahead. Duane donned the extra helmet and began talking to ASAC Danversen on Danversen's cellular phone. He was already en route.

"Paul, I'm closer than you, so I'm on my way to the site. Head into the office and take charge there. I want a local command post established at the church, first thing. Get on the horn and arrange to have the Winnebago brought over from the city. We'll put it as near to the church as we can safely get."

The "Winnebago" was a twenty-four-foot recreational vehicle that had become government property thanks to one of the West Coast's largest drug raids. It had been retrofitted with television monitors, communication links to every city, county, and state police agency, and the latest in cellular gadgetry, tracing and recording equipment. It would serve as the on-site command center.

"Steve has called in the SWAT team. They may get there before I do. This could be a bad one, Paul. I talked with Joe Randle, the local PD guy on the scene. He's worried. Thinks there may already be one down. If they really intend to hold an entire crowd hostage, we've got major problems.

"Gene's our best negotiator, but he's on vacation. Back east somewhere. He's out then. Let me check when we get there. The rest of the team will be there. Baytown won't have anybody. Listen. Patch me through to SIOC. I need to let someone there know what's coming down."

He looked over at the pilot. "How much longer?"

"Five."

"Sir, the SIOC director is on the line."

"Hello, this is Duane Webber, SAC in San Francisco."

"This is Supervisory Special Agent Lawford. What can I do for you today?"

"I'm en route by chopper to a Bay Area suburb called Baytown. Local PD is already on location. They think they've got a hostage situation in a church."

"A church? How many involved?"

"Don't know for sure. Report is at least four people, well armed. Word has it they may be Arabs. They are holding an entire crowd. We don't know the exact number, but probably several hundred."

"When are you on the scene?"

Webber glanced over at the pilot. He held up three fingers.

"ETA is three minutes."

"I'll notify Sam Johnston. He's section chief at the International Terrorist Section these days. When will you verify what you have coming down?"

"Soon. We'll establish a command post on-site, first thing."

"Keep us in the loop as soon as you verify what's happening."

"Roger."

They skimmed the top of the last hill that loomed between them and the campus of Baytown's Calvary Church. Duane had been in Baytown several times before. It was the first time he had flown in, however. Houses were neatly laid out in typical suburban tract fashion. The downtown area consisted of numerous stores and office buildings, the tallest of which was only five stories. Schools, playgrounds, city parks. It was a nice new upscale community. The sort of place people moved to in order to get away from crime and violence somewhere else. Twenty-six thousand people within the city limits. Several larger contiguous communities surrounded it on three sides. The west side ran back up into the golden hills for which the Bay Area is famous. In a few months, with any decent amount of rainfall, the gold would turn into a rolling carpet of verdant green.

The pilot pointed. Just ahead, several police cars could be seen near the front of a large structure, the highest point of which was a cross, mounted on a steeple.

Calvary Church.

"Set 'er down in the parking lot, Sam. Over there." Webber pointed to the north side of the large lot. He was not much of a churchgoer and so was impressed with the number of cars. However, it meant that a lot of people were at risk here. The helicopter had barely touched down when Duane unbuckled his safety harness, opened the door, and dropped down onto the asphalt surface. He walked briskly in the direction of three police cars. Several uniformed patrolmen were standing around the cars, looking in his direction.

"Hi, Joe," he greeted one of them, extending his hand.

"Hello yourself, Duane. You're looking fit. Sorry to have to call you out today but this one looks like we could use a little help."

"Glad to oblige," Webber answered, his eyes on the main entrance as he wondered what might be happening beyond the closed doors. "What do we know for sure?"

"We know there are at least four people inside, armed with automatic weapons. Maybe others. Can't tell yet. Looks like they have plenty of firepower and are planning to stay for a while. We saw one of them working on a door. My guess is the doors are loaded with explosives by now. It looks like they've killed already. A man. Can't say about others."

"You say this is all coming over on television?"

"Yep. The church televises its morning service live every Sunday. They're on the air right now."

"Do you think these guys know they're on the tube?"

"At first I didn't. But now I don't see how they can help but know. They've made no effort to shut it down. Maybe that's part of the deal."

"Could be. If they're who you think, these people love putting on a show. And the bigger the audience, the better they like it." Duane stared at the building. "Our boys will be here within the hour. We'll set up a mobile command post in the Winnie. Then we can watch them ourselves. Who's your main man going to be?"

Randle glanced up at a car turning into the parking lot entrance. "Chief White's coming in right now. He's the boss."

"Okay then. Let's get to work. Have your men spread out and cover the exits. Maybe they don't plan on coming out any time soon, but let's not take the chance. All the roads shut down?"

"Tight," was Randle's terse response. He wished that he could be the main man in this operation, but knew he would take a backseat the moment Chief White stepped out of his car.

"Good. You've done everything possible and you've done it well," said Webber, sensing the frustration in Randle's voice. He rested his hand on Randle's shoulder. "Now introduce me to your boss."

56

18 September, local time 1145
Baytown, California

The Winnebago RV was parked about thirty yards from the church's main entrance. It was rapidly being turned into a Central Command unit. The whirring of a power generator could be heard each time the door opened. Inside, agents squeezed back and forth past one other in the narrow space. The air-conditioned interior of the vehicle was crammed with electronic gear, telephones, radio sending and receiving equipment, and several television screens.

At the moment, all three screens showed the same picture. Webber was watching over a technician's shoulder. The scene being transmitted by Baytown's Channel 17 looked forbidding.

"Are we ready to talk to SIOC yet?"

"Yes sir."

"Okay. Tell them I'll get with them in a few minutes. Just as soon as we can figure out for sure what's going down. Give them what you see on the screen. I'll be right back."

Webber stepped outside the trailer and started around the corner. Suddenly one of the agents stuck his head out of the door.

"Sir. One of the bad guys wants to talk."

Webber whirled, ran back up the steps into the trailer and stood in front of the screens. He saw the face of a handsome young Arab.

Can't be very old. Twenty-five? Twenty-six, maybe.

He was speaking into the camera.

". . . So, I assume by now that the Great Satan's law enforcement agencies are at the door. Let me warn you against doing anything heroic. All the entrances to this place of worship have been seeded with enough explosives to take out anybody trying to enter. The explosion will also kill the people located at each door."

The figure on the screen paused as his image dissolved and another took its place. Webber saw a group of at least ten men and women. One had a baby in her arms. They were huddled together on the floor in front of a door.

He swore softly.

The speaker's face then reappeared on the screen.

"If any of these people do not cooperate with us, they will be shot," he continued matter-of-factly. "If you try to overpower us, you will force us to kill them. I hold the detonator in my hand for the doors, as you can see." He held up a small black object with several red buttons.

Once again Webber swore under his breath.

"If the people here with us, or others from the outside, try to overwhelm us, we will shoot them. But first I will push this. The result will not be one you would wish to be responsible for." Webber's face tightened as he watched the man's finger brush across the buttons.

"I have but one small request, to begin with. I would prefer to speak with you over a cell phone. I am prepared to do so when I hear from you. On the chance you do not hear my voice, I have written the number on this card." The man took a card from the front seat and held it up. It contained a series of handwritten numbers. "You will tell me what is your number. I will also require the provision of a television set. I'm told there is one in the church nursery. Bring it to me, please." The man smiled at his own politeness. "Knock when it is available. We will disarm the door and retrieve it. Once this is done, I will speak with you further.

"Please do not do anything more or less than what I have indicated. All the other doors will remain armed and ready to detonate. Anyone trying to force entry will be summarily shot. If the television is not at the door when it is opened, someone here will die. Do not tamper with it in any way. I have an electronics and explosives expert with me. If there is evidence of tampering, I assure you, people will die." The man smiled into the camera once more. "In fact, the possible loss of life in here is tremendous, so please act with the greatest of care. You have fifteen minutes. Do not disappoint me."

Chief White watched along with Agent Webber and the others.

"Communicating directly by phone will be an advantage. But why does he want a television set? You think he just wants to see himself on the screen?"

"No," Webber answered, "he's got other plans. And he's got the upper hand. I think we have to give this character what he wants this time around. Did you see that guy on the platform? He was alive when he went to church this morning. Now he's dead. They're serious and probably suicidal. We've got to establish communications with them."

Webber looked at Lieutenant Randle, standing beside his boss, then back to Chief White. "How about it, Chief?"

Chief White frowned as he watched the images on the screen. Then he grunted affirmatively. "Joe, take Steve with you, get that television out of the nursery, and pound on the door. But be careful."

Randle nodded affirmatively and ducked through the RV door.

—~—

Joe Randle's heart was pounding double-time as he and Officer Steve Smith walked up the steps and onto the large Spanish-style patio. The midday sun was warm, but it was far and away the secondary cause for the beads of perspiration he wiped with the sleeve of his uniform. Before entering, the two officers checked each of the four double doors as best they could from the outside. There did not appear to be anything unusual.

Randle looked at Smith and nodded. He reached for the door handle and opened it. Stepping inside, they stared at the sanctuary doors, then crossed the lobby, looking back and forth in both directions. Randle motioned to Smith. There was a sign to the left identifying the nursery.

Opening the door, Randle's heart skipped a beat. Three startled and very frightened women stood in the middle of the room, a small baby in each arm and two more babies in cribs. A wall-mounted television conveyed the scenes from inside the sanctuary.

"Oh, thank God! We thought . . ."

"I'm Joe Randle. This is Steve Smith. Baytown police. How many children are in here?"

"Eight. All babies," one of the women answered, tears spilling from her eyes.

Randle glanced at his watch. Seven minutes left.

"Steve, take the television down. I'll get the children and these women out of here."

Randle carefully scooped up the two remaining infants. They were both asleep. He smiled at the attendants. "You've done great so far. These are the quietest eight kids I've ever seen. Follow me and let's see if we can keep on being quiet."

The three women followed Lieutenant Randle out of the room and across the lobby to the exit. With his hip, he pushed the crash bar and opened the door, both arms full of babies. The women followed him outside and started running across the patio.

"Careful," Randle called after them.

Three police officers came forward to meet them. Randle handed the two babies he carried to one of them and started back into the church.

"Officer," a female voice called.

Randle hesitated and looked back. One of the women was running toward him, with a policeman right behind her.

"What is it?"

"There are more children inside."

"You mean in the nursery?"

"No. Upstairs. In the classrooms."

"Upstairs?"

"Yes. We have a children's Sunday school during this hour in conjunction with the worship service. They must still be up there."

Randle looked at the other officer.

"Get some men together. Let's get in there and check it out. Thanks, ma'am. You've been very brave. Now go on back and take care of those babies."

Less than a minute passed before eight uniformed patrolmen jogged up the steps and into the main entrance. Four went up the steps on the right. The other four followed Randle across the lobby and up the steps to the left.

The stairs opened onto a landing and a hallway with doors on both sides. The hall was silent and empty. Randle opened the first door. Inside, a group of small children sat in a circle, heads bowed, holding hands. A man and a woman, sitting cross-legged on the floor with the children, looked up and smiled with relief at the sight of the policemen.

"See, children? We asked Jesus to send help and these nice men have come."

Randle stood in the doorway.

"I want you to follow us down the stairs and outside. Okay? Here, young fellow. You take this policeman's hand. Form a line and stay together. Walk very quietly. Understand?"

Twelve heads nodded gravely, eyes big as plates. They looked frightened, but did exactly as told. One little girl looked at Randle.

"Are my mommy and daddy all right?"

"They are fine. Everything will be okay. Now you do exactly what I asked. Okay?"

The little girl's eyes remained on Randle, as though trying to discern whether or not he was telling the truth. Then she headed down the hall with the others.

Door by door, the officers repeated the same procedure. Some children were crying, but there was no panic. The adults had kept them together and comforted them while waiting for help to come.

Randle was amazed at how well this was going. Not a sound was heard as orderly lines of children of varying ages passed through the halls on either side of the lobby and down the steps. Randle hurried down the stairs as children and their adult workers streamed out of the building.

By this time, Officer Smith had taken the television to the main sanctuary doors and placed it on the floor. Randle looked at his watch. Less than a minute left. Children were still coming down the stairs. Randle motioned for them to hurry.

Fifteen minutes gone. Exactly.

Patrolmen appeared on both landings at almost the same time. The last of the children were on their way out.

Randle hesitated, adrenaline pumping as he watched the human stream flow through the exit doors.

As the last child's foot touched the lobby floor, Randle checked his watch. Thirty seconds past the deadline! He pounded sharply on the door. Then he followed the others outside. Standing on the patio, he watched at least two hundred children and the workers who had remained with them scatter quickly across the parking lot between two lines of policemen. There was a chorus of frightened voices mixed with cries of relief.

Randle looked back at the lobby. Through the glass doors, the television set looked strangely out of place, like a small animal with its plug-in tail trailing off to one side. Then he noticed another sign he had not seen before. It was an attractive, free-standing wooden sign, to one side of the sanctuary doors: Thank you for being quiet. Service is in session.

Randle turned and headed for the trailer.

You're welcome.

—∾—

Akmed checked his watch again. It had been eighteen minutes since he had spoken into the cameras. It was unnerving not to be able to see outside. He said nothing to the others, but his stomach was churning. He was bothered. What was going on out there? Was he talking to the wind? Was anybody there?

He motioned to Mamdouh, who was leaning against the back of the last row of pews, gun in hand, watching the small group of people that were huddled near his assigned door.

Mamdouh walked up to the group and poked one man with the barrel of his gun. "Move away from the door."

The man started to get up.

"No. Do not get up. Move!"

They stared at each other for a moment, silently measuring one other as antagonists sometimes do. Slowly the man scooted forward, the others following his example, clearing out a space in front of the doors. Mamdouh looked to see that Akmed had disarmed the explosive charge. Then he pushed the crash bar down and cracked the door open, just wide enough to peer outside, wary of some sort of trap. The lobby was empty.

He pushed the door open all the way. There it was. As ordered. A television set. Reaching out, he grabbed the electric cord and dragged the television inside the door. Before closing the door, he looked across the lobby and through the glass on the far side. What he saw took his breath away.

A large black recreational vehicle was parked directly opposite the main entrance. It was surrounded by police cars. Men in blue or brown uniforms could be seen everywhere.

He closed the door.

We've done it. We've awakened the Great Satan. Allah u akbar!

—∾—

Joe Randle watched from the corner of the RV. He saw the sanctuary door open and a man, crouching down, reach through the opening and drag the television inside. Before going back inside, the man stood and looked out on the scene in the parking lot. A few seconds. Then he disappeared behind the door.

Randle cursed and walked around to the RV door.

57

18 SEPTEMBER, LOCAL TIME 1230
BAYTOWN, CALIFORNIA

Two hours and thirty minutes after the first shots had been fired, the local Command Center was well on its way to being established. Baytown Police Chief Jim White and the FBI's SAC Duane Webber, were operating as top commanders, representing both local and federal law enforcement. Assistant SAC Paul Danversen had arrived at the San Francisco office. Lieutenant Joe Randle had been cast in the unofficial role of advisor to the commanders. The California Highway Patrol had taken over responsibility for traffic control around the perimeter, and several officers had joined the vigil outside Calvary Church. Baytown's mayor was on the way to the scene and would undoubtedly demand a role in the process as the community's elected leader.

The pieces were beginning to come together.

Two behavioral specialists were being called in from Oakland. They had been part of a recent negotiating training seminar for law enforcement personnel that Webber's negotiating team had attended. Dr. Dale Hummel served as an on-call consultant for the Oakland PD. Dr. Sandra Hinkle worked with the Alameda County district attorney's office as an expert in the field of hostage negotiation. She was also a professor of criminology at the University of California in Berkeley.

Police calls were being routinely monitored by the offices of both the *Oakland Tribune* and the *San Francisco Chronicle*. Media representatives were beginning to arrive on the scene at a hastily established communications center near the entrance to the church parking lot. Sergeant Frank Castor was assigned duty as press officer.

Public utilities personnel arrived with blueprints describing the various gas, water, and electrical underground routes leading into the facility. The location of cutoff valves was being determined. The mayor ordered City Planning Department personnel to find and deliver blueprints of the church facility to the Command Center. Emergency medical teams and equipment were arriving.

Hospitals in the area were being alerted to a possible massive emergency. Weapons and tactics specialists from the Baytown PD and the FBI were arriving in a steady stream. The tactical squad was marshalling in a parking area about a block away.

Inside the Command Center, Webber, White, and Randle, together with FBI technicians, continued to monitor the television screens. They watched two men conscripted from the congregation carry the television to the platform and plug it in. Another congregation member was stringing a long cable down the aisle, apparently from a TV cable source off-camera. He attached the cable to the set. The one who seemed to be in charge turned on the set and watched a picture appear on the screen.

"What channel are we on?" he asked.

"Seventeen," responded the man who had laid out the cable.

The terrorist changed channels until he reach 17. He stopped, looked up and smiled. He had just seen his own picture.

He waved his cell phone at the camera.

Webber swore, smacking the work bench with his fist. "We didn't give him a number to call! Come on, fellas. Help me out here. That's what he's waiting for. And where is our negotiating team?"

They watched as the man dropped the phone in a chair next to him.

"Dial 9-1-1," suggested a young man sitting near the front between two women. "Then ask to be connected with the police."

The man on the platform eyed the young man for a moment, as if he were evaluating what had just been said. Then he picked up the phone and dialed. In a few moments he was on the line with Duane Webber.

"Good morning . . . or should I say good afternoon?" The man's tone was cheerful. Almost carefree. "Time flies, doesn't it?"

Randle wondered how fast time was flying for the people who had been sitting in the pews for almost three hours.

Probably not very fast. And by now I'm sure that more than a few of them need to use the restroom. How's he going to handle that?

"Who am I speaking to?" the man asked, leaning back in the chair.

"My name is Webber. Duane Webber."

"Well, Mr. Webber. Who are you? What qualifies you to be talking with me just now?"

"I'm with the FBI."

"Ah, the FBI. Good. And what is your position with the FBI?" His voice carried a mocking tone now. "Are you one of those trained negotiators we hear so much about? If you are, forget it. I do not wish to speak with a negotiator. *I* am the negotiator. I am also the leader of this team and I wish to speak only with the leader of the FBI. Are you the top man?"

"I am Special Agent in Charge of the San Francisco office. And yes, I am in charge of this region. Now that I've introduced myself, perhaps you would be kind enough to do the same?"

"Of course. You'd like to know who we are. I will tell you in a moment. And from now on, I will speak only with you, Mr. Special Agent in Charge. No one else. But first we have some personal needs to attend to. It may be of interest to you that we have counted six hundred and eighty-seven people who remain here as our guests. We are very much like a jumbo jet filled with passengers, are we not? Only we are not flying anywhere."

The man paused, then continued.

"That is not exactly true." He motioned toward the body lying on the platform. "You can see that one individual has already been judged by Allah. He is in hell with the rest of the world's infidels who refuse to acknowledge Allah as the one true God. There will surely be others if you decide not to assist us in meeting our demands. But for now the comfort of our guests is important to us."

"Look at him sitting there with a dead body, talking about the 'comfort of his guests,'" the Chief muttered.

Shhh. Listen. Webber pointed to his lips and then to his ear.

"We have been here together for about three hours now. There is a need to use the restrooms. Here is what we will do. One of my associates will be in the lobby for purposes of security. Our guests will be numbered off in groups of twenty, and permitted to use the restrooms. Once they have returned, the next group will be permitted to go. We will do this until everyone has completed the task. Should anyone fail to return . . ."

He paused, looking around, his eyes growing dark and hard. "Two of those remaining inside will be killed for every individual trying to escape. An eye for an eye.

"So this is the plan. The doors are charged with explosives. We are deactivating one of them. Twenty people are ready to leave. Let them do so without endangering those who remain. Oh, there is one other very important request. While we are caring for these mundane personal needs, I want you to see to it that we are linked to the networks. CNN, Fox, NBC, ABC, and CBS. This must be accomplished within one hour. If it is not done, five people will die. For every hour of delay thereafter, five additional souls will be deposited in hell until you comply. This is not a threat. It is a promise. This is a nonnegotiable request, so do not waste precious time talking. We have many here from which to choose. Just do it."

Webber and Randle looked at one another.

Chief White swore again, a look that almost bordered on admiration in his eyes.

"They've got us," he said. "And they know it."

They watched as a group of twenty people shuffled out of the door to the far left of the main entrance. Webber knew that this was going to take some time.

"I still don't know your name," he said into the telephone.

"Ah, yes. How impolite of me. But first, we must attend to the needs of our guests."

"He's taunting us!" growled White.

"We will need diapers and some baby food. There are three small infants with us here."

"Why don't you just let them come out with their mothers?" asked Webber.

"Perhaps later. Not just yet. It is also past the noon hour. We are getting hungry."

"What would you like to eat?" asked Webber.

"Something quick. McDonalds. Tell them to bring enough for all these people. Oh, I almost forgot. You will want to add to that number your own people outside. How many extra will we need?"

"Don't worry about us, but thanks for your concern."

"It is my pleasure," the man responded with a smile. "Don't forget. You have fifty-five minutes left to establish a national news hookup."

Webber could see people returning now from the restroom. Others stood waiting, forming a line near the exit.

"Can you believe this?" Randle asked as he watched the screen. "There's an exit to the outside about twenty or thirty feet from that door. If someone went for it they could probably get away. But they are going back inside."

"That's okay for now," said Chief White. "Let's not get anyone else killed." He turned to face Webber. "What's your plan? What are we going to do?"

Duane Webber sat quietly, staring straight ahead.

I don't know. I don't know what we're going to do.

For the first time since arriving on the scene, his mind drifted back to Janice. He saw her standing by the car, her lithe form growing smaller as the helicopter lifted off the ground and flew away.

I love you, Janice Webber.

He mouthed the words silently as he watched a steady stream of people file in and out of the auditorium.

"Food and drinks will be delivered within the hour." Webber was back on the telephone. "We're working on the network links. But I will not continue our conversation until you have identified yourself. In our culture we do not carry on discussions with people we do not know by name."

"Ah, you are very perceptive, Mr. Agent Webber of the FBI. You know that we are not your people. Is it our skin color? No, there are many in your country with our skin color. How do you know we are from a different culture?"

"I repeat, I will not continue our conversation until you give me your name."

"Yes, of course. Please. My name is Akmed el Hussein. My friends and I are members of Islamic Jihad. We represent the poorest and most oppressed people on earth. Our mothers and fathers and children are exploited and left to suffer at the hands of the Jews, armed by the Great Satan, the United States of America. I'm sure you know of us. You have occupied our land. Now we are occupying yours."

White looked at Webber and shrugged. Webber said nothing. He knew a great deal about Islamic Jihad. The group was on the FBI security threat list. It was linked with Hamas and was viewed as an extremely radical and dangerous organization.

"Of course I have heard of the great Palestinian people," said Webber, "and I am sympathetic to their plight. Perhaps I know something of the organization you claim to represent, but I'm not sure. Can you enlighten me?"

"Of course. The Islamic Jihad is committed to the creation of an Islamic Palestinian state. The Jews have shown themselves to be our enemies by usurping our land and suppressing our people. In spite of the recent efforts of the PNA, we must tell you there can be no meaningful negotiation with the Jews. They can never be trusted. They are determined to keep us enslaved, due in large part to the strong support received from America. So we come because you leave us no other choice. And make no mistake about it. We are ready to die if necessary.

"The *jihad* used to be a condition of faith among early Muslims. It was their sacred duty to engage in holy war; to kill anyone who did not embrace the one true faith. Today, some of our Muslim brothers have left the path of our ancient forefathers. It is for this reason that Allah has called a new generation of the faithful to assume the task of restoring the faith in our day."

"So just what is it that you want from us? May I call you Akmed?"

"If you wish."

"Why are you holding these people?"

"Because your government ignores the plight of our people. Our people are held hostage in our homeland, but no one cares. It is the only way to gain your attention and that of the rest of the world. It is for this reason, and this reason alone, that we are here, Mr. Agent Webber. We also remember 9/11. We remember the selfless sacrifice of our heroes who brought down your twin temples of greed. Now you will remember another day. Day 18 of September. A glorious day for the oppressed of the world. And here are our demands.

"We demand that America compel Israel to release all Arab political prisoners. It must be done immediately. Within twenty-four hours.

"We demand that the United Nations Security Council force Israel to retreat from the Gaza Strip and the West Bank and restore it to its rightful people, the Palestinians.

"We demand further that the UN establish a Committee of the People, together with a strict time limit for the restoration of all lands that were wrongfully usurped from the Palestinian peoples in 1948.

"We demand that Palestine be accorded full statehood by the nations of the world.

"We demand the immediate removal of all Israeli armed forces and police from these territories.

"And we demand that the United States cease its interference with these goals through its financial and military aid to our enemy, the illegitimate nation of Israel."

"They don't want much, do they?" whispered Joe Randle.

"You have exactly twenty-four hours to accomplish these tasks. After twenty-four hours, if all has not been completed, or at least adequately undertaken with agreed-upon limits ensuring their timely completion, two persons will die every hour until all of them or all of us are dead. Am I being clear enough, Mr. Agent Webber?"

"You are being quite clear, Akmed, though I cannot imagine that one human being could do such a heinous thing to another."

"Imagine it, Mr. Agent Webber. You will do well to imagine it, for it will happen if we do not achieve our worthy goals. And not only two each hour, but thousands elsewhere."

"Thousands elsewhere? What do you mean?" asked Webber.

"Exactly what I said," Akmed replied. "Listen to your newscasts and you will see."

The Command Center door opened and Stacey Jones, Travis Stentz, and Laine Cole pushed their way into the crowded interior. Three of the five-member FBI negotiating team had arrived. Webber shrugged.

"Nice to have you guys here. But you're a little late. He won't talk to anyone else but me now. Stacey, you start gathering information from the tactical unit. Travis, you're in charge of the situation board. Keep track of what is happening and what is said. Laine, listen in. Feed me your thoughts on sticky notes. Harry's out of town anyway, so I'll stay on point with this guy. Let's see what we can do here."

—m—

While Akmed continued his diatribe, a seemingly endless procession of men, women, and children, made their way to the restrooms. Ken Ralsten's mind was racing as he stood in line. He was angry. And he had never been more frightened in his life. These fools were crazy enough to kill them all. He was sure of it.

Wouldn't you know something like this would happen while Cain is off cavorting about in Israel with his little fan club? When I told him in the board meeting that he shouldn't be going on this trip, I had no idea . . . We've got to get out of here!

As they shuffled nearer the door, he whispered into his son Geoff's ear. "Get ready. As soon as we get through the door, run for the side exit."

Geoff looked startled.

"But, Dad, what about—"

His father squeezed his arm until it hurt.

"Pass the word to your mother. Be ready and don't let anything or anyone stop you."

"But—"

"Be ready!"

Geoff leaned close to his mother and whispered in her ear. Her face blanched, but she said nothing.

They were almost to the door.

—∾—

Mamdouh was tired of standing in the hallway watching people move back and forth between the restrooms and the auditorium. He reached into his shirt pocket and found the pack of cigarettes. It had been a long time. He tapped one out and fumbled for a match, striking it on the matchbook cover.

As he leaned forward to touch the flame to the cigarette, he glimpsed two figures darting for the side exit. A third person stumbled out of the line, half-dragged by one of the escapees before falling to the floor. Before Mamdouh could react, the exit doors flew open and the two were gone.

Suddenly there was pandemonium!

Mamdouh fired his gun into the ceiling. There were screams. Some people dropped to the floor. Others pushed their way back inside the sanctuary. Mousa came running out into the lobby, stumbling over people who had fallen on top of one another in their panic.

"Back inside. Everyone, get back!"

People scrambled to their feet and hurried back into the sanctuary.

Elizabeth Ralsten was the last one in before the door closed.

—∾—

"What is happening, Akmed? We heard shots." Webber leaned forward, trying to ferret out corners of the television screen that were off-camera and left to his imagination.

Akmed stood watching the commotion. Then Webber saw one of the other terrorists run down the aisle and say something to him.

"A small problem. It seems two of our guests chose to leave us without requesting permission," Akmed said. "You know what that means."

—∾—

In a matter of moments, the door to the Winnebago opened and a policeman stuck his head inside. "Two of the hostages managed to escape, sir."

Webber stepped to the door and looked down. The teenager was weeping uncontrollably, oblivious to the strangers around him. "But, Dad," he cried, shaking the shoulder of the man at his side, "you said we had to get away. I did what you said to do."

The man's face was pale. He appeared to be in shock.

"What's your name, sir?" Webber asked.

The man looked blank, staring straight ahead.

"Sir?"

"Ralsten. Ken Ralsten. This is my son, Geoff. My wife didn't make it," he added dully. "Elizabeth didn't make it."

He looked at the boy.

"She should have gotten out with us." His voice was shrill. "You let go of her, Geoff!"

"I tried, Dad. Honest. I pulled her with me. She wouldn't come. Let's go back. Something terrible is going to happen to her. You heard what that man said about people trying to escape. Let's go back, please."

"I'm sorry, son," Webber injected. "I can't permit that."

"But—"

"Officer, take these two over to the medical unit."

Webber turned and ducked back inside. He was fuming. He overheard the man saying to the boy, "It was our only chance, Geoff. You should have had a better hold on your mother!"

Webber closed the door and looked at the others. They shook their heads.

"The shrinks are going to have their work cut out with that kid," Randle declared. "His old man is dumping a truckload of guilt on him."

"I can't blame them for wanting out," White mused, "but what a price to pay."

Webber said nothing. He returned to his seat and stared at the picture on the screens as he fought to maintain control of his emotions.

58

18 SEPTEMBER 1245 LOCAL TIME
BAYTOWN, CALIFORNIA

"You know our policy is not to negotiate with hostage takers, Duane." The FBI director's voice sounded adamant over the direct line hookup between the Command Center and Washington, D.C.

"Yes sir. I'm well aware of our policy. But I'm here in the middle of something with over six hundred people's lives in my hands, and I believe we need to give them something in order to buy time. If we don't, this has the makings of a disaster that will make Waco look like a walk in the park. They've killed one already and are threatening more. If we don't give them network television access in forty minutes, they say they will kill five hostages. I believe them. They're going to do it."

"And if we give it to them, they may do it anyway. Hold on just a minute, Duane." The line went dead.

Webber looked at the others. Their unanimous recommendation a few minutes earlier had been to permit a network linkup. Was there any way to make them think they were on network television without actually doing it? None of those present knew. They had sent a runner to the media corps at the Communication Center to ask about the possibility. The runner had not yet returned.

Webber took a long sip from a soft drink can, sat back in the chair, and stretched. With every passing hour, tension was increasing inside the black trailer. He could feel it building all around him.

The young man who spun dials, listened with earphones, and operated most of the equipment surrounding them turned to Webber.

"It's for you, sir. Washington."

"Hello. Webber here."

"Okay, Duane. Sorry to break away like that. It looks as though we're in even deeper than we thought. We just received a call from Boston. Some guy called WBZ, the NBC affiliate there, and told them Boston should 'prepare to die.' He declares the city is going to be the victim of a biological holocaust unless their demands are met within twenty-four hours. Said they had already exposed some people as a kind of 'living illustration,' at Boston Common. Over by Frog Pond. You ever been there?"

"Sure. A couple of times."

"Well, at first they thought it was a hoax, but they sent a couple of uniforms down to check it out. When they got there, they found two families showing symptoms. They're all in the hospital now. The littlest one is very sick. Apparently whoever this was used a form of inhalation anthrax. A fellow from up in Maine was able to ID two potentials. They stayed for several days in his guest house. Get this. He put the finger on Marwan Dosha."

"Dosha. Are you certain, sir?"

"Ninety-nine percent."

"You think there's a connection with what's happening here?"

"Possibly. Ask your friend there."

"Dosha," he repeated, half to himself. "Shall I use the magic name, sir?"

A pause.

"Yes. Go ahead. Let's test the water."

"We'll keep this line open, sir. Can you give us a permanent tenant there on your end of things?"

"Will do."

Webber looked at Laine, who shook his head. They turned back to the screen. Akmed was sitting in a chair on the platform, smoking a cigarette. There were no ashtrays, so he flicked the ashes onto the carpet. The irreverence struck Webber as so out of context. Was that part of the message they were trying to get across as well? Webber dialed. He could hear the phone ring over the television monitor at the same time it was heard in the room. He watched Akmed pick up the receiver.

"We're working on the network hookups, Akmed. I'm doing the very best that I can. I'm not sure I've got the clout to force such a decision."

Akmed made a point of looking at his watch. "There is not a great deal of time remaining. Rest assured that if you fail, five people will die. That is not an idle threat, Mr. Agent Webber. It is a promise."

Just then, the runner stuck his head inside the trailer. He moved it from side to side and motioned thumbs down. They could not pull off a phony hookup.

"The networks are ready, but it's too iffy to try to fake it," he whispered to

Randle. "They may have someone outside who will let them know whether or not they're really on."

Randle nodded. "Thanks. Stand by in case we need you again."

—m—

"Our recommendation at this end still stands, sir. We're unanimous on it and we're running out of time." Webber could hear a murmur of voices on the other end of the line. Then it was silent.

"Okay," the director's voice came through, wrung out with resignation. "This is a mess, Duane. We may be dodging driftwood just so we can hit an iceberg, but get busy anyway and set it up. Try for something big in return. Like a few hundred hostages. I've got to talk to Ellis up in Boston. Hang tough."

"Yes sir. And good luck with Boston."

Webber motioned to Joe Randle.

"Take charge of getting the media hooked in. Make certain they don't go off half-cocked. Remember Harry's Bar."

Randle remembered. How many years ago had it been? In Berkeley, some nut with a gun had taken over a local bar and was holding the patrons hostage. When television crews arrived to provide live on-the-spot coverage, the gunman saw what was happening outside the building by watching the television in the bar.

While news reporters described police activity, complete with pictures documenting their commentary and revealing members of a SWAT team positioning themselves for an assault, the perp began killing everyone inside. Eventually, he too was killed, but the fat had already been dipped into the fire. Lives had been lost unnecessarily and fingers of guilt were pointed in all directions. Coverage of the tragedy came under major scrutiny, resulting in more stringent guidelines for cooperation between law enforcement agencies and the media.

As he headed for the Communications Center, Randle tried to mentally prepare himself for what was ahead.

59

Look, Akmed, I'm doing everything I can." Webber's tone carried an edge of frustration as he spoke. It was the exact mood he wanted to convey. "I'm pulling all the strings I've got. Give me something to negotiate with. Give me the hostages. Let me come in and take their place."

"Are you serious?" sneered Akmed. "These people are our ticket. If we gave them up, you wouldn't begin to meet our demands!"

"If you won't give them all up, then give us some of them as an act of good faith. Without that, I'll not be able to pull together enough support for hooking you into national TV."

Akmed's eyes wandered over the crowd seated before him.

The other two operations should be well on the way by now. It's time to play the next card.

"Mr. Agent Webber, here is my deal. When I see proof that we are linked into the major networks, guests will be released."

"How many hostages can I say will be coming out?"

Akmed placed his hand under his chin, feigning the appearance of giving the question thoughtful consideration. In actuality, he had already decided his next move days ago.

"NBC, CBS, ABC, Fox are each worth fifty. CNN will be worth a hundred. That is my best and final offer. Not one more or less. Do not attempt to stall or negotiate further."

"Akmed, this is very difficult. How about giving us an extra hour to work out the details?"

"No."

"Thirty minutes. Surely you can give us an extra thirty minutes?"

"Mr. Agent Webber, you are beginning to get on my nerves. The answer is, and will continue to be, *no.* Not an extra hour. Not an extra half hour. Not an extra minute. And please do not try to fool us with treachery or dishonesty. By now you must be aware that ours is not the only matter before you."

Webber knitted his brow and licked his lips.

"What do you mean?"

"Come now, Mr. Agent Webber. Have you been in contact with your headquarters in Washington?"

Webber hesitated, wondering where this conversation was headed.

"Yes," he answered, finally.

"And have your people there expressed concern over the welfare of the city of Boston?"

Webber looked at White and the mayor.

"Well?"

"Yes. An unverified threat has been received. What do you know about it?"

"I know that you would do well to consider it seriously. If the United States requires of Israel their acquiescence to the righteous demands of the Islamic Jihad, there need be no further lives lost. If she does not, then your troubles have only begun.

"If our demands are not acceded to, we will be forced to release a weapon of incredible death and devastation on the people there. You may also be interested to know that we have in our possession the pastor of this church and twenty-four of the church's members, who have been sightseeing in our homeland."

Akmed gave a dramatic pause as this unexpected news had its intended effect on the Command Center. Webber stared at the screen, his mind racing. Then Akmed continued.

"So we are ready. If this demand is not met on time, we will proceed with executing five persons here immediately. We will continue to do the same every hour after that until you fulfill our demand. One way or another, you will have your wish regarding the release of our guests. You get to decide if you prefer them handed to you dead or alive. You don't have much time left, Mr. Agent Webber. The hour will soon be up."

—m—

"He knows about Boston, sir. Says they've got some incredible weapon of mass destruction and that they're ready to use it. He also claims that they've got the pastor of this church and twenty-four church members hostage in Israel. Apparently they're on a tour."

"Unbelievable. If that's true—," the director hesitated. "All right, I'll have it checked out. What is going on here? Why do you suppose they picked this church?"

"The word is that the pastor has taken groups to Israel before. Maybe they just arbitrarily chose. I think the fact that they have television access is also key. And it is not so large a crowd that they can't manage it, but large enough to threaten devastating results if we don't give them what they want."

"You could be right."

"I decided not to mention Dosha just yet, though I'm not exactly sure why," Webber added, wiping beads of sweat from his forehead. Even though the trailer was air-conditioned, perspiration continued to pop out in various spots on his body. He knew it was an indication of the stress he was feeling.

"It's just as well. Let's play our cards as carefully as possible. It looks like the deck has been stacked against us," the director responded. "If no point is served, there's no purpose in divulging everything we know. We've verified anthrax as the weapon of choice on the little boy at Frog Pond. An inhalation variety. He skinned his elbow earlier in the day. The doctors say that, together with his chronic asthma, is the reason he is so sick so soon. The prognosis is that he and the others are goners. It's only a matter of hours. A day or two at the very most. Doesn't seem to be much the doctors can do once the spores are ingested."

"This is much more sophisticated than a run-of-the-mill terrorist operation, sir," said Webber. "It also looks to be more deadly. You know the stats, sir. Religious terrorism usually proves to be much more lethal than when it's just political. These people are asking for some political stuff, but the fact that they've chosen a church and maybe a pastor over in Israel makes me believe we've got the worst of the worse on our hands. I don't know about the Boston situation, but these people appear to be ready to die for the cause."

"What's your overall status, Duane?"

"Our Command Center is one hundred percent. We've set up a Communications Center a couple of hundred yards away and out of sight. I've not been down there, but I'm told it's already loaded with media peeps. We just delivered hamburgers, fries, and Cokes enough for seven hundred, inside the church. We've gotten everyone out of the periphery rooms; you know, all the Sunday school kids and the adult workers that were with them. Must have been two hundred or more there. I guess it pays to volunteer for Sunday school work. At least it did today. Two other people escaped about a half hour ago; a man and his teenage son. His wife is still in there. And in five minutes we go on live network TV."

"You got a SWAT team there?"

"Came in about twenty minutes ago. They've taken up positions near the building."

"What about the building layout?"

"Got the blueprint copies from the Planning Department fifteen minutes ago. The SWAT team leader is checking them out now."

"Who is he?"

"Hendrickson."

"Don't know him. Is he good?"

"The best."

"Good. Stay in touch."

—∿—

Esther had remained seated quietly in her pew from the beginning of this whole bizarre event. The only time she had moved was to use the restroom with the others. Then back to her seat again.

At first she had prayed. Because no one was permitted to talk to their neighbor, a good number of the hostages were spending their time in conversation with God. She glanced out of the corner of her eye in both directions, something inside her needing the reassurance of others being present.

No, it was more than that.

It was an inner longing that she recognized, but one with which she had never fully come to terms—the need to be reassured that, somehow, everyone was all right. It was a feeling she had talked about with other pastors' wives—how that even after sometimes being ground into powder by congregational criticism and thankless behind-the-scenes tasks that nobody else would do, there was a need to know that everybody in the church family was okay. Even if the wives themselves were not.

Now Esther Cain was experiencing that same mysterious concern. It drove her once again to her silent vigil of prayer. Surrounded by frightened souls, rendered helpless by armed and dangerous people whose cause she did not understand, she sought and found her refuge in communion with God—*the God who is truly there.*

Glancing at Jeremy sitting next to her, she caught his eye, then looked away, not wanting to draw attention to their relationship. Next to him was Allison Orwell. Beautiful Allison. She seemed so strong in her faith. A standout in terms of physical attractiveness, she carried within her a spirit that was equally beautiful. Esther tried to think of a time that she could remember seeing her in church without her Bible open and taking notes. In fact, there it was in her lap this morning. A young girl, undergoing the transforming metamorphosis from adolescence to womanhood. She possessed what Esther liked to call a fair beauty, one that spoke of purity, flawlessness, and freshness.

Why am I thinking like this? Why is my mind wandering so? Come on, Esther, pull it together. You've got to stay calm and alert.

As she let her gaze move beyond those seated next to her, there were others with heads bowed, obviously praying. Some were busy comforting family members and keeping an eye on the intruders. Surprisingly, more than a few pairs of eyes were on her. Watching. She knew they were wondering what she was thinking, what she would do.

Esther tried to read the lips of the man on the platform, sitting there in her husband's chair. He was talking with someone, she did not know who. She hoped it was a negotiator. She had read about such people in the newspapers. Their verbal heroics had seemed so otherworldly, however, that it had never been more than a passing curiosity. Now she found herself straining to interpret any discernable lip movement and praying that the world's best negotiator was on the other end of the line.

What's going to happen now that Ken and Geoff have escaped?

Esther remembered the terrorist's threat. She could not bring herself to even think what the outcome might be.

If only John were here.

60

18 SEPTEMBER 1830 LOCAL TIME
THE ROAD TO JERUSALEM

The sun hung low over the Judean hills as the orange and blue Israel Tours bus made its way along Highway 90, coming to the main road between Jericho and Jerusalem. Turning left, they began the long, winding ascent, from 250 meters below sea level to 820 meters above. It was slow going. The passengers were silent, lost in their own thoughts. Talking among themselves had been forbidden by the terrorists. No one was to speak unless first spoken to.

John's last question to Yazib remained unanswered.

"What do you mean you have my wife and our congregation? You expect us to believe you have taken them hostage, too? That's impossible."

The sun readied itself for the day's final encore by turning cumulus clouds into fiery curtains throwing giant shadows across the ancient hills. Under normal circumstances, it would have been a grand climax to another glorious day of adventure. But today the audience was unappreciative as their commandeered ride turned off the main highway and bounced over potholes onto a side road. They passed a marker announcing that Nebi Musa was just ahead. Shortly thereafter, they pulled into a deserted parking lot in front of an ancient mosque.

"We will enjoy a brief rest here while waiting for darkness to come. This is a good place, no?" asked Yazib, looking at John Cain. "Do you know where you are?"

John stared at Yazib, choking back the resentment and anger he felt at their predicament. He nodded once.

"You may speak to your people now, Reverend Cain. Tell them where we are. I'm sure they would like to know."

John turned his gaze slowly, pain shooting through his head and shoulders as he shifted in the seat. His eye and cheek had swollen, as well as part of his lower lip. It was hard to speak clearly, yet he wanted to bring words of comfort to these frightened disciples, these friends who had followed him halfway around the world.

They had often stood together on the threshold of eternity back home. As funeral dirges echoed in their ears, they had waited for their pastor to make some sense out of death's senselessness. And somehow, by digging deeply into his soul and into the Scriptures, he had come up with a word time and again. But no words came to mind that could erase the collective fear he saw staring back at him today.

"Tell them!" Yazib spoke sharply. "That is, if you even know where we are," he added with a smirk.

"We are at Nebi Musa," John began, flinching at a sudden stab of pain under his eye. "Muslims believe that this is the site where Moses is buried. From here you can see Mount Nebo, across the Jordan Valley. According to Deuteronomy 34, that is where Moses was shown the Promised Land by Jehovah God. It is where he died. Because Muslim tradition holds this to be Moses' final burial place, there is a large cemetery here in which many of their people have chosen to be buried. If I remember correctly, Muhammad's favorite wife, Aisha, is also buried here."

Yazib and the other team members were attentive to John as he spoke.

"Very impressive, Reverend Cain," said Yazib. The others nodded their heads appreciatively. "I am surprised that you are so aware of our Muslim beliefs."

"Your beliefs and traditions are an important part of the history of this land," John responded, grimacing at the pain, wondering if his cheekbone had been broken by Yazib's blow.

"Where are you taking us?" Evelyn Unruh suddenly demanded, in a loud, clear voice, from two rows behind John.

"Shut up, old woman," Yazib answered curtly.

"I will not shut up, young man," Evelyn snapped, her eyes flashing defiance. "I have lived too long to be treated this way. Furthermore, I am an American citizen, as are we all. You may think you are making some kind of political statement by taking us hostage, but the way you are acting is most certainly not in keeping with your own Muslim traditions."

"I said be quiet," repeated Yazib.

But Evelyn was on a roll as she leaned forward in her seat, her finger pointing and slicing through the tension in the bus, to emphasize her words.

"I don't know a great deal about your beliefs, but I do know about mine," she said hotly, "and I am not afraid of you. I also want you to know that I deeply resent the way you have treated Pastor Cain. He is our spiritual leader. We would never strike one of your spiritual leaders. I cannot imagine

Muhammad respecting what you are doing to us. He would certainly show an old woman some respect!"

Yazib seemed at a loss for words, put off guard by this elderly woman's challenge.

It was Pasha who finally stood and approached Evelyn slowly.

"What is your name?"

"My name is Evelyn Unruh."

"Where are you from, Evelyn Unruh?"

"I was born in Omaha, Nebraska. My family moved to California when I was six years old. I've lived there ever since. I have a son and three grandchildren."

"I see. Do you have some pictures of them?"

"Yes, as a matter of fact, I do. May I show them to you?"

"Of course."

John watched in amazement as Evelyn worked her grandmotherly charm on this gun-wielding, female terrorist. She reached into her purse and withdrew a well-worn picture, laminated in plastic, and handed it to the woman.

"They are very beautiful," she said quietly, handing the photo back to Evelyn. "How old are you now, Evelyn Unruh?"

"I am seventy-seven," she answered emphatically.

"Come with me. Some fresh air will be good for one as old as you."

"I am fine just where I am, thank you," Evelyn answered emphatically.

Pasha suddenly grabbed Evelyn by the hair and yanked her from the aisle seat. Screams of surprise and protest erupted from the other group members. Three men nearby rose to stop her.

"Sit down!" ordered Yazib, pointing his gun at them. "You must sit down. Now!"

Pasha continued dragging Evelyn down the aisle by her hair. John, aghast with horror, reached out to stop her, only to be brutally hammered back into his seat by Fathi Adahlah's pistol chop to the back of his neck. Pasha hurled Evelyn through the open door.

Pain from the blow paralyzed John momentarily, making further intervention impossible. As he was slammed against the window, he heard something pop. Then another. Was it a bone? Had he broken something? He was too stunned and in too much pain to tell.

"Oh, God, please, no!" John heard Patricia Hansen's voice. He heard others sobbing uncontrollably. John wanted to tell them that he was all right, they didn't need to worry. But he could not move. He gritted his teeth as a hot current of pain streaked through his body.

Out of the corner of his eye he saw the woman they called Pasha. As she moved away from the door, John saw the weapon in her hands. Her face was expressionless, her eyes dark and cold. He forced his mind to concentrate, as a stab of apprehension jarred him. Pushing himself up from where he had fallen, he peered out the side window.

There in the dirt by the side of the bus, Evelyn lay motionless, her eyes open to the darkening sky, the faces of her grandchildren clutched in her hand.

Name: Evelyn Unruh.

Born: Omaha, Nebraska.

Lived in California from the age of six.

Died: Nebi Musa, Israel.

Age: Seventy-seven.

Cause of death: Two shots fired at close range.

Another victim of Pasha Bashera, terrorist.

John stared at the lifeless form of his dear old friend. He lifted his hand to brush at the tears in his eyes and was surprised to discover there were none. The tears spilling over were on the inside of his soul, dropping on the floor of his heart.

Lord, what have I done? We should not be here. We should be home with our families, in America. What is happening to us?

He heard quiet weeping behind him. Regret came crashing down like falling rocks. He wanted to tell everyone how sorry he was. He wanted to help everyone make some sense out of Evelyn's senseless death.

But it was no use.

It was too late.

61

The sun had completely disappeared behind the hills by the time Imad restarted the engine. Grinding the gears noisily in place, he turned the bus in a tight circle and headed back across the parking lot in the direction they had come.

Every head turned, every eye strained, to catch a final glimpse of Evelyn.

And then she was out of sight.

John looked at her empty seat. Inches away sat Mary Callahan, her seat partner and roommate. Mary's face was chalky white as she continued wiping tears away with nervous hands.

The kidnappers said nothing.

After a while, the bus turned left and continued westward up the Jericho-Jerusalem Highway. They had gone only a few kilometers when Yazib took the guide's microphone in his hand and turned to face the group. His face was grim. "You see what happens when you show disrespect. Such tragedies are unavoidable in war. And you must understand, we are at war. What part do you play? You are merely pawns in a game of chess. You are property. Chattel for purposes of negotiation. Your lives mean nothing to us. Remember this. Unless your country understands that the only way to get you back is to meet the demands of our people, you are worthless."

He paused, but no one moved or spoke up.

"Fathi is coming among you now. He will bind your arms and tape your mouths. I warn you not to panic. Do not attempt any heroics. If anyone does anything out of the ordinary, that person will be shot just like the old woman. And one other person as well, for good measure. If some of you die, it does not concern us. Enough of you will remain alive for our purposes. And if you cooperate, you will all live. It is as simple as that."

Fathi moved silently among the hostages, beginning with those seated in the back of the bus. Pasha's eyes never left them for an instant, her weapon held in firing position.

Each person's mouth was taped over with a wide brown adhesive. The tourists were made to stand while the same tape was wrapped around them, binding their arms to their upper body, from shoulder to wrist. Returning to a sitting position was difficult, forcing each individual to sit up straight or lean forward with hands tucked behind their backs.

John was the last to be bound.

"Do his arms, but leave his mouth free for now," Yazib ordered.

Fathi quickly drew the tape around and around John's torso. John's shirt was short-sleeved, and the tape clung tightly to his bare arms. He knew that almost every man and woman was dressed similarly, all in short sleeves, several in walking shorts. When the tape was removed, it would be painful. If it was removed . . .

John looked into the eyes of the man wrapping the tape. They were cold. Matter-of-fact. Telegraphing no inkling of concern for their welfare. This was a man seemingly devoid of the feelings that were slamming around inside John's head. A skilled employee, well trained and dedicated, busy with the day's work.

John felt another stab of remorse.

What if it's true? What if Esther and the church back home are being held hostage? How could they possibly have done it? It's probably just a bluff to make us more uneasy, more willing to cooperate. Still, how did they know about us? About the church? Poor Evelyn. She will never see it again. Will any of us ever see it again? And what about Boston? Is it possible? Could they really have a bomb?

The more his imagination ran amok, the more concerned he became. Finally his thoughts returned to the hotel by the sea, where this nightmare had begun. To Jessica. Both relief and concern spilled over in his mind as he thought about his sweet, beautiful Jessica.

What has happened to her? She's a resourceful twelve-year-old. She won't panic. At least I hope not. Obviously these people expected her to be on the bus. And I almost gave her away. Will she know what to do?

He prayed silently.

Thank you, Lord, for allowing her to not feel good today. Thank you for keeping her there in the restroom during all of this. This is one more time in my life that you've taken something bad and turned it into good. Help her find someone at the hotel who will take care of her and keep her safe. And, Lord, please watch over Esther and Jeremy back home. I don't know what is happening there, but you do. Keep your protecting hand on them. Help Jessica reach someone by phone soon so they can arrange to get her home.

Burning concern and genuine physical pain swept through John once again.

If what these people say is true, Lord, I beg of you, keep my family and the church family safe. Remove them from danger. Watch over them until we are all together again.

His thoughts veered to Evelyn. He was haunted by her lifeless form, and the picture of her grandchildren clutched in her hand. Regret hung like a dark cloud. Suddenly the bus veered abruptly to the right onto another road. John peered into the darkness, then back at the road again, dimly lit by the bus' headlamps. He thought he saw a sign identifying the road as Highway 437.

Where would they be taking us? We must be close to Jerusalem, but I don't remember ever having been on this road.

After what seemed about five or six miles, the driver, the one they called Imad, made an abrupt left turn and pushed the accelerator to the floor once again. Along the edge of the road, another sign caught John's eye.

Ramallah. We must be circling Jerusalem, coming around to the north.

"Do you know where we are?" Yazib asked as he shifted his legs. He sat directly across from John, leaning against one of the large canvas bags that John assumed was filled with ammunition and other weapons.

John shook his head. He was not going to reveal that he had any idea of direction or location. Anyway, his sense of where they were was sketchy at best.

"We are coming soon to a small village. We will be met by other soldiers of the revolution. Ten of your group will be taken into their custody. The rest of us will continue on."

"Why are you separating us?" asked John.

"We are, as you say in America, hedging our bets. We cannot be too careful when it comes to dealing with the enemies of Allah and of our people. If you are all in one place and that place is discovered, we are much weaker than if only a few of you are lost to us. Our power is heightened by keeping some of you on the black squares, and others on the red." Yazib paused, then asked, "Do you like chess, Reverend Cain?"

John said nothing.

"It is a game forbidden by some of the most strict in our Islamic community. However, I have found it to be great mental exercise. Perhaps we can play together one day, when this is all over and done with."

John continued looking straight ahead, watching for road signs that might reveal a familiar name. Before long, another flashed by, indicating an interchange. It pointed out Highway 60, Ramallah to the north, Jerusalem to the south. Highway 60. John knew where they were now. It was a relatively short distance to Jerusalem. Ramallah and Shechum/Nablus lay along the highway to the north. They did not turn north or south, however, but continued along in a westerly direction another two or three miles before the bus slowed and eventually rolled to a stop, its right wheels on the road's shoulder.

Shadowy figures emerged from the darkness, gathering at the side of the bus. Imad opened the door and a man stepped up into the entry well.

Yazib strode down the aisle, tapping first one passenger, then another on the shoulder.

"Move. Hurry." Yazib spoke roughly to the first few until everyone got the idea of what they were supposed to do. Patricia Hansen, Mary Callahan, Shad Coleman, and Debbie Sommers stood to their feet and shuffled toward the exit.

Nick Micceli stood, expecting to see Yazib tap his wife, Patricia's, shoulder as well. It did not happen. John watched as concern etched more lines on Nick's face, visible above the tape that circled his head and covered his mouth.

"Move!" shouted Yazib, giving Nick a shove. There was no opportunity for pleading to be removed from the bus together. No time for good-byes. Nick staggered under the force of the blow, then made his way along the aisle.

Adele Smith, Dan Wilson, Jill Anderson, Dan Watson, and Sandy Mitchel.

John watched each person quietly move past the man standing in the door and disappear into the night. Finally, with a broad smile and a wave of his hand, the man followed Sandy out the door.

The door closed. The bus roared to life, lurching back onto the roadway. There was more grinding of gears as they headed west. But only for about a mile and a half. Imad turned left and John was certain they were now headed south, toward Jerusalem. He felt a sudden flush. Every bone seemed to ache. He was consumed with weariness.

Lord, I'm begging you. Keep each of those people safe. I'm responsible for their being here, but there's nothing I can do to protect them. I don't know where they are being taken, but you do. Keep your strong arm of protection around them. And around the rest of us, too.

The deployment of the ten hostages had taken no more than a minute, maybe two. It had been only a few hours since they had left the hotel on the Dead Sea.

But it seemed like an eternity.

62

18 SEPTEMBER, LOCAL TIME 2314
JERUSALEM

Two more stops were made. John was not sure exactly where in either case. At each stop, shadowy figures came out of the night to meet them. Each time, a few more of his flock were swept into the gloomy depths of the city.

Ruth Taylor, Larry Mitchel, Susan Cloud, Harold Eiderman, Donna Thomas.

John was heartsick as he studied how carefully Yazib selected and separated husbands and wives.

What is his purpose in doing this? Does he think we will be easier to control this way? He's probably right. Does he expect increased cooperation from us?

John did not know.

Now he wished he had taken more time to read about the psychology of hostage taking. He remembered scanning articles on Stockholm Syndrome, Pan Am 103, the New York Trade Center bombing, and, of course, the riveting losses of 9/11. Some years ago, he had watched a film about Terry Anderson's seven-year saga as a hostage in Lebanon. But it had evoked only a passing curiosity. The prospect of any real-life involvement with terrorists seemed no less improbable than being tapped for Harrison Ford's role in *Patriot Games.*

Who would ever imagine that a pastor and parishioners would be taken hostage? Was this designed to be some diabolic blackmail scheme? John tried to remember what he had learned from news reports about radical Muslim terrorism around the world. He knew the Intifada was not simply a racial or political issue, spawned by mutual hatred and distrust between Arabs and Jews. Listening as these youths spoke among themselves, mostly in Arabic but occasionally in English, John was becoming increasingly aware of one thing. Their kidnapping was not just about a piece of dirt. It was more than that. This was a battle with roots in religion. A *jihad.* And at its core a zealous commitment to Islamic ideals of spiritual reawakening and moral purification. A return to the soulish roots of the Muslim faith.

Apparently John and his group had been chosen as human vouchers, flesh and blood currency, with which the terrorists hoped to barter their way out of Gaza's rock-strewn streets and the refugee communities of Israel's West Bank—places where the Palestinians had suffered for decades under the relentless boot of poverty and the domination of their hated enemy.

John knew this much. He knew that radical Muslims craved a platform, a springboard from which to launch an Islamic renaissance throughout the world. And because Islam is not a pluralistic religion, it offered little room for people of other faiths to coexist in mutual harmony. The most radical Muslims held that all outsiders were infidels who must either be converted or destroyed.

John watched the woman called Pasha and her companions as the bus started to move again.

We are more than currency to these people. We are symbols. Symbols of a false religious group, an immoral society that has befriended the Jews and blocked Middle East Muslims from having their day.

John quickly pushed the thought from his mind. It was not one that fostered optimism.

At the second stop, along one of Jerusalem's narrow side streets, John could see the familiar, well-lit, ancient walls of the Old City, with the Jaffa Gate and David's Tower in the distance. Phyllis Watson, Greg Sommers, Jerry Cloud, and Patricia Micceli disembarked and were quickly loaded into two vehicles that drove away in opposite directions.

John looked toward the back of the bus. The only group members still onboard were Edgar Anderson, Bob Thomas, Gisele Eiderman, and him. They were rolling again, moving out along Karen ha Yessod, past the YMCA and the King David Hotel. They turned onto Hativat Yerushalayim, took a right turn down the hill and then left along Silwan Road. Eventually they came to a stop at a place that was familiar to John, even in the darkness. They were in the parking lot in front of the Gihon Spring, at one time the sole water source for ancient Jerusalem.

Around 1000 BC, King David had captured the city and made it his capital. Although his son Solomon eventually built the temple on higher ground above it, the main residential portion of the ancient city clung to the hill called Ophel, located just above the Kidron Valley. The site had been chosen because the Gihon Spring ran through a cave at the foot of the slope.

On previous trips, this had been a favorite place of John's, one he had hoped to visit this time. But definitely under different circumstances.

The location of the natural spring on the floor of the Kidron Valley meant that Jerusalemites of old were in constant danger of being cut off from their water source when the city came under siege. However, about three hundred years after the reign of David, King Hezekiah carried out a stunning engineering project connecting the spring to the Siloam Pool, more than a quarter of a mile inside the city.

On several occasions John had tramped through the dark connecting tunnel, candle in hand and knee deep in water. Now he wondered if this was to be their final destination. And if so, why? What was the purpose in all this?

Pasha, still dressed in her hotel clerk's uniform, stood beside John, tugging on the role of adhesive tape in her hand. Without a word, she wrapped it several times around his head, covering his mouth. Then she drew a knife from the bag she had carried when leaving the hotel. The knife startled him, especially in the hands of one as calloused to killing as this woman appeared to be. She reached around his torso and cut through the tape that bound his arms. "Do not attempt to remove the tape over your mouth. Just the tape from off your arms."

She repeated the task with each of the others, giving them the same instruction. John removed the tape as gently as he could, but much of the hair on his arms came with it. The same process was being repeated by the others behind him. He rubbed his forearms. They were tender and sticky where the tape had been, but it felt good to be able to move again.

The terrorists gathered up their gear in preparation for leaving.

"Everybody out," Yazib ordered, looking at John.

John went first, followed by Gisele, Bob, and then Edgar. It wasn't until everyone was off the bus that John noticed the old car parked near the entrance to the tunnel. It was an ancient Mercedes taxi, filthy dirty, with license plate numbers beginning 666.

That figures.

He could not make out the rest in the darkness.

"Over there." Yazib pointed toward the car, his voice gruff and tense.

They walked rapidly to the cab. John assumed they were about to leave the area in it.

"You men, inside quickly. In the back." He motioned to Gisele. "You. Stand here. Fathi, keep your knife near the woman's heart. Anyone tries to escape and she will be killed first." Yazib looked at John. "Do you understand?"

John nodded.

"All right." He looked at Imad and Pasha. "Let's get busy. You know what to do."

They opened the canvas bags, removing automatic weapons, grenades, and ammunition clips. What looked like a large amount of explosives came next, then two radio-controlled detonators and a few other nondescript items. John was surprised to see a coil of rope with a grappling hook, each prong covered with a rubber substance.

What are these people up to?

Pasha withdrew some clothing from the bag, tossing pieces to Yazib, Imad, and Fathi. Then she moved behind the car and began undressing. With what appeared to John to be an unusual amount of feminine immodesty for an Arab woman, she removed the hotel clerk's uniform and dropped it to the ground, kicking it under the car together with her shoes. A moment later, she had donned the uniform of an Israeli officer, her feet ensconced in combat boots. She shrugged her way into a backpack the color of her military blouse. Yazib smiled at her and patted her shoulder in approval.

By the time she was finished, the others had also changed. Only they were in the uniforms of Arab policemen. The remaining contents of the larger bags were transferred into packs and strapped on each of the terrorist's backs. At last they were ready.

"Come," Yazib motioned to them. "We are going."

John and the others, their mouths still taped, got out of the car.

"You will follow me. We will walk single file. Watch your step. The stairs are uneven. One could easily injure himself in the darkness. If you fall and hurt yourself so that you cannot continue to keep up, we will go on without you." Yazib spoke very matter-of-factly, but the sinister implication of his warning was not lost on anyone.

They moved out from the vehicle and trudged up a series of irregular steps carved out of earth and stone. John remembered having walked down these steps from the upper part of the Ophel, some years before. It was much more difficult in the dark, however, with no illumination other than moonlight. The temperature was cooler here in the Judean hills, but the night air was still warm. No need for a jacket.

Yazib led the way, moving steadily up the side of the hill. After a few minutes on the steep incline, all the hostages were breathing heavily. John wiped perspiration away from his eyes. A sharp ache in his side made him feel his age. Though he exercised regularly back home and was in better than average physical condition, the strain of the last few hours and the physical exertion required by the climb were taking their toll. He wondered about Gisele and the others. They were likely at the end of themselves as well. Did they have enough left to endure? John experienced a wave of emotion. His family was so far away, in another life altogether than the one he was living now.

Will I ever see Esther and Jeremy and Jessica again?

A feeling of hopelessness added its weight as he climbed. He forced himself to turn his attention back to what was at hand, not what might never be again.

Focus. Pay attention to the present. Let the future take care of itself.

At the apex of the climb, they stopped to catch their breath. The City of David archaeological excavations had been going on in the area for some time. John knew this was a site of great controversy and even occasional violent protests staged by religious zealots claiming that ancient Jewish graves were being violated. Diggers refuted the accusations, declaring that in any case the site was too important to leave buried.

As a result, ever so gradually, the earliest incarnation of Jerusalem, some three thousand years old, continued to be unwrapped by the tools of the experts.

Its ragged stone steps and high walls were bathed in the glow of bright lights. A broken pillar could be seen still standing upright on its base. Several others nearby were horizontal, where they had fallen centuries before. Even tonight, in their danger-filled circumstance, John could still feel the allure of the glories of the past reach out to him from these ruins.

As he surveyed the scene, John also believed he was beginning to see where the terrorists were headed. But their ultimate goal still eluded him.

"We are going over there," Yazib pointed across the road to a part of the wall that formed a forty-five degree corner and, unlike the rest of the area, remained in dark shadows. John wondered why the darkness, then noticed that two of the lamps pointing toward that area had been broken by vandals. Or by someone. This really was beginning to feel like a well-organized, sophisticated operation. The mix of daring and detail was impressive.

These people must have major backing from someone. This is not a few hotheads running a slam-bang program of indiscriminate terrorism. If what he says is true about other teams in America, this is shaping up to be a major international event. And I'm so close to the middle of it that I can't gain full perspective.

They waited for a couple of minutes. There was very little traffic on the road at this hour.

"Now!" hissed Yazib.

As the last vehicle to be seen in either direction passed by, they dashed across the road. For a full minute they were out in the open, Yazib leading the way, then the hostages, followed by the others. It was an opportunity for someone to see them, to question their presence, to stop them from going further.

Sixty whole seconds!

Where is everybody?

They reached the shadows of a wall that stretched above them into the inky blackness of the night. The Old City. They leaned against the stones to catch their breath and to verify that no one had seen them. Nothing happened to indicate that they had been discovered. No shouts. No sirens. Nothing.

John was consumed once again with disappointment.

Where are you, God, when we need you? Here we are, in the very place that you yourself walked. Have you forgotten us?

Off to the left, around the corner from where the band of intruders huddled in the darkness, was the Dung Gate, so called because the area in ancient times was the local rubbish dump. Now it provided the nearest access into the Old City. Two young IDF soldiers leaned against the corner of the wall, their weapons hanging loosely from their shoulders. They were bored with another uneventful tour of guard duty.

"*Yesh mashehoo?*" asked one. "Do you have something to eat?"

"*Khafisat shokolad,*" the other soldier answered, reaching into his pocket for a candy bar. He broke it in half and handed one of the pieces to his partner.

"*Ani rotseh bakbook birah,*" the first man mumbled as he bit down on the candy. "I'd like to have a can of beer."

"*Ken,*" agreed the other, licking his lips.

"Remember those two American girls that came through here a couple of hours ago?"

"The blonde? And the one with the tan?"

"Yes."

"How could I forget?"

"Nice looking, huh?"

"The best today. I wonder what they're doing now?"

"I know what they're *not* doing."

"What's that?"

"They're not having as much fun as they could be if we were off duty."

Both guards laughed and strolled into the center of the gateway. The *Bab el-Magharbeh*—its official name, meaning "Gate of the Moors"—was typically quiet at this time of the night. The only activity had been a few tourists moving in and out of the Old City through the gate. Mostly Japanese and American. Occasionally a young woman worthy of a second look. And the two Americans. Other than that, nothing.

A short distance away, the unwelcome visitors whose discovery might well have earned these two soldiers medals and accolades from their superiors went unnoticed.

63

Fathi had practiced for this moment many times.

He had hurled stones and chunks of driftwood high and far, letting them fall into the sea off the Gaza coastline. He had coiled and thrown this very rope and grappling hook a hundred times under a desert sky.

He was ready.

With one expert fling, he watched the hook fly upward and disappear, soundlessly hitting the rampart floor. He pulled back on the rope until it was firmly anchored against the upper wall. The group waited, straining to hear sounds above them that would indicate an unseen guard might have noticed, looking up to see if an accusing face stared down at them. There was none. John sensed the tension gripping their captors as they huddled at the base of Suleiman the Magnificent's sixteenth-century legacy to the City of Gold.

In shocked disbelief, John now understood they were about to climb this ancient edifice.

It looked like from where they were crouching, the thick Ottoman walls rose more than one hundred feet straight up into the dark shroud of the night. Scrub brush, broken pillars, and fallen stones lay scattered along the base. One false move and it was all over. This was not the best way to enter the Old City.

"I will go first," said Yazib, looking up to where the rope disappeared in the blackness. "Fathi, you are next. Then you, Reverend Cain, followed by the other men and Pasha. The American woman comes last. If you do anything but cooperate fully, her throat will be cut immediately. Understood?"

The men nodded.

Gisele's eyes were wide with fear. Unintelligible sounds were coming from behind the tape across her mouth. She made desperate motions with her hands as she shook her head.

Yazib stepped up to Gisele. "Be quiet. You must do it!"

Gisele was shaking now. Tears rolled down her cheeks.

"There is only one other choice," said Yazib, his hand resting on the knife handle in the sheath on his belt. He paused.

"What will it be?"

John moved to where Gisele could see him. He put his hands together in prayerlike fashion, fingertips pointing heavenward. He nodded as if to say, you can make it. Then, with a glance at each of the terrorists, he walked over to Gisele and put his arms around her, holding her until he felt her stop shaking. Stepping back, he nodded affirmatively again.

Gisele brushed back her tears and nodded. She had no choice. She would try to climb.

John watched as Yazib grasped hold of the rope and put his weight on it. It held. He climbed slowly, but steadily, always careful to remain in the shadows. From even a short distance away, the climber would be invisible to all but the most discerning onlooker. From the base of the wall, one had the illusion that Yazib's body was growing smaller as he climbed, until he disappeared from view altogether. A moment later, the end of the rope jiggled, signaling the next climber to begin the ascent.

Fathi took hold of the rope and began climbing. All too quickly, John thought, he was at the top and it was his turn. He took the rope in his hands and placed both feet against the base of the wall as the others had done. With one last encouraging look to the others, he began to climb.

One hand over another. *Don't look down, John.* Pain from the blows he had been dealt earlier in the evening now surged through his body. He tried to fight off the pounding in his head. Then his foot slipped, throwing him off balance. The rope started sliding through his hands. Desperately he held on, his elbows scraping raw against the wall. The thought of free-falling onto the stones below pumped fresh adrenaline through his system. Not able to open his mouth, he struggled to breathe as he fought to regain his upward momentum. Just then his foot brushed against a large crack between the stones. He jammed the toe of his shoe into it. His heart was hammering. *Up! Keep going up!* The rope tore into the flesh of his hands. *Don't look down!*

The rope was tighter against the wall now. *I must be nearing the top.* The thought of airplanes flashed randomly through his mind. *Flying should be a piece of cake after this, if I make it.* Sweat ran in rivulets down the inside of his shirt. He forced himself not to panic at the thought of how far he was from the ground. *How is Gisele ever going to make this climb?* Then there were hands under his arms, another tugging at his wrist. Yazib and Fathi dragged him over the side and he fell exhausted onto the rough surface. He was on the roof of the El Aksa mosque, at the place where it served as part of the fortress wall.

After a few moments, John rolled over and sat up, leaning back against the wall as he sucked air. *One more thing they didn't teach me to do in seminary,* he said to himself as he braced his hands and knees to get up. The two terrorists were leaning over the side, their weapons propped up against the wall. John began a stealthy crawl toward the nearest one. His inner voice whispered, *It's your chance. Do it!*

Then Edgar's hand reached over the wall's top edge. Yazib and Fathi pulled him over the top. John stood, his legs still shaky from the climb. He glanced again at the AK-47s. It was not to be. Even if he saved himself, the others would never make it. And that, John realized, he could never live with.

Bob Thomas was over the top now, and he was soon followed by Pasha. That left Gisele and the fourth terrorist. Edgar, Bob, and John all looked at each other, the same thought etched in their faces. *Can she do it?*

John closed his eyes and silently prayed for Gisele.

When he opened them, he saw that Edgar and Bob had followed suit. They were sitting with their backs against the wall. Pasha had unshouldered her weapon and stood a few paces away, facing her hostages. Yazib and Fathi were leaning over the side.

John started toward the wall's edge.

"Stop." Pasha, her voice low and threatening, lifted the barrel of the rifle and pointed it at him.

John hesitated, putting his hands up, palms forward and about shoulder high. With a look of determination in his eyes, he walked over to the edge of the wall. Yazib glanced at him but said nothing, his attention focused on the woman clinging to the rope below.

Gisele was struggling. She was more than halfway, but she had slowed considerably. She was waiting longer between letting go with one hand and crossing over the other. To gain some leverage, she attempted to place her foot in a crack between two stones.

When Gisele had dressed in the morning, she had decided against pants or shorts. They were going to Jerusalem. She would wear a skirt. She had chosen a multicolored, lightweight cotton skirt that came to mid-calf, thinking it would meet the day's requirements very nicely. She also put on a short-sleeved cotton blouse and canvas walking shoes to complete her outfit.

Now, as she placed her foot in the crack, the toe of her shoe became entangled in the fold of her skirt. She looked down, attempting to pull loose. That's when she saw just how far up the wall she had come—and she froze.

John watched in horror as she dangled awkwardly about thirty feet below the top of the wall. With each passing second, it became obvious she was not going to make it. Without thinking, he reached for the tape around his head, tearing it away, pulling hair and skin at the same time. Yazib heard the sound, but by the time he turned, the gag was hanging limply around John's neck.

"Gisele!" John called, in a low voice. "Hang on. I'm coming to help!"

Yazib grabbed at John's shoulder to stop him, but John shrugged him off.

"You are not going anywhere!" Pasha hissed, moving forward until the black barrel of her rifle was inches from John's face.

"Shoot me if you wish. You'll wake up Jerusalem if you do. That woman is my friend and I intend to go after her." John turned to Yazib. "Is there another rope?"

"Yes, a shorter one. I don't think it's long enough to reach her."

"Get it."

Yazib hesitated, his surprised gaze never leaving John's face.

John let out a long, anxious breath as he tried not to think about the height or the danger. "Come on. You people should have thought about something like this happening."

"Wait." Yazib bent down and reached into his pack. He withdrew a coil of rope, thinner than the one they were using to climb. John took it from him and tossed one end over the side. It barely reached Gisele's shoulders. Not enough to tie around her.

Why didn't I think of this before she started up? We could have pulled her up. Now it's too late.

John knelt and tied the rope to the grappling hook, wedged tightly against the lip of the ledge by Gisele's weight. He wondered if it would be strong enough to hold them both.

"It's too short to tie around my waist. I'd never reach her. I'll have to climb down to her and you'll have to pull us both up together."

Edgar and Bob scrambled to their feet, unable to speak, but concern filling their eyes. John flashed a grim smile and said, "Pray, fellas. I'll be right back."

He dropped over the edge into the dark shadows. The rope burned into his hands as he made his way down to where Gisele still clung helplessly. He knew she wouldn't last much longer. By the time he reached her, both of his hands were raw and bleeding.

Holding on as tightly as he could, he came to a stop inches above her.

Not too fast now. You'll knock her off the rope.

Shoving the toe of his shoe into a crack in the wall, he looked down.

The world turned!

Oh Lord, what am I doing?

The height was dizzying. Going up, he had purposely not looked down. Now he had to, in order to see what he was doing. What he saw made his stomach turn. His arms ached as he adjusted his grip, but the foothold gave him a brief respite, releasing some of the tension while he got a better hold. He managed to wrap the end of the rope twice around his left hand. Looking down again, he spoke quietly.

"Gisele. Nod your head if you hear me."

John was surprised by the sound of his voice. It was calm, quiet, confident. The same voice he might have used in a counseling session in his office. It did not betray the fear and anxiety that flowed like molten lava into every part of his body as he clung to the rope.

Her face was against the wall, her eyes closed.

"Gisele?"

Her head moved. She nodded, but did not look up.

"I'm close to you. I'll help you. I'm coming down beside you now. Do you hear me?"

Her head moved again.

"Hang on tight. I may bump into you, so, whatever else you do, don't turn loose! Okay?"

She didn't move.

John put his face against the wall and took a deep breath.

"Jesus," he whispered, "you're all I've got."

He slipped his toe out of the crack and inched his way down. When he had gone as far as he could, Gisele's head was even with his waist. He felt around until he drove his left foot into a narrow crevice beside her. A stab of pain shot up his leg as he reached down and placed his arm around Gisele, desperately hanging onto the rope with one hand.

They pressed against the rock wall, their bodies swaying precariously with the impact of John's movements.

His left arm felt as if it were pulling out of its socket and the rope wrapped around his hand dug into his flesh. With his right hand he fumbled for the rope underneath Gisele's body.

There!

Grabbing it, he hung on with every ounce of energy until they stopped swaying.

"Gisele," John whispered through gritted teeth, "listen to me. We're going to make it, so hold that thought and listen carefully to what I want you to do. Keep your feet where they are for now. Then turn and face me and put your arms around my neck."

She turned her face toward him. He saw the fear in her eyes. She wouldn't last much longer.

"That's right. You have to turn loose of the rope now and put your arms around my neck. Hurry. Do it. We'll apologize later to Harold for this."

John felt her body tighten against his as she released one hand. Then she turned lose from the rope altogether and her entire weight bore down on him. Clinging to his neck, she cradled her head into his shoulder.

"Don't look down, because we're going up. Push upward with your feet when you can, but mostly, just hang on tight. You're a lightweight, so they'll pull us both up really easily. Not to worry!"

Liar. You're a dead man, Cain, and you know it. Your hands are torn up and your energy is spent. How do you think you are ever going to hang on long enough to make it back to the top?

John leaned his head against the wall. Then he looked at Gisele.

"What did you say?"

She returned his look inquisitively.

Even as he asked, he remembered the tape covering her mouth. She couldn't say anything. *But, I could have sworn she said, "We'll do it together."*

"Okay, Gisele. Here we go."

Come on, Lord. You know how much we need you now. We'll never make it without you.

Gripping the rope as hard as he could, he looked up, feeling the added strain as the men above began pulling them up. Every ounce of energy was focused. Slowly they inched their way higher. John's and Gisele's world had become a tiny place in which only the two of them existed. It was a simple world, consisting of a few rough-hewn, centuries-old stones piled on top of each other. The stones were fighting back, resisting his effort to overcome them, scraping his knuckles with every move upward.

Suddenly, he felt her slipping away.

No. Hang on, Gisele!

And then she was gone.

"Gisele!"

She had turned loose.

Oh, God, no. I've lost her!

Strong hands reached under his arms, dragging him up and over the rampart's edge for the second time.

Almost . . . almost, Gisele . . . I'm . . . so . . . sorry . . .

Evelyn Unruh's lifeless form flashed before his mind. Now he'd lost another. And then he gave up altogether as darkness fell in upon darkness.

64

The right side of his face felt the blow . . . then the left.

What's happening . . . ?

John forced his eyes to open. Edgar was hovering over him, his big hands slapping first one side of John's face, then the other. There was a look of relief as John came around.

"Edgar . . ." John tried sitting up, only to slump back onto the rooftop. He waited a moment, gathering his strength, then rolled over and pushed himself into a kneeling position. With Edgar's help, he stood up.

He must have passed out. Imad was on top with the others now. In low voices their captors talked in Arabic among themselves, casting an occasional glance in their direction. Bob was sitting nearby, Pasha's gun pointed at him in a threatening manner. Then John remembered Gisele. Tears filled his eyes.

"Gisele . . . ," he choked out her name. It was all he could say, overcome with remorse at his failure to rescue her.

Edgar gave him a puzzled look. Then he understood. Putting his hand on John's shoulder, he turned him around.

Gisele was sitting by herself, knees drawn up, face buried in the folds of her skirt.

She lifted her head and saw John standing there looking at her. Slowly she got to her feet and came toward him. Her mouth was still covered with tape. There could be no words, but her eyes, brimming with tears, said it all. She placed her head against his chest.

"I'm so glad to see you," John whispered hoarsely. "I thought . . . I thought I lost you at the very last. Thank God you're safe!"

Her arms went around him, holding onto him tightly.

Reaching up, she touched his face with her hands. Then she drew him toward her until her cheek touched his. First one side, then the other. He started to put his hands on her arms, but hesitated when he saw how dirty and bloody they were. She noticed them, too, as she stepped back. She stared at his hands, then looked up again as more tears began spilling down her cheeks.

"Don't worry, Gisele," John said. "These hands will heal fast. If there are scars someday, they'll just remind me that you're alive!"

—~—

"What do you mean, an empty bus?"

Elijah Pazer leaned forward in his chair, gripping the edge of his desk so hard that the knuckles of both hands turned white.

"Just what I said, Eli. It's confirmed. An Israel Tours bus was reported missing this evening at 2145. The group was more than two hours overdue for dinner at their hotel. The hotel manager finally contacted the tour company. They had no word of any problem, so they called the Salt Sea Hotel & Spa in Ein Bokek. The group stayed there last night. The manager said the bus left around 1630. No one noticed anything out of the ordinary. That was the last anyone saw of them or the bus until about twenty minutes ago."

"So what happened twenty minutes ago?" Pazer inquired of his young associate.

"IDF reported sighting an empty bus parked along Silwan Road near the Gihon Spring."

"Any signs of life?"

"None."

"No explosives involved?"

"They weren't sure at first, so before they opened it up they brought in the bomb squad. As it turns out, there was nothing."

"Well, an entire busload of tourists can't have just disappeared!" Pazer exclaimed. "How many are supposed to be in the group?"

"Twenty-five, plus the guide and driver."

Just then the phone rang. Elijah Pazer picked up the receiver.

"Halo!"

The young man watched nervously as his colleague's face grew somber, his countenance darkening noticeably. "*Todah, le-hitra'ot,*" he said at last, putting the receiver down gently while staring at the desk.

"Eli?"

Even though Benjamin Hertzel was a generation younger than his commanding officer, he felt free to call him by his first name. It was often this way in Israel, where there were more open collars than ties worn by men, and informality was a way of life. In this unique land respect was earned, not simply accorded to someone because of age or position. And Benjamin knew that Eli had long ago earned the respect of his peers.

"They found the driver of your bus, Ben. Tied, taped, and stuffed under a pile of laundry in a maid's room at the Salt Sea Hotel." Pazer rose from his chair and walked around the desk, cracking his knuckles at the same time. "So they sent someone up to check each of the rooms that the group members had used. They were all empty. Except for one. The guide's room. It was David Barak. I know him . . . I *knew* him. My wife and I had dinner with him and his family two weeks ago."

Benjamin Hertzel stood silently, disheartened by what he sensed was coming, waiting as Eli struggled to continue.

"He's dead. They found his body in his room. Three bullet holes."

Hertzel swore. "That means—"

"That means," Eli interrupted, "that twenty-five American tourists are somewhere in this city being held captive. Or maybe they're dead by now. Only God knows. This looks like an unholy mess."

"So what shall we do?"

"Put out the word. Close the city down. Tight! Shut down all routes in or out. Lock up the borders. Call in all off-duty personnel. Oh, and impound that bus!"

"The bus is already secure," Benjamin replied, jotting the instructions on a notepad as was his custom, using the same ancient Hebrew script that had been used centuries earlier by law keepers in King David's day.

"Good. Have it dusted. We probably won't get anything worthwhile, but do it anyway."

"Done. Anything else?"

"See if the tour company has any pictures of the people. I'll pass the word along to the chief. He'll probably want to contact the PM."

"The prime minister? This early in the process?"

"Yeah." Pazer walked over to take his jacket from off the wall hook. "There's more to this than you know, Ben. I took a call around eight o'clock from Mossad HQ. They had just been contacted by the Americans about a hostage situation out in California. Some terrorist nuts, who claim to be members of Islamic Jihad. They've got over six hundred people rounded up in a church."

The younger man followed his superior to the door. "Did you say California?"

"Yeah," Eli looked at his assistant. "Why?"

"That's where the group in the bus is from."

"California's a pretty big place, Ben."

"They're from a place called Baytown, somewhere near San Francisco."

"Baytown?" Eli paused, then began walking down the hallway toward the situation room. His steps were slow, but his mind was racing. "That's where the hostages are from."

"Eli," a female voice called out from an open side door behind them. "Another message from Mossad."

The uniformed woman's heels clicked on the marble floor as she entered the hall and handed a piece of paper to Elijah Pazer. He scanned it swiftly, then looked at Benjamin Hertzel.

"Now the word from Washington is that Boston has received a threat from terrorists. They claim they're going to cover the city with anthrax spores if the USA doesn't put the pressure on Israel to meet their demands."

"Are they taking it seriously?"

"They've got people in the hospital. A couple of families. Kids and parents. Some kind of high-grade inhalation anthrax is confirmed. They aren't sure about too much else, but they are sending their findings to their disease center. If they've got anthrax, you know what will happen if they're crazy enough to actually release it. That stuff is lethal enough to kill everyone for miles around and years to come!"

"Do you think this is tied together?"

"Is our father Abraham? I think we have another 9/11 on our hands. Only a lot worse, if that's possible. Let's go. We've got work to do!"

65

MONDAY, 19 SEPTEMBER, EARLY MORNING
JERUSALEM

Light and shadows. That was all.

No guards appeared to be on the rooftop tonight. At least not at the moment. John didn't know whether to be disappointed or relieved. Though he said nothing to the others, he was certain their lives were inconsequential to their captors. What he did not know was why such a great effort had been made, why extra chances were being taken, to get them into the Old City. He didn't understand what they were after. It would have been much easier for them to climb the wall without these inexperienced Americans. *Why keep us with them? Why not just kill us and move on?*

Imad, Fathi, and Pasha were crouched together, engaged in animated discussion with Yazib under cover of the darkest shadows of Al Aqsa's circular, silver-capped dome. The tone of their voices was subdued, but intense, and the language of the moment was Arabic. John could not understand what they were saying.

Yazib was shaking his head vehemently. Then he turned and spoke to John in English.

"You must continue to do exactly as you are told. Do you understand?"

"I want my friends to have their gags removed," John countered.

"Impossible."

"No. It's not impossible. We have cooperated. But we refuse to go any further until you take the tape from their mouths."

Yazib glared through the dark shadows at John.

"You are an interesting man, Reverend John Cain. And a surprisingly brave one, too, I'll give you that. Is this woman"—he nodded toward Gisele— "your special friend?"

"I understand what you are implying. No. She is not my *special* friend."

"Why else would you risk your life for her?"

"She and her husband are members of my church. She and I have two things in common. We are human beings and we are Christian friends. That is our relationship."

Yazib continued watching him, his eyes gleaming in the starlight.

"They might call out."

"I assure you upon my word, we will not call out."

"Your word," sneered Yazib. "The word of an American infidel pastor? It is not much."

"It is all we have remaining."

"This is true." Yazib pulled a revolver from his belt and touched the barrel against John's lips. "You make a single sound and you're a dead man. Furthermore, I assure you, the woman will die more slowly than you and much more painfully."

John nodded, feeling both apprehension and triumph.

"Remove the gags," Yazib motioned to Fathi.

Fathi hesitated for a moment, then moved to follow orders, though a look of concern crossed his face. He slipped a wicked-looking combat knife from its sheath. Gisele shuddered as the cold steel touched her neck. A moment later the tape was cut. She began pulling it away from her face and hair, grimacing as it tore loose. The others followed suit. When Fathi finally stood in front of John, knife in hand, their eyes locked. There was such hatred in the man's eyes, a kind of hatred mixed with triumph. Then he sliced through the tape that hung loosely around John's neck.

"Put the tape in here," ordered Fathi. He held out his open backpack. "We do not want to leave waste matter lying around, now do we?"

John and the others dropped the sticky strips into the bag.

"Come. Follow me and do exactly what I do. Our guns will be trained on you and we will use them if you try anything stupid."

"You've made your point," John retorted.

Yazib stepped out of the shadows of the dome. Bending low, he moved swiftly across the rooftop, careful not to get too close to the wall's edge where they might easily be seen from below. The others followed after him in single file.

John had a strange impression of déjà vu as they walked across the Al Aqsa rooftop. The familiarity of these surroundings was uncanny. He had been inside the large, plain-looking mosque on several occasions. Plain, that is, in comparison to the eye-catching Dome of the Rock, just off to their right, with its gold leaf aluminum dome rising majestically over the *Kubbet es-Sakhra,* the sacred rock, on which Abraham prepared the sacrifice of his son, Isaac. This same rock is venerated as the place from which, during his mystical journey to Jerusalem, Muhammad is said to have mounted his steed and ascended into heaven. The great Dome looked magnificent tonight. Silent. Not a soul in sight.

Directly underneath them, the Al Aqsa mosque was a vast complex accommodating up to five thousand worshipers at one time, and serving essentially as a prayer hall. Many believe it was built on the remains of an ancient Byzantine basilica. Below the mosque are the huge underground chambers of Solomon's Stables. John remembered some Jewish friends calling it *Midrash Shlomo,* the School of King Solomon.

John looked across to where, in a few hours, hundreds of Muslim worshipers would stop at the fountain in front of the mosque. There they would ready themselves for prayer by ceremonially washing head, hands, and feet. Once inside, each man would prostrate himself until his forehead touched the carpeted floor in acknowledgement of the majesty of Allah. Tonight, however, all was quiet.

Without hesitating, as if he had done this many times before, Yazib slipped over the wall, dropping down to the roof of the Islamic Museum, a long rectangular structure attached to the west side of the mosque, holding exhibits depicting the many centuries of Muslim life in Jerusalem.

About three-quarters of the way along the roof, facing into the vast esplanade known as *Haram Esh Sharif,* the Venerable Sanctuary, the slender lofty tower of a minaret pointed the way to a Muslim heaven. Near the top, a square balcony covered by a miniature dome marked the place where the muezzin stood and called the people to prayer each day at sunrise, midday, afternoon, sunset, and evening, reciting the *Adhan.*

Allah u Akbar.
God is greater.
God is greater.
I witness that there is no god but God.
I witness that Muhammad is the prophet of God.
Rise to prayer.
Rise to felicity.
God is greater.
God is greater.
There is no god but God.

As a Westerner, John had encountered the beauty, the mystery, and the mysticism of the call of the minaret the first time he had come to Israel. His soul-expanding emotions had been tempered somewhat by the discovery that ancient mystery had succumbed to modern technology. In most minarets, an electronic recording had long since taken the place of the muezzin. Progress.

John followed Yazib, dropping down onto the museum rooftop and waiting while the others followed. The strain of the past few hours was starting to take its toll. John was exhausted. Still, adrenaline flowed from some unknown reservoir as he watched Yazib motioning to the others. He signaled for quiet as they walked to the edge of the roof and looked out upon the esplanade. Responding to another hand motion, they dropped onto their stomachs and peered over the edge into the area below.

Haram esh-Sharif, known to Jews and Christians as Mount Moriah, or the Temple Mount, stretched out before them, a fantasy of long shadows and moonlit plazas. John understood that they were looking down at a locale with the potential of igniting the religious and political passions of a billion people around the world. Tonight, however, it was a place of solitude, of quiet gardens, where a gentle breeze sighed its way through tall trees.

The narrow Morrolo Gate, one of two gates through which tourists could enter during the day, was closed and under guard. Patrols of plainclothes Muslim guards, uniformed Arab police, and IDF soldiers maintained security. Tonight, as on other nights, they watched. But no one could be seen moving about.

Yazib attached the grappling hook to a lip that protruded up from the roof. Throwing the line over the side, he quickly rappelled to the ground. John went next. One by one the others followed. Then with a practiced flip of the wrist that would have made Clint Eastwood proud, Fathi snapped the rope in a manner that caused the hook to release and fall to the ground.

"Come quickly," whispered Yazib, tension and excitement cracking his voice. He ran to the southeast corner of Al Aqsa mosque, the area identified by tradition as the site of the ancient Hebrew temple's pinnacle. Here, according to the accounts in Matthew 4 and Luke 4, Jesus was tempted by the Devil. John had never been here before because it was off-limits to the public.

They made their way down a stairway leading to a solid wooden door, one that was always locked and could be opened only by an official of the Supreme Muslim Council. Well, almost always locked. Yazib pushed on the door. Whoever had turned the key earlier had done it well. The door opened immediately and the small group of captors and captives crowded inside.

They found themselves in a large underground area, full of damp, musty odors. Yazib produced a flashlight, revealing a few of the dozen pillars supporting the esplanade above. They walked single file across to the far side. At first, John did not see where they were headed. Not until they came close did he become aware of a door, tucked in behind one of the pillars. Yazib pulled it open far enough for everyone to squeeze through, closing it after the last person was inside.

Yazib ran his flashlight back and forth until finding a single bare bulb and a pull-chain hanging down from the ceiling. Reaching up, he grasped hold of it. A dim light filled the room, the bulb small but adequate.

John guessed the room to be about 20 x 20 in size. Two of the walls were earthen. The other two had been roughed in by carpenters more intent on finishing in a hurry than they were on quality of craftsmanship. Bare boards, no insulation, and no windows. It gave the appearance of having been thrown together hastily and probably quite recently. A makeshift room built for one purpose alone. And they were it!

To one side was a table and four chairs. Opposite were three cots, outfitted with blankets and thin mattresses. A stack of bread, cheese, and several bottles of mineral water had been piled unceremoniously on the table. The sight of food and water reminded John that it had been many hours since any of them had eaten. Then his eye caught something else. Chains, looking to be six or eight feet in length, were attached to one of the walls. Each complete with a steel ankle bracelet. A crude bucket, filled with water, was located near the door.

"Sit down," Yazib commanded, motioning toward the chairs. "We will remain here for the next few hours."

"Why did you bring us with you?" John asked at last, standing near Yazib.

"Patience, Reverend Cain. You will be made aware of everything in time." In spite of the coolness of the room, Yazib wiped perspiration from his brow, turning his attention back to his team of kidnappers and killers. He spoke to them in Arabic.

"Congratulations. We have done well, my friends. We have crossed the desert and the sea. We have entered, undetected, into the heart of the land of our people. Praise belongs to Allah."

His teammates nodded.

"He has enabled us to do what others thought impossible, by bringing us safely into the Sacred Zone. Now we wait. Our brothers are at work, tightening the noose around America's neck. By this time the world has been awakened to danger. We can no longer be ignored. They will be forced to meet our demands or mortgage their own future."

Imad and Fathi smiled as they soaked up the words of their leader. Pasha's eyes were on Yazib, but her face was a mask. John could not tell what emotions were gathering there. He wished he understood what was being said.

In English, once again, Yazib gave instructions. "These two beds are for use by the Americans. Imad. Fathi. Move the one on the right away from the others. We will use it. We will perform guard shifts of four hours' duration. You two will be first. Pasha and I will remain here. I want one of you just outside this door. The other will stay nearer the outside entrance. Hide behind a pillar. If someone should come, do nothing unless absolutely necessary. But kill if you have to. We must keep our presence unknown as long as possible. Understand?"

Heads nodded.

"In four hours, come and wake us. We will spell each other this way."

"Some of us need to relieve ourselves," John mentioned as the others prepared to leave.

"I regret the absence of the privacy to which you are accustomed, Reverend Cain. You may go outside, in the larger area that we walked through. One at a time. These two will be with you," he said, glancing at Imad and Fathi. "Take the bucket."

Gisele looked at John, puzzled.

"There is no toilet paper," said John. "This doesn't appear to be a five-star facility."

Her puzzled look faded into a stare of incredulity, followed by a shrug of resignation, and a tight smile. It was a moment for earthy humor. Unfortunately, the seriousness of their plight did not permit its full exercise. Gisele hoisted the bucket and gamely followed the two guards out the door.

Yazib looked at John.

"You and the others may take turns when she returns. You see the chains attached to the wall? As each of you return, you will be fettered with one of those. Pasha will personally see that it is securely locked around your ankle. Then I believe we should all try to get some sleep. Do you agree?"

John said nothing.

"Pasha, break open some food and water while I move these packs nearer to the table. Please, gentlemen, relax and make yourselves at home." His countenance suddenly turned hard and unyielding. "Do not even think about escaping. I am sorry, but for you there can be no escape."

His words struck John with foreboding finality. He looked over at the others. Their faces mirrored his own fears. The full import of Yazib's threat, veiled in polite conversation, had not been lost.

At that moment Gisele returned through the door opening, bucket in hand.

"Next?" she said, offering a weak smile to the men.

66

18 September, local time 1330
San Francisco

We're coming to you live from Baytown, where shortly after ten o'clock this morning, at least four gunmen invaded the worship service at Calvary Church. Authorities have moved rapidly to close off the area surrounding the church, but, as you can see, a large crowd has gathered at the far side of this rather large parking lot, near the field Communications Center set up by local police and the FBI. Both agencies are working together to resolve what has been described as an extremely dangerous situation. Many among the crowd are church members who were on their way to the eleven o'clock service at the church, which you can see behind me now. Some are friends and relatives of the hundreds still inside. The California Highway Patrol has cordoned off the surrounding streets, but onlookers continue to arrive on foot, drawn to this macabre scene by the extraordinary media coverage, of which we are a part. Reporting live for KFOR . . ."

" . . . as part of the negotiation process, network news coverage around the world has been agreed to by officials at the Command Center located in the recreational vehicle you see on the right-hand side of your screen, and by a consortium of news bureaus. Our reporters are on the scene to bring us the latest developments. Off-duty fire department, emergency medical crews, and Baytown law enforcement personnel have been requested to report immediately to their duty stations. The FBI's presence continues to grow as well. This is Ann Stewart at CNN. We'll be going live to the scene in just a moment. . . ."

"With the nation placed on red alert by the Office of Homeland Security, ABC News is taking you live to Baytown, California, a suburban community southeast of San Francisco, where earlier this morning gunmen, believed to be Middle East terrorists, entered a church and have taken several hundred people hostage. . . ."

"This is a special CBS News bulletin. I'm David Shaw. We are taking you directly at this hour to Baytown, California, where shortly after ten o'clock this morning, local time, an undetermined number of gunmen claimed an entire church congregation hostage during a morning worship service. Little else is known at this hour, but Sherry Ellison of affiliate station KGNA is on the scene and ready to give us a live report. Sherry, what can you tell us about this situation?"

"Well, David, as you were just saying, at approximately ten o'clock this morning . . ."

"Our NBC affiliate in San Francisco, KFOR, is joining us now on a national hookup as we break away from the game to focus coverage on yet another bizarre act of terrorism perpetrated on our shores. Several gunmen, believed to be Middle East terrorists, are currently holding hundreds of people hostage in a church in suburban Baytown, California. We are going live now to KFOR news anchor Tom Bernstein. Tom, fill us in with what you know."

"Well, what we know at this hour is that a quiet Sunday morning church service in the middle-class East Bay suburb of Baytown has been shattered by the staccato of gunfire. At least one parishioner is dead. Calvary Church is an interdenominational church that has served its community and the surrounding area for more than thirty years. At about ten o'clock this morning . . ."

Duane Webber shook his head as he watched the television monitors light up with news reports of the crisis he was facing. It had to be done—but he didn't have to like it. Score one for the bad guys. The eruption of coverage across the globe was not going to make his task any easier, which was exactly what the terrorists wanted. It was a brilliant move, really. And he had no other choice but to comply. Right now it was the currency he needed to buy more time. And time was what he needed most right now.

The RV door opened and Special Agent Todd Hendrickson poked his head inside.

"We've got a couple of ideas, boss. Take your pick." Hendrickson held up a partially folded blueprint of the church building in his hand.

"Let's have a look," Webber said, motioning the SWAT commander inside.

—ɯ—

Akmed appeared to be nearing the end of a rambling oratory that included a list of demands directed at the United States, the UN, and the enemy state of Israel. He had been in front of the cameras for forty minutes. His gun was propped against a platform chair, next to the one he'd been sitting in before he began his "conversation with the world," as he so modestly dubbed it.

In front of each door, small groups of ten to fifteen people sat huddled on the carpet. A few, weary of the strain and discomfort, leaned against the end of a pew or stretched out on the floor itself. Directly in front of the central entrance, thirteen people had been herded into position as human fodder in case of a surprise attack.

Earlier, row by row, individuals had been required to pass purses, wallets, keys, and any other personal belongings to the aisle. These were gathered under the supervision of the woman they called Aziza. As the parishioners divested themselves of their possessions, every man wearing a suit jacket had been made to stand and open it, confirming that no dangerous weapons were hidden. No weapons had yet been found, but hundreds of purses, cell phones, pagers, car keys, and checkbooks—anything and everything that would normally be carried to church—were piled indiscriminately in the altar area between the platform and the first rows of pews.

The process had been thorough, but it had not been complete. At the edge of the group gathered near the central entrance, Connie Farrer reclined on the carpet, propped up on one elbow. When the confiscation procedure was first announced, she had managed to slip her cell phone out of her purse and push it under the folds of her full skirt. Before she was ordered to the back of the sanctuary to join the other hostages at the door, she had secured it under the belted portion of her skirt, making it possible to carry unobtrusively. She had been carrying the phone only for the past five weeks, ever since landing her new job, and now she decided it was time to put it to use.

She glanced around, taking stock of her situation. There were two young children, four men, and six women in the group. The female terrorist was standing barely a half-dozen paces away. The children concerned her the most. If they saw what she was about to do . . .

Can't think about that. Just do it!

Connie sucked in her waist and tugged at the hidden phone. A quick glance around, just to be sure. She reached under her skirt and slipped it out, sliding it under the arch of her arm and shoulder. She felt her heart beating against her ribs. Nervously, she ran her fingers over the buttons until she was sure of their position. Then she began punching in numbers she had only recently committed to memory.

Pause.

A glimpse of the cellular phone startled the man next to her. Then he slowly edged to his right to try to shield Connie from the female terrorist's direct line of vision, turning his head so that he could watch Connie out of the corner of his eye. Connie's heart skipped a beat as she glanced up at the woman with the gun. She had noticed nothing yet. In fact, she was totally absorbed in the speech that her leader was giving, momentarily drawing her attention away from the group huddled to her left in front of the doors.

Perfect, thought Connie as the phone rang the third time.

"Hello. Jody Ansel here."

Connie froze, then quickly punched down the volume. She looked over at the female terrorist. She was still watching her leader.

"Hello. Can I help you?"

"Jody, it's Connie," she whispered.

"Hello. This is Jody Ansel. I can hardly hear you. Can you speak up, please?"

"Jody. It's Connie Farrer."

"I'm sorry. We're very busy now and I can't hear what you are saying. Can you call back later?"

An explosion of fear spread through Connie's stomach.

She's going to hang up. No! Don't! Please!

Connie leaned forward until her mouth was almost touching the instrument cradled on the floor, beneath her arm.

"This is Connie Farrer."

"Connie. Where are you?"

Thank goodness she remembers me!

Connie was the newest kid on the block. She had been afraid that Jody Ansel might not even know who she was. They had only talked briefly a few times since Connie had gone to work for KFOR. Her feeling of relief was overwhelming.

Get control of yourself, Connie.

"I'm in church."

"In church?" A long pause followed. When Jody spoke again, her voice had taken on a new, quieter tone. "You mean *the* church? You're at Calvary in Baytown?"

"Yes," Connie whispered.

"Oh, my—" She heard Jody swear softly. "Just a minute, Connie."

Connie could hear muffled sounds of conversation. Then a male voice.

"Connie, this is Tom Bernstein. Are you okay?"

She looked around her. Others in the group were becoming aware of her whispers into her armpit. Looks of concern and fear spread on their faces.

"In a manner of speaking," she whispered.

"What can you tell me?"

"Not much. Talking is dangerous. I'm only a few feet from one of the terrorists. There are five altogether. Four men. One woman. We are stacked in front of the doors to discourage rescue attempts. They aren't fooling. The doors are set to blow. One guy is already dead."

"We're getting pictures from inside the auditorium, Connie. We're linked with NBC now. And CNN. I still can't believe we've got a reporter inside the church!"

"Believe it. And answer the phone next time on the first ring. Got to go." Connie pushed the *end* button and returned the phone to its private hiding place in the folds of her skirt. As she did, a drop of perspiration surprised her as it fell into the crease of her eye.

She wiped it away.

67

But you've got to go with it, Tom. So far the word is that four terrorists are holed up in that church. Now we know there are five. This is incredible! We have someone inside. With a phone, no less. We'll absolutely scoop everyone else!"

Betty Filtcher, the station's senior vice president, stood in front of Tom Bernstein, her back to the eyes of three large robocams staring vacuously at the news desk. No matter. At the moment, KFOR was showing the live feed from inside the church, with a voice-over interview between NBC anchor Joshua Carey and Dr. Al Zenbari, a professor at UC Berkeley with expertise in Middle East history and culture.

"What we should do is let the FBI know what we know." Tom was looking, not at Betty, but at Jody. Jody nodded in agreement.

"No!" Betty's voice rose slightly, fists clenched at her side.

Tom and Jody both looked at Betty, shocked by the vehemence in her voice. Her eyes were a bit too close together and when she became angry they narrowed, giving her face a squinty, hard sort of look. It was the only uncontrolled reflex that Jody had ever seen in her. And then only on those rarest of occasions. Every hair remained in place. Her makeup was classically faultless. The royal blue suit and burgundy blouse didn't have so much as a wrinkle that showed. Only her eyes—and now her fists—revealed anything other than perfect control.

"No," she said again, quickly regaining her composure, fists unclenching. "Not yet. Not until you've done your job, Tom. And your job is the news. We've got her number. Call her back. Find out what's really happening inside that place. Then report it. Don't you understand what we've got here? We've been scraping the bottom of the ratings barrel for a solid year. Finally, it's our turn!"

Their eyes locked in battle. It was going to be very interesting to see who won this war of power and restraint.

"Betty, if we call Connie," Tom replied calmly but firmly, "unless she remembered to put it on silent ring, it will expose the fact that she still has a telephone. If we go on the air with this now and the terrorists see it, we will put that girl's life in danger. To say nothing of the others. This is a delicate hostage situation, not just a news piece. Those people are in grave danger. She risked a lot just to get in touch with us." Tom glanced up at the monitor. "Look at the pile of stuff they've lifted from the rest of those poor souls. Somehow she managed to keep her cellular hidden. If they find out who she is and that she's been in contact with us, who knows what they'll do to her."

Jody could feel Tom's total identification with the pictures on the monitor; his mental absorption with the circumstance and the people. She knew that his uncanny ability to "feel a story" was what set him apart from so many other newspeople.

Despite the tense circumstances, Jody couldn't help but smile as she looked at Tom Bernstein. He didn't look a bit better than when he had jogged in a few hours ago. His shirt was still open and his five-o'clock shadow looked more like seven or eight o'clock now. His sandy hair was tousled and looked as if he had jumped out of bed and never put a comb through it. Which, of course, was exactly what had happened.

Still, she said to herself, *he has an honest face, a face for the moment at hand.* His unkempt look sent a message of urgency and sincerity to the viewing audience. He reminded her of a younger Dan Rather during the days of Desert Storm. Tom made the audience come together around their television sets. He connected with them. They identified with him, as if he were their husband or brother, favorite uncle or father. Right now, he was all of these and more. He was their link to a world that was, at the same time, both familiar and strange.

"Then what good is she to us if we don't use the stuff she gives us?" Betty Filtcher's eyes were squinty again.

"We're on again in ten, folks." Floor director Matt Hershey's big voice cut through the tension surrounding the studio desk.

"Just do it!" ordered Betty. She opened her immaculately manicured hands in a gesture of ultimate disgust. "And for goodness sake, Tom, get some makeup on. They can't see your eyebrows!"

"Five, four, three . . ."

His eyebrows? Jody wanted to laugh at Betty and hit her at the same time. *All of this and you're worried about the man's eyebrows?*

" . . . two, one."

"We're back in San Francisco again . . ." Tom Bernstein's unshaven face filled the screen. "You've been listening to a discussion between Joshua Carey and Dr. Al Zenbari, Middle East expert and professor at the University of California at Berkeley. We continue to bring you live coverage of this morning's unprecedented takeover of a church's worship service by terrorists.

"The number of hostages claimed by a terrorist spokesman inside the building has been set at 687. One person is known dead, though we still have no word as to that person's identity. There is confirmation that two people have escaped from the church sanctuary and an unknown number of children and their adult teachers have been rescued from Sunday school classrooms located in the building.

"*Sanctuary.* It's a word that usually describes a protected place of refuge—or a house of worship. Today, however, the sanctuary at Calvary Church in Baytown has been turned from a haven of tranquility into a house of terror.

"At the scene now, standing in the church parking lot, is Sandra Marshall. What's the latest from your vantage point, Sandra?"

"Tom, the only words that can adequately describe this situation . . ."

Betty Filtcher stomped out of the newsroom, furious.

Tom Bernstein, KFOR's chief anchor, remained in a quandary.

Jody Ansel, assistant news director, felt guilty.

She was glad to see someone stand up to Betty Filtcher. She had wanted to do it herself many times. She felt a growing concern over Connie Farrer's life-and-death circumstance. Connie was young and new in the business and could easily make a tragic mistake. But these were not the reasons that Jody was feeling guilty.

The real reason was that this had turned into the most exciting day of her entire career.

And she was loving every minute of it!

—w—

Jim Brainard stared at the television.

The night before, an FBI agent had deposited him at the Sonesta Hotel, along the banks of the Charles River. Get some sleep, he'd been told. He was tired all right. And despondent. When he let his thoughts return to Booth Bay, it was not his beautiful Hill House that filled his mind. It was beautiful, faithful, and . . . tragic Rosa. Then came the faces of the murderers of this beautiful child who had become the daughter he'd never had.

As he watched the news from California, he became angry. *How dare these people disrupt our society. We've worked hard to become the nation that is the envy of the world. Why don't they just leave us alone? What did we ever do to them? What will they do next?* He wanted to turn off the television. Go to bed. Get some sleep. But he could not.

By Sunday evening, all the networks were giving round-the-clock coverage. How they managed to gather information and package it into on-the-spot news stories was beyond Jim's understanding. But he recognized that television news was a medium of tremendous power. No wonder that Arab in the church out there was determined to get airtime. This kind of coverage was unprecedented. There had been nothing like it since those terrible attacks on the Trade Center and the Pentagon.

He was watching NBC. Anchorman Joshua Carey had just finished interviewing a professor of Middle East affairs from Berkeley. The San Francisco anchor, Tom Bernstein, was back. Jim liked this young man. Today was the first time he had seen him.

He guessed that Bernstein was probably in his late thirties. Pretty sensitive when it came to reporting. Jim liked that.

Doesn't pander to the sensational. Maybe his station manager has put the screws on him. Who knows? I like the guy, though. Doesn't look like he's taken the time to shave all day. Wonder how long he can stay with this without being spelled off? Looks pretty tired. There is something disconcerting about the man, though. What is it?

He watched the newscaster more closely.

Maybe it's his eyebrows. You can hardly make them out.

68

Monday, 19 September, early morning
Jerusalem

John Cain leaned his head back against the makeshift wall and stared up at the lightbulb. It couldn't be more than forty watts. Add to that a layer of dust on the bulb, and the resulting light in the room was minimal. The fixture, if it could be called that, hung from the ceiling at a crazy angle. John's eye followed the cord to a small hole in the makeshift wall, where it disappeared.

It must be attached to a long power cord, probably plugged into an outlet somewhere outside.

Yazib and Pasha lay close together on the bed farthest away, her back turned toward him, his arm thrown across her waist. Yazib's heavy breathing confirmed that he was sleeping soundly.

John sat on the floor, knees pulled up as a headrest. He was huddled between the two beds designated for the prisoners. His body ached. His face was bruised and cut from the earlier beatings on the bus and the climb over the wall. Every muscle cried out in protest over the way they had been treated during the last hours.

Gisele Eiderman was asleep on one of the beds. Edgar, Bob, and John had argued over who would use the other one—each man desperately wanting to lie down for a rest, but also not wanting to appear selfish. Finally, they agreed that Edgar and Bob would share the bed and John would take the other one when Gisele woke up. Even though John was exhausted, he could not bring himself to share the bed with her. He had always taught his congregation to avoid even the appearance of impropriety, and he was determined to practice what he preached, even under the circumstances. Holding on to each other while climbing the wall of the Old City was one thing. That had been a matter of life and death. This was not.

Besides, he had discovered something. The place where his chain attached to the wall contained a small crack in the mortar. John figured the work had probably been done recently. After the others had fallen asleep, he tried to wiggle the fixture. At first there was nothing. Then just as he was about to give up, a small piece of sand and mortar broke loose and fell to the floor. Heartened, he continued his efforts with renewed energy, checking every so often to be sure that his captors were still sleeping.

Both Edgar and Bob were stretched out in the deep sleep that accompanies emotional and physical exhaustion. Each had an eight-foot chain securely fastened to one leg.

John looked over at Gisele, curled in fetal form near the far edge of the mattress. She, too, wore the ankle chain. As he watched, she shivered, whether from the cold or from the stress of the day's events he could not tell. He scooted along the floor until he reached one of the blankets at the foot of the bed. Unfolding it, he laid it carefully over her shoulders. She stirred, but did not awaken.

John returned to working the bracket on the wall, but no more mortar broke loose.

I don't know what I'd do if it came loose, anyway. Can't imagine I'd get far with this chain trailing behind me.

"John?"

He looked over his shoulder to see Edgar leaning up on one elbow on the far bed.

"John. Either you get up on that bed or I'll do it myself. Goodness knows I could use some room with this big lug I'm stuck with." He gestured over his shoulder at Bob, who was still fast asleep and snoring lightly.

John shook his head and smiled briefly. "Keep talking, Edgar. Your words are long, but your chain is short. You couldn't, even if you wanted to."

"John, I know what the Bible says about modesty and propriety and all, but there's nothin' immoral or immodest about you gettin' up on that bed and gettin' some sleep. The rest of us need you to be at your best and you ain't goin' to be if you keep sittin' down there. Now what's it goin' to be? Either you get up there or I'm movin' over."

John nodded but remained seated.

"I'm just trying to set a good example, that's all."

"John, you *are* setting a good example. For Pete's sake, Gisele is still alive because of you. But we need you to set a good example of using common sense, too, and common sense says you need to get some sleep while you still can. No one's gonna think twice about you climbing up on that bed and gettin' some shut-eye."

John looked up from where he was sitting, sighed, then pulled himself up until he was sitting on the edge of the mattress. He knew Edgar was right. He was exhausted. Carefully, so as not to awaken Gisele, he lay down. Slowly stretching out, he let himself begin to relax. Every bone in his body affirmed that this was a decision well made.

"Good night, John."

"Good night, Edgar. And thanks."

—w—

All four prisoners were sound asleep when the changing of the guard took place. Had they been awake, they would have seen Yazib and Pasha check the contents of the backpack on the table, making certain one last time that everything they needed was there. Had they been awake, they would have been awed by what they saw. And they might have understood what was going to happen.

For the umpteenth time, Yazib counted the small, very compact packages, each with an adhesive back covered by thin strips of treated paper, containing powerful explosives, then placed them carefully back in the pack, along with the miniature radio detonating device, a lightweight, collapsible telescopic apparatus with a magnet on one end and a release button on the other.

Yazib fastened the top of the pack and threw it over his shoulder. With one arm, he gave Pasha an affectionate hug. Their heads touched briefly. Then they went out together.

69

18 SEPTEMBER, LOCAL TIME 1635
BAYTOWN, CALIFORNIA

I've just been handed this special news bulletin." Tom Bernstein glanced down at the sheet of paper in his hand, then looked off-camera. "Are we certain of this?"

He paused while the response came through his earpiece, "*The White House confirmed it five minutes ago.*"

Bernstein turned back to the camera.

"Earlier today, terrorist spokesman Akmed el Hussein, the leader of the group that is holding hostages at Calvary Church in Baytown, indicated that other terrorist activities were under way in other locations. He specifically mentioned Israel as a target.

"It has now been confirmed by the Israeli government that an American tour group visiting in that country for the past seven days is missing. The Israel Tours bus in which they were traveling was found abandoned near the entrance to the Gihon Springs, just outside the Old City in Jerusalem. Further investigation has determined that this same bus left a hotel near the Dead Sea, at about four-thirty Sunday afternoon Israeli time. That would have been eight-thirty this morning here on the West Coast. Lending a further bizarre twist to this day's incredible events, authorities in Israel have confirmed that the missing group is being led by Dr. John Cain, the senior minister of Calvary Church in Baytown."

Bernstein paused, rubbing at the side of his cheekbone.

"This is truly unbelievable. Authorities in Jerusalem have heard nothing from any member of the group, nor from any would-be kidnappers. However, Israel Tours in Tel Aviv has verified that there are twenty-five persons in the group, including Dr. Cain. All of them are missing. It seems they have simply disappeared. Vanished."

He sagged back into his chair, sighed, then looked straight into the camera.

"It doesn't take a genealogical researcher to determine that with a name like

Bernstein, my roots and heritage are Jewish. Both my wife, Ruth, and I are proud to be American-born Jews. A little over a year ago, we visited Israel for the first time. When we arrived there, we observed a small group of Yemenite Jews in the airport, engaged in the process of entering their new homeland. Yemenites. Russian Jews. Jews from Poland. Jews from Hungary. Even Jews from the United States. All coming to Israel because, for them, it is their true homeland.

"I remember that moment as if it were yesterday. As a Jew, I can tell you it was a strange, discomforting feeling. Ruth and I are Americans. We've always been and always will be. I served for six years in the Marine Corps. We pay our taxes and complain about them like everyone else. We're proud to be Americans.

"But my heart went out to these people, many of them with nothing more than what they had on their backs. Happy to be in a place they could finally call home. A little piece of planet Earth not much larger than the greater San Francisco Bay Area. I can tell you, it was hard for my wife and me to fully comprehend.

"Later we saw a group of pilgrims at the Western Wall, the most sacred spot on earth for the Jews. Ruth and I watched as they stood for a long time with their eyes closed and faces inches from the wall, bodies swaying back and forth, offering prayers up to God. Then I went to the wall. I wrote out my prayer on a little piece of paper and stuck it in a crevice between two stones. Many others had done the same. It was an indescribable feeling for me to stand there, where millions of other Jews have stood throughout the years. To know that in that moment, I belonged. That at some time or another, perhaps my cousins or great-great grandparents had stood in that very place and had done the very same thing.

"I walked back to where Ruth was waiting and we held hands together for a long time. We prayed for the peace of Jerusalem. Tonight—" His voice faltered. He rubbed his eyes with the back of his hand, clearing his throat at the same time. "Tonight . . . it all seems so long ago and far away. What we have seen today is not an answer to our prayer. It is instead the prelude to our worst nightmare."

Bernstein opened his mouth to continue. Then, as if suddenly remembering where he was, he leaned forward, eyes glistening with a sadness that fully transferred to the minds of millions of viewers and said, "This is Tom Bernstein reporting from San Francisco. I'll be back in a moment."

It was quiet on the set.

Off camera, Jody wiped at her eyes.

Sally choked back a sob and ran toward the restroom.

Betty sat on the edge of a nearby desk, stunned by what she had just seen.

Upstairs in the control room, the director had been momentarily caught off guard. He'd been absorbed by the anchorman's sudden, heartfelt monologue. He moved quickly to fade the newsroom from the screen. Then he punched up KFOR's signature and viewers heard a voice-over say, "You're watching KFOR's 24-hour news coverage of the Baytown hostage crisis. Stay tuned for up-to-the-minute reports from our studio and on-scene reporters."

It was an unnecessary request. No one was leaving.

Tom Bernstein's emotion-packed comments had riveted NBC and CNN viewers to their television screens across America and around the world.

—⁂—

"Tom, listen, you deserve a break in the action." Matt, the floor director, leaned over the news desk, looking sympathetically at his favorite anchor. "Go lay down for a while."

"I'm tired, but I'm okay. Let's keep going a little while longer."

"You're starting to crack, Tom," Betty Filtcher chimed in. "That last bit was over the top. Too personal. You probably just ran off all of KFOR's Muslim audience with your remarks."

Tom's eyes ignited with anger. "Get off my back, Betty. I'm fine. I expressed some personal feelings, that's all. It doesn't hurt our viewing audience to know that their news team has feelings. Once in a great while, it's okay not to come off like a wooden Indian. And you'll probably say that's a racist comment, guaranteed to wipe out our Native American viewing audience. Get a life, Betty!"

Tension crackled like electricity between the two until Betty turned on her heel and stalked out of the newsroom.

Just then, a slight man in work clothes made his way up to the desk and stopped in front of Tom. Hesitantly, he reached out a bronzed hand, his dark eyes brimming with emotion.

"Mr. Bernstein, my name is Beni Hamill. I am called in today, especially for purposes of security. They say for me to lock the doors downstairs and double-check everybody coming in. Paulo and I have been doing this all day. We watch you just now on the monitors downstairs. I asked Paulo, could I come up to tell you that I am also sad today? He say, yes.

"I am an Arab, Mr. Bernstein. My people are Palestinians. They are living in terrible circumstances. It is not right what they have to suffer. But, Mr. Bernstein, it is not right what is happening today either. It just brings us all more pain and suffering. I pray for peace in the world, as well as you. I am sorry that Allah has not chosen to answer our prayers."

Tom looked at the man for a long moment. Then he came around the corner of the desk. First they shook hands. Then they put their arms around each other, each man patting the other on the back.

For a brief moment, in a place normally brimming with cynicism, confusion, and chaos, there was peace on earth.

—∞—

"The Voice of Palestine, Algiers, reports that today in the Gaza Strip, IDF soldiers shot four Palestinians dead, among them a twelve-year-old mentally handicapped boy. A Palestinian youth stabbed five students and a principal in a Jerusalem high school. The IDF has sealed the assailant's home. Students and other Israelis are rioting. West Bank automobiles are overturned and burning and at least two bystanders have been injured. The September 24 signing of a Permanent Agreement between the PNA and the State of Israel appears in grave jeopardy."

"The Israel Television Network in Jerusalem indicates that in the Gaza Strip, the IDF today quelled an unprovoked attack initiated by as many as a dozen young Palestinians. Rocks were thrown, and at least one assailant fired a handgun at Israeli police while running down Gaza's main street. Two Palestinians are confirmed dead and two more were wounded during the clash.

"In Jerusalem, a Palestinian youth stabbed five students and critically wounded the principal in a Jerusalem high school. The assailant's home has been sealed off. Protesters rioted in a West Bank suburb for about an hour this afternoon. The IDF reports that two persons sustained minor rock injuries. No other substantive damage was reported.

"A missing Israel Tours bus was discovered earlier today near the entrance to the Gihon Springs. The driver of the bus was later found bound and gagged at the Salt Sea Hotel & Spa in Ein Bokek. Dr. David Barak, the tour guide, has been confirmed as a shooting victim in what appears to be a hostage-taking incident. He is survived by his wife and son. Hotel management has verified that the group of twenty-five are United States citizens here on a religious pilgrimage. If anyone has information regarding this bus, or its occupants, please contact . . ."

70

18 September, local time 1730
Boston

This is not a test. We repeat. This is not a test. Please check immediately with your local radio or television stations designated to provide Boston's citizens with emergency information. Those stations are . . ."

". . . received the threat earlier this afternoon. Police have confirmed the members of two families have been diagnosed with a virulent form of inhalation anthrax. The deadly anthrax spore was apparently released near Frog Pond in Boston Common. . . . Please remain calm. . . . The Office of Homeland Security in conjunction with the governor of Massachusetts has requested that all citizens of the Boston metropolitan area begin an orderly evacuation of the city. To ease the process of evacuation, the following thoroughfares, turnpikes, and expressways will be reserved for outbound traffic in all lanes: All Masspike lanes will be for westbound traffic only. I-93 from the central artery north of Callahan tunnel is reserved for northbound traffic only, and south of Callahan tunnel for southbound traffic only. Follow the instructions of emergency officials stationed at entrance points. . . ."

"Logan International Airport is diverting all incoming flights to Newark and New York City's LaGuardia and JFK airports. Commercial and privately owned aircraft will be permitted outgoing flight status only until advised otherwise. Fares are being suspended."

"All MBTA Orange, Blue, and Red Lines will continue moving passengers away from downtown. You may board at any station. The Green Line will offer southbound-service-only from Lechmere to Boston College and Cleveland Circle. All of MBTA's 162 bus routes will provide outbound service until further notice. Fares are suspended. Amtrak trains will be operating outbound service every hour from North Station, South Station, and Back Bay Station, beginning at 6:00 P.M."

"The following is a further list of public transportation being made available in your area. Greyhound Lines . . ."

". . . lock your doors and windows. If you choose to remain in your home, duct tape the windows and doors of a room. Stay inside until further notice. Be certain you have bottled water and food with you for three days. Turn your car radio to the emergency band for traffic updates and other information. . . ."

". . . and so the decision to evacuate was issued following a closed emergency session in the mayor's office, after receiving a terrorist threat concerning the use of a biological weapon with deadly anthrax spores as its base. At least nine people are being treated as a result of exposure to inhalation anthrax spores at Boston Common earlier today. . . ."

". . . here are the pictures of two individuals wanted for questioning regarding the alleged terrorist threat to the citizens of Boston. Mohammed Ibn Ahmer, also known as Nicolas Hondros, is believed to be living and working in the Boston Area. This second picture is the most recent likeness available of Marwan Dosha, one of the world's most wanted terrorists. It is now believed that at least four men, of Arab descent, may be working together here in Boston in an effort to carry out this threat. . . ."

". . . medical authorities confirm that only small amounts of anthrax spores are necessary to create a catastrophic situation here in the city. . . ."

". . . a small island off the coast of Scotland was the location for a secret study regarding the use of anthrax as a potential offensive weapon during World War II. Every living animal was killed. Today, this island is still off-limits to all visitors as a result of the lingering effects of contamination. . . ."

". . . please, do not panic. . . ."

—∾—

Jim Brainard glanced over at Special Agent Daniel Morse. "Now there's the media understatement of the year. 'Please, do not panic'?"

They sat staring at the pictures on the screen, listening to the commentary. They had been at this for a while. Suddenly, Jim straightened up and shifted to the edge of the couch.

"I've got an idea," he exclaimed.

The younger man smiled.

"I know. I think getting you out of town is a good idea, too. I'm going to check with my boss and see what he wants us to do."

Jim shook his head emphatically.

"No. That's not what I mean. I know where they are," he declared, pounding his fist into an open hand. "Why didn't I think of it earlier?"

The young agent watched him carefully.

"Are you serious? You know where they are?"

"Come on," Jim shouted, jumping to his feet. "Get your boss on the phone. I've got to talk to him!"

Morse hesitated, sizing up this exuberant senior citizen who was fairly bouncing up and down in front of him. It was difficult to know how seriously he should take the man. Jim suddenly stood still, his eyes boring into those of the young agent. His look had become determined, his countenance rock hard.

"Don't just sit there, man. Come on. Hurry!"

Morse hurried.

—∾—

Twenty-seven minutes later, Special Agent in Charge Jerry Ellis, of the Boston office, was wrapping up a five-minute, emotion-charged conversation with the FBI Director. Ellis had already laid out his options with a team of strategists at SIOC, the FBI's Strategic Information and Operations Center, and then reviewed his recommendations with the Section Chief of the International Terrorist Section.

"It makes sense," the director was saying, his voice sounding detached, almost casual, as if he were discussing the merits of a business deal with an associate. "I've shared your idea with the attorney general. He's at the White House with the president and the NSC people. It's a go. I'm sending you every agent within three hours of Boston. Anybody we can drive in or fly in. Logan has been notified that we're coming. I'll have an HRT underwater unit on its way within the hour.

"Meanwhile, keep your buddy there under close wraps. What's his name? Brainard? He sounds sharp enough and he's the only witness to have seen these vermin firsthand. Concentrate on this Ibn Ahmer character. I'd like to be wrong, but I'll put money on Dosha already being long gone. He's not going to stick around for the party. That's why he's got these other three nuts. He's on his way somewhere to watch it all happen on television. We'll cover all the airports, train stations, and rental cars. We've alerted U.S., Canadian, and Mexican border agents. Maybe we'll get lucky.

"I've got an HRT unit on its way to California, too. It may be too late to do any good, but we're leaving nothing to chance. This is war. Nothing less. We've been saying this for years now. Maybe this time they'll believe us.

"And listen. Do your best to keep your troops on point. That's all I ask. We don't need another 9/11 up there. What we really need is a win. I'll guarantee, if we don't, the world isn't ever going to be the same again."

---

18 SEPTEMBER, LOCAL TIME 2047
QUANTICO, VIRGINIA

At exactly 2047, a C-130 Hercules lifted off the runway at Quantico Air Force Base headed for Boston. It climbed rapidly into the night skies, the lights of the nation's capital flickering in the distance. Three hours earlier, an identical plane had headed west toward the crisis in California.

Inside, a full array of the latest equipment, including a jet black Messerschmitt twin engine helicopter and a high-speed power boat, both equipped for night surveillance and surrounded by a small core of the nation's most uniquely trained federal officers. They were members of the FBI's Hostage Rescue Team, a cadre of agents trained in the skills needed to accomplish exactly what their name implied, together with the ability to do it anywhere they were needed in America.

The team sat quietly, listening with rapt attention as their leader laid out the possible options once their team arrived at Logan Airport in Boston.

71

18 SEPTEMBER, LOCAL TIME 2047
BOSTON

Downtown Boston had become a virtual ghost town. Only the most rumor-hardened citizens remained. Like the legendary Harry Truman who perished in the Mount St. Helen's eruption, nothing was going to dislodge them. Not even the prospect of impending death.

From Faneuil Hall Marketplace to the Prudential Center, from Old North Church to the Bull & Finch Tavern, only the occasional shadowy figure could be seen running toward a subway station. Even emergency and rescue workers were starting to clear out and find shelter for themselves.

Boston Common was empty.

Traffic was creeping along in every outward direction on the inner-city streets and avenues.

Even the Combat Zone along Washington Street between Avery and Stuart, normally buzzing with its strip shows, porno films, and other sleazy diversions, was devoid of patrons tonight.

Across the river, the campuses of Harvard and MIT were deserted.

Inexpensive studio apartments and finely appointed row houses—all were vacant.

Theaters were dark.

Restaurants were empty.

Hotels were locked.

Massachusetts General Hospital was almost entirely evacuated.

Buses were full.

Trains were jammed.

MTBA Lines were packed.

The Massachusetts Turnpike was bumper to bumper for miles.

Fitzgerald Expressway was a virtual parking lot.

Gridlock reigned.

Tempers were flaring.

An occasional fight broke out.
Random gunshots could be heard.
The Cradle of Liberty was under siege.

—∾—

At the Sheraton Hotel in downtown Montreal, Canada, a man sat by himself in his room, sipping from a bottle of mineral water and toying with the Caesar salad he had ordered from room service. The television was tuned to the latest on Boston's evacuation crisis.

He watched thoughtfully, his finger lightly touching the scar on his cheek.

—∾—

LOCAL TIME 2105
BOSTON

At Logan International Airport, the C-130 rolled to a stop as the giant cargo door in its belly dropped open.

The jeep was first out. Without stopping, its occupants raced out onto the runway and through a nearby open gate. The boat and trailer were next. Then came the helicopter. Men surrounded the machine, making ready for flight, while others rushed to attach lines to the boat. Within a few minutes the helicopter's engines sputtered to life. Moments later it lifted into the air, hovering noisily overhead. Lines were linked to a cable lowered from the helicopter. Carefully the boat was lifted from its trailer bed and disappeared into the darkness.

A television traffic report helicopter suddenly appeared over the terminal building and touched down near the C-130. Four men dressed in scuba gear trotted down the ramp and climbed on board. The red and white machine lifted from the runway and it, too, was soon gone from sight.

72

We've located them, sir. They rented a powerboat at one of the marinas along the Charles. We found the fellow who rented it to them just before he split with the evacuation warning. He recognized the one guy. It's Ibn Ahmer. He's been trying to reach the boats he has out. Says he called these two and alerted them to the danger. Ordered them to hightail it in. They told him they might try to land at a dock closer to where they're located."

"How far away are you?"

"Distance-wise? I'm not sure exactly. Couple of miles, maybe. The subjects have been sighted by our agents in the TV station chopper. You got a Boston map there?"

"Right in front of me."

"Right now, they're about a quarter mile beyond the Harvard Bridge. Do you see it?"

"Yep."

"They're not moving. I don't know what they may have going, but we've dropped our boat in further upriver, about a mile beyond them. We'll approach SEAL-style and put our men in the water as we go by. They'll hear us, maybe even see us. But because lots of other boats are heading in they'll think we're just one of them, anxious to get back to a landing and out of the area."

"You say there are only two on board?"

"That's the word."

"Be careful."

"Thank you, sir. We'll do our best."

—∾—

The boat's engine roared to life at the first touch of the ignition. The pilot looked at the men in black. All four gave a thumbs-up. He pushed the throttle forward and headed upriver, Cambridge on the left and Boston to the right. Solid ribbons of light on the main traffic arteries stood out against the unusual semidarkness of the cities on either side. The pilot turned his attention back to the river and to the task of finding the craft that had been spotted a short while ago by an agent with night-vision field glasses.

There!

The pilot lifted a hand and pointed in the direction of the target, floating silently, well ahead and off to the left. He stayed on course now, keeping his boat at the same speed and to the right side of the target. There could be no slowing down, nothing that would cause suspicion that he was anything other than just another poor victim trying to escape with his life before it was too late.

One!

Two!

Three!

Four!

The strike team was swallowed up by the river like stones from a child's hand.

The powerboat roared on into the night.

—~—

Mohammed Ibn Ahmer and Yusif Shemuda extinguished their cigarettes and returned to their preparations. Both men were wearing nylon windbreakers over knit pullover sweaters, which not only provided warmth against the chilly night air but also offered protection. And protection was what they were interested in. They understood the gravity of what they were doing, at least as much as anyone could. And in spite of the special rewards promised to martyrs of the holy war, both men had decided they still wanted to live. They pulled on protective masks and gloves to cover their face and hands, then set about the task of checking—one more time—the assembly of the two balsa wood model airplanes they would use to launch the attack.

Both aircraft were flight ready.

"There can be no turning back now," said Mohammed. "The infidels think we are fooling. They do not believe we will destroy their empire. This will be the biggest victory yet achieved. It will strike fear worldwide. People will know. Allah is greater!"

From a cloth-covered plastic container, Yusif carefully withdrew one of the two square objects located inside. Cautiously, he attached it to the specially designed aluminum mounts on the top side of one of the model airplanes, just behind the single propeller.

He paused when he heard the approaching sound of a motorboat coming at high speed in their direction.

Both men stared into the darkness until they saw it. Mohammed checked the seat beside him, where a fully loaded, silencer-equipped Cobray M-11/9 submachine gun lay inches from his hand.

This inexpensive, but very reliable and deadly weapon had been created specifically for close military combat. Mohammed liked it because it did not need to be aimed, only fired. Anyone within range would be snuffed in an instant. Like the two young Israeli soldiers he had murdered with a similar weapon three years ago as they strolled along a sidewalk in Jaffa.

The boat roared past without letup and continued on into the darkness. There appeared to be only one person on board. Mohammed smiled and turned his attention back to the task at hand. When the second airplane had been outfitted, he set it down on the deck and looked at his watch.

11:57.

Three minutes to the appointed hour.

—∞—

The four HRT frogmen swam swiftly and silently beneath the surface of the river, closing on their target. The lead agent checked his watch.

11:58 and counting.

—∞—

Yusif stood to his feet, grasping one of the model airplanes by its underbelly. He primed the motor and sent the signal to the starter. In a moment it would rise into the darkness, headed toward downtown Boston.

Mohammed watched expectantly, his eyes glistening with excitement. In his hand he held the airplane destined for Cambridge.

Taking hold of the controls in his left hand, Yusif lifted his airplane high. He looked at Mohammed and nodded.

—∞—

The four swimmers broke the surface of the water without making a sound, two on either side of the boat. They saw one of the men on deck stand up, holding a model airplane. The light from the boat's cabin illumined the scene, revealing in an instant the method of delivery planned for Boston's demise. With one hand, the lead frogman ripped off his scuba mask; with the other hand he reached desperately for his knife.

73

Allah u Akbar!" shouted Yusif as he released the model airplane with its deadly cargo. A second later, grunting with surprise, he turned toward his companion. Mohammed stared in disbelief at the handle of a knife protruding from Yusif's chest.

Desperately, Mohammed twisted away from the side of the boat, fumbling for the weapon that lay on the nearby deck chair. It was all a blur of motion. A dark face rose behind the spot where he had been sitting. He pulled the trigger, releasing a hail of bullets. The face disappeared.

Yusif fell forward against Mohammed, knocking him off balance.

Then they were on top of him, a fist pounding into his mouth, a chop to the neck.

Then darkness.

As Yusif fell, the radio controller fell from his hand and bounced off the edge of the hull. It sailed past the outstretched hand of one of the frogmen, who dove in a desperate effort to catch it.

Too late!

The small box disappeared into the dark waters of the Charles River.

"It's what?" shouted the director. "The stuff is on a model airplane headed for Boston? Are you serious? A model airplane? How long ago?"

"Our team hit them at 11:59."

The director stared at the clock on the wall.

12:02.

"I'm sorry, sir. We were a split second too late." The agent's voice sounded like that of a condemned man seated in the electric chair. "One of the terrorists is dead. The other is in custody. We lost Abramson. He caught some rounds from a submachine gun. And the airplane's radio control unit was lost during the operation."

There was a long silence. When the director responded, his voice was distant and hollow. "I'm sorry, too. Dear God in heaven, I'm sorry, too."

—∞—

Frogman Tom Riley put down his radio pack. He watched as the others took Abramson's body below and placed it gently on the bed. He had died instantly, three terrible bullet wounds to the face. Tom looked away toward the remaining lights of the city.

Somewhere . . . in the darkness . . . more death was on the wing.

The tail section of the second model plane had been broken in Yusif's fall. Riley bent down and picked up a cloth-covered plastic container. He folded the cloth back.

"Hey. Check this out."

The other two frogmen moved in to take a look at the small square container with a spray valve protruding from the top. It was obvious what the container was and how it would be attached to the aluminum mount on the plane. So ingeniously simple. But there was also something else. Riley lifted it out.

"A transmitter."

"For the second plane," he said, turning it over in his hand. "Do you suppose it would work with the first one?"

"If they haven't altered the radio frequencies," said Larry Becker. "My kid's got one almost exactly like this at home. I've flown it a few times. Want me to give it a go?"

Riley handed the unit to him.

"Be careful. Even if it works, can you bring it back?"

"I don't think we want it back," Becker responded dryly. "We just need to find it. Then . . . maybe . . ."

"Maybe what?" Riley gripped Becker's arm.

"Maybe if we can find it, we could land it somewhere in one piece. It's a long shot."

"Let's try. Gene, get this tub going and head for shore."

"Which shore?"

"Wait a minute!" Becker said. "Be quiet and listen." He was staring up into the dark sky.

The others stopped, listening. There was only the lap of the water against the boat, together with night sounds from the city and the constant flow of traffic in the distance.

Then they heard it.

"Look for lights! Look for lights!" Becker exclaimed excitedly.

"Lights?"

"Yeah, this plane on the deck here has wing lights. The other one probably does, too. Do you hear it?"

"Yes. Yes, I do," said Riley.

"It must be circling. That lowlife didn't have time to get it headed off to—"

"There, see? It's right there! About ten o'clock. See the lights? Going away. The red would be to the right; green on the left. Coming toward us, vice versa. Got it?"

"Got it, Larry. Looks like red is left now. It must be coming our way."

"It is. And look. I've got control!" Becker moved the control lever back and forth. The wings wiggled a bit and the lights bobbed up and down.

"All right! Okay then. What shall we do? Let's head for shore, Gene. The Boston side. Okay?"

"You got it."

Becker focused on the device in his hands. "I'll work the plane and keep it up until we get to the riverside. Then we'll try to land her." He paused for a moment, then added, "There is one more problem, though."

"Another problem?"

"I'm not sure what triggers this baby off, but I've got a feeling it's this button here. There's no way of knowing for sure. And we don't know when or how it's set to disperse. We may get there just in time for the shower."

"That's a happy thought, old buddy," Riley answered. "I tell you what. Just be careful. And do your best to make sure we don't all go home in boxes."

74

18 SEPTEMBER, LOCAL TIME 2124
BAYTOWN, CALIFORNIA

Yes, I believe we should go with the SWAT leader's recommendation. It's our best chance. But I have to be honest. The operative word here is *chance*."

Webber was looking at the television monitor as he talked to the U.S. attorney general, who was standing in the FBI's Strategic Information & Operations Center at Tenth and Pennsylvania in Washington, D.C. With the attorney general were several high-ranking Justice Department staff members, SIOC analysts, the International Terrorist Section Chief, and the FBI Director. It was about as high a level of response as one could get without the president himself being there.

"Duane, I know time is critical there, but do you think we've done all we can do in negotiation? What if someone higher up could talk with them? Or how about a local Muslim leader there in the Bay Area? Have we exhausted all our good ideas?" His voice was quiet, but firm and thoughtful at the same time.

"We'll do what you decide, of course, sir. But I hear you asking for my opinion, so I'm going to give it." His face tightened as he continued. "I don't believe further 'wait and talk' tactics are going to get us anywhere. We've bit into the apple already, sir. The longer we wait, the less apple we have left. We need to get in there as quickly as possible."

"I know you do. But we're still living in the shadow of the Twin Towers here. And the Pentagon. Those are mighty long shadows, Duane. People are really beginning to wonder about us. And about Homeland Security. It looks mighty grim.

"On top of all this, the director tells me we've got a model airplane in the air in Boston ready to drop an anthrax bomb on the city. A model airplane! Can you believe this? And there's a busload of Americans missing in Israel. Word has it they're from your church out there. What is that all about? These people have gotten way ahead of us again. And your church people are living on borrowed time. Other than that, it's business as usual here in D.C."

Webber sat watching a scene of relative inactivity currently being projected from inside the church. Akmed was pacing back and forth in front of the first row of pews. He stopped to whisper something to one of his male counterparts. The man smiled and nodded, backing away. It looked like he was speaking to someone seated in the congregation. He was not near a microphone, so it was difficult to figure what he was up to. Webber wished he could hear what he was saying.

"Are you still there, Duane?"

"Yes sir, I'm still here." Webber shifted his feet as the attorney general's voice came through the speakerphone. "I hear you. And I don't envy you one bit, sir." Webber waited. Finally he broke the silence between them. "So what will it be?" he asked softly.

"Duane, I'm ordering you to get in there and get those people out. Do it as quickly as you can. Put your SWAT team to work. Do whatever you have to do. We'll talk again when you're finished."

"Yes sir. Right now we're still waiting for the release of the hostages that were promised when we got the networks involved. A couple of hours ago our friend indicated they would be coming out. But so far nothing. It will really help if they do turn some loose. If and when that happens we'll execute your order immediately," he responded, leaning forward in his chair. "I will stay in touch as things unfold here. Oh, by the way . . ."

"Yes?"

"Good luck on your end, sir."

"Thanks, Duane. Good-bye."

Webber heard a sigh on the other end of the line. He looked over at the others. "It's a go. Let's find Hendrickson and make sure we're ready to take these characters out when the time comes." He got up from his chair and stretched. "I could also use something to eat."

Turning his back to the monitors, he headed out the door with Chief White following close behind.

75

MONDAY, 19 SEPTEMBER, LOCAL TIME 0025
BOSTON

Special Agent Gene Jones guided the boat slowly and steadily across the river, all the while keeping an eye on his partner. Becker was braced against the cabin railing, head cocked back, peering up into the blackness, his concentration locked onto the red and green wing lights blinking feebly above him. Sweat beaded on his face, even though the night was cool.

Handcuffed and with his feet bound together, Mohammed Ibn Ahmer observed the unfolding drama from the bottom of the boat. He was going to die. He knew it. They were all going to die. There was no way these fools would be able to bring that model airplane down without disaster. The dreaded spores were sure to get them all. This was not the way he wanted to go out.

As they drew close to shore, Jones maneuvered the boat in alongside a small floating dock. The moment they bumped the dock, Jones shut down the engine while Riley leaped out and secured the tie lines.

Becker never let his concentration waver. While Jones and Riley helped him out of the boat, Becker kept his eyes riveted on the model airplane. The whine of its tiny engine could be heard clearly now as it circled overhead. Jones kept a hand on Becker's waist, guiding him as they walked barefoot along the dock toward the river's edge.

The dock moved unsteadily under their feet as they neared the shore. Becker swayed and started to lose his balance. Jones tightened his grip, at the same time staying low and away from the transmitter's controls.

"You're doing great," Riley said encouragingly as they stepped on shore. "This way."

The red and green lights on the plane continued in a tight circle as Becker endeavored to control it from below. Walking at a fairly rapid pace, they came to the edge of the street paralleling the river.

"Okay, Larry, take your pick," Riley said. "We've got a paved street, a cement sidewalk, and some grass here between the walk and the river.

Becker glanced around quickly, then back at the red and green lights. His fingers were not as limber as he would have liked. They had never quite warmed up after being in the Charles. The level meter looked okay and so far he had managed not to bump the power switch. The only button he did not recognize from his son's model airplane he had to assume was the trigger device that would release the spores.

"Grass. Let's do grass. It's softer. I'm going to try to bring it in tail down, nose up. If you guys would like to leave, now's your chance."

"Hey, Larry. You do this right, we'll all go home together. Mess it up and it won't make much difference where any of us are standing when you bring it down." Riley gave Becker a gentle pat on the rear. "No pressure, though, buddy. For an old model airplane man like you, this is a piece of cake."

Becker forced a smile at Riley's effort to ease the tension.

"Okay, frog people, here we go."

The shrill sound of the tiny airplane engine could be heard clearly as Becker adjusted the throttle trim lever. Every eye was riveted on the running lights as he moved the rudder lever and began the final delicate adjustments on the aileron and elevator trimmers.

"Okay, easy . . . easy," Riley breathed. The plane was dropping into the light projected by street lamps and the office buildings across the way.

Becker was in a world within a world now, carefully maneuvering the plane toward the strip of grass along the shore. It continued dropping, coming straight toward him. At the last second, it suddenly veered toward the sidewalk. *No!* He touched the control, pulling it back. *Tail down. Nose up. It's coming in too fast . . . too fast!*

Stall! Stall!

Power off!

Drop!

At the last possible moment, the tail dipped down and the nose lifted. Becker cut the engine and the plane dropped onto the grass. It bounced once, twice, then nosed into the turf, falling off to one side and twisting part way around on the tip of one wing.

No one moved at first. They simply stared at the child's toy that had been turned into a lethal bomb. Waiting to see . . . no one was exactly sure what. Becker carefully lifted the strap from around his neck and placed the control box on the grass. Then he sat down beside it and began shaking uncontrollably.

Riley and Jones walked over to the plane. There, attached to the upper part of the model, was the lethal payload, still intact.

The two of them looked at each other and grinned.

"Yes!" they exclaimed, high-fiving and pounding each other on the back. They ran back to where Becker sat on the grass. Both men stopped as Riley picked up the control box and laid it carefully on the sidewalk. Then they pounced on Becker, three incredibly relieved FBI agents rolling in the grass like boys playing in the park.

"You did it!" Riley said. "Becker, you did it, man! How does it feel to have saved the world?"

The three agents broke into howls of laughter.

"Stupid Americans," Ibn Ahmer muttered to himself as he listened from the bottom of the boat.

76

When Special Agent Daniel Morse received the message that two of the terrorists had been apprehended, but that a model airplane carrying an anthrax bomb was on its way toward the city, he and Jim Brainard ran to catch the MBTA Subway Green Line at Science Park. Morse had just been told in no uncertain terms to get Brainard out of the area as quickly as possible. Morse was surprised at how agile the older man was. He thought of being sixty-something as old. His father had died of a heart attack at sixty-two. Of course, he had been a lifelong smoker. Still, Morse had never seen a man who seemed more fit for his age than Jim Brainard.

Both men, of course, were highly motivated. Fear of the unknown surrounding this invisible, deadly disease—a disease that could fall like rain in the night and kill an entire city—was indescribable. There was no time left to warn anybody still trapped inside the Boston city limits. The worst-case scenario had just been confirmed. They both knew they were probably dead. But they ran anyway. The Green Line was the only train carrying passengers toward the downtown area. All other lines were running empty into downtown, then racing back along their respective lines, gathering up evacuees at each outbound station. The need to move people out of the area between the Charles River and downtown had prompted MBTA officials to schedule the Green Line to run empty to Lechmere Station, then reverse back through downtown, picking up evacuees along the way, and then on to Boston College and Cleveland Circle.

Science Park Station was the second stop.

Jim Brainard and Agent Morse scrambled on board just as the departure signal sounded and the doors closed. They had expected the train to be packed. Surprisingly, there were still a few seats available. Jim surmised it was because the majority of people had already been evacuated. No one really had known before this crisis just how rapidly a large population, numbering in the hundreds of thousands, might be removed from the central point of danger.

He looked around. Few people were talking. Most sat huddled in their seats, looking out into the night or staring across the aisle at their neighbors or their children. Jim saw two vacant seats across from a mother and her young son. The boy looked to be eleven or twelve, and was wearing a baseball uniform and a cap with the Red Sox emblem. Agent Morse was behind him as they reached the seats. Jim smiled at the mother and patted the lad on the shoulder. Then he slid in so that Morse could have the aisle seat.

That's when he saw him.

—~—

Safwat Najjir sat hunched down in a side chair from which he could see everyone as they entered. He had boarded the T at Science Park Station just moments ahead of Jim Brainard and Agent Morse. In the small case resting in his lap, he carried enough anthrax to turn Boston into a mass graveyard.

Beginning at North Station, the next stop, he intended to take up a position near the doorway. At the precise moment the signal indicated that the doors were closing, he would toss out a small egg-shaped object, barely two inches in circumference.

The object looked very much like a small lightbulb and was just as fragile. It was an ingenious, innocent-looking device that would break on impact against a railing or a wall, delivering anthrax spores into the city's underground system where huge air-conditioning units would automatically pump the virus into the streets and buildings above them. Aboveground stations would receive the same gift of terror and death, with nature's wind currents doing the rest.

When Najjir saw Jim Brainard board the very same car in which he was sitting, he could not believe his eyes.

How can this be? It's the old man from the fishing village. He's the one person who might recognize me. But will he connect me with tonight's events?

The train began moving. Najjir opened the case and withdrew his first egg. He held the device delicately, covering it with his other hand so as not to break it by chance. He was ready for the toss. It was for this very moment that Allah had called him. He would not fail.

He glanced again at the innkeeper.

He's coming right toward me!

It appeared that a younger man behind him was also making his way across the car. Involuntarily, Najjir tightened his grip on the death device. He watched out of the corner of his eye and then exhaled with relief as he saw the innkeeper prepare to sit down.

He hasn't seen me.

The old man smiled at a little boy across the aisle, patting his shoulder. Then he looked up.

And their eyes met.

Najjir saw the old man turn and whisper to his companion. Now both men were staring at him. A rush of anxiety caused him to tighten his grip on the egg. Slowly he stood, clutching the case in his left hand. In his right hand he held the egg. He knew that they knew. He was no longer a secret.

—~—

The train began to slow down as it approached North Station. In a few seconds, it would stop and the doors would open. People would crowd into the car. It would be impossible to fire a weapon.

Daniel Morse had never been in a situation like this. If Jim Brainard was right and this was the man, he had to take him out—*now*. His mouth felt like cotton and perspiration broke out underneath his shirt. He stepped past Brainard, never taking his eyes off the Arab. The man was standing now, clutching a small case with one hand. It looked like he had something in the other hand, too, but if he did, it was not a gun.

Morse drew his Glock .22 from the belt holster beneath his jacket. Even before he said a word, passengers nearby caught sight of the weapon. One young woman screamed.

"Don't move, fella," Morse called out. "FBI."

The train rocked slightly as it continued to slow down.

What happened next became headline news across the nation.

—~—

Jim Brainard was standing in the aisle only a step or two behind Agent Morse. His emotions ran unchecked as he glared at Safwat Najjir. He remembered the first day he had opened his doors to this man at Hill House. Anger welled up as he thought of what this man and his companions had done to Rosa Posadas. This man was a rapist and a murderer! Jim caught sight of the small object in the man's right hand and fear clenched like a fist in his stomach.

"Stay back," Najjir cried out, sliding out of the seat and moving nearer to the door.

"FBI," Morse repeated. "Give it up!"

He steadied his gun with both hands and pointed it at the man's heart.

The train was barely moving now, as it rolled into North Station.

"Don't come any nearer," Najjir shouted back. "This is anthrax. If I drop it, we all die!"

A man next to Najjir dropped into the aisle and began crawling desperately to get away.

The train jolted to a stop.

The door opened.

Najjir glanced around quickly.

None of the other passengers moved.The crowd of people on the platform jammed the doorway, pushing and shoving to get inside. Underhanded, Najjir tossed the egg well back into the car.

In the same instant, Agent Morse fired his weapon.

Passengers screamed.

Najjir crumpled to the floor.

Transfixed, Jim watched the flight of the egg. The cruel instrument of death was coming right toward him. It seemed to take forever.

Arching over Agent Morse's shoulder, the tiny missile continued its slow-motion airborne journey of death and destruction.

Without thinking, Jim Brainard reached up for the egg. At the last moment, he was jostled by a passenger trying to board and he lost his balance. All he saw was a flash of brown in front of his face. And then it was gone.

Jim regained his balance and steeled himself for the inevitable.

But there was nothing. Only a split second of stunned silence.

Then pandemonium.

Screaming and yelling, the passengers scrambled over each other, trying to reach the aisle. Sheer bedlam ensued. Then, as quickly as it had begun, it stopped. Jim looked to his right and there, standing on the seat, was the young lad in the baseball uniform. On his hand was a well-worn first baseman's mitt.

Carefully the boy opened it. He glanced down at his mother who sat, horror-stricken, unable to move. Then he looked over at Jim Brainard and grinned. In his glove lay the unbroken egg.

Timothy O'Neil had just made the catch that would forever be known as The Final Out!

77

19 SEPTEMBER, LOCAL TIME 0147
WASHINGTON, D.C.

Are you sure? You're one hundred percent certain? That's wonderful!" The director jumped up from his chair. "Thank you *very* much. Congratulations! This is the best news I've had all day. Maybe in all my life. Yes . . . yes . . . all right. I'll see you boys when you get back."

He put down the phone and looked around the room, smiling from ear to ear. He lifted his hands in the air and said in a loud voice, "Let's wrap up Boston and give it back to the people, folks!"

All activity stopped as the men and women turned their attention to the director. They had been hard at work laying various contingency plans for sealing off the doomed city of Boston.

"Special Agent Ellis has confirmed that the model airplane has been recovered and its cargo contained."

A cheer broke out as people clapped and hugged with a spontaneity seldom seen before in that room. Next came the questions. "How did they do it?" "Have the people been told yet?" "When will they be allowed to return?"

"What about the other two terrorists?" asked the attorney general. "Any word?"

"They're pretty sure Dosha is long gone. He's not the sort to stick around for the dirty work. His past pattern has been to put things in motion and then skip. The educated guess is he's probably three states away by now. Maybe even in Canada. We'll concentrate every effort toward finding him, but he's a cool one. The fourth terrorist was recognized and apprehended on a subway by one of our agents and the citizen from Booth Bay. You remember him? The fellow that owns the bed-and-breakfast where these lunatics stayed for a week?

"Wait until you hear this, though. Talk about your miracles."

The group of high-level government officials listened intently while the director recounted the capture of Safwat Najjir and the heroics of a young lad named Timothy O'Neil, who possessed the softest touch with a first baseman's mitt in all of Boston.

The room was buzzing as people gathered in groups to discuss the latest turn of events, the feeling of relief washing over them like the first rains of summer.

The director was already back on the phone, this time to California.

—w—

The mayor of Boston went on radio and television at 3:15 in the morning to make the momentous announcement. The tone in his voice and the huge smile on his face underscored the good news.

"The need for evacuation is over. Good citizens of Boston, it is safe to come home!"

Along auto-clogged expressways and turnpikes, horns began honking. In homes crowded with friends, relatives, even strangers who had been taken under roof, cheers went up. There was hand-clapping, hugging, and dancing among what was perhaps the largest late-night listening and viewing audience in regional radio and television history. Old-timers reminisced that they had not seen the likes of it since the end of World War II.

—w—

19 SEPTEMBER, LOCAL TIME 0525
BOSTON

At Logan Airport, Jim Brainard found himself being congratulated by the mayor of Boston and the FBI's Jerry Ellis. Television lights took the edge off the early morning chill as newspeople and cameramen stretched cables—and tempers—across the runway pavement. In the background, the Hostage Rescue Team was already reloading their equipment on board the plane they had arrived in a few hours earlier. The huge turbines on the C-130 were just starting to turn over.

A stretcher, shrouded in black, was lifted from a police van and carried solemnly up the ramp, disappearing into the plane's belly. Television cameras captured the tired faces of the three surviving agents who had overcome impossible odds and saved the city. None of them was available for comment. Agent Daniel Morse also slipped quietly around the media crews and made his way up the ramp.

Following his moment in the media spotlight, Jim took Jerry Ellis's arm and pulled him to one side.

"Do you have any idea how long it will be before Logan opens up to commercial flights?"

"No, but I can find out. We'll get you home. Don't worry about that."

When Jim hesitated, Ellis asked him, "Did you have something else in mind?"

"I want to go to California."

Ellis looked at him quizzically.

"It's hard to explain, but a couple of hours ago, I began feelin' as though I need to go out there. To California. It's got something to do with that pastor's family and the church situation there."

"Do you know those people, Mr. Brainard?"

"Nope. Haven't ever been to California. Besides that, I'm Catholic. Never met a Protestant preacher in my whole life. But before my wife died, God love her, she would get like this once in a while. She used to call it a 'leadin' of the Lord.' More often than not, she was right."

Jim paused for a moment to zip up his jacket. "Well, I have to be honest. I don't actually know much about 'the Lord's leading.' Now that I think of it, that's kind of a sad thing for a man in his sixties to have to say, don't you think? Middie'd get determined, though, and follow through on whatever it was she believed God might be tellin' her to do. I know it sounds kind of outrageous and all, but it's almost like she's here again."

Jim looked up at the stars twinkling above the terminal lights. "I guess the good Lord's talkin' directly to me now. I think he's tellin' me to go to California and be with that family. It doesn't make much sense, but . . . well, it just seems like the right thing to do."

Ellis studied the older man's face. An honest face, clear-eyed and earnest. He shook his head, partly in disbelief, partly in admiration. Then he made a decision.

"Mr. Brainard, if it weren't for you, this city would be a graveyard tonight. The entire country owes you a debt of gratitude. The more I think about the last couple of days, the more awesome it all becomes. I go to church regularly. I've always believed in God and I pray every day. But this experience has me thinking that there's something about my faith that I haven't tapped into yet. So, I'd say if the Lord is telling you to go to California, we'd best get you out there, if we can."

Ellis stopped to consider his options. "I'll tell you what, Mr. Brainard. It could be hours before commercial flights resume here at Logan. And then, who knows how long before you could book a flight out. But we've got a C-130 here that's just about ready to leave for D.C. If you'd like, I'll get you on board. You can fly with us down to the capital, and by the time we arrive, we'll have a first-class seat for you on the next flight out to San Francisco, with our thanks for a job well done. How does that sound?"

"I like the way you work, Ellis," Jim chuckled as they shook hands. "Would you mind walkin' me up that ramp so your boys don't decide to toss this old geezer out on his ear?"

78

19 SEPTEMBER, LOCAL TIME 0845
BAYTOWN, CALIFORNIA

Word of the events in Boston reached Special Agent in Charge Webber and his team early in the morning hours. An apparent tragedy of monstrous proportions had turned into an incredible victory. The news lifted the spirits of the tired men inside the Winnebago Command Center. Now if only they could catch a few breaks of their own. Nearly twenty-four hours had passed since the first shots rang out in Calvary Church's sanctuary. In spite of every effort, nothing had changed, no hostages had been released. Webber had sent in more food, but kept the SWAT team back while he urged Akmed to release those that had been promised freedom earlier. But Akmed wasn't dealing.

Finally, at 8:45, Webber left the RV to stretch his legs and get some fresh air.

Almost exactly one hour later, Akmed was pacing back and forth at the front of the sanctuary. Finally, he laid the AK-47 on the communion table and motioned for Ihab Akazzam.

Ihab listened as Akmed whispered instructions in his ear. He nodded, smiling as he stepped back.

Akmed then turned and looked at the weary crowd sitting before him.

"Mrs. Cain!"

Esther jumped involuntarily at the sound of her name.

"Ah, Mrs. Cain. There you are. Come here, please."

"What—" Esther's voice wavered. She swallowed and cleared her throat. "What do you want?"

"Please do not ask questions, Mrs. Cain. What I want is for you to come here. Now, come!"

"Let her alone. She's not been well."

Jeremy was on his feet, even as Esther tugged at his sleeve.

"Jeremy. Sit down. Please!" Esther drew him down into the pew. Then she stood and began working her way past the others between her and the aisle.

"Wait!"

Esther froze.

"And who might this young man be?" asked Akmed, his eyes fixed steadily on Jeremy. He recognized him as the same person who had directed him earlier to dial 9-1-1.

Esther cast a desperate look at Jeremy and then back to Akmed.

"Who is he? What is he to you, Mrs. Cain?"

"My son," she whispered, her head down, hating herself for divulging the information, not knowing what else she could do.

"What? Speak up so that I can hear you clearly, Mrs. Cain."

"He is my son," she said again, this time clearly and distinctly.

"Ah, Jeremy. Jeremy Cain. And, Jeremy Cain, who is this young lady sitting next to you? Your sister perhaps?"

Jeremy stared back silently.

"You will answer me, Jeremy Cain, if you know what's good for you. Is this your sister?"

"No."

"Then who?"

Jeremy remained silent. Esther saw Akmed reach for the weapon on the communion table. Her eyes filled with horror and in desperation she started to say something. But she was interrupted by another clear, steady voice.

"My name is Allison Orwell."

Startled, fear squeezing the breath out of her, Esther looked over and saw both Allison and Jeremy standing together.

"Orwell, Orwell." Akmed rolled the name over, his hand releasing the weapon on the table. Then his face lit up with recognition. "Ah, your father is the good doctor, sitting back there. Is that correct?"

Allison looked back at her parents.

"Yes. My father is the good doctor. He spends every day saving lives, not taking them," she answered firmly and with a touch of defiant pride.

"Very good," Akmed said, admiringly. "A fine answer indeed and your point is well taken. Am I to assume that you and young Mr. Jeremy are good friends? Perhaps even best friends?"

There was no response.

He waited for a moment, his eyes flitting across the crowd that was now at attention, weariness forgotten as this new scenario unfolded before them.

"Mrs. Cain. Please come and sit here in the front row." He looked around again. "Mrs. Ralsten!"

Elizabeth Ralsten stood to her feet.

"Thank you, Mrs. Ralsten. Please join Mrs. Cain here in front. No, don't sit down." He motioned to Jeremy and Allison as they started to be seated. "I want you to come here also."

Jeremy and Allison looked at each other, uneasiness etched clearly on their faces.

—w—

"You'd better get the boss. Something's going down in there." The technician turned away from the monitors and looked toward Lieutenant Randle as he spoke.

But Randle was already headed out the door.

—w—

"There is another couple that my associate and I met while visiting with you last week," Akmed said smoothly. "I do not recall their names, but I recognize them both sitting over there." Akmed pointed at the Heidens. "Aziza, would you be so kind as to escort them to the front, please?"

Esther turned to watch as the young couple stood and started down the aisle, followed by Aziza, her AK-47 held ready. Esther did not know the Heidens, but she recognized their faces. John had mentioned that they were from the Seattle area. They had not been at Calvary Church for long. And Mrs. Heiden was obviously very pregnant. Esther wondered what effect all this tension might have on her and her baby.

"Please. Come up here with me." Akmed turned and mounted the three steps onto the platform. "You too, Jeremy Cain and Allison Orwell."

The four followed him up the steps.

"Turn around, please, and face your friends." Akmed took the microphone in his hand. To the Heidens, he said, "I apologize for not remembering your names?"

"Heiden," Phil responded nervously. "I'm Phil. This is my wife, Sherri."

"I am pleased to meet you again," Akmed responded warmly. "It is regretful that it must be under such trying circumstances."

Esther tensed. Though his tone was polite and his manner warm and cordial, there was a steely look in his eyes.

This man is evil. He's capable of anything.

79

What's going on?" Webber demanded as he stepped up into the Command Center vehicle, his eyes riveted immediately on the monitors. Chief White and Lieutenant Randle were close behind him.

"I'm not sure. We couldn't hear at first. He just now picked up the microphone. He called out a young couple that he and the woman apparently met last week at church. Akmed and the Aziza woman must have been here checking the place out. That's the couple, I didn't catch their names, standing there on the platform. She's the pregnant one. The young fellow over there is Cain's son. Name is Jeremy. The one next to him looks like a girlfriend. They were sitting together before Akmed called them up. She's Allison Orwell. Her father was the doctor who checked out the dead guy earlier on."

"Any idea what he's up to?"

"I'm not sure, sir. But a moment ago, he ordered those two down to the front pew." He pointed them out on the screen. "One is Mrs. Cain, the pastor's wife. The other is Mrs. Ralsten."

"Uh oh."

"Is the SWAT team going in, sir?"

"Yes. I just hope we're not too late!"

"We have tried to make you comfortable during this stressful experience," said Akmed, his tone cool and sinister. "We have even permitted all of you to go to the restroom to relieve yourselves. It was extremely disappointing to note that the first time this courtesy was extended, it was taken advantage of by . . . I believe it was your husband and son, Mrs. Ralsten. Am I correct?"

Elizabeth Ralsten's eyes were downcast. Her lip trembled.

"Mrs. Ralsten?"

Elizabeth felt a hand slip into hers. She glanced over as Esther squeezed and then released it. It wasn't much, but it was the courage she needed.

Elizabeth stood up straight and looked Akmed in the eye. "Yes," she replied. "It was my husband and my son."

"Mrs. Ralsten. Do you not recall that I said anyone who attempted to escape would result in the death of two?"

Elizabeth stared at him.

"Do you?"

Numbly, she nodded.

"Your husband and your son escaped. I am told they tried to take you with them. Is that true?"

Again she nodded.

"Why did you not go with them?" asked Akmed, curiously. "You would be safe now."

"I could not," she replied evenly, her eyes still locked onto Akmed.

"Why?"

"Because I believed you. I could never live with myself, knowing that as a result of saving my life, others had died."

Akmed studied her for a long time. At last he nodded his head as though he clearly understood her motive. "You are a brave woman, Mrs. Ralsten. You have in you the spirit of a Muslim warrior. Sit down."

Elizabeth Ralsten sat down. She was visibly shaking and near to tears.

"Mrs. Cain."

Esther had been silently praying,

Oh, Lord Jesus, let me be strong for you just now. Help me honor you through your strength and not disappoint you with my weakness.

She stood up.

"Mrs. Cain, it is important that you and all these people, as well as those making decisions outside these walls, know that Akmed el Hussein is a man of his word."

Akmed paused. Esther said nothing.

"Our people have nowhere else to turn. We are ignored, killed, deprived of our possessions, our land, our self-respect. We are seeking an end to the pain and suffering of our families. But it continues on to this day. Your people have contributed to our tribulation. Regretfully, we must come seeking relief in the only way left open to us. An eye for an eye, a tooth for a tooth.

"It is your political and religious leaders who are at fault," Akmed continued. "They have caused this disaster because of their refusal to heed our repeated warnings. Politicians like your president. Religious leaders like your husband, Mrs. Cain. All are guilty. All must repent or be severely punished by the fires of hell.

"Just look at what has happened here. Even in such a simple thing as using the restrooms, you are guilty of unbelief. You do not take us at our word. Or perhaps you thought I had forgotten. But I assure you, I am a man of my word, and I have not forgotten. Now it is time. Punishment is at hand. I told you at the beginning that two people would die for every one who tried to escape." Akmed paused and smiled beneficently. "Two plus two equals four, does it not?"

Esther's knees buckled, then she caught herself. She realized what he intended to do. It hit her with hammerlike force. Jeremy and the others were going to be sacrificed.

"However," Akmed went on, "to show you just how generous I can be, even though four deserve to die, I am presenting you with a gift, Mrs. Cain. A gift of the undeserved mercy of Allah."

He smiled, looking at the four young people before him.

Esther caught her breath.

"Two may live, according to the mercies of Allah," he declared, looking down at Esther. "Only two need to die."

Fear shot through her brain.

"And you, Mrs. Cain, will now decide which of these two will live and which two will die."

—⁓—

Duane Webber swore, pounding an open hand with his fist. "This guy is an animal. He is a cunning, diabolical madman!"

"Here, sir. This headset. Put it on. Hendrickson wants to talk."

Webber grabbed the headset and put it on.

"What is it?" he growled angrily.

80

Ah, sir," Hendrickson hesitated. He could tell by the tone in Webber's voice that something was wrong. "Our man has been in the air-conditioning duct for ten minutes. The rest of us are in place and ready."

"How much longer?"

"I can't be sure, sir. He's got to move carefully in order to avoid making noise."

"What's he using?"

"A .308."

"Is this guy the best you've got?"

"Absolutely. He's the best, period. He can shoot the eyes out of a snake at a hundred yards."

"Good. He's about to run up against the biggest snake he's ever taken out."

"Yes sir."

"By the way. What's his name?"

Hendrickson groaned. He had hoped Webber would not ask that question.

"It's Hamdi, sir."

"Okay, then, let's . . . say again?"

"Hamdi."

"But that's an—"

"I know, sir. Hamdi is an American-born Arab. He's also proven himself with five years of excellent service. And he's the best there is."

"But do you think it's wise to put him in this situation? For his sake, if nothing else."

"He's the best I've got, sir. For Hamdi it's not an issue of race. It's a matter of duty and honor. If he makes it all the way in, he'll do the job."

"I don't know . . ."

"Sir, remember what happened in the Second World War," Hendrickson plunged ahead. He'd already planned what he would say if it came to this. "We told a lot of American Japanese that they couldn't fight, that we didn't trust them to even walk on our streets. But after all was said and done, they turned out to be some of the best soldiers on the battlefield."

There was silence at Webber's end.

"Sir?"

"You did the right thing, Hendrickson. We're staying with you from here on until you're inside." Webber kept his eye on the scene unfolding in front of him. "We'll let you know where the bad guys are when you're ready to move. Looks like something may be happening right now. He's pulled some people out of the crowd. Says he intends to kill two of them as retribution for those two who escaped. I don't doubt for a minute that this guy thinks this will be great theater. We need your man in position, pronto. Let me know when he has a clear line of sight."

"Yes sir."

Hendrickson took a deep breath, then calmly gathering his team together in the church lobby.

One way or another, it was almost over.

—w—

In the Winnebago, Webber stood and tried to stretch the weariness out of his body. Every muscle felt like a tangle of knots. He listened to the sounds of Hendrickson deploying his team across the church lobby. He watched Akmed and the others on the screen, weary of this drama with no commercial breaks to relieve the tension. Soon every citizen in America would begin exercising their constitutional right to second-guess the FBI's latest action. And it would all come back to him eventually.

He heaved a long sigh and wondered what Janice was doing.

It was almost over.

81

Esther was numb with disbelief, yet she knew without a doubt he was serious.

Deadly serious.

He intends to kill Jeremy. And the others, too. Oh God, how could you let this happen? You've already taken Jenny. I don't know where Jessica and John are, or if they're even alive!

Just then she heard a voice.

Quiet, firm, composed.

It was Elizabeth Ralsten.

"Sir, it is not right that these people should die for something done by my husband and son." She paused, taking a deep breath before continuing. "Let me take their place. It's not right that anyone should have to die here today, but if you feel you must kill someone, then kill me."

A look of amusement came over Akmed's face.

"I will say it again, Mrs. Ralsten, I am impressed with your bravery, even if it is utterly foolish and misguided. Your husband and son would do well to examine themselves in the light of your courage. It is more than I would expect from the likes of any of you. But I'm afraid I must decline your most generous offer."

"It is not just a generous offer. It's what Jesus did for me. For all of us," Elizabeth continued, still on her feet. "He died for my sins. And yours, too. He took our place, though he did not deserve to die. The only 'sin' my husband and son have committed is wanting to escape from this terror. If that is a sin, it is a sin of which all of us in this room are guilty in our hearts. Perhaps they were unwise to act as they did. Perhaps they lacked courage at a particular moment. But I am certain that they would not wish for anyone in this room to die needlessly and without just cause for something that they did."

Akmed's gaze never left Elizabeth.

"And so I ask you again," she said softly but firmly, enunciating each word. "If someone must die to appease your word of honor, then let it be me. Let these young people go."

The room was still, the atmosphere electric.

Esther felt a flush of pride as she watched Elizabeth.

"Sit down, Mrs. Ralsten."

Elizabeth did not move.

Akmed took a step toward her. "If you do not sit down, Mrs. Ralsten, I will make you sit down. And I assure you, it will be painful. Learn from your husband and your son's errors. Obedience is best."

Esther took her arm. Elizabeth sat down.

Akmed smiled. Then he turned to Mamdouh Ekrori.

"Make certain the cameras are facing the wall until I say otherwise. We will use them again later." He put the microphone down on the floor and moved away. "What we must do now will best be done without our friends outside looking on. Aziza, Mousa, Ihab. Come."

82

Hendrickson, he's getting ready to kill some people in there. What's your status? I need your shooter locked and loaded."

Webber paused, listening for a response from inside the church building.

"The outside lobby doors and windows leading to the parking lot are blacked out. Our entry teams are ready. Hamdi thinks he's maybe two-thirds of the way. Ten more minutes. He can hear voices, but the turns are tight to get through. He's got to go slow. If they hear him, it's history. And so is he."

"I know, I know," Webber sounded weary, resigned to accept the unacceptable. "Look, we've got more trouble here. Akmed has just turned all the cameras toward the wall. The only thing we can make out are the bumps on the wallboard. He's away from the microphone, too. Whatever he intends to do, he's not about to show and tell. At least not until he's finished. I think he's moving his troops, though, and we're not going to be able to tell you where they're at."

Hendrickson swore and bit down on his lip, hard enough to draw blood. In this business, everything was timing. Timing down to the second. If they did not know where the bad guys were, the rescue plan was never going to fly.

Webber's voice crackled over the radio. "Any bright ideas?"

"Yeah. Pray for a miracle!"

83

Connie Farrer desperately wanted to call the station again. But Aziza was too close. She did not dare risk further exposing the fact that she had a cellular phone in her possession. But suddenly the miracle she'd been praying for happened.

Akmed was calling the others forward. Each of the groups remained huddled in front of the doors, but the terrorists were well removed from where they were sitting. Connie reached beneath her dress and once again pulled her "secret weapon" from its hiding place. She punched in the numbers to Jody Ansel's desk.

"Hello," the voice answered before the first ring had finished.

"Jody?" Connie whispered, conscious of the anxious looks being given her by others in her group.

"Yes! Oh thank God, you're okay and you've still got the phone."

Yes, Connie agreed silently. *Thank God.*

"What's happening? They've turned the cameras and shut down the microphones. We're not getting anything from inside."

"I know. Listen carefully. They're getting ready to kill some people. I think it's going to happen in the next few minutes. Is anybody out there going to help us?" Connie's voice was filled with desperation.

"The police and the FBI are all outside, Connie. I'm sure they're doing everything they can. But, now they can't see inside, so—"

"They can if I can talk to them."

"What?"

"Patch me through to whoever is running the show, Jody. I can tell them what they need to know. I can see everything from here. They really are getting ready to kill somebody!"

"I'm putting you on hold, Connie. Don't hang up. I'll be right back."

Connie looked toward the front of the church. The five terrorists were still standing there, talking to one another in Arabic.

—~—

Jody Ansel looked at the circle of anxious faces around her desk.

"Well?" demanded Betty.

"They've shut the world out because they are going to kill some people. Connie's watching it all and hoping somebody comes quickly."

Betty swore softly, her face alight with excitement, her hands clenching and unclenching. "It's what we've been waiting for."

"What do you mean?" asked Jody.

"Get her back on the line. We can give a blow by blow report of the situation. We'll scoop every network with the biggest story we've touched in years. This is it, Jody. It's our big break." Betty threw her hands in the air. "The ratings game is about to be won by KFOR!"

"You're insane," Tom Bernstein replied angrily. "You're talking ratings and people inside that church are about to die. Good grief, woman, have you no soul?"

Betty stared at Tom, spitefulness boiling into pure hatred in her eyes.

"Tom Bernstein, I want—"

"He's right, Betty."

Jody could hardly believe whose voice she heard speak up next. It was her own.

Betty's jaw dropped as she turned to face Jody, but she quickly recovered. "You're fired, Jody. And so is the great Tom Bernstein. Both of you get out of my studio!"

"I'll be happy to leave," Jody heard herself saying, gathering courage with each word, "but only after this is over. Right now I'm calling the FBI, so get out of my way and stay off my back!"

Betty started to say something, stopped, then looked again at KFOR's lead anchor. Everyone else remained frozen in place, watching the off-camera drama work through to its climax. This was better than prime time.

Tom smiled. "I'm with her, Betty," he said with mock innocence, nodding toward Jody. "I'm staying until this is over."

Betty's face turned crimson. Her hands went to her hips. Her narrow eyes darted back and forth between the two mutineers. Then without another word she turned and stalked out of the studio.

—m—

In less than five minutes, Jody Ansel was talking with Special Agent in Charge Duane Webber, explaining the situation to him.

"You have a what?" was his incredulous response.

"A reporter from KFOR went to church there yesterday morning, before coming in to work. She's still in there and I've got her on the phone."

"Hold on . . . what's your name again?"

"Jody Ansel."

"Hold on, Jody. I'll be right back."

Webber flipped on his radiophone.

"Hendrickson!"

"Yes sir."

"I think we just got our miracle."

"Sir?"

"Channel 4 has a reporter inside the church. She's been there all along. And she's got a cell phone. I'm going to talk with her right now. Hang in there a bit longer. Where's Hamdi?"

"He needs another five, sir."

"I'll be right back."

He picked up the cellular phone.

"Hello. Who am I talking to?"

"My name is Connie Farrer," whispered a female voice.

"This is Duane Webber, FBI, Connie. Jody Ansel vouches for you that you're the real thing and not a plant, so here's the deal. We're ready to send in a SWAT team, but I need your help. I need you to be a part of the entry team. Okay?"

"Yes."

"We need your eyes. We can't see anything in there right now. I've got a sniper moving into position. Maybe three or four more minutes. There are SWAT teams at each door. We think the one called Akmed has the only detonator. Can you verify?"

"I haven't seen anyone else with one."

"Good. We have to take the leader out so he doesn't have a chance to blow the doors. Do you understand?"

"Yes," the voice whispered.

"Connie, when we come through the doors, we have to know where the bad guys are. By the way, we count five of them. Can you confirm?"

"Yes."

"All right. Tell me exactly where those five people are located and give me an idea of what's happening in there. Why did they turn the cameras away?"

Connie Farrer whispered her story into Duane Webber's ear.

84

Mrs. Cain? You must not delay any longer. What is your decision?"

Esther stared helplessly at the four people standing on the platform. The attention of every person in the room was riveted on the wife of Calvary Church's senior pastor, the mother of one of Akmed's chosen victims.

"Please," she pleaded. Her voice was low and strained. "I cannot do this. I can't make such a decision. What you are asking is impossible."

"Then all four will die," Akmed said abruptly, motioning toward one of the terrorists standing near by.

"Wait!" Esther cried out.

Akmed stopped, then turned back to Esther.

"Oh, please. Don't do this terrible thing."

"Then decide, Mrs. Cain! Who should live? Who will die?"

Akmed waited.

Tears fell down Esther's cheeks as she looked at the chosen four.

"Mrs. Cain, you are wasting our time. Let's not protract the inevitable any longer. It is within your power to save two lives. Isn't that what you and your Christian husband do? Save lives?" The evil smile that crept over his face was accentuated by the hard glint in his eyes. "That is what you claim to do, is it not? So I am giving you an opportunity to fulfill your vocation. If you refuse, I assure you, all four will die. Two unnecessarily and all because of you. This will remain on your Christian conscience for a long time, will it not?"

"But this is my son. My own flesh and blood. And Allison has done nothing to deserve dying. And the Heidens. What have they done to you? Can't you see that this woman is with child? Take her life and you take the life of her unborn baby. These are innocents. What purpose will be served? In the name of God, what can you people possibly hope to achieve with such madness?"

Esther's voice was strong. Her tears fell to the floor.

Akmed's eyes were darker now, foreboding, like some terrible thundercloud. His voice stirred with sudden passion, his hand twitching involuntarily as he spoke.

"What purpose will be served, you ask? I will tell you what purpose. We will show the world that it has no alternative. Palestine must be granted the right to live again or every one of her enemies will remain under the sentence of death. Not just two or four," his hand swept dramatically toward the congregation, "but six hundred or six hundred thousand! The enemies of our people are the enemies of Allah. We will strike you again and again, until justice prevails at last!"

"But we are not your enemies," Esther cried. "Can't you see that? We don't even know you."

"Ah, yes," Akmed smiled grimly, "perhaps that is the problem. You do not know us. But you will. That I can guarantee you. And you will give us what we want. Sooner or later. Now, Mrs. Cain, you must choose. And you must choose quickly. I have had enough of you."

Esther started toward Akmed. Numb. Desolate. Defeated.

"Akmed," she spoke his name softly.

She had heard others call him by name. But she had never let it cross her own lips. To do so would turn this evil intruder into a person. It would give him a mother. A father. Perhaps brothers and sisters. It would permit the inhuman to become human. Esther had not allowed herself to think in those terms.

Until now.

Now she knew she must. She did not understand what drove these persons to such desperate deeds. But they were people. They were not things. They were not animals without souls. They were flesh and blood people.

And they had names.

85

From his cramped location in the air-conditioning duct, Hamdi carefully sighted in his .308 high-powered, silencer-equipped rifle on Akmed el Hussein.

"I have him, sir," he said softly into his radiophone.

"Hold it," came Hendrickson's reply. Hamdi's high-pitched voice always reminded him of a young boy's, not yet past the age of puberty. A boy's voice for a man's job.

Hamdi saw the detonator and considered for a brief moment the possibility of shooting it out of the man's hand. He knew he could do it. But what if his shot set off the explosives? No. He could not take that chance.

His concentration was nearly total now.

Until the conversation directly below him entered his consciousness. He could see the woman who was talking. She was pleading with the terrorist leader. His hand wavered slightly as he listened.

"Let these children live . . . You will serve your purpose far better by taking my life . . ."

Hamdi swore under his breath. *That woman, whoever she is, is bartering her life!*

He readjusted his aim.

—ʍ—

Hendrickson took a last look around at his men. At each of the three doors he could see, the five-member teams stood ready. He knew the scene was identical at the two doors beyond the periphery of his vision.

Each man wore Kevlar headgear, a solid piece looking a little like a biker's helmet, fitted with goggles. Fatigues, worn in a pants-in-boots style. Combat boots. A flack jacket. And a radio pack on their back with a receiver attached firmly in the ear. From head to toe, they were dressed in black.

Each team was now positioned less than three feet from their respective door entry. Like dominos, they were stacked together, every man pressed against the one in front. Attached to the hip, each one wore a SIG-Sauer P226 handgun, loaded with a fifteen-round clip. The team leaders carried a sawed-off shotgun in one hand, with a Heckler and Koch MP-5 fully automatic submachine gun, capable of firing thirty rounds in a matter of seconds, strapped on their shoulder. The others held submachine guns in their right hand. Attached to each weapon was a slender laser light to enable their finding targets in total darkness. With his left hand, each man held on tightly to the battering ram.

Jim Corry was the lone agent assigned to the entry plan who was not a regular member of the SWAT team. He had been relegated to the electrical control panel located in the basement. His hand was on the master switch that provided power to the sanctuary. It tightened as he listened over the receiver in his ear.

Hendrickson nodded.

"Everyone is in position," he spoke into his radiophone.

"Go when ready," Webber responded from the Command Center.

"Team One?"

"Ready."

"Team Two?"

"Ready, sir."

"Team Three is ready," Hendrickson said for the benefit of the others. He would be leading Team Three through the center doors himself.

"Team Four?"

"Ready."

"Team Five?"

"Ready."

"Corry."

"Ready."

"Hamdi?"

"Ready, sir."

"All right. We'll do it just like we rehearsed. Tell me when he's down, Hamdi."

—∾—

In his earpiece, Hamdi heard the entry team checking off one by one.

The woman below him was still pleading, "If you must kill someone, kill me."

"No!"

"Please, Akmed. Hear me out. Let these children live. Let them live to understand the plight of your people. Think about it. My death will serve your purpose in a far greater way than theirs ever could. You'll be killing the leader's wife. You claim that my husband is in your hands in Israel. Perhaps he is dead already. Don't you see, Akmed? You will serve your purpose far better by taking my life than by killing them. Let the children live!"

Akmed hesitated, folding his arms. He held the detonator in his left hand, running a thumb across the switch as he considered what Esther said.

Hamdi pushed everything from his mind and focused on one clear objective.

His heart slowed its beating. A last deep breath. *Let it out slowly.*

His finger tightened on the trigger. The scope's crosshairs were steady, just above the man's eyes.

Pffpht!

Akmed staggered backward.

The detonator dropped to the floor.

On his face was a look of disbelief.

"He's down!"

Hamdi quickly scanned his sight lines, looking for a secondary target.

86

"He's down!"

The boyish voice in Hendrickson's earpiece was sharp, precise. The team leader's response was instantaneous. "All teams—Execute! Execute! Execute!"

In the basement, Special Agent Corry slammed the master switch down on the electrical panel, plunging the building into total darkness. Hendrickson felt the surge of the men behind him. They struck the double doors with enough force to tear the left side door off its hinges while the right side splintered and sagged. The SWAT team rushed headlong into the darkness, stumbling over bodies that were scrambling to get out of the way.

As they led the charge, the team leaders for teams three and four hurled "flashbangs" into the center aisles. The explosions were deafening and the flashes bright enough to momentarily blind unprotected eyes, giving the SWAT teams a temporary edge over the enemy.

"Down! Down! Down!" the officers shouted as they moved forward, their laser scopes crisscrossing the room in a quick, methodical search for the gunmen.

Gunfire erupted near the front of the sanctuary, followed by cries of pain from those who were hit.

With the aid of night-vision goggles, the team specialist directly behind Hendrickson located the shooter and fired at the same time another shot sounded from the left side of the room.

The terrorist went down.

On the far right side of the auditorium, another terrorist was taken out by a single shot as he ran for the exit door, his AK-47 firing wildly until he hit the floor.

—ʌʌʌ—

On the platform, Esther defied the order to get down, throwing herself instead in the direction she had last seen Jeremy, Allison, and the Heidens. She stumbled over Phil Heiden, who was kneeling protectively over Sherri, shielding her body with his. She collided with Jeremy and like broken sticks they fell, Jeremy toppling onto Allison as Esther rolled between them and Aziza.

Uneven streams of light bobbed and weaved around them as the terrifying staccato of gunfire echoed in the large auditorium, interspersed with the cries of the wounded and the fearful screams of those who were desperately trying to find cover from the fusillade of bullets.

Esther fought to untangle herself. She scrambled to a kneeling position in time to see Aziza's face suddenly caught in a thin red stream of light. The young female terrorist had stumbled during the first confusing seconds of the attack. Now she was on her knees, barely an arm's length from Esther, submachine gun in hand, her beautiful face transfixed with fright. Her eyes were darting back and forth wildly, seeking a way of salvation from this terrible day of judgment.

And then Esther was illuminated by one of the light pencils. A flicker of recognition passed between the two women.

Esther had often heard that the events of people's lives flash across their memories just before they died. But that was not what Esther saw. Instead, another drama raced through her thoughts at the speed of light, at the same time leaving every frame indelibly imprinted in her mind.

A young girl skipped through the rock-strewn streets of a Middle East village, her freshly washed dress bobbing up and down at her knees. With bare, sandaled feet, she kicked a pink and blue ball against a high wall, then chased after it through the dirt and dust. The child's laughter was familiar, yet Esther knew she had never seen her before. The young girl pirouetted gaily, hands raised toward the sky. So familiar. Yet so strange. Suddenly a soldier stood in the street, pointing his gun at the girl.

"No."

It was a mother's cry, surging up from the depths of her heart.

"No!"

The child stopped her dancing to look at the soldier. Then she turned and looked at Esther.

Her eyes were full of sadness and pain.

Her lips formed two words.

"Help me."

Then her beautiful face exploded!

Esther felt the pain.

It ripped through her mind and slammed the breath from her body.

She reached for the face that was no longer there. And she began falling . . . falling . . . into darkness . . . as the pain gradually . . . disappeared . . .

—~—

Search!

Rapid fire on the right!

Search! There he is, running to the left. He's shooting.

More screams!

More shouts!

Three lasers found the runner simultaneously. Another burst of rapid fire and he was gone.

Search!

The woman!

She's on her knees on the platform. She has a gun in her hand. It's up. She's firing!

Hendrickson squeezed off three quick shots.

In that same split second, another person entered Hendrickson's line of fire. Reaching toward the woman with the gun.

"Cease fire! Cease fire! Cease fire!"

—~—

The sudden stillness was deafening.

The laser scopes continued their macabre dance, like strobes at a rock concert, but the hellish sounds of gunfire in the chambers of the Lord were at last silent. It seemed as if the entire room held its breath.

Waiting.

A little child whimpered.

A low moan was heard near the back of the sanctuary.

"Power on," Hendrickson spoke quietly into his radio mike.

The SWAT team assault, which had seemed like a nightmarish eternity to the hostages, had lasted exactly forty-three seconds.

87

19 SEPTEMBER, LOCAL TIME 1950
JERUSALEM

John awoke with a start.

Where am I?

He stared up at the bare lightbulb, then looked across to the opposite bed where Edgar and Bob were snoring loudly. Turning the opposite way, he looked into the face of Gisele Eiderman. She was awake. She gave him a weak smile.

"We've got to stop meeting like this," she quipped.

John rolled over, letting his feet drop to the floor. He sat up, embarrassed by the intimacy of their situation.

"I tried the floor, Gisele," he whispered. "It's hard."

"I know," she replied hastily. "I didn't mean anything by what I said. Just my attempt to lighten up these long tour days with a little levity."

"I know," replied John with a pained look. "Don't stop, whatever you do."

Edgar stirred, licking at dry lips as he opened his eyes.

"Bad breath alley over here, folks," he said. "And Bob snores a whole lot worse than Jill, that's for sure."

"Oh, yeah?" came Bob Thomas's muffled voice from the far side of the bed. "Well, the last few hours on this rack have given me one more reason why I married Donna and not a horse like you, Ed."

Like battleworn soldiers, they reached for whatever humor they could muster as a fundamental means of surviving their situation.

The three men were sitting up now and Gisele had turned over on her side to face the others. Their banter sounded good to John.

This is healthy, given the circumstances. It's amazing what a few hours of sleep will do for one's outlook.

He glanced over at their two male captors. They were asleep, with their rifles propped nearby.

His mind turned to Jessica.

Where are you, sweetheart?

Then thoughts of Esther and Jeremy crowded in and knocked the wind out of his sails.

What is happening to them? Are they safe? Lord, please keep your hand on my family. I can't do anything. You have to do it. Somehow, please, get us all through this mess and bring us together again.

He slid down onto the floor facing the wall and resumed the task he had been working on earlier. The others watched with growing interest. When they saw that John seemed to be making some progress, they each quietly checked the fixture to which their own chain was attached. Eventually, though, the other three gave up and turned their attention back to John. Silently, he twisted and pulled for another hour. It began to look hopeless.

When they heard voices approaching the door, talking in low tones, John hurried to twist around until his back was against the wall fixture. The door opened and Yazib and Pasha entered the room.

Pasha placed a backpack on the table while Yazib walked over to where John was sitting.

"You like it down there, Reverend Cain?" Yazib smiled. "It does not look very comfortable to me."

"I'm not very comfortable, actually," John answered. "Would you like to remove these chains? That would go a long way toward making me feel more at home."

"Ah, yes, I am sure it would," Yazib responded agreeably. "All in good time, Reverend Cain. All in good time."

Pasha stood next to Yazib. John decided she had the coldest eyes of any human being he had ever known.

"Lean forward, Reverend Cain," Yazib commanded.

"What?"

"Lean forward. Quickly."

He cuffed the side of John's head with his hand. John leaned forward, still in a sitting position. Yazib gave the fixture and chain a visual check, but did not try to reach in behind and pull on it. John was grateful. The small flat plate, which lay flush against the wall, kept its weakened condition a secret.

—m—

TUESDAY, 20 SEPTEMBER, LOCAL TIME 0015
JERUSALEM

Time continued to drag on, with no sign from the terrorists that they were in any hurry. After what seemed to John to be several hours, there was a sharp knock on the door and a man he had not seen before came into the room. He was dressed in a rumpled white shirt and unpressed pants, with leather strap sandals on his feet. He looked to be about thirty years old, but John could not be sure.

He had been in the room for only a few minutes, whispering to Yazib, when Yazib suddenly grasped his arm roughly. Their conversation grew louder and more heated as Yazib led the man out the door. A messenger perhaps. But with what message? John wished he could understand their language as well as they understood his. But he didn't. He didn't even know what time of day it was.

When Yazib returned, he was alone and appeared agitated. He motioned to Pasha and they went back outside, leaving the door partially open. Because the others were outside as well, on guard duty, it was the first time the prisoners had been left alone since their arrival. Yazib and Pasha's muffled voices could be heard rising and falling. It sounded like they were arguing about something, but they spoke in Arabic and it was impossible for John and the others to tell what was happening.

They looked at one another quizzically.

"What do you suppose is going on?" Bob asked.

"I wish I knew," John replied. "They seem upset, so something is not going well."

"I wonder if that's good news for us or bad?" mused Gisele, staring at the door.

Edgar glanced down at John, still sitting on the floor, his back against the side of the bed.

"How's it going down there?"

John smiled. He glanced at the door to reassure himself that their captors could not hear, then turned his attention to the fixture to which his chain was attached.

"Look."

He pulled the plate back about an inch from the wall. Behind it, Edgar could see that the crack in the mortar had further deteriorated and the first threads of the eye were visible. It looked more like a large screw than a bolt. That was encouraging.

"How long do you suppose this thing is?" John asked.

"Who knows. A couple of inches? Probably more like four or five," Edgar answered.

"Unfortunately, I haven't anything to dig with other than my fingers."

"Maybe this will help," Gisele said. She began removing her belt.

"Thanks anyway, Gisele. If they catch me with that belt . . . well . . ."

"I'll take care of the belt, John. I should have thought of this before. This is the part you need. The buckle just snaps off. See?" Gisele smiled as she held it up.

John took it from her. It was V-shaped. He turned it over in his hand, then pulled back the plate and inserted the buckle behind it. He began digging and scraping, using the buckle as a chisel, while the others watched. John looked up and smiled.

"This is much better. It just might work. If I have enough time."

"They're coming back. Get rid of that belt," Edgar exclaimed, looking over at Gisele. She lay back, pretending to be asleep, while her hand worked the belt under the thin mattress. Enough of a space around the eye screw had been dug so that John could push the buckle in behind the plate. He leaned back against it just as their captors came through the doorway.

The three men and the cold-eyed Pasha stood near the table looking at the prisoners.

"The news for you is not good," Yazib began. "The Great Satan and your infidel leaders have been unwilling to meet our demands. As a result, the city of Boston has been destroyed with a biological weapon. Hundreds of thousands are dead!"

John and the others stared at their captors incredulously.

"I don't believe you," John said finally, breaking the silence.

Yazib stepped forward suddenly and kicked John in the ribs.

Then again.

John doubled over in pain, gasping for breath.

Yazib kicked him a third time.

Edgar yelled, "Stop it!"

The two guards with guns lifted them to the ready position. Realizing their captor's nerves were on edge and that anything could happen, Edgar slowly sat back on the bed.

"You would not know the truth even if it was about to destroy you," Yazib snarled angrily, his focus still on John. Twice more he lashed out savagely with his boot, catching John in the stomach and then across the side of his face. John lay still, doubled into a fetal position, trying desperately not to groan, not wanting to give Yazib the satisfaction of knowing just how much pain he was inflicting. Most of all, not wanting to reveal the weakened plate and screw in the wall behind him.

"Anyway, for you, Reverend Cain, it is worse. Much worse."

Gasping for breath, John squinted up at Yazib, who stood over him now, hands on his hips.

"Your FBI attempted to dislodge our team of freedom fighters in California. We were given no alternative but to blow up the church. Our people gave their lives as martyrs of Allah. Your congregation is no longer, Reverend Cain. They rejected the cry of reason and the call of Allah. They have been doomed to spend eternity in hell." Yazib paused, watching the impact of his words sink into the soul of the man doubled over on the floor. Then he smiled a slow, wicked smile. "I regret to inform you that your wife is among the dead."

John tried shutting the words out by pressing his eyelids tightly together. Through his own physical pain, he fought to control the groan of anguish that screamed out silently inside him. He knew now. They were all defeated. He felt as if he would explode.

It was a moment he would never forget.

Never.

For the first time in his life, he wanted to kill!

Then something unexpected happened as John lay there on the floor. Something that defied any real definition.

He felt . . . a presence.

Something . . . no, it was more than that. *Someone* had entered the room.

What's this?

He had never experienced anything like this before.

Maybe I've taken one too many hits on the head.

Lying on the floor, he curled up in pain and an aching grief that went beyond the physical bruises and tortured his soul. But the undeniable presence was there alongside him. And not just standing. Kneeling.

Suddenly John knew something else.

He knew that this mysterious presence was feeling his pain. Touching it. Absorbing it!

John was not a man given to visions or mystical flights of fantasy.

That's why this was so incredible.

He knew *Who* this presence was.

He was still in the world of reality. He knew that he was dirty and bloody and beaten. But he was not broken. Not completely. Not yet. He opened his eyes and looked up just in time for Yazib to spit in his face.

"Come." Yazib turned away from John and spoke to the others. "I want to finalize our plans with the rest of you."

Their captors slowly backed away, still watching the crumpled form of their prisoner. Then they turned and followed Yazib through the doorway.

Edgar, Bob, and Gisele were too overwhelmed for words.

They looked at one another, tears of concern filling their eyes. Quickly they scrambled to help John up from the floor. Bob's chain did not permit him to move that far, but Edgar and Gisele were able to reach him. They reached for him wordlessly and eased him up onto the bed, not knowing what to say. It was almost as if they had taken the beating themselves. Carefully they turned him over.

When they did, they were surprised.

John was trying to smile.

His lip was cut and already beginning to swell, his face looked badly bruised, but there was a familiar twinkle in his eye. At least in the one that remained fully open. Edgar and Gisele looked at one another apprehensively. Had he finally been pushed over the edge? Had the beatings and the pressure caused him to snap at last?

"John, are you all right?" Edgar asked, concern etched in each word.

"I'm okay," John answered through gritted teeth, straining to resist taking a deep breath, knowing he might pass out from the pain. "I could use a new rib or two, but I'm okay, thanks."

Gisele wiped at blood oozing from his broken lip. John winced and mumbled "I suppose I could use a face-lift, too."

"You'll be okay," Gisele responded, but her voice sounded flat and unconvincing. "John, did you hear what that man said?"

"I heard him."

"I'm so very sorry . . ." Her voice trailed off, tears spilling out on her cheeks.

"It's not true."

The others stared at John.

"It's not true. He's lying," he said again.

"How can you be so sure?" asked Bob uneasily. "Why would they say such things if they weren't true?"

"It hurts to talk," John mumbled. "Can you understand me?"

They nodded.

"At first, I heard what you heard. Yazib caught me off guard. But then I watched him. And the others, too. Did you notice how the others looked while he was telling us of their 'great victory'? They looked like Oakland Raider fans when they lost the Super Bowl. If they've had such great success as terrorists in America, don't you think they'd all be gloating? My guess is that something has happened all right. But it's not to their liking."

The others pondered . . . listening . . . wanting to believe . . . but . . .

"They're not telling us the truth. I'm sure of it, but it's hard to explain." John formed each word carefully. "Something happened a moment ago while I was being kicked around. I felt something. It was a presence. Right here with me. I've never experienced anything like it before.

"For a while I thought I was dying and going to heaven. I'm telling you, that's what it felt like. And the most incredible assurance came over me. No voice, nothing specific. But I knew Jesus was here in this room, guys. In a way I have never experienced him in all of my life. I believe he's still here right now. I don't honestly know how everyone back home is faring. I don't know if Esther is alive or dead. I don't even know where Jessica is or if she is okay."

A shadow of anxiety passed over his countenance and his voice wavered. Clearing his throat, he continued. "All I can honestly say to you is that I have put them all in God's hands. I don't know any details, but the assurance that God is with each member of my family . . . and yours, too, is very strong. That may not make any sense, given what we're facing here, but that's what's happening as I see it."

They were all leaning forward, studying his face as he struggled to talk to them. Edgar was the first to respond.

"Pastor, I know times have been hard for you this past year. Jill and I have been prayin' every day for you and Esther and the kids. Even comin' over here on the plane, I felt this sudden burden to pray for you. And I did, too. Now here we are in one really deep mess. But I want you to know somethin' 'bout how I feel. I been followin' you as my pastor for the last twelve years. I've seen others come and go in our church. But you've been a good shepherd to Jill and me. If she were here right now, she'd say the same. For what it's worth, I'm glad to be here with you. Whatever happens, I want you to know that this situation ain't your fault. There's no surprises with God. Remember? That's what you've been tellin' us back home. I don't know why all this has happened to us, but God knew this was comin' down even before we left town.

"I say let's pray for strength and wisdom. And courage, too. Didn't you tell us once that Martin Luther used to say, 'Pray as though everything depends on God, but work as though everything depends on you'? We're not the first Christians to be locked up in this town. We may not be the last. So let's do it. Let's pray as though it all depends on God, because it does. Then let's think and work as though getting out of here all depends on us!"

The others nodded in agreement. Chained to a wall underneath Jerusalem's Al Aqsa mosque, they joined their hands and called upon God.

After Edgar led in a brief, heartfelt prayer, John lowered his battered body back down to the floor. He sat facing the door, expecting their captors to return at any minute.

Meanwhile, he lifted the plate and began working Gisele's belt buckle further and further into the hole.

Jerusalem Post, International Edition:

Prime Minister Wallach issued a direct appeal to the Palestinian leaders of the PNA and Harakat al-Muqawama al-Islamiyya [Hamas], urging them to use every means at their disposal to bring about the safe return of the American hostages believed to be held by extremists within their organization. "It is a time for action," the prime minister said early today. "We are on a bridge leading to peace and progress between our peoples. We must not return to the brink of war."

Twenty-five persons are believed to have been taken hostage by Arab terrorists belonging to the Palestinian Islamic Jihad, a fundamentalist terrorist organization with roots in Hamas. The Americans were last seen boarding their tour bus at Ein Bokek. The bus was recovered late Saturday night near the Old City in Jerusalem.

Yesterday morning, the body of an unidentified elderly woman, believed to be an American, was found in the parking lot at Nebi Musa. According to an unnamed source in the government, she had been shot twice in the head at close range.

Confirmation of her identity is unavailable at this time. The authorities will not say whether or not they believe she was part of the missing tour group.

Security has been tightened at all borders and at Lod International Airport. All military leaves have been cancelled. The IDF and other security forces have been placed on full alert. House to house searches continue. So far, no trace of the missing Americans has been found.

88

19 September, local time 1005
Baytown, California

Todd Hendrickson and his men moved about slowly, surveying the chaos throughout the sanctuary. People began crawling out from under the pews and picking themselves up from the aisles. They stared in amazement at the ominous-looking men dressed in black, watching with a kind of reverent deference as SWAT team members checked the bodies of the five fallen terrorists, who only moments before had appeared to be irrevocably in control.

"Sir?" Hendrickson spoke to the Command Center.

"Yes?" came Webber's anxious voice.

"We're secure. We need medics."

"They're on the way."

Uniformed police and FBI personnel rushed in through the entrances. Medical teams hurriedly began to work with the wounded. In less than a minute, Webber strode into the building and paused, looking for the first time at what he had only seen on television screens.

"How are we?" he asked, coming up to Hendrickson, who stood in the center aisle, near the front.

"I've got one man down. But he's alive. Johnson says the perp he's working on is still alive. Barely. The rest are dead. We've got some civilian casualties. I don't know yet how many." He hesitated. "There's a woman on the platform. At the last second, when we took out the female terrorist, she came into the line of fire. I'm not sure about her."

"Medic!" It was Dr. Orwell's voice. He was looking up over the back of a pew. "Over here quickly. We've got an irregular heartbeat. Bring some oxygen with you."

Hendrickson walked with Webber toward the platform. The shot of adrenaline that had peaked at the beginning of the assault was beginning to subside. He watched three medics on their knees, working with the woman who had been caught in the line of fire.

What was she doing there anyway? Why didn't she stay down?

"Oh, no," groaned Webber, catching sight of the woman's bloodied face.

Hendrickson looked over at him.

"You know her?"

"It's Mrs. Cain. She's the pastor's wife."

They lifted her onto a stretcher. An agent was ordering one of the Baystar helicopters to get ready for a run. Closing ranks, the evacuation team hoisted the stretcher and headed down the aisle to the exit.

"What's her condition?" Webber asked the supervising medic.

"Barely alive. She took one in the head, another in the shoulder. A third one went through her back and out her chest. She's lost a lot of blood."

"Will she make it?"

The medic sighed and shrugged. "Doesn't look good. Excuse me, gentlemen. I've got another situation here."

"What's with her?" Webber asked, seeing several medics gathered around a woman lying near the choir loft.

"She's pregnant. Her water broke. The kid is on the way. Looks like we're going to have to deliver right here."

Webber looked at Hendrickson. They shook their heads.

"Life and death. I guess they're never far apart," Webber said.

The wail of sirens sounded a mournful lament through the streets of Baytown as a steady procession of ambulances and patrol cars made their way up Washington Avenue toward Calvary Church. The wide thoroughfare, normally filled with shoppers and delivery trucks, was blocked by motorcycle police at every intersection. Bright yellow fire department emergency vehicles thundered by, warning lights flashing and air horns blaring as they headed up the hill.

Bystanders watched from the safety of store windows or stood under awnings out of the afternoon sun. Other spectators sat in the outdoor patio at the Coffee Bean, drinking lattes and cappuccinos, engrossed in the show. Conversations alternated between speculation about the five Arab terrorists and the hostages at Calvary Church, the terrible weekend events in Boston, and the missing tour group in Israel.

Shortly after ten o'clock, word began to spread like wildfire down Washington

Avenue that an FBI SWAT team had broken through to the hostages. Rumor had it there had been some sort of explosion, followed by sporadic bursts of gunfire inside the church. Radio and television reporters soon confirmed the news and spoke of possible dead and wounded, though the reports were unconfirmed and no one seemed to know how many.

A new phalanx of motorcycle officers now swept down Washington Avenue, securing the route to East Bay Hospital, the largest and closest medical center, which fortunately also housed a trauma unit. Blood reserves had been bolstered earlier in the morning in preparation for possible casualties. Trauma surgeons and emergency medical personnel were on standby at EBH and other area medical centers. The possibility of hundreds of dead or wounded was very real. Whatever the outcome, they were determined to be ready.

High overhead, television helicopters circled the city, monitoring the events and sending live reports to their respective studios, which then flashed the images by satellite to millions of viewers across the nation and around the world.

Three Baystar medical emergency helicopters settled onto the church parking lot, quickly lifting off again after taking on the most seriously wounded. Next, two Army medical helicopters joined the evacuation efforts, flying regular sorties between the church and nearby hospitals. On the ground, fire department EMTs and other ambulance units tended to the injured inside Calvary Church, transporting those in need of further care to East Bay Hospital.Less than thirty minutes after it all began, the streets were silent. Motorcycle officers could be seen standing at street corners, talking with each other and conversing on their radios. Time seemed to slow as bystanders waited for final word of what had happened at the church.

As if on command from some unseen source, the motorcycle officers along Washington Avenue mounted their Harley Davidsons and roared noisily up the street toward Calvary Church. Someone remarked that the only thing missing was the rolling of movie credits.

89

When Hendrickson and Webber walked outside, they found themselves in the middle of parking lot pandemonium. The first Baystar helicopter was lifting off the lot, while another idled nearby, waiting for a stretcher to be secured inside. A uniformed policeman shouted orders into a battery-powered megaphone. Ambulances were lined up in the handicap zones. The blue van in which the terrorists had arrived was marked off by yellow crime scene tape. Two policemen stood guard.

Television crews rushed to reposition their cameras at the wide base of the patio steps. A short distance away, Agent Webber could see Joe Randle talking with news reporters.

"What can you tell us?"

"How is it in there?"

"Are all the terrorists dead?"

"How many casualties?"

"Where did these people come from?"

"What did they hope to accomplish?"

Webber looked at Hendrickson. "Joe did a good job with those people. I need to remember to tell White. He's a good man."

Hendrickson nodded.

"Ladies and gentlemen, if you'll be patient, we'll give you a statement in just a minute," Lieutenant Randle was saying. Webber turned to Special Agent Corry, who at that moment happened to be walking past. "Hey, Corry, get Chief White and the mayor out here, will you? I think I saw them inside the building. If they ask why, just tell them we're having a press conference. That'll bring 'em out."

"Yes sir," Corry answered.

—∾—

Connie Farrer felt pretty much like a floating doll. Whatever the medics had given her was starting to work. They said her left leg looked like a clean break, just below the knee. Her ribs would need to be X-rayed. They surmised her injuries were not caused by the battering ram that had fallen on her. More likely they were the result of being trampled by the SWAT team as they entered the sanctuary. She had been directly in their path with no time to get out of the way.

Connie clutched her cell phone with both hands, resolved that nobody would take it from her. This was her first "game ball" and she was determined to keep it on her shelf of memories. Five weeks at the station and a star in the biggest story she would probably ever cover.

What's more, I'm still alive to talk about it.

She could feel herself relaxing, getting sleepy.

"I'm keeping this, okay?" she said to the nearest fireman.

He looked at her and smiled. "Lady, I don't care if you keep the offering plate. I heard what you did with that cell phone. Pretty gutsy. You just take it easy now, 'cause your job is over for today. Leave the rest to us. The next stop for you is a nice clean bed and a room with a view at EBH."

Connie closed her eyes.

"It sounds glorious," she murmured. "I always wanted a room with a view . . ." Her voice trailed away.

She heard the firemen laugh as they lifted her from the floor.

90

Jeremy sat on the floor, his back against one of the choir pews. Allison was cradled against his chest, his arms encircling her protectively, though there was no longer a need to protect her. She cried softly in his arms. He stared vacantly at the scene, watching as the medics worked on his mother.

Mrs. Orwell sat next to them in the pew, her hand on Jeremy's shoulder, eyes tearing with sadness as she prayed quietly.

Like a prairie brushfire, the rush of pent-up emotion burned its way through Jeremy's mind. He could not stop rehearsing the events of the last few minutes.

I thought for sure they were going to kill us. Me. Allison. The pregnant lady and her husband. But no. Not all of us. Only two. How could they expect Mom to choose which ones would die? That was completely insane. Then Mom offering to die in our place. How could she do that?

All of a sudden, that terrorist is flat on his back and he ain't moving. I don't even know what happened to him, it was so quick. And then the lights go out and all hell breaks loose.

And then Mom—what happened to her? One second she was there on top of me, the next second she was gone, rolling away, lost in the darkness. Then for one split second I saw her in the laser light. She was facing the Arab woman. It was . . .

Jeremy flinched involuntarily. He'd never seen anybody die before. But he had looked over just in time to see Aziza get hit. *She was dead before she hit the floor. No doubt. It was terrible. But Mom was a victim, too. They say she's still alive. But she doesn't look like it. Oh God, don't let her die. Please. Please. Please!*

The paramedics were lifting Esther's still form onto a stretcher. They carried her off the platform and headed up the aisle toward the exit. Jeremy pulled himself up to a kneeling position. Wordlessly he looked at Mrs. Orwell, then at Allison who sat beside him, still clinging to his hand. He rose to his feet and stumbled after them.

"Wait, Jeremy," called Mrs. Orwell, helping Allison to her feet. "We'll come with you."

They hurried up the aisle after the stretcher team, following them onto the parking area and to a waiting helicopter.

"She's my mother," Jeremy shouted. "Let me go with her."

The medic looked at him sympathetically.

"We can't take you, son. Not enough room. But ask that fellow over there." He pointed to Lieutenant Randle. "He'll arrange a ride for you. East Bay Hospital."

The man pulled himself inside the helicopter and called to the pilot, "Okay. Let's go!"

Jeremy stood back, watching as the air rescue helicopter rose and banked away, heading across town with its precious cargo.

—~—

19 SEPTEMBER, LOCAL TIME 1345
WASHINGTON, D.C.

"That's great. Tell everyone there they have my deepest congratulations. I'm proud of all of you. You figure out who and I'll determine how to honor your troops publicly and appropriately later."

"Thank you, Mr. President," the attorney general replied. "I'll let them know your feelings."

"What's the word on casualties so far?"

"In Boston, two dead terrorists and we lost an agent. One from the HRT unit that we sent up there. It's too early to tell what problems the evacuation itself may have created. Dosha is still at large, and the best guess is he's out of the area. Maybe the one we captured will shed some light on that, but I doubt it. He probably doesn't know anything. The mayor has been on the air most of the morning with the news. Reports are that the city is settling down a bit, but it will be days before they're back to normal up there.

"Where the SWAT units cleared the church in California, we have four dead terrorists and one on the critical list. He probably won't make it, but they're trying. One agent was wounded, but is in satisfactory condition. Amazingly, only one civilian dead. One in critical condition. She may not make it. Unfortunately, it was the pastor's wife and it may have been from 'friendly fire.' She took three hits. Didn't look good at last report. They rushed her to the local trauma center and are working on her right now.

"Altogether, nine airlifted with serious injuries, mostly bullet wounds. There were a lot of bullets flying around. Fifteen more with minor to moderate injuries. A lot of these were the ones crowded in the doorways when the SWAT teams entered. The television reporter with the cell phone that you heard about has a broken leg and some banged-up ribs. Two elderly heart attack victims. Both of them are in local hospital CCUs. One stable. The other critical. And there was the one male civilian who was killed at the outset by the terrorists.

"All in all, as bad as it was, it could have been much worse. I believe we contained this with the absolute minimum losses. They tell me that it looks a bit like a war zone inside that church. They're putting together a TV pool camera crew even as we speak. They will be allowed inside within the hour."

"Good work," the president affirmed warmly. "Have you heard any more about the ones in Israel?"

"That's out of our hands, of course, sir," the attorney general responded quickly. "The CIA is in touch with Mossad. We're ready to assist in any way we can, of course. No one is certain what the terrorists' objectives might be. Could be just another headline grabber. But they've definitely disappeared. That's for certain. This entire operation appears to be Hamas and Islamic Jihad."

"Well, I wonder what this will do to September 24? Things were going so smoothly. Think they'll still sign?"

"You know them, sir. The CIA will give you more definitive stuff on what this will mean, but all appearances indicate nothing has really changed. Islamic Jihad has made Palestine its central issue and their strategy for reform—if it can be called that—is armed struggle, not the signing of agreements. Now that the PNA has indicated a willingness to negotiate for peace and for the creation of a Palestinian nation on the West Bank, these guys are saying, 'Forget that. We want it all. Let the Jews go somewhere else.'"

"Too bad."

"Yes sir, it is. The State Department is putting out a new travel warning for tourists headed for Israel, Jordan, and Egypt. We've already done the same to Syria, Lebanon, and Iraq. Pretty soon, it may only be safe for Americans in the U.S. and Canada."

"And that hasn't worked out too well even at home recently, has it?"

"You're right, sir. But we'll do better. Homeland is working hard at coordinating our terrorist information. I think we'll win in the long run. It just takes time. We'll let you know if anything further develops regarding this Dosha character.

"Tell your team thanks again. And congratulations for a job well done."

"Thank you, Mr. President. Good night."

91

Tuesday, 20 September, local time 0110
Jerusalem

Why have you brought us here, Yazib?"

John leaned back against the cool concrete wall and squinted through eyes swollen half-shut. He watched Yazib busy himself with the materials spread out on the table. Pasha sat on the edge of the far bed, filing her nails, an assault rifle resting on the mattress beside her. *This was something you didn't see every day.*

Yazib stepped back, his attention still focused on the table. Each item had been repositioned like chess pieces in a tournament. Everything seemed to have its special place. Slowly he turned around and faced the others in the room.

"Why have we brought you here, Reverend Cain?" he repeated. "You are here because you are going to help us."

"And how will we do that?" John persisted. "We don't even know why *you're* here. How can you assume we'll help you when we don't know what you intend to do?"

"Ah, you are a very curious person, Reverend Cain. And a very interesting one, I might add. I commend you again for your courage. It is far greater than I would ever have expected. But like all other Americans and all your Jewish friends, you are in a final word, *fools.* Forgive me if I offend you, but clearly that is what you are. You did not even realize that a war was in progress when you came to this land.

"You came on a lark. A religious pilgrimage. It is what you call a 'vacation.' However, what is mere diversion for you is life and death for us. Our days and nights have been taken up for months in planning and training for this attack on the enemies of Allah. We have joined our souls with the souls of all the *mujahedin* who have striven in the past to free Palestine. We are one with our forefathers who gave their lives for this land, ever since it was conquered by the companions of the Messenger until today.

"For you this was a vacation. A religious odyssey. For us it is the continuation of a long and dangerous war with the Jewish devils. It requires all our effort and dedication until the enemies of Islam are overcome and the final victory of Allah descends."

"But what purpose can we four possibly serve? And where have you taken the others who came here with us?"

"It will do no good for me to answer your last question. The four of you will not see your companions again until you all meet in hell." Yazib's eyes suddenly grew narrow and cold. "You want to know why you are here? Now, I will tell you. You are here to destroy the Western Wall."

John and the others stared at Yazib in disbelief. Yazib began pacing back and forth in front of them.

"Outside it is dark now. Pasha and I will be leaving you shortly to set in motion the final stage of our glorious mission. The items you see here on the table have been generously supplied by our supporters. These small containers are filled with a new and very powerful explosive. See?"

He lifted one from the table and held it up.

"When we peel away the protective layer on the back, it permits the explosive to adhere to any substance it touches. We will place these units at various points on the Wall. Both the containers and this installation arm are of a color that blends in well with the Wall. It is possible that we may succeed in placing all six without being seen. Then when the explosives have been planted," he held up the ominous-looking, black detonator, "Boom!"

John's heart sank.

"Surely you can't believe you will get away with something as crazy as this. And for what purpose? Even if you succeed, you'll touch off a wave of hatred and anger against the Muslim world that will never be stopped," John exclaimed. "The Jews will retaliate by destroying the Dome of the Rock. They may even bomb Mecca. Then where will you be? You will spark a religious war with horrible consequences for your own people."

Yazib smiled crookedly, enjoying his moment of glory.

"Precisely. We must take the chance with the Dome. It is the price we pay to arouse our people, to shake them from their sleep and inspire them to overthrow the occupiers of our land. But you are mistaken in one thing, Reverend Cain. Hatred and anger will flow like a river, it is true. However, it will not be directed toward the followers of Islam. It will be poured out instead upon Christians and upon the Great American Satan, that dark and distant enemy of Islam, without which Israel would have long since crumbled in weakness.

"Think about it. The destruction of this most sacred religious site will be the end result of a diabolical plot against Israel, designed and carried out by American Christians. Three men and a woman, to be exact."

He paused, savoring the shocked looks on the faces of his hostages, while he relished the ingeniousness of the plan. He looked at his watch.

"Within the hour, the world will be informed that you were shot by IDF soldiers and Arab security guards, who vainly attempted to stop you from completing your wicked plan. You will be killed in the very act of destroying the Zionists most unifying and holiest symbol. Unfortunately for them, you will have succeeded in blowing up the Wall before you are stopped. What a tragedy. But your bodies will be found nearby, and all the evidence for this terrible deed will confirm that it was carried out by Christian Jew-haters from America."

Now John understood why the terrorists had changed into military and police uniforms. He had thought it was simply so they would look like they belonged at *Haram esh Sharif* if they were seen entering the compound. Instead, they were planning to kill their American prisoners and then slip away by melting into the confusion that would inevitably follow.

"When it is over, Reverend Cain, the Jews will find you with this detonator." Yazib held it up, turning it slowly in his hand. "And by the time you are discovered, it will have only your fingerprints. The prints of a right-wing Christian fanatic. The pastor of an American church, no less. Do you have any idea of the importance of this night? You should be honored. You will each play a significant role in our success. My only regret is that you will receive credit for this accomplishment instead of the Islamic resistance movement. But this is a small price to pay."

Yazib laughed, his eyes ablaze with excitement as he turned back to the table.

"Come, Pasha. Let us gather our tools and be gone. Imad, you will come with us and remain in the shadows to watch for security personnel. We want no surprises until we say so, yes?"

Imad nodded soberly. He picked up a Galil assault rifle that was leaning against the wall and began stuffing extra clips of ammunition into his pocket.

"Fathi, it is as we agreed earlier. You will stay with the prisoners. As soon as Pasha and I are ready with the charges, I will signal Imad. He will help you bring the prisoners to us at the Wall. If they refuse to cooperate, shoot them here and carry them outside. Understand?"

"I understand," said Fathi.

"Good. Now, Imad, help Fathi tape their mouths. And remember, the tape must be removed as soon as they are dead."

"Should we tie their hands?" asked Imad.

Yazib thought for a moment.

"Yes. Keep your knife ready, however. We will not have time to untie them later, so be prepared to cut them loose. Be careful not to leave any rope behind. If this place is discovered later, it will look like somehow the Americans hid out here before they destroyed the Wall. If they try anything early on, just shoot them. You have the silencer on your weapon? Good. If you must kill them sooner, it will be of little consequence. No one will hear."

Yazib's back was turned to John and the others as he spoke. Now he turned to face the group.

"Reverend Cain, I am confident that you understand what is about to happen. Cooperate and you will live longer. Not much longer, I grant you, but a little. And every minute of life is precious, don't you agree? Do not resist Allah's will and you will all die quickly. If you do not cooperate . . . I assure you, that you will each die an exceedingly slow and painful death . . . beginning with her."

Yazib smiled broadly at Gisele.

Her eyes reflected apprehension, a sense of the inevitable rolling in upon her.

She knows she is going to die, Yazib said to himself with smug satisfaction.

Pasha moved around the corner of the table and paused in front of Gisele. She waited until the men had finished taping her mouth. Then she tied Gisele's wrists behind her back. With an air of calculated indifference, she pushed her down onto the bed and walked away to stand by Yazib.

The underground room grew still as Yazib scooped up the backpack and began placing the last few items carefully inside. He had the air of a priest presiding over the elements on the communion table.

"Allah u Akbar," he said, passionately.

"Allah u Akbar," the others responded in unison.

"Good-bye to each of you. And especially to you, Reverend Cain," Yazib said, pausing at the door. "It has been a pleasure making your acquaintance. Come, Pasha. Our triumph is only moments away."

The door closed behind them.

92

Fathi Adahlah moved over to the edge of the bed on which he and his cohorts had taken turns sleeping during the final countdown hours. He looked at the American men on the bed opposite. Their leader remained on the floor. He seemed to prefer that position, though it looked uncomfortable to Fathi.

His eyes wandered to where Gisele lay bound on the other mattress. Very nice. He'd had an eye for her from the very beginning. Too bad there was not more time. She could have been a very enjoyable diversion.

He turned the AK-47 over in his lap, checking it carefully, wiping it down with a handkerchief he withdrew from his pocket. Additional clips were stacked on the bed. The light was not good where he sat, but it did not matter. He could see well enough for what was needed.

For hours, John had worked patiently, but with a foreboding sense of desperation. He had scraped with Gisele's belt buckle and with his fingers until they were raw, careful not to arouse suspicion, all the while fearful that his efforts would be in vain. Now the moment of truth was at hand. Time was running out.

He applied pressure to the chain. It remained firmly stuck.

Again.

No success.

A third time.

The sound of bits of concrete falling to the floor echoed like cannon fire across the room. At least it seemed that way to John. The chain broke free. He held the eye hook in his hand.

He looked across to where Fathi was sitting. Apparently he had heard nothing. He continued staring off in the distance. John breathed a deep sigh of relief. Time to go into his act. It was nothing more than a desperate gamble. But there was no other way.

He started coughing into the tape gag, making terrible choking sounds.

Startled, Edgar leaned over the edge of his bed to see what was the matter. John struggled, as if trying to get to his feet, as he twisted around into a crouching position.

Edgar instantly sized up the situation and turned back toward Fathi, doing his best to make pleading noises that would attract the lone terrorist's attention.

—~~—

Fathi looked up at the prisoners, drawn by the muffled choking sounds of their leader. Cain was writhing on the cold floor, hands tied behind his back, the tape still over his mouth.

The black man was making sounds, too, his eyes pleading with Fathi to do something.

He is choking. It will be funny if he dies before I get to kill him. It doesn't matter. In an hour, he'll be dead anyway. But better if he can walk on his own and I don't have to drag his body all the way to the Wall.

With an air of disgust, Fathi unsheathed the Walther 7.65-millimeter PPK that he wore on his belt and stepped across the room until he stood between the two beds. The man was struggling to breathe, the back of his neck was turning red.

Fathi bent forward to get a better look.

John transferred his weight to his left leg, but stayed crouched with his head forward, as if trying to dislodge something from his throat. Out of the corner of his eye, he saw Edgar shift ever so slightly forward on the edge of the bed. In his mind, John warned him to *wait . . . wait . . . now!*

Spinning around on his pivot foot, John swung the chain with all his might. It caught Fathi just above the knees and wrapped around his legs. With surprising quickness, Edgar lurched forward from the edge of the bed, throwing all his weight—backed by hours of pent-up frustration—into the body of their startled captor.

Fathi fell, his gun hand flailing upward, spitting several bullets from the silenced weapon into the ceiling and the top of the wall. Edgar stumbled as he reached the end of his chain, but all the years he'd spent as a much younger man honing his footwork in the boxing ring served him well and he managed to keep his balance in an awkward twirling dance.

John scrambled to his feet and yanked hard on the chain, dragging Fathi forward. Edgar delivered the *coup de grâce,* a well-placed kick to Fathi's neck and jaw that rendered him unconscious. John quickly unwrapped the chain from around the fallen man's legs.

John and Edgar were perspiring and breathing hard, but there was not a second to lose. They turned their backs to each other and began feverishly working on the ropes that bound their wrists.

The knots were tied too well.

Dropping to the floor and wriggling in close to Fathi's inert form, John managed to pull the man's combat knife from its sheath and then struggled back to his feet. When Edgar and he were again back-to-back, Edgar worked the rope on his wrists back and forth along the knife's edge.

The last threads gave way at last. Success. He was free!

Quickly, he cut John loose.

Fathi began to stir.

Edgar leaned down and picked up the Walther.

"You move, mister, and you are one dead, misguided soul." His voice was calm, but cold with fury. "On second thought, roll over very slowly onto your stomach. Now."

With Fathi facedown on the floor, John rummaged through his pockets.

"I hope he's got the keys," Bob said anxiously. He had leapt to his feet at the beginning of the fight for freedom, but the length of his chain had prevented any involvement.

"He does," John replied, his hands moving from one pocket to the next. "He has to. He was supposed to take us outside. Ah, here they are."

John pulled the small key ring from Fathi's side pocket. He tried first one, then another. The third key did the trick, opening the ankle brace that had kept him chained to the wall since their arrival. Quickly, John moved to the others, releasing them from their fetters as well.

Bob walked to where Fathi had been sitting moments before and picked up the remainder of the tape.

"This is going to be a pleasure."

He wrapped a long strip around Fathi's face and mouth. Tightly.

"Stand up and take off your shirt," ordered John. Edgar kept the Walther pointed steadily at Fathi's head.

Fathi looked at him questioningly, apprehension etching new lines on his young face.

"Your shirt. Take it off!"

His eyes never left John's as he removed his shirt. John took it and then slipped the man's leg into Edgar's ankle brace and locked it. The last of the tape was used to bind Fathi's hands tightly behind his back.

The four stared at each other with looks of disbelief.

"Good job, John," Bob exclaimed. "I can't believe it. We're free!"

"'Free' is a relative term," Edgar said philosophically. "We are a long way from 'free.' Take it from a brother who knows."

"Edgar's right. Are you ready for what we have to do?"

"Do we have a choice?" asked Bob.

Both Edgar and John shook their heads. Gisele said nothing, her eyes still on the man who until a few minutes ago had been her designated executioner.

"We all go home. Or we all stay. It's as simple as that," John answered. "If we can capture the others and make them talk, hopefully they'll tell us where the rest of our people are located. Maybe we can even get to them before they finish putting those charges in place."

John took the Walther from Edgar.

Bob cradled the AK-47 in his arms. "I trained on one of these when I was in the army," he said.

"Ever kill anybody?" asked Edgar.

"No," was the quiet response. "But after what these bozos have put us through, I think I'm ready."

They opened the door cautiously. It was dark, but on the far side the exit leading to the staircase and the courtyard had been left cracked open.

"Chances are pretty good that this Imad character isn't far from that door, so be careful," John whispered. "Let's go."

A cool breeze greeted them as they moved stealthily up the stairway and out into the starry Jerusalem night.

93

20 SEPTEMBER, LOCAL TIME 0145
JERUSALEM

Yazib and Pasha moved through the long shadows with catlike quickness. They darted past *El-Kas,* where Muslims come to wash each day before prayers, and made their way along the stone esplanade, swiftly, quietly, ever watchful for security personnel. They stayed close to the trees, although for the moment they were not concerned about encountering any Jews. There would be little chance of that on the mount, especially at night. Despite the rancor and hatred between them and their implacable foes, the Jews still gave respect to these favored shrines of Islam.

They walked out into the open, casual and confident as they strode toward the Western Wall. That was when an Arab policeman saw them from across the way. He dropped his cigarette on the ground and crushed it with his heel. Smoking in this area would be interpreted by those more devout than he as desecrating the holy shrines. Then he started toward them. Coming closer, he recognized the Israeli uniforms and was startled by their blatant disregard of protocol.

Both Israeli soldiers smiled and saluted their greeting.

—m—

John led the way up the stairwell. Outside, they made their way along the edge of the building. To their right, the magnificent Dome of the Rock stood out against the night.

According to popular Arab tradition, the original purpose of this grand mosque was the commemoration of Muhammad's ascension to heaven. However, like so many other Middle East contradictions, a more recent structure known as *Qubbat el-Miraj,* the Dome of the Ascension, also stood nearby. And there was another, more cynical, theory about Ommayad Khalif Abdul Malik ibn Marwan's motivation in building the Dome. According to this theory, the mosque was built between 688 and 691 to overshadow Christian churches in the vicinity that were attracting Arab converts. Whatever the truth was, the Dome was indeed an impressive structure.

Daily prayers had ended hours ago, so no one was about. John finally spotted Imad, who was crouched down in the shadow of *El Aqsa*, cradling an AK-47 and looking off in the direction of the Western Wall.

John signaled with his hand for Edgar to circle around and come along the edge of the *El-Kas* fountain. "Bob, you approach him from the other side," he whispered. "Stay in the shadows."

Bob nodded and furtively edged his way along the side of the building. A moment later, they saw Edgar advancing steadily past the far edge of the fountain.

Imad saw him at the same instant. He tensed, his total concentration focused on the shadowy figure coming toward him. Lifting his rifle, he pointed, then lowered it again, apparently uncertain as to who it was and what he should do.

The decision was made for him.

Bob saw his opportunity and accelerated his pace toward the crouching figure. Hearing a sound behind him, Imad turned.

It was too late.

The stock of Fathi's confiscated AK-47 came down swiftly at the back of his neck. He dropped to the ground with a groan. Edgar joined Bob and the two dragged Imad's unconscious body further back into the shadows. A handkerchief was stuffed into his mouth and secured with a piece of cloth torn from Fathi's shirt. Two more strips bound his feet and hands. A rapid search of his pockets turned up an assortment of small items. Cigarettes. A Swiss army knife. Matches. A pocket flashlight. Some ammunition clips.

John turned the flashlight over in his hand.

"Bob, you stay here. At some point, one of the others will probably signal or come back and tell this guy to bring us out and kill us. If they come back, do what you have to do."

Bob nodded grimly. "If one of them comes back, I've got no choice. I'll be ready, but praying for another way out."

"My guess is they'll signal in some way," John said. "That's probably what this flashlight is for. Answer back with the same signal you receive. If it's supposed to be anything other than that, the game's up anyway, so don't worry about it. Edgar, get that guy's gun and the clips and let's go. Come on, Gisele."

They continued moving swiftly but quietly until they came to the edge of the open esplanade. There was no cover here. John peered across the way, trying to spot the remaining two terrorists. Finally he saw them, off to the right, almost invisible in the inner court shadows of the Western Wall, the most holy shrine of the Jewish world. It was all that remained of the retaining wall built by Herod around the second Temple in 20 BC. Ninety years later, when Titus overran the city, he spared this part of the temple wall with its huge stone blocks, in order to show future generations the greatness of Rome that had destroyed the rest of the building.

The Wall! Lord, please don't let them succeed in blowing it up.

John had been to the Wall on numerous occasions and had felt its awesome power. From Byzantine times forward, the Jews had come here to remember the anniversary of the Temple's destruction and to lament the dispersion of their people. Standing before the face of the high wall, they wept and prayed, a tradition that led to the Western Wall coming to be known as the Wailing Wall. The practice continued for centuries until 1948, when Jews were forbidden access to the Wall by the Jordanians, who claimed the site as their own.

Then came the Six Day War of 1967. When it was over, the city had been liberated and overnight the Wailing Wall became a place for national rejoicing and worship. Tonight, John realized that the unspeakable was about to happen. The Wall was destined for destruction.

He studied the two figures, who stood less than fifty feet from where John and the others were hiding in the darkness. Could these young Arabs, filled with such hatred and bitterness, really pull it off? They evidently believed they could. And John believed it, too. There was a good chance they just might do it.

John assumed the explosives would be powerful enough to collapse the Wall. But that would be a small explosion compared to the conflagration of pent-up fury among the Jews that was sure to follow. Somehow these two disasters had to be stopped.

John took stock of the situation. Maneuvering deeper into the shadow of a tall pine tree, he stopped abruptly, staring into the darkness. He caught his breath.

There was an Arab policeman, sitting quietly, leaning back against a tree barely ten feet from where John was crouched.

He was looking straight at them!

Why doesn't he say something? Surely he sees us.

But the policeman did not move.

Carefully, John edged closer. He grimaced when he realized the man was not watching them at all. He had been propped in a sitting position against the tree.

The front of his shirt was sticky with blood.

His throat had been cut from ear to ear.

John looked back across the open space between himself and the Wall.

Yazib and Pasha were nowhere to be seen.

Where are those killers now?

A light breeze swirled from west to east. The night was cooling rapidly. Yazib placed three containers in Pasha's hand. Her hands were cold. He felt familiar stirrings as they touched. The same feeling he'd had in the hotel at Ein Bokek; when they had kissed in Eilat; and while watching her change on the beach. This was a woman he could love. He had little doubt of that. He wondered how she felt about him. It would be nice to know. He felt certain she was attracted to him, but their time together had been spent in such extraordinary circumstances that who could know if it was really love?

Perhaps when this is all over . . .

"I am ready, Yazib."

The sound of her voice drew him back to the moment at hand.

"You will be all right?"

"Yes," she said, placing the containers in the pack, then strapping it over her shoulders. Pasha reached for the Galil assault rifle leaning against the Wall, removed the safety, and looked steadily at Yazib, her eyes eager with excitement.

"Remember," he said, "from the time you lift your hand and signal, you have five minutes. Two minutes to take out the guards and the next three to place the explosives and get away. If you take longer . . ." Yazib shrugged.

"I understand. I will not be late."

Yazib withdrew a pencil flashlight from his pocket and pointed in the direction of the Al Aqsa mosque. Three quick flashes. The signal to Imad. He waited. No response.

Where is he? Surely he can see the signal from there. He flashed again.

There! Three quick flashes from out of the darkness.

Yazib breathed easier. He turned to Pasha. "Make your way carefully. Just before you reach the Gate, wait for two minutes. By then, Fathi and Imad should have had time to bring the prisoners out. Make certain that I can see your hand signal. From that moment, it will be exactly five minutes and the charges will be detonated. Run swiftly. Join the soldiers when they rush the Gate. Then slip away. You remember the address where we will meet?"

She nodded. "It is well into my memory."

"You must be there by three o'clock."

She nodded again. If any of the team failed to arrive by that time, they were on their own. The likelihood of their escape would be greatly diminished if they failed to enter the escape route door at the appointed hour.

"Once we have regrouped and no longer need the other hostages, we will dispose of them and then we can declare our mission to be a success. Unfortunately, if the news we have heard is true, it will not be so great a success as we had hoped for, but we will have done our part well."

Pasha smiled warmly, then reached up and briefly touched his cheek with her hand. "It is all the more reason that we must succeed with this part of the plan."

"*Ilael liqa,* Pasha. See you later."

"*Hazz sae'id,*" she whispered. "Good luck."

94

John tensed as he saw the small flashes of light coming from the direction of the Wall. He watched for a response from Bob.

Nothing.

He glanced at Edgar, then back to where Bob was supposed to be waiting.

The signal was repeated from the Wall, followed by three flashes in response.

Good!

John waited to see what would happen. He was startled by a sharp intake of breath, then realized the sound was of his own making.

Was it the right signal to send back? There was nothing from Yazib to indicate otherwise. Nothing out of the ordinary.

Slowly, he let out his breath. *It must have been what they were looking for.*

Edgar and Gisele crept up to where John was waiting, and the three continued their vigil, staying deep in the shadows, squatting alongside the dead policeman. John guessed they were no more than fifty feet from the two terrorists. Yazib and Pasha were lost from view in the shadows, but John knew they were there.

What are they doing? How are we going to get to them or past them to tip off the authorities?

Something in the shadows caught his eye. A figure moving stealthily through the darkness along the Wall, toward the Morollo Gate. He couldn't tell who it was. Then movement on the Wall as the other terrorist scaled to the top and quickly dropped down out of sight. But not before John caught a glimpse of the person's physical features.

Yazib!

"It's happening then," John whispered. "Either we find a way to stop them or they get away with this devilish plan. What are we going to do?"

John looked at Edgar.

"I say we finish what they started." The old prizefighter's eyes shone. He had heard the bell and he was ready to fight.

Gisele looked anxious. She swallowed once and gave the others a weak grin. "I'm with you, guys."

John looked back toward the Wall. "I'll take Yazib. Gisele, you come with me. Edgar, go after the woman.

"Here, Gisele. Take this and use it if you have to." He thrust the Walther into her hands.

"But I don't know anything about guns," she protested. "You take it."

"No. I'll need both hands to get to the top of the Wall." John was not certain he could use the pistol himself unless at very close range. Even then he was not really sure. He had never fired a handgun. "I've got this knife. That will have to do."

"Here, hon," Edgar stepped closer and took the gun, turning it over. "This is the safety. It's off now. So if you pull the trigger, be sure it's pointed at one of the bad guys 'cause it will fire. If one of 'em comes at you, aim and shoot. Don't hesitate. I mean it!"

Gisele nodded lamely, scared out of her wits. She looked down at the weapon in her hand, making sure her fingers were nowhere near the trigger.

"Let's go do what we have to do," John said quietly. He turned and began moving cautiously toward the Wall, with Gisele trailing behind him.

Pasha looked back into the shadows along the wall. She could not see Yazib but knew he must be able to see her. She lifted her hand and then dropped it, walking out of the shadows toward the Morollo Gate. As expected, the heavy wooden gate was locked. But it was not going to keep her out. With practiced agility, she scaled the wall next to the gate and peered over the edge to the other side. Two soldiers were standing guard below. One of them looked up just as she stood, surprised to see an Israeli soldier staring down at him from atop the Wall. A woman no less, dressed in olive Class Alephs complete with sergeant's stripes, and carrying the standard Galil assault rifle at her side. He motioned to his companion. The soldier on the Wall smiled and waved.

They had barely recovered from their surprise, when the soldier nearest to the Gate noticed the silencer attached to her weapon. Definitely not standard issue. But by the time he was able to react, it was too late.

Ppfft, ppfft.

Pasha's sharpshooting skills made quick work of the two soldiers. They dropped onto the pathway without a sound. Pasha leaped down from her perch above the Gate. Stepping over the dead soldiers, she raced down the path, glancing quickly at her watch as she ran. Fifteen seconds behind schedule. Now she was at the bottom of the short path. From here on in there was no cover. Pasha ran out into the open toward the floodlit Wall.

Looking up, she saw Yazib at the center of the Wall, lowering a second explosive charge into place.

No alarm yet. Amazing. Anyone who looks this way will see us.

She tore the protective strip away from the adhesive base and placed her first explosive charge as high as she could reach on the right-hand side, the small southern section reserved for women. Then she ran around and came to the center of the Wall.

She checked her watch again.

Forty seconds.

Glancing up, she saw the telescopic arm being retrieved directly above her. Standing on her tiptoes, she pressed a second package against the Wall. Her heart was beating now with crescendo force as she ran toward the barrier in front of Wilson's Arch, to the north of the exposed portion of the Wall.

Twenty-five seconds.

She shifted the rifle to her left hand and reached for the last explosive package. As she did, she saw a soldier running toward her. He was calling out, "*Khaki! Khaki!*"

For a second, she hesitated, then reached up and pressed the final package in place.

The first soldier was joined by another and they hurried toward her, yelling and shouting. She waved, as if to say everything was fine. They continued shouting and running toward her. She stood next to the Wall, waving her hand. One of the soldiers was speaking into a radio pack as the two came closer. When they were about thirty feet away, the woman in the sergeant's uniform leveled her weapon and fired. Both men went down.

Just then, a third man appeared, off to her left.

"Stop," he shouted in English.

I've got to get away from here. This place will blow any second now.

"Drop your gun, Pasha," the man called out. Startled to hear her name, she looked over. The man was black and he had a weapon pointed at her.

Is that the American? Impossible. But it is. Something has gone wrong!

She turned and began firing wildly. Before she could take aim, a searing pain swept through her chest. Then another in her abdomen. A split second later, she heard the muffled gunfire.

Ppfft.

Ppfft.

A third bullet drove her backward onto the huge stone esplanade. The Galil dropped out of her hand as she landed on her back, hands groping awkwardly at her body. Her army blouse was sticky with warm blood. Her eyesight began to fade as she stared up into the blackness of night.

—~—

As John darted across the open area toward the Wall, every movement, every breath sent a knifelike pain through his chest.

That hooligan must've cracked some ribs when he kicked me.

When he reached the shadow of the Wall, he paused for a moment to catch his breath. Gisele pressed in close beside him. They had not been seen. John looked up. The wall appeared higher than it had from across the way, much too high to simply jump up onto. Especially in his condition.

How did he get up there? he asked himself, knowing that Yazib had managed it only a short while earlier.

"Gisele," he whispered. "It's too high. You'll have to help me. Can you give me a boost?"

Gisele gave him an "are you kidding?" kind of look, but she gingerly put the Walther down on a flat stone, squatted down close to the wall, and cupped her hands together. "I'll try."

"Lift with your legs, not your back," John said. "Okay? We've only got one chance."

She nodded and John could see her gathering everything she had for the attempt. He put his foot in her hands and whispered the countdown.

"Three, two, one!"

John launched himself with all the energy he could muster. Gisele thrust upward, a low growl of determination punctuating her effort. It was just enough. John hit the upper edge with his stomach, almost blacking out from the pain. For a second his feet dangled precipitously, but then he pushed himself the rest of the way up onto the flat surface of the Wall, landing with a force that knocked the wind out of him and drove another shooting stab of pain through his body.

Yazib was at the far end of the Wall, his back turned to John, working the telescopic rod with both hands. Amazingly, he heard nothing.

Keep moving!

Getting to his knees, John looked over the opposite side of the Wall where, in a few hours, hundreds would gather to pray. It looked a long way down. He hated high places! No railing, nothing to keep him from falling. This was the worst.

Focus!

Scrambling to his feet, dismissing his fears and the sharp pains in his chest, John ran toward Yazib. At the same time, he heard shouts from below.

Yazib looked up and saw him coming. He dropped the rod over the side, into the public area below, and turned to face his onrushing attacker, blinking unbelievingly, his concentration momentarily broken. His hand swept across the top of the wall, feeling for where he had placed his weapon. In his haste, he turned away from the rifle rather than toward it. As Yazib started to stand, John lunged at him.

Grunting from the physical force of the attack, the two men wrestled back and forth. Grabbing the collar of John's shirt, Yazib managed to roll him onto his back and then broke free. He scrambled a short distance away, climbing awkwardly to his feet, his eyes sweeping the surrounding stonework in desperation.

Where is the detonator?

John crawled after Yazib, but the younger man pivoted and jammed his foot viciously into John's rib cage. Gritting his teeth at the searing pain, John grasped Yazib's ankle, twisting it sharply. He heard a crack and a cry of pain as Yazib pitched over him and fell hard onto the rough stone surface. John yanked on his leg to keep him down, then rolled about and came to his knees.

Just then he saw it.

The detonator. There it is!

The tiny trigger box of destruction lay near the Wall's edge. John looked at Yazib. He had seen it too, and lunged for it. John threw himself at Yazib, pounding him with his fists, then grasping at his face, twisting it around to the side. He fought with a fury he had never felt before. Then he saw Yazib's hand reach out and enfold the detonator.

With his last ounce of energy, John lashed out with his foot and caught Yazib just below the sternum. He heard a groan of pain. He kicked again, and this time his foot hit Yazib's elbow, causing the detonator to skitter away from both men. It came to a stop at the center of the Wall, near the western edge.

With a hammerlike blow, Yazib jammed his other fist into John's stomach. He pounded John's face and ribs. He worked on him like a man gone mad. Suddenly he was off of John and standing over him with a gun in his hands—

a gun exactly like the one John had left with Gisele. As John stared into the business end of the barrel, the Walther 7.65-millimeter PPK took on cannon-like proportions. Still, he could see that Yazib's hand was wavering.

"You!" Yazib gasped, sucking for air. "I don't know how you got loose. But you have become a definite liability, Reverend Cain. You have come very near to ruining our grand cause. However, I shall now complete this task in the name of Allah, and we shall die together."

Yazib backed away, edging over to the detonator. He bent to pick it up, his eyes never leaving John.

With the gun in one hand and the detonator in the other, he rose to his full height. His fingers ran across the surface of the black box, searching for the button.

Where is it?

He glanced down and saw that the device had flipped over in the melee. The button was on the underside.

In the moment that he glanced away, John slipped the knife from his belt.

Yazib sensed his movement and glanced back at him. As he did, the detonator bobbled in his hand. Instinctively, he used his gun hand to try to steady the other, shifting his aim away from John.

John threw the knife.

He had never thrown a knife before.

It flew past Yazib's shoulder, disappearing harmlessly over the edge of the wall, but it came close enough to make him dodge and take a step back. As he did, his ankle turned on a loose stone and he stumbled toward the western lip of the wall. Fighting to regain his balance, he was still trying to find the button on the detonator. Then the little box fell from his hand as he teetered at the edge of the precipice. John lunged for the deadly device, scooping it up.

Yazib's gun hand was high above his head now as he frantically tried to stop the inevitable. He fought desperately to regain his balance, his hand waving helplessly in the air as his foot lifted slowly from the top of the Wall. His face registered disbelief as he went over the edge.

A long, hollow scream signaled the end. Yazib landed facedown with life-crushing force, inches away from where Pasha lay bleeding, unmoving, her eyes locked open in death.

From atop the wall, John heard sirens. A burst of gunfire sounded from somewhere nearby. Yelling. The roar of approaching vehicles. The pounding of running feet.

Then he collapsed and darkness settled in all around him.

PART FIVE

The Islamic Resistance Movement [firmly] believes that the land of Palestine is an Islamic Waaf [Trust] upon all Muslim generations till the day of Resurrection. It is not right to give it up nor any part of it.

Those who are on the land have the rights to the land's benefits only, and this trust is permanent as long as the heavens and the earth shall last. Any action taken in contradiction to the Islamic Shari'a concerning Palestine is unacceptable action, to be taken back by its claimants.

—from the Hamas Charter
Article Ten, Chapter Three

Glory to [Allah] Who did take His servant for a Journey by night from the Sacred Mosque to the farthest Mosque, whose precincts We did Bless—in order that We might Show him some of Our Signs: for He is the One Who heareth and seeth [all things].

—The Qur'an
Sura 17:Isra:1

But on Mount Zion will be
deliverance;
it will be holy,
and the house of Jacob
will possess its inheritance.

—The Holy Bible
Obadiah 17

95

20 SEPTEMBER, LOCAL TIME 0555
JERUSALEM

The first rays of early morning sunlight crept into the room, painting the sterile white walls with a warm glow. John swiveled his head in both directions, unexpectedly becoming aware of a soft pillow cradling his skull. A clean white sheet covered his body. A bottle with some sort of clear liquid dripped a mysterious substance through a tube and a needle that had been inserted into his arm. Across the room was a mirror and sink. Beyond the window there was sky. Blue sky. Nothing else. In front of the window, a small table on wheels. And a vase with brightly colored flowers.

He forced himself up on his elbows and attempted to shift to the side of the bed. Pain shot through his chest. With an involuntary groan, he fell back onto the pillow.

"Hello, cowboy." The voice was low, but musical and a bit provocative with its heavy accent. He turned his head to the right again. An attractive young woman in a nurse's uniform was standing nearby. Black hair. Face a deep bronze. Dark eyes.

How did she get here? Who is she? "Where am I?"

"You are a guest of the Hadassah Hospital. I am your hostess. Well, actually, I am your nurse. My name is Katya. How are you feeling?"

"Great, so long as I don't move, breathe, or talk."

She laughed. "You have not lost your sense of humor."

"How did I get here? I don't remember."

"An ambulance brought you here several hours ago. You are a celebrity, Reverend Cain. I understand that you are Israel's hero."

"Hero?" John tried to grasp what she was saying.

"You and your friends. You saved our Wall. You risked your lives for our people. More than that, you have kept us once again from the mother of all wars, as our old nemesis in Iraq liked to call it."

John forced his mind to focus. At first his thoughts were scattered in kaleidoscopic disarray. Then gradually they moved together. The hijacking of the tour bus. The climb over the ancient wall. The room beneath Al Aqsa. Overwhelming their captors. The dead policeman. The fight on top of the Western Wall. Yazib falling . . .

"My friends?" John leaned forward, grimacing again as he did.

"Please, Reverend Cain, try to remain still. You have some cracked ribs and two broken ones, not to mention a fractured collarbone. Your friends are all well and asleep in their own rooms here in the hospital."

"All of them?"

"Two men and a woman. You all appear to have been through a great deal."

"Just three? No others?"

"I'm sorry, I'm not aware of any others."

"What time is it?"

She looked at her watch. "Five minutes until six in the morning. The doctor will be in shortly. You must rest now. I believe the authorities are also outside, waiting for you to awaken and fill in the details of your adventure."

John reached over and grasped Katya's hand. "Please, will you have someone check to see if there is any news about my daughter at Ein Bokek, and the rest of my group here—and also regarding my family and the church in America. I was told by our captors that . . . that my wife . . . has been killed. I need to know what has happened."

Katya's eyes darkened with sadness. "You have been through so much. I will ask for you, Reverend Cain. Perhaps the others will have some word. I will pray for you that this is not true about your wife. I only know what is to be read in the papers."

"The papers? It's in the newspapers?"

"Of course. And on television. But you must lie back and rest for now. I will find Dr. Kamen."

Katya exited quickly. John settled back into the pillow and stared disconsolately at the ceiling, his mind whirling with random images. Fragments of thoughts. Bits and pieces. Nothing seemed to connect. It was all too overwhelming.

The door opened and a short, heavyset woman in her fifties came into the room. She had the weathered face of someone who had seen it all and was no longer impressed. Her eyes were deep brown, her salt-and-pepper hair cut close. The salt appeared to be winning.

"How do you do, Reverend Cain? I am Dr. Yudit Kamen. I have been assigned to see to it that you get well, starting immediately." Her English carried an accent typical of one whose first language is Hebrew. She smiled a crooked, toothy smile. "You will cooperate with me, of course, yes?"

"Of course." John forced a smile.

For the next few minutes, the doctor poked and pinched and prodded the full length of John's body.

"You are sore, yes? You have pain?" she said, after an extended silence.

"Only from my head to my feet," John answered honestly.

The doctor stepped to the head of the bed and placed a stubby hand on his forehead. It felt warm. There was kindness mixed with the seriousness in her eyes. "First of all, from what I understand, you can thank God that you are alive. Two broken ribs. We have them taped already. You will heal. One fractured collarbone. We'll position your arm in a sling for a couple of weeks. You will heal. Multiple bruises and a slight concussion. Again, Reverend Cain, you will heal. This is not my opinion. It is an order. Are you understanding?"

John could not help smiling. The word that came to mind was *biddy*. Yet in spite of her gruff bedside manner, Dr. Kamen exuded a warmth and a professionalism that could not be concealed.

"I am understanding. And my friends?"

"Bruises, minor injuries, nothing major. Looks like they had a cakewalk compared to you. Or else they are much quicker on their feet. Don't worry. They are resting and they are well. And to hear them tell it, you are the reason that they are alive."

"No," he assured her, looking up at the ceiling. "I am not the reason. It was the God of Abraham, Isaac, and Jacob. He is the reason we are alive."

Dr. Kamen reached out and gripped his hand, patting his arm with a tenderness that embarrassed them both. Her eyes were glistening.

Just then the door opened and a man in uniform, along with two others in plainclothes, strode into the room.

"I will leave you for now," said Dr. Kamen, backing away. She turned to the three strangers. "Don't be too long with my patient. He needs rest, not government interrogation."

"No, please wait, Doctor." The man who spoke extended his hand, palm down. Dr. Kamen stopped at the door.

"Reverend Cain." The man who spoke was dressed in a blue sport jacket and gray polo shirt. He approached John's bed and extended his hand. "My name is Noel Kupperman. This is Peter Dintz and Colonel David Ribbut.

Colonel Ribbut is with the IDF. Peter and I are with Mossad. You are familiar with these organizations?"

John nodded.

"Reverend Cain, you have our deepest thanks for what you and your friends have done. If it were not for your heroic efforts, this day might well be the first day of an all-out war. You have saved the most sacred symbol of our nation. More importantly, you saved her soul."

The others gazed at John intently but said nothing.

He tried to think of an appropriate reply. Nothing came to mind, so he remained silent. He was about to inquire regarding Esther, Jeremy, and Jessica, when Kupperman continued.

"Now I must ask of you another favor still. I have just spoken to my headquarters by telephone. We have a most unusual situation that has developed in the last few hours." He turned to Dr. Kamen. "We must take Reverend Cain with us immediately. He is needed in the city."

"Absolutely not!" Dr. Kamen took a step toward the Mossad agent, both hands planted indignantly on her ample hips. "This man is injured. Do you understand that? He needs rest. He should not be moved for several days. No. I will not hear of such a thing."

Kupperman took the doctor by the arm and led her to the far side of the room. With their backs turned to John and the other two men, the pair conversed in quiet but heated tones in Hebrew, punctuated with abundant hand gestures. Abruptly the doctor turned to look at John. She was obviously angry . . . and . . . what else? Without a word, she opened the door and left the room, pausing long enough to give Kupperman one last withering glare. Kupperman came back to the bed.

"The doctor is making preparations for you to go with us now. I sincerely believe you would agree with this decision if all the facts were before you. The simple truth is, we cannot accomplish what must be done without you. Please do not ask questions. Just relax and let us make you as comfortable as possible. We will travel together in an ambulance. Dr. Kamen will come with us."

Kupperman turned and left the room.

The other two men stood quietly to one side, looking at John, saying nothing. He stared back. Inside, a gnawing apprehension began to mount.

Once John had been made as comfortable as possible, the ambulance departed under full police escort. The ride lasted about half an hour, during which time John tried to gather his energy and speculated about their intended destination. Dr. Kamen, along with Agent Kupperman and the colonel, rode in back with John. The other man from Mossad sat in front with the driver. There was little small talk. Dr. Kamen inquired as to whether or not he was in any discomfort. He was, but he said no. After about fifteen minutes, she asked again if he would like some pain medication. Again, he declined. He wanted to be alert for whatever was ahead.

When the ambulance finally stopped, John heard excited voices outside, some Arabic, some Hebrew. The door opened and two men prepared to remove the stretcher.

"Hold it!" John said emphatically.

They stopped, everyone looking at him.

"I'm not going unless I walk."

"Reverend Cain," protested Dr. Kamen. "You are still going through a period of severe shock trauma in your body. I'm afraid I must insist that—"

"And I'm afraid I must insist that I walk," responded John. "Wherever we are and whatever we are doing, I intend to be standing when it happens."

A slight smile broke across the colonel's face. He said nothing.

Everyone waited for someone to take charge.

"Help this man up." commanded Dr. Kamen.

"Thank you, Doctor." John tried not to groan as they eased him out of the ambulance and helped him to his feet. He was unsteady and surprised at how weak he felt. The pain in his ribs was sharp and his head felt like it could easily drop off and roll away. *Maybe this was not such a good idea.*

"I may need to lean on somebody, but let's go."

He took a first hesitant step. Then he looked up and scrutinized the surroundings.

"What are we doing *here?*"

John recognized the alleyway in which they were standing. He had walked here many times before.

96

You know where we are?"

"Of course. This leads to Gordon's Calvary."

"That is correct. Let us walk slowly, Reverend Cain, for your health. Can you put a hand on my shoulder, please?" asked Dr. Kamen. John steadied himself and they walked slowly along the alley behind a squad of police officers who formed a wedge to move the crowd of onlookers out of the way. Curious Arab children and teenagers followed the party, some trying to sell their first customer of the day a postcard or a cheap, olivewood camel. The police stopped at the entrance to Gordon's Calvary.

"A very strange thing has happened during the night," Kupperman said as they neared the end of the alley. "As you know, this is a religious site operated by a Christian mission organization. Early today when the first employee arrived, she heard singing coming from inside. The door was still locked so she did not know what to make of it. She ran down the road and got a policeman. Together they went into the garden and, well, here we are. Let's go in and see for ourselves."

They walked through the mission store entrance. It looked familiar to John, exactly as it had appeared the last time he had visited, several years ago. Books and pamphlets in simple, wooden racks. Religious trinkets and Holy Land pictures on display. The woman behind the counter smiled nervously, but said nothing as the entourage moved past. Beyond this room through the far door was one of his favorite places in all of Israel.

"Good morning, gentlemen." A tanned and well-groomed man stepped from behind one of the book displays. He looked to be in his sixties, balding, with brown and gray flecked hair brushed neatly along the sides of his head.

"And you must be Reverend Cain." He spoke it, not as a question, but as a matter of fact, a crisp British accent augmenting the resonant tones in his deep voice. "My name is Carson. Gerald Carson. I oversee the mission. I must admit that I don't normally get up this early, but when our staff member called, I hurried right over. I'm pleased to meet you. Your heroic deeds are filling the airways and the newspapers this morning."

John was weary of hearing the same "heroic" commendations repeated over and over. He didn't feel heroic, but he nodded politely and tried to smile. He was becoming annoyed with the feeling that these strangers knew more about what was going on with him than he did.

"All right. Out with it. Why are we here?" John's voice was edged with impatience.

"Come with me." Carson led the way, talking over his shoulder as they walked through the doorway. "They may have told you that when our staff member first arrived, she heard singing from inside. The place was still locked from the evening before. It has to be kept very secure in this neighborhood. And so she went to find a policeman. When they finally walked into the garden . . ."

Mr. Carson led them outside.

Birds were singing. Flower blossoms along the pathway glistened with the dewdrops of early morning. This was indeed an oasis nestled in the heart of a bustling city. Only the roar of buses leaving the nearby station on their first run of the day reminded John and the others that thousands of people were coming and going all around them.

". . . this is what they found."

John stopped and stared in astonishment.

He could not believe his eyes!

Patricia Hansen, Mary Callahan, Jerry and Susan Cloud sat directly in front of him on a stone bench. On a low wall nearby, Nick and Patricia Micceli were sitting next to Harold Eiderman and Jill Anderson.

Shad Coleman, Adele Smith, the Mitchels, along with Greg and Debbie Sommers had formed a circle on the small stone patio. Ruth Taylor, Donna Thomas, the Watsons, and Dan Wilson were standing in front of the entrance leading into the open tomb that many believed was the one in which Jesus was buried and from which he rose on the third day.

"Thank God! You are here. I can't believe it! You're *all* here! This is incredible. How on earth did you get to this place?"

Jill and Ruth ran up to him, wordless concern etched in their faces as they stared at their bruised and bandaged pastor, who was obviously in a great deal of pain. It was Harold Eiderman who asked the question on everyone's lips.

"Are the others . . . Gisele . . . ?" he halted in midsentence, unable to continue.

"They are all fine," John said, breaking into a smile. "And they don't look nearly as bad as I do. They are resting at the Hadassah Medical Center."

A cheer went up as people began hugging and laughing and crying, all at the same time. They rushed up to John, wanting to touch and hug him, but he held up his free hand.

"There's nothing I want to do more right now than hug and kiss every one of you. I still can't believe you're all here. It is just too wonderful. But take it easy, okay? Most of me hurts right now, and with the drugs that the good doctor here has pumped into me, I'm not sure where the safe-to-hug places are."

Everyone laughed, though their eyes remained filled with concern.

"Can we sit down for a few minutes? I want to know exactly how all of you managed to show up here of all places. What has happened since I saw you last?"

"Actually we are also very interested in that question being answered," added Noel Kupperman, the man from Mossad. "The policeman who found you says the door was locked when he arrived. Did someone give you a key? Our belief was that you were being held around the city in different places. Were we wrong in that assumption?"

The group grew silent, casting uneasy glances at each other, apparently uncertain as to who should be the spokesman. Finally, Nick Micceli stepped forward.

"Well, John, as you know, the terrorists initially separated ten of us out of the group that first night. Once we left the bus, we were taken across what looked to be farm terraces, and then through an old cemetery. We walked along a path until coming to an opening in a huge rock. Someone came up with some flashlights and candles and they led us inside.

"I remember a dark hole to the right of the opening. I couldn't tell how far down it went, but it looked deep. I was afraid that was where we were going. Once inside, though, we began climbing up some sort of an underground room with stone steps. Eventually, we got to a place where it appeared like an avalanche had closed the stairs off from wherever they used to go. I don't think anyone had been in there for a long time. There were two small cave-like rooms off to one side. They put us in these rooms and kept us tied up. All the while, our mouths were taped. Then they left us in the darkness.

"Because it was so dark, we sort of lost track of whether it was day or night. They took our watches and valuables. None of us have our passports. They're all gone. At that point, we were just grateful to be alive. We could hear the guards outside and caught a glimpse of flashlights or candles every now and then. They brought us something to eat, which we accepted as a hopeful sign.

We thought they probably wouldn't bother feeding someone they were going to kill right away."

"If you were gagged, how did you eat?" asked the colonel.

"They removed the tape so that we could eat. Two of them stayed until we were finished. Then they retaped our mouths. We decided that maybe we were close to civilization and they didn't want to take a chance that we might yell for help. We prayed a lot for one another—and for the rest of you.

"Then, sometime late last night, two men came in. They didn't say a word at first. They just entered the rooms and began untying us. When we were all free they ordered us to follow them, but to be quiet.

"When we walked out, the other guards were there, but they were sleeping. We couldn't figure what was going on, but we followed the men anyway. I thought they must be relocating us to a new hiding place. We went down the same steps we had walked up earlier, and as nearly as we could tell retraced our path to the same highway where they took us off the bus. When we got there, two vans were waiting."

"Did the vans have markings? Did you notice the license plates?" asked Kupperman.

"No markings. They were what I would call army green. Wouldn't you say, Dan?"

Dan Watson nodded affirmatively.

"I didn't have a chance to look at the license plates. Did anyone?"

The others shook their heads.

"All right," Kupperman said, obviously disappointed. "Please go on."

"That is really all there is," Nick said. "We were driven here in the vans. The men got out, unlocked the door to this place, and led us out here into the garden. They told us we should wait. They said that the others would be coming and when we were all together, we should wait here until a woman arrived. When she came, we were to ask for our pastor by name. They gave us the feeling that you were well known here, John. Then they admonished us not to talk to anyone else or to leave until you arrived. So here we are."

A hush fell over the group. Only the sounds of birds and the noise of the nearby city awakening to a new day broke the reverie. No one seemed to know what to say or do next. John was still trying to absorb what he had just heard when Larry Mitchel spoke up.

"We had pretty much the same experience," he said, looking around at his group. "We were taken off the bus here in the city and stuffed into old automobiles. There were only five in our group. They took us to two separate rooms, two in one, three in the other. We were tied or chained, I guess whatever seemed to be handiest. The room I was in had no windows. We had our gags removed only once for very small food portions—some sort of sandwich. So some of us are kind of hungry, now that I think about it."

"I assure you, my friends, we will provide you with the best breakfast you have ever enjoyed," said Kupperman with a smile. "An American breakfast. At least as American as we can make it here in the land of lox and bagels. Lunch and dinner, too. But tell me, who freed you?"

"A man with brown hair and a blonde-haired woman," said Donna Thomas. "I would say she looked Scandinavian. I remember wondering what she could possibly be doing here and how she got involved in this."

"We've been discussing this among ourselves since arriving here in the garden," said Nick Micceli. "We all showed up at different times. Our group was the first, and we were brought here by the two men I mentioned. I thought initially that they were Arabs. Dark hair, dark eyes, bronze skin. Could have been twenty-five or thirty years old. They spoke perfect English, though. No identifiable accent. Later we decided they might have been Jews. To be real honest, though, we don't have a clue."

"For us, it was two men, one with red hair and the other I would say was African-American, but being as we're not back home, he was probably not American, so maybe just African," said Jerry Cloud.

"Red hair? African? Scandinavian? Did these people give you any indication as to who they were? Any names? Did they indicate where they were from?" asked Colonel Ribbut.

"No. We asked, but they didn't answer."

"Where were your guards?"

"Sleeping," replied Jerry. "Just like Nick said his guards were doing."

"Was this true for all of you?" the colonel asked incredulously, looking from face to face.

Everyone nodded.

"This is amazing," declared Peter Dintz, who up to that point had made no comment, but had been scribbling notes on a small writing pad. "I've never heard of anything like this."

Again there was a lull in the conversation.

Finally the silence was broken by John Cain.

"I have," he said quietly.

The others looked at him.

"I've heard of something like this happening before," he continued, grimacing as he lowered himself gingerly onto the edge of the low garden wall. "In fact, it happened right here in Jerusalem."

"I don't quite follow you, Reverend Cain," said Noel Kupperman, a questioning look on his face. "I've never heard of anything even remotely like this happening in our country and I've lived here all my life."

John smiled.

"I suppose not. But it did. There's a record of it in the New Testament, in the Acts of the Apostles. Chapter 12. One of Jesus' disciples was named Peter. Like Mr. Dintz over here. He'd been thrown into prison by Herod. The church was praying earnestly for him. The night before his trial, while he was sleeping between two soldiers, bound by chains, with sentries at the prison door, someone entered his room.

"This person awakened him, ordered him to get dressed and follow him out. At first, he thought he was dreaming. He didn't believe it was really happening. Then when he found himself outside the prison, he realized an angel of the Lord had delivered him. He went to a house where he knew friends would be present. They were so surprised, they could hardly believe their eyes when they saw him, even though they had been praying for him all night."

"Reverend Cain," said Colonel Ribbut, chuckling in protest. "Are you trying to tell us that *angels* did all this?"

"Colonel, I'm not trying to tell you anything. Perhaps when your investigation is complete, you'll find some other answer for these events. Did anyone in the IDF or Mossad have a clue as to where these people were being held?"

The three men were silent. Dr. Kamen was staring at John.

John looked around. "I need to say this to all of you. A kind of confession, I guess. In recent months, I have been wondering whether or not God was really there. Every member of my family has been under unbelievable stress and pressure. Since little Jenny's death, our prayers all seemed to hit the ceiling and bounce back unanswered. It has been the most difficult period in my life. And it's not over yet. I don't know what the situation is back home. I don't know if Esther and Jeremy are safe . . . and . . . and I don't know where Jessica is."

John cleared his throat, forcing back the emotion that was rippling to the surface.

"But I have to say that seeing all of you here this morning—safe, and hearing about the miracle of your release, has certainly blown away the shadows of doubt in my heart. Unless and until another answer can be proven, Colonel, I'm going on record as believing that the God of Israel and his Son, Jesus, sent the angels of heaven to take care of us all."

"Reverend Cain," Kupperman interrupted. "My sincerest apologies. In the confusion of all these events, I believe we have committed the gravest of errors. I was unaware that you had not already been informed about your family. According to reports we have received from your FBI, your wife is in serious, but stable condition in the hospital. I'm sorry to say that she received gunshot wounds when the FBI stormed the church in which she was being held hostage. You have a son, also. He is well and uninjured. Please forgive us for not informing you sooner."

John was overcome with a mixture of gratitude and fresh concern for Esther. He took a deep breath, fighting back the tears by keeping his eyes focused on the stone pavement in front of him.

Esther was shot? My Esther in serious condition?

"Is . . . is she . . . out of danger?"

"That is the report we have received," Kupperman assured him. "Her condition is serious, but stable. As for your daughter, Jessica, I am sorry. There is no news."

John closed his eyes and leaned back. He felt someone's hand touch his shoulder. He opened them again. It was Noel Kupperman.

"We have everyone in Israel looking for her, Reverend Cain. I am confident we will find her soon."

"Does anyone know what happened to her?" asked John.

"Our best reasoning is that she has been kidnapped by the same group that took you hostage. Your guide, Mr. Barak, was shot and killed. The driver of your bus was found bound and gagged in a laundry room at the hotel in Ein Bokek. We have questioned all the hotel personnel. However, one of them is missing. A desk clerk. He was last seen on the afternoon your bus departed. Another clerk remembers a young girl coming to the desk and asking for assistance, saying she had been left behind by her tour group.

"The missing clerk assured the girl that he would contact you as soon as you arrived at your next destination. He even offered her a room in which to rest until you came for her. About a half hour later, he told the other desk clerk that he had an errand to run. It is the last anyone has seen of either of them. We believe that this man is probably a sympathizer or a member of the Islamic resistance movement. It could be Hamas or Islamic Jihad, the group that took you prisoner."

John stared at the open doorway leading into the empty tomb. With a sigh, he stood to his feet.

"Let's join in a circle and thank God for bringing us safely together again, shall we? We have so much for which to thank God." John looked over at Gerald Carson, the mission administrator who had been quietly observing the reunion. "We're on your turf this morning, my brother. Pardon us for barging in like this, but on behalf of all of us, thank you for receiving us with such graciousness. Would you mind leading in prayer? The God of Israel has been mighty good to all of us."

Mr. Carson beamed.

There in the garden near the empty tomb, Jew and Gentile alike joined hands, some awkwardly, others with the familiarity of having done so many times before, and offered up thanksgiving and praise to the Lord for his mysterious and wonderful works and beseeching his protection over little Jessica Cain.

97

Saturday, 24 September, local time 0800
Jerusalem

The next four days passed quickly. John returned to his room at Hadassah and for two days continued his recuperation under the watchful eye of Dr. Kaman. Gradually, the pain from his injuries subsided and he regained his strength. A steady stream of visitors came to his bedside, or took short walks with him along the hallways, asking questions, taking notes, and recording John's account of his harrowing ordeal.

Imad Safti and Fathi Adahlah were taken into custody and incarcerated in Tel Aviv. Yazib Dudori and Pasha Bashera were identified and returned to Gaza for burial, following an autopsy.

Evelyn Unruh's remains were transported to Tel Aviv and prepared for the flight home.

Gisele Eiderman, Edgar Anderson, and Bob Thomas were released from the hospital and reunited with their spouses. All of the hostages underwent thorough examinations at Hadassah and everyone was given a clean bill of health. Telephone calls were made to reassure anxious family members at home.

When John spoke with Jeremy, his report about Esther sounded worse than what Kupperman had said. She was not being permitted visitors other than Jeremy. The doctors were encouraged by her progress, but indicated that she was still not out of danger. Her eyes had opened once and it seemed as if she was aware of her surroundings. Then she slipped back into a comalike sleep. The doctors were hopeful that this would change for the better in the next twenty-four to forty-eight hours. Thankfully, her vital signs were strong.

Late Thursday morning, Dr. Kaman said good-bye to John as he exited the hospital into a bright, sunny day. Noel Kupperman drove him to the Hilton Hotel in western Jerusalem, where the rest of his group was staying.

John was torn between rushing home to be at Esther's side and remaining in Israel to search for Jessica. No one should have to make such a choice. *What shall I do, Lord?* After talking with Jeremy, John decided to remain in Israel until Saturday. In the meantime, he determined to turn over every rock in Israel in order to find his daughter.

Each of the Americans was debriefed at IDF and Mossad headquarters. There were repeated interviews with the Israel Television Network, CNN, and numerous other radio, television, and newspaper reporters. *Time* and *Newsweek* were preparing cover stories for their next editions.

The Israeli government provided chauffeured limousines, each with professional guides, enabling the group to visit the sites they had missed in and around Jerusalem. Armed security was always present. At first it was uncomfortable, but soon Israel's best-known American guests adapted and actually enjoyed finishing out the balance of their interrupted excursion. This left John free to look for Jessica.

After several hours talking with Kupperman and other law enforcement personnel, it was becoming apparent to John that finding Jessica would be like finding a shooting star out in the heavens somewhere. It was not impossible. It could be done. But to be successful one needed to know what to do, where to look, and how to properly use all available resources.

John was fully aware that he knew nothing in this regard. He was a foreigner in a strange land, the victim of circumstances he still did not fully comprehend. His moods ran the gamut from hopefulness to utter despair. By Thursday, he was becoming resigned to the possibility that he might have to go home without her.

Late Thursday afternoon, 118 of the 120 members of the Knesset met in special session to acknowledge the nation's gratitude to the Americans who had risked their lives in order to preserve the Western Wall. John and his intrepid group of travelers were invited to the parliament building to hear the reading of a proclamation honoring their courage. They were acknowledged with a standing ovation. John overheard a reporter say that it was the first time Israel's parliament had ever been united on anything.

The special session was followed by a state dinner in the Great Hall where, on other occasions, many leaders of the free world had dined, including Egypt's Anwar Sadat, who had once been the honored guest of Golda Meir on a historic evening.

At last, emotionally drained and physically exhausted, the tour group arrived back at Lod Airport. It seemed to John that at least a year had come and gone since their Israel odyssey had begun here at this same port of entry.

Security was extremely tight, even by Israeli standards. Packages and suitcases were rummaged through with aggravating thoroughness. A small crowd of fellow travelers and well-wishers stood about, trying to catch a glimpse of the Americans as they departed. Officials from both Jerusalem and Tel Aviv were present, though John was never sure exactly who most of them were or what they represented. Media people followed them as far as security would allow.

John looked around, wishing sadly that he could say good-bye to David. Devora Barak had gone to the country to stay with her family. She was not taking calls. John sent her flowers and a letter of condolence. Returning here would never be the same. He missed his Jewish friend.

And Jessica!

He choked back his emotions at the thought of leaving the country without her. He could be back in a matter of hours. And he was convinced that a grateful nation was leaving nothing undone in its efforts to recover the missing twelve-year-old daughter of their country's latest hero.

He made the decision. He needed to be with Esther.

At last the boarding call came.

John did not look back.

---

24 SEPTEMBER, LOCAL TIME 1330
SAN FRANCISCO INTERNATIONAL AIRPORT

San Francisco International Airport was overrun with media and news personnel. The pilot of the Calvary Church group's plane had been notified about his special passenger list in advance of their boarding. After discussing it with John during the flight, he had radioed ahead to ask that someone take charge of preparing for a brief press conference. Airline personnel on the ground proceeded to make arrangements for a meeting area and the necessary security.

John and his group were taken off the plane first, even before the passengers in first class were permitted to exit. The fact of their presence on board had quickly circulated among the passengers. For the most part they had been left to themselves. Now, as they walked past others who politely remained seated, people reached out to touch them and offer congratulations. Spontaneous applause broke out in the cabin as John and his group waved good-bye.

A reunion of tour participants with family members took place in the V.I.P. lounge. When John entered, he saw Jeremy standing off to one side. They walked toward each other without a word, until they stood inches apart. Then they stopped, faces struggling with emotion, both remembering the way they had parted two weeks earlier.

"I love you, Dad."

"I love you, too, Son."

With one arm still in a sling to protect his broken collarbone, John gave Jeremy the hardest hug he could muster with the other.

After a few minutes, John called for the group's attention. "Let's go, gang, and get this over with. The sooner we do this, the sooner we get to go home. Next year in Jerusalem!"

A chorus of groans greeted the familiar old saying.

"Tonight in our own beds!"

Cheers and hoots filled the room in response.

Each person pulled away from their family members and formed up behind John in the way that had become so familiar during these past days.

"We're ready, Pastor," a voice called from the back. "We'll follow you anywhere."

"I think we just did!" another voice yelled back.

The rest laughed as John started through the door.

A cheer from the crowd of onlookers went up as John Cain emerged from the pedestrian tunnel, followed by the group that had set off unnoticed from this same location two weeks earlier. Cameras flashed and whirred. Questions were shouted. For the next twenty minutes, their faces and stories were carried across the nation on every major television network.

98

John's initial assessment was that the man had a "good face," creased by the accumulation of life experience. The eyes contained some sadness, but a twinkle, too. And the lines around his mouth suggested that laughter lurked behind the concern that was now a part of his countenance. Here was a man who had been touched by life's sorrows without being fatally wounded by them.

As father and son stepped out of the hospital elevator, the man stood, his eyes on Jeremy. He started forward, then hesitated, as if embarrassed at his intrusion.

"Dad, this is the man I told you about on the way home. Mr. Brainard, this is my father."

The two men shook hands, smiling at each other.

"I feel like an intruder, Reverend Cain," Jim said, stepping back, still sizing up the man whose face had become familiar through countless newspaper photos and television reports over the past few days. "When I left to come out here, you were still missin', and I just had to come. I know it sounds strange, but I felt like God wanted me to be here with your family for some reason. So I came."

John studied the older man for a moment, then reached out and took his hand.

"I'm thankful that you came, Mr. Brainard."

"Please, the name is Jim. And no thanks is needed."

"Okay, Jim. And my name is John. Jeremy has been telling me about you. I can't begin to understand how God placed my family on your heart like this, but I'm glad he did. To think you would leave everything and fly all the way across the country in order to come to the aid of total strangers in our greatest time of need, well, that is incredibly special. I'm grateful beyond what words can express. Your presence here has meant so much to Jeremy. And now that I know about it, to me as well."

"Thank you, John. Now I want to let you go to the room. Your wife has been through as much as you have. They say she's sleepin' but I'll bet she'll be glad to wake up and see your face."

"Thanks. I'll see you in a little while."

"I'll be here. In a convoluted kind of way, we've been together in this thing, even though we never met before. I'm lookin' forward to gettin' better acquainted."

"So am I."

"I'll stay here with Mr. Brainard," Jeremy offered.

"No, son, you go with your dad. This is a time for you all to be together."

They parted, John and Jeremy heading down the hall. Jim Brainard went back to his chair and began thumbing through the sports pages to check on how his Red Sox were doing.

—∾—

A nurse opened the door to Room W212 and then stood to one side. John stepped past her, with Jeremy close behind. Sunlight streamed through the large picture window, reminding him of another hospital room, half a world away. *Déjà vu.*

John walked to Esther's bedside and stood quietly, noting how the white sheet gently followed the contours of her slender form. Her eyes were closed. Her hair fell loosely across the pillow, accenting her pale face and lips. Carefully, as if fearful she might break, John reached out to touch her hand.

The nurse came around to the other side of the bed and bent close to Esther's ear.

"Mrs. Cain."

Esther stirred.

"Mrs. Cain. You have a very special visitor."

Esther's eyes fluttered. At first she seemed unable to focus. Her eyes closed again. Then, eyes still closed, her face softened with awareness.

"John? . . . John? You're home?"

Her eyes opened again, this time rimmed with tears.

"Hello, sweetheart."

Esther moved her hand out from under the sheet, touching his cheek as he gently kissed her lips.

"I love you, John."

"I love you, too."

"I thought . . . for a while there . . . I thought I might never see you again."

John tenderly kissed her hand. A tear from his eyes dropped onto her wrist.

"Hi, Mom," Jeremy stood at the foot of the bed. "How are you feeling today?"

"Oh, Jeremy. Hi. Better now that Dad is home." Esther looked back at John. "You are home." Her look was suddenly serious. "Is there any word about Jessica?"

John hesitated.

All the way home, crossing the Atlantic and the North American continent, John had wondered how much Esther knew of Jessica's situation. It was one of the first questions he had asked Jeremy on the way to the hospital from the airport.

Jeremy told him the story had been in all the newspapers and on television, too. It was the lead story on every newscast. Esther's doctors had decided it would be best for her to be informed, once it became known that John and the others were safe. They waited until Friday, when she finally awoke from the deep sleep into which she had slipped on Monday. Then, with Jeremy present in the room, they had told her. Her response had been one of surprising inner strength, given her history of depression. Jeremy said the doctors were very pleased.

"Everyone in Israel is looking for her," John replied at last, watching to see how she would handle the news.

Her eyes closed. A tear trickled out and ran down her cheek onto the pillow. She opened her eyes again and offered up a weak smile. "I know God is watching out for her, darling." Her fingers wrapped around John's hand.

John could not speak.

"Honey," she said, "try not to worry. I'm glad she was with you. Somehow God is going to be glorified in all this. Who can tell? If she had been here with us, she might have been killed."

John hadn't thought about that possibility.

Jeremy shifted in the chair where he was sitting on the opposite side of the bed.

John stroked Esther's hand, his eyes never leaving her face.

"I'm a different woman than when I saw you last," Esther said.

John certainly could not disagree. From all he had read and heard, there was no doubt she was a heroine. A look of serenity had replaced the tight lines that he remembered from before he had gone away. His last sight of her leaving the airport, the haunting look of emptiness, had lurked in his memory every day until now.

"Jesus has really touched me, dearest. Like you, I've been to the edge and looked over. And now I'm not afraid anymore. I'm not afraid of death. I'm not afraid of life, either. I know that God must have some purpose in all of this, though I can't begin to understand what it might be. I've had to resign myself to his will. It's been hard—and, honestly, every now and then I still try to take it back.

"While we were being held in the church, I didn't know what to do. I so desperately needed you to be there. Then, when I realized they had taken you hostage, too, I almost went crazy. There was only one thing that I had in my power. One thing they could not take away. Prayer.

"When I began to pray, I suddenly felt connected. With God *and* with you. I had to put you and Jeremy and Jessica into God's hands. And myself and the rest of our people who were trapped there. Whatever was going to be, I knew that I couldn't control it. I could only trust God. There was nothing else.

"Darling, I can't really tell you what that act of surrender did for me. I've lots I need to tell you. But that's for later. Right now, I want to hear you tell me everything you've been through. Don't leave out a single detail. I love you so much."

John looked into his wife's eyes, trying to fathom the depths of her obvious transformation. What had all this trauma done to her? What had God done for her? She was definitely a different woman from the one to whom he had said good-bye.

It was not false bravado.

It felt genuine.

Carefully, he leaned forward and kissed her again.

—ʍ—

Jeremy had said nothing to his father about the personal crisis he and his mother had lived through together, leading up to that fateful Sunday. He had thought about it every day, but on the way to the airport he decided that would come later, if and when his mother chose to share it.

For now, watching the bedside reunion of his mother and father, it was enough just to be together again.

Really together.

99

SUNDAY, 25 SEPTEMBER, LOCAL TIME 0800
BAYTOWN, CALIFORNIA

By eight o'clock Sunday morning, Calvary Church was already packed to the doors. Normally the early service had the lightest attendance of the day. Not this Sunday. Today, people chose to come early, to be there when Pastor John Cain returned to his flock.

Newspeople were in abundance, some who could not remember the last time they had been in an actual church service. Anyone with a camera was asked to check it at the visitor's information center, which ruffled the feathers of the news photographers, as well as some of the local gawkers and guests from out of town who had come hoping to capture a memorable photo of this momentous occasion. Security at the doors of the church was as tight as a Super Bowl game. Chief White was taking no chances on another crisis. Bags and purses were searched and every face was scrutinized by law enforcement personnel on duty at every entrance.

An arrangement with NBC, ABC, CBS, Fox News, and CNN had resulted in a pool of equipment and crews to provide live national coverage of this first gathering of the congregation following their extraordinary and unnerving experiences at the hands of foreign terrorists.

Connie Farrer sat on the aisle, third row from the front. The ushers had encouraged her to sit on the front pew so that she would have more room for her leg splint. She declined, still feeling self-conscious from the notoriety she had experienced the past several days. Jody Ansel sat next to her and beyond Jody were Mr. and Mrs. Tom Bernstein. Both Connie and Tom had notepads in their laps.

Always the reporters, thought Jody, smiling to herself.

Later in the evening, Tom was hosting a KFOR news special recapping the Baytown hostage events. Kris Lauring, a popular Bay Area talk show host and son of a local minister, would be Tom's coanchor. It would be Channel 4's lead-in to their 7:30 news, followed by an hour-long, prime-time NBC special called *Without Warning.* The special also was being hosted by Bernstein and Lauring in San Francisco, and by NBC's Joshua Carey in the beleaguered but euphoric city of Boston.

On the front row, side section, Jeremy and Allison sat together with John Cain and Allison's parents. Jeremy had asked Phil Heiden to join them. Sherri Heiden and little Suzanne Esther were at home this morning, watching on television. Many of the regular attenders sitting in this section were curious about the identity of the white-haired gentleman sitting next to John. No one seemed to know who he was. Both John and Esther's parents had flown to the Bay Area to be with their children and grandchildren. They sat in the row directly behind John and Jeremy. Jim Copeland, Sherri Heiden's father, was also present, sitting next to Phil. Phil's mother, Suzanne, was at home with Sherri and her new granddaughter.

Elizabeth Ralsten and her son, Greg, were sitting next to Esther's parents. When they first arrived, they had slipped unobtrusively into seats near the back of the sanctuary. When someone mentioned to John that they were present, he asked Jeremy to bring them forward to sit with the family. It was important to John to honor Elizabeth publicly, and to convey, both to her and to the other members of Calvary Church, that no ill will remained over Ken and Greg's escape. Ken had elected to stay at home, still too ashamed over what he had done in his desperate bid for self-preservation. John knew he would need to reach out to Ken very soon and help him begin the healing process.

Thelma Lunder and her daughter, Laura, whose husband and father had been laid to rest on Tuesday afternoon, sat quietly in the pew beside Mrs. Orwell. Most of those returning from Israel with John had already experienced enough media mania to last them for a lifetime. All but Edgar and Jill Anderson had opted for a later service. The Andersons sat just across the aisle from their pastor, heads bowed in silent prayer for the morning.

At exactly eight o'clock, Terri White stepped to the pulpit and invited the congregation to stand. The choir entered from the rear doors, singing the processional, *"A mighty fortress is our God, A bulwark never failing,"* as they made their way steadily down both center aisles. As the song echoed across the bullet-pocked sanctuary, the congregation spontaneously joined in singing the familiar words:

Our helper He, amid the flood
Of mortal ills prevailing.

For still our ancient foe
Doth seek to work us woe;
His craft and power are great,
And, armed with cruel hate,
On earth is not his equal!

There did not appear to be a dry eye in the house, even among the most jaded newsmen.

When the congregation had been seated, Edgar Anderson walked slowly up to the platform and stepped behind the pulpit to lead the opening prayer. In his simple, direct style, the former prizefighter gave thanks to God for his faithfulness. He asked the Lord to put his arms around Thelma and Laura Lunder and Evelyn Unruh's family in these days of their sorrow. He prayed for the families of those whose lives were lost in Boston, and for the injured still recovering in hospitals and at home. He prayed for people of Arab descent, especially those who were suffering the present animosity of the world community as a result of the actions of their radical Islamic brothers. He concluded by asking God to help the Israeli authorities find Jessica Cain and bring her safely home—and he prayed for peace to come to Jerusalem.

Applause greeted Phil Heiden when he stepped to the microphone and told of the birth of their first child. The congregation laughed and applauded again as he pointed out the exact location on the platform where his daughter had been born. A murmur swept through the sanctuary when Phil went on to announce that the church board, with Pastor Cain's encouragement, had decided that the day's offerings, in their entirety, would go to support a local mission to people of Arabic descent in the Bay Area, both Christian and Muslim, who were jobless or faced with other genuine needs.

To guard against public criticism, a special fund had been established at a local bank, to be overseen by an independent group of Christian, Jewish, and Muslim community leaders from the area. Phil encouraged the community at large to join with the members of Calvary Church in contributing to the fund as a symbolic act of reconciliation, Christian love, and goodwill. By the time the offering plates reached the back of the sanctuary, they were overflowing.

Handkerchiefs were again in evidence when the soloist began to sing:

When peace, like a river, attendeth my way,
When sorrows like sea billows roll.

Whatever my lot, Thou hast taught me to say,
It is well, it is well with my soul.

Then as was his normal practice, without introduction, John stepped to the platform and looked across the sea of faces gathered before him. As he opened his Bible, the congregation rose in unison and began a thunderous applause. Embarrassed, he looked down, gripping the pulpit, attempting to gather his emotions. Then he held up his hands to quiet the people. The applause continued. Tears ran freely throughout the sanctuary in a release of pent-up love, relief, and gratefulness to God for what he had done.

When the crowd finally quieted, they were still standing as Dr. Orwell walked up the steps to where John stood and put his arm around his shoulder.

"Pastor," he said simply, "I think you can see that I speak for us all when I say it's good to have you home. I love you, John, as do we all. You've led us to our Lord and taught us how he would have us live, week after week, for the last twelve years. Last Sunday, I guess we all wondered if we would ever see each other like this again. It's much too early to sort out all the purposes that God may have had in mind in this. But I'll say it again, John, it's good to have you home!"

More applause punctuated Dr. Orwell's heartfelt words, followed by a chorus of affirmation from the congregation.

"Amen."

"That's right, Pastor."

"Bless you, Pastor."

"Welcome home, John."

100

When the congregation had again been seated, John located his place in the Scriptures and began his sermon.

"These are the words of Jesus to all who would hear them today," he said. "You will find them in the New Testament, chapter six of Luke. I can think of nothing else this morning that is more important for us to hear.

"'Love your enemies, do good to those who hate you, bless those who curse you, pray for those who mistreat you. . . . If anyone takes what belongs to you, do not demand it back. Do to others as you would have them do to you. If you love those who love you, what credit is that to you? . . . Be merciful, just as your Father is merciful. Do not judge, and you will not be judged. Do not condemn, and you will not be condemned. Forgive, and you will be forgiven.'"

John paused, looking up from the Bible that he held in his hand. Every eye was riveted on him. Sensing his emotion, his pain. Waiting.

He closed his Bible and laid it on the pulpit. With his hand, he made a sweeping gesture across the room.

"This is a sanctuary," he began. "A place dedicated to the worship of God. Last Sunday, for most of you who gathered here at the nine-thirty service, it began as a refuge from the grind, a sacred site, where perspective could be regained, hope rekindled, God's grace experienced.

"Unexpectedly, it was turned into a place where predators hunted without rules and what we call precious they treated as profane. Cowardice and death took charge for a while. But heroism and honor won out. The bullet holes in the furniture and in these walls can be repaired. This carpet, stained with the blood of victims and the vanquished, can be replaced. Visitors will one day join us in worship and never know of the carnage that was here, unless we tell them.

"But you will remember," John declared, "because you must. Not so that you can hate, but so that you can love again.

"This morning, I confess to you that I know something I never thought I'd know. Never wanted to know. I know what it feels like to want to kill." His voice softened, his eyes grew sad. "On Jerusalem's Western Wall, I experienced feelings I had never known before. I was determined to kill one of our captors.

There was no other answer to my situation. Nor to yours here in this sanctuary. The brave men who set you free last Monday, and who put their lives on the line for the city of Boston, had no other choice but to kill so that you and others like you might live.

"But for a moment, I was truly frightened. Not alone because of the fearful circumstances. No. I was frightened because I actually *wanted* to kill. It burned like a fever in my body. I was angry at what was happening to all of the people for whom I felt such responsibility there in Israel. I was angry at what I had heard was happening to you here at home and to the people of the great city of Boston. I wanted to hurt someone, to hurt them the way they had hurt those whom I loved."

The people listened attentively. They remembered their own fears, their anger, and disbelief. And, for some, the desire to kill.

"Today, however, I am a different man than when you last heard me speak in this pulpit. I am forever changed. I have not yet learned all the lessons God has for me as a result of this extraordinary event. That will take awhile. I do understand some things, however. I understand as never before that you and I cannot remain isolated and insulated from the rest of the world any longer. Ordinary people like you and me are being affected by the extraordinary circumstances of our times.

"I had thought at one time that nothing could move me so profoundly, so emotionally, as the events of 9/11. Now 9/11 has come home to me and to us all in a way I could never have imagined. I can no longer see a rock thrown, or a soldier die for freedom, without being moved. I cannot pass by a fireman or a law enforcement officer without feeling grateful. I cannot look at those who hunger without doing something to help feed them. I cannot see the faces of missing children on milk cartons without praying for them and looking for them in crowds. I cannot let the rest of the world go to hell—morally, physically, or spiritually—and say, 'It's not my problem, there's nothing I can do.' It *is* my problem. It is *our* problem. And we must *all* do something about it.

"I am still learning what it means to love my enemy. I thought I used to know. That's when my *enemy* was someone who disagreed with me or treated me spitefully in the church or misrepresented me with malicious gossip. That, dear friends, was another life. Now I've discovered I am unable to resist passively. Not when innocent people are endangered and killed. I'm sorry. I wish I could turn the other cheek more effectively, but as yet, I cannot. There is one thing I am learning, however. I am learning not to hate.

"The psalmist wrote, 'O Israel, put your hope in the LORD, for with the LORD is unfailing love and with him is full redemption.' Let me urge you to discover for yourself the unfailing love and the full redemption of our great God."

John continued speaking quietly, thoughtfully, every word clear and distinct. His words, wrapped in resonant tones, struck chords of response in the hearts of his listeners. He commended the people for their courage. He spoke of Esther's progress in the hospital. He consoled the Lunder and Unruh families and promised to visit this week all those who had been wounded or who were still in the hospital after last Sunday's incident. He encouraged any who might be suffering emotional trauma as a result of their terrifying ordeal to seek professional help or to spend some time with one of Calvary's pastoral staff.

He acknowledged Jim Brainard, the crucial role he had played in Boston, and the "leading of the Lord" that had brought this Roman Catholic layman to the side of the Cain family.

Then he asked them to keep Jessica in their prayers. This was the one moment that he acknowledged the presence of the television cameras.

"Whoever or wherever you are in the world, if you know of Jessica's whereabouts, I ask you to contact us so that we can arrange for her safe return. And, sweetheart, if through some miracle you are watching . . ." John paused and the cameras panned the audience, many of whom were dabbing at their eyes again. "Remember, Jessica, God knows where you are. God always knows where we are. Your mother and daddy love you, honey, with all our hearts. And God loves you even more."

The camera moved in until John's face filled the screen.

"Look at that," the program director said softly, shaking his head over what he had just seen and heard.

John Cain was smiling.

Epilogue

The night was cool, with just the slightest touch of a breeze. Stars stood out like tiny torchlights and the half moon pointed to the presence of the Big Dipper suspended above their heads.

John and Esther, wrapped cozily in soft cotton pool robes, leaned back in their chairs and gazed at the dark sky. Esther's hand reached out to touch John's. He smiled and covered it with his own.

His arm sling had been discarded two weeks ago. The dark bruises on his face were mostly reddish now, some completely gone. A small scar remained visible under his right eye, a reminder of the traumatic events of more than a month ago.

On this quiet October evening, low garden lights cast their inviting glow, creating lacelike shadows among the flowers and trees around the pool. The pool, lit like this at night, had always been a favorite place for John.

He glanced over at Esther.

She was looking up into the night sky, smiling.

"What's the smile about, darling?"

Esther didn't move or shift her gaze.

"See that moon? And all those stars? When I see them, I feel as though we are close to her. Somewhere tonight, our little girl has been looking up at that same moon and those same stars."

John squeezed her hand. She turned toward him, her eyes glistening bright.

"I know she is alive, John. I just know it!"

"I believe it, too, darling. I don't understand how or why the Lord permitted this to happen. Of all the people not to make it safely home from Israel, it had to be the eldest and the youngest. I can't see any purpose in it. I'm afraid for her. But I know she is alive. I can't tell you how, but I know it."

They continued gazing up at the stars.

"Remember me telling you about stumbling into Amsterdam's red light district with Jessica?" Both of them laughed. "She was determined to pray for that one particular girl in the window."

"For a little girl, she does have a great heart for people," Esther agreed.

"What I didn't think to mention before is that the next morning, Jessica and I went to Anne Frank's house. I was determined for her to see it. It was like I had this great need to take her. At the time, I thought it was just to give her a better perspective on the Dutch people than I had the night before. Now I'm not so sure."

"What do you mean?"

"She's been kidnapped, that is for certain. For all we know, she may be held somewhere all by herself." John halted, clearing his voice as it broke with emotion. "Sometimes I can hardly stand the idea of her being there without us."

"I know. A year ago, this would have destroyed me," Esther mused pensively.

"Now I think perhaps God led me to take Jessica to Anne Frank's hiding place. I wish you could have seen her. She was so taken by it all. Not fearful in any way, just deeply moved. Maybe when she thinks of Anne Frank, that little girl's episode will help her take courage."

"You may be right," Esther agreed. "I've been thinking about the apostle Paul's words these past few days, 'And we know that in all things God works for the good of those who love him.' Maybe you're right. Maybe that experience will help her. Paul said something else that's been like a personal promise to me since this all came about. 'And the peace of God, which transcends all understanding, will guard your hearts and your minds in Christ Jesus.' I have a strength that I've never known before. I find it hard to believe myself sometimes. And amazing as it seems, I'm more at peace right now than I have been in months.

"When I think about Jessica, which is most of the time, I have this strong feeling that she is in danger, but she is alive." She paused, her voice plaintive. "Oh, John, what are we going to do? How will we ever find her?"

"I don't know. I honestly don't know. But as soon as we get any word at all as to her whereabouts, I am going after her."

"I'm coming, too!"

"We'll see about that when the time comes. First, you've got to heal up completely."

Esther stood and began untying the belt around her robe.

"What are you doing?"

"While you were gone, I experienced a very unusual time in prayer with the Lord. He let me see how much he loved our Jenny. How much he loves us all. I have truly been in a healing mode ever since. The most deadly wound that I've been carrying all this time? Well, the Lord has brought a total healing. But there's one thing I used to do that I've not done since Jenny died."

John sat perfectly still, watching and listening.

"For so long, I could not forgive myself. I felt so responsible for her death. I had no joy and there were no tears. Everything was locked inside and I couldn't get at it. You remember how we used to come out here and enjoy this yard and the pool? I loved swimming with you and the children. It was one of my favorite things. But I lost all that when Jenny died. I couldn't bear even to come out here. I used to watch you stand here at the edge of the pool. I felt so terrible, my darling, because I knew how much you were grieving. And my guilt just kept growing greater."

"I'm so sorry," John said, getting to his feet and reaching his hand toward her. "I've never blamed you. Please accept that. It was a horrible accident, that's all. It was no more your fault than mine. It just happened and only God knows why."

"I know. I knew it intellectually a long time ago. It was my heart that couldn't accept what had happened. Can you forgive me for the way that I've been these past months?"

"Oh, sweetheart, of course I can. I do. But can you forgive me for not sensing where you were in all this? I was so wrapped up in myself that I failed to be there for you."

Esther smiled.

"You are forgiven. I put all that away weeks ago. Dr. Benton has helped me process a lot of this as I've continued counseling with him. But a part of the healing process is being able to talk with you like this. For so long I couldn't do it. Thank you."

"For what?"

"For coming home, safe and sound. For being my husband. My best friend. My lover."

She dropped the robe onto the chair and walked to the edge of the pool.

"Be careful," John cautioned. "Those bullet wounds have barely had time to heal."

She turned to face him and held out her hands. In the low garden lights, he could see each one of the small scars. She smiled again. Then without a word she turned back to the water.

When she dove, hardly a ripple broke the surface.

John watched as she swam slowly and easily to the far end. Then turning toward him, she started back.

So graceful. So relaxed and beautiful.

John laid his robe on the chair and stepped in to meet her.

They stood in the water, inches apart, eyes on each other.

"She is October's child, you know," Esther said softly.

"What?"

"Jessica. Her birthday is July 23. That makes her October's child."

John looked at her for a moment, puzzled, then slowly nodded and smiled with understanding.

Their lips touched.

They held each other for a long time.

Hand in hand, they walked up the pool steps and out of the water. John held the robe for Esther. She drew it around herself while he put on his own robe.

They embraced again under the half moon and the Big Dipper and the stars.

Then they went inside.

If you would like to correspond with Ward Tanneberg,
he can be reached at wardtanneberg@kregel.com.

Vanished!

Sequel coming in 2004

SUNDAY, 18 SEPTEMBER
SOMEWHERE IN ISRAEL

Jessica was positive her eyes were open.

So why can't I see anything?

She shut them again, felt her eyelids press tightly together, opening once more just to be sure.

I must be in bed.

No. The surface was too hard for that.

Did I fall out onto the floor?

Her head throbbed with every pounding heartbeat.

She lay perfectly still, feeling the darkness, straining to see something.

Anything.

But there was nothing.

No light in the window.

No stars in the sky.

Only the darkness.

And voices.

At first they were nothing more than a quiet murmur. Jessica couldn't make out what was being said. She closed her eyes again, pushing everything to the back side of her mind. Her head swirled. She felt groggy.

But the voices were still there. Low. Distant. Unintelligible.

Their words sounded strangely . . . foreign.

Maybe Daddy's watching television in the other room.

The voices were getting louder, like when people quarrel. Though she could not understand what they were saying, Jessica discerned the argumentative tone. Then it came to her. She recognized the language.

Arabic. They're speaking Arabic.

But how do I know . . . ?

At last the mental cobwebs that had spun into all the dark corners of her mind slowly detached, and in their place one terrifying memory leaped out, quickly devouring every other thought.

The bus. They left the hotel in the bus.

Without me!

Her thinking became jumbled again, running together and falling apart in a kaleidoscope of indefinable patterns. She tried to grasp the slippery, incomprehensible fact that her father had left without her. It did not make any sense.

Why? How could he have missed seeing that I was not in the bus? I'm always right there in the front seat, nearest the door.

She recalled the strange feeling as she stood in the entrance to the hotel lobby, staring in disbelief at the place where only minutes before the bus had been parked.

Bewildered and frightened, she had approached the desk clerk. He appeared as surprised to see her as she was at being there.

"How did you miss your bus, Miss Cain?" he asked, his eyes never leaving her, while he fumbled for the handle of an open drawer.

"I don't know. I told my father where I would be. I don't understand how they could have left without me. What should I do now?"

Reading the concern on her face, the clerk's demeanor had changed rapidly from startled disbelief to benign kindness and sympathy. With a smile, he assured her that she was not the first person to miss a bus. He was confident that as soon as her absence was discovered, the driver would return for her. If, however, the hotel did not hear anything within a couple of hours, he would personally contact the tour agency representative. They would make whatever arrangements were necessary to reunite her with her father and the others. He had even volunteered an unused room in which she could watch television and rest while she waited.

He offered me a glass of orange juice . . . and then . . .

Try as she might, Jessica could not remember past the orange juice.

She wasn't feeling well. That was why she had gone to the restroom as the others were walking out to board the bus. Her father had reminded her that it was a two-hour journey to Jerusalem from the Dead Sea resort at Ein Bokek and there were no facilities on board. Having had an upset stomach all day, she wanted to be ready for the journey. But when she came out they were gone. She had not been ready for that!

The juice.

It was such an uncomfortably hot day, a glass of orange juice had sounded great. Besides, it was probably the one thing she could get to stay down. Earlier, stretched out in the shade by the pool, her father cautioned her not to get dehydrated.

"Drink lots of liquids, honey. If you don't, this heat will make you feel even worse."

Now as she lay in the darkness listening to strange voices, she struggled to remember what came after the orange juice.

But she couldn't.

There was nothing.

Had there been something in the juice?

And then fear tore through her, clawing and flaying at her insides. Jessica tried sitting up, but for some reason she couldn't.

What's the matter with me? Why can't I get up? If only I could see. . . . What is going on?

Like pirouetting ballerinas, the questions danced randomly across her mind, only to disappear, whisked away by an invisible magician's hand.

And then the awful realization hit her.

She couldn't move because her arms and legs were tightly bound.

Wrapped with tape like an Egyptian mummy.

Packaged for delivery.

Totally stricken now, with fear rising like a gigantic ocean wave, Jessica shut her eyes and cried out for help. For an instant there was nothing. Then the wave came crashing down inside her mind. She heard only muffled sounds. No words traveled beyond her lips. The tape over her mouth barricaded her cry.

A motor started up.

A door slammed.

Seconds later, she felt herself moving. She was not in a room after all.

Is this a truck? Maybe that's why the air smells funny. What am I doing in a truck?

She bounced helplessly with each merciless pothole in the road as the vehicle lumbered along, gathering speed.

Panic pierced her brain.

Fright played the boogeyman in the darkness.

Who are these people? Where are they taking me? What are they going to do? Daddy, where are you?

But Daddy couldn't save her now.

Jessica's unprotected head banged painfully against the truck bed, while the roar of the engine, the scraping of gears and the sounds of wheels on pavement filled her with such terror that she began convulsing involuntarily. She fought back the bile that threatened to erupt from her stomach, sensing she might choke if she didn't get control.

Concentrate. Calm down. For goodness' sake, don't throw up!

Jessica closed her eyes tightly. Slowly the panic receded as she breathed deeply through her nose. Again. Once more. Her heart hammered as if it were attempting to escape her body.

Oh, God. What is happening to me?

The nightmarish horror of her predicament came rushing in with sickening force. Her worst fears were being realized. She had always been careful never to get into compromising or dangerous situations. Never to get too close to strangers. Yet in spite of this, here she was.

I want to go home. Daddy, where are you? Dear God, please help me. Don't let this keep happening!

Jessica desperately longed to be home in her cozy bed in California. Her natural ebullience and enthusiasm for adventure was gone, replaced by a consuming terror that stalked her mind like a character from a late-night horror movie. But this new reality was more terrible than any monster that had ever waited beneath her bed to carry her off in the night.

Tears broke free now, running unchecked into her hair and ears as the silent screams of all the world's missing children fought to escape her lips.

Daddy? Please. Help me!